Confessions of a Rookie
CHEERLEADER

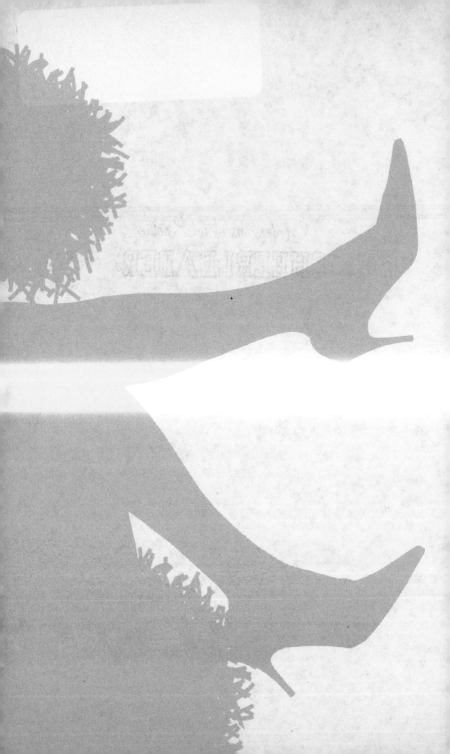

Confessions of a Rookie

CHEERLEADER

a novel

Erika J. Kendrick

ONE WORLD
BALLANTINE BOOKS / NEW YORK

A One World Books Trade Paperback Original

Copyright © 2007 by Erika J. Kendrick

Published in the United States by One World Books, an imprint of The Random House Publishing Group, a division of Random House, Inc., New York.

ONE WORLD is a registered trademark and the One World colophon is a trademark of Random House, Inc.

ISBN 978-0-345-49486-3

Library of Congress Cataloging-in-Publication Data
Kendrick, Erika J.
Confessions of a rookie cheerleader : a novel / by Erika J. Kendrick.
p. cm.
ISBN 978-0-345-49486-3
1. Cheerleading—Fiction.   2. Basketball players—Fiction.
3. African Americans—Fiction.   4. Chick lit.   I. Title.
PS3611.E537C66 2007
813'.6—dc22   2006049359

Printed in the United States of America

www.oneworldbooks.net

2 4 6 8 9 7 5 3 1

Book design by Susan Turner

To the Rookie in us all who endlessly endures.
With each lesson learned and every stripe earned,
the seasons of life are won.

Acknowledgments

They say it takes a village to raise a child. Meet my fabulous village.

Triple smooches to my agent extraordinaire, Stephany Evans, who has been relentless about releasing my voice to the world. You absolutely rock, darlin'!

Thank you to one of the smoothest editors in the game, Melody Guy. They said you were the best. I understand why. Thank you for raising the bar!

An incredibly righteous thank you to my very own RockStars: My father Benjamin Kendrick (Papi) and mother Estraleta Kendrick, who stand behind me in case I fall. You are the epitome of patience, understanding, and damn good parenting. Daddy, you are the man every little girl wishes would piggyback her into the sky so she can pick crab apples in autumn. She dreams of standing on your shiny shoes while you whisk her round and round the dance floor in spring. Thank you for keeping my dance card full. And mommy, you single-handedly keep my soul whole. I'm infinitely better with you by my side, shaking the world free and catching pockets of sunshine as they fall. If I can play in your league when I grow up, then I will have pulled off something exquisite. You've done well and I'm rather proud of you, too. Team Kendrick scores big—HUGE!

My step-goddess, Judy Walker-Kendrick, who peppers my life with love, support, and exceptionally sound business advice. There should be more queens like you for the princesses fist-fighting for their just due.

Narlan (my Gail) and Aliyah, I love you as much as God allows. You are my happy place.

A hundred hugs to my very best friend, flight instructor, and doublemint twin, Cari (my Care Bear). I love you just the way you are—now change! Thank you for saving my life.

My sister and lethal legal counsel, Karetha Dodd. I couldn't have asked for a groovier role model. My neck hurts from looking up to you!

Tricked-out thanks to Yvette, Paul (Big Poppa), Jazmine (Jazzy), and Jackie (my Jackpot). Having you in my life has made me complete. Yvette, every woman dreams of having a gorgeously glammed girl-friend complete with steadfast uncompromising love like yours. I often wonder how I got so lucky. Jackie, my perfect angel, thanks for remind-ing me that God always remembers to sprinkle a little extra pixie dust. You were right . . . we just clicked!

To Tasha, for always loving me no matter how far into left field I de-cided to go. You've been an amazing sister. Thank you for making mom's bacon so I didn't have to.

To my second mothers who always opened the door when I ran away from home: Rochelle (mama), Ms. Loggins, Aunt Georgia, and Ms. Free. I promise to pay it forward.

To all my sisters in the GSC (Girl Scouts Crew) where it first began twenty-five years ago: Latoya, Aldina, Noani, Carmen, Toi, Joi, Alaina, and Arlina. I'm down for an old-school campfire complete with mess kits and sleeping bags.

Thank you, Uncle Bob, for carrying around that folded, crinkly magazine article and believing/knowing that you'd see my name in print again. Your devout belief in me has kept me steady. It's not quite the story you told me to write, but I think you'll like it.

Thank you to my phenom family: Gertrude Jones (my Grandma, the Godmother of the Jones mafia who holds it down), your undying love has been my lifeline. To my way-too-cool cousins: Kristy, Tisha, and Jennifer, thanks for finally letting me in on all the big-girl secrets. To my Uncle Junior, Aunt Tula and Beene, Charbrielle, Jamila, Saidia, Haidia and Aqeel, Nickie, Uncle Chuckie and Ida, John John, Esko, Big Michael and Little Michael. To Juanita Dawson, Adero, Khari, Gloria

Kendrick, Gloria, Michelle, Nita, and all my little cousins. And to the rest of my family, thank you. I've learned the invaluable tough-love lessons along the way.

To the incredible men in my life whose unflagging presence and encouragement have made me a better lead singer and frontwoman: Alvin Bowles, Jr. (my mentor), Douglas Jones, Jr. (my Diggy/producer extraordinaire), Rahsaan Brothers, and Leo Gatewood. It was always enough.

Primo thanks to Team NABFEME (National Association of Black Female Executives in Music and Entertainment): My boss and NYC mom, Johnnie Walker. I've come a long way since jonesing for a gig in your corner office at Def Jam. I promised I wouldn't disappoint. To Karen, Lynette, Leah, Drennna, and Shana, the New York officers for NABFEME, I couldn't have asked for a more brilliant team! Heather Nelson, Kim Cooper, Tanisha Tate, Tamekia Flowers, Kristian Buchanan, and Unique Webster, thanks for all the inspiration and being a constant reminder of what it means to tastefully take it to the top!

A groovy thank you to the following RockStars (old and new) who have invited me into their jam sessions over the years. We've created some beautiful music together: Erika (Ewok) Watkins, Collin, Freddye, Reverend Barbara Heard, Nia and Aunt Sylvia, Dee, Danielle Bennett (thx for the hair and therapy sessions!) Kenneth, Imani and Willis, Tony and Angela, Big Rob, Henry Dunlap, Reuben, Claudia and Thomas, Laura and Jason, Gingi and Jason, Aunt Alice and Uncle Joe, Harold Walker and Jean, Judge Everett Braden, Judge Preston Bowie, Dawn, Myata (my Mizza), and Vershawn (Do or Die)! To my rockin' Karaoke family: Brandon (the Karaoke King), Emily (thx for always listening), Meghan, Mandy, LeAnna, Sunshine and Lydell (NYC's finest). And the sickest Stanford rock band: Michelle Foss, Anastasia, Dee Dee, and Courtney.

Words cannot express how completely rad it was to grow up with my Newberry family. You are, and will always be, truly exceptional in my girly book: Danita Smith, Karen Love, Rhonda Craven, Diane Collins, Debra Kelly, Jacqueline Kelly-Smith, Fred Matthews, Reverend Robert Storme, Gladys King-Lucas, Annie Washington, Drue Haynes, Terrence Bell, Samuel Lee Heard, Lamarr "Juice" Springs, George Cole, Pauline Reynolds, Brenda Baxter, Jannie Jamison, Reverend Margaret

Ann Williams, Vernado "Rock" Parker, Homer Lyons, and Anna Bell West. You make the West Side the best side!

To the million-dollar gang at the Ramada: Ken Hennings, Jerry Woodard, Gary Williams, Phillip T. Hardiman, Charles G. Guevo, John L. Suber, Rose M. Clay, Harry L. Sampler, Sr., Samuel C. Jordan, James Myks, Jerry Bell, Tami Tisdale, and Toni Thomas. Sam Malone and Cheers ain't got nothin' on us!

A crimson-and-cream thank you to my mind-blowing sisters of Delta Sigma Theta, especially the red-hot ladies of Omicron Chi. I see you, Sands. To my Soror/Mentors Dr. Reggae McClinton-Jackson and Patricia Watson. And to my Naledi, you are fiyah!

A very special thank you tagged with shiny big bows to my beautiful Toya Rose for always holding me up, particularly when I was down. We go way back, Sands/friend/x-roomie! You never had to, but you always did!

To Tia Williams, thank you for inspiring me from a distance and embracing me up close. Your tiniest gestures helped me navigate my way. Knowing you inherently makes me better.

Dr. George Smith, thank you for teaching me early on that I am "The Prize."

To Frosty, Jessica, and Precious, I know what each and every purr means.

And to Cody, the furry ruler of my world, thank you for snuggling beside me all those life-changing nights while I dreamed scenes to the sweet sound of your snores. I fancy I'll stock up on cat nip and treats now! We did good.

Confessions of a Rookie

CHEERLEADER

1
Pregame Warmups

IT WAS MY VERY FIRST TIME.

My legs were spread-eagled in the air, and my heart raced into overdrive, heaving and palpitating, while my itty-bitty baby Bs glistened with beads of perspiration. Stretched out on my back, I stared down at the patch of long curlies, which ironically I'd trimmed for this special occasion after toying with the notion of designing little hearts and arrows into them. I wiped my clammy hands on the sheet beneath me and wondered whether I should leave my feet in the air, soles facing the ceiling, or bend my knees and lay my size tens flat beneath me. I'd seen this done before in the movies but couldn't remember proper positioning to save my life. I shut my sea-green eyes and winced at the thought of the painful experience I was about to endure.

Neither of my best friends had enjoyed their first time. They had strongly urged me to just do it and get it over with. "It hurts at first, but once you get used to it, you wonder how you could've gone twenty-eight years without it," the two of them had said. The thought of the hot wet rod rubbing between my thighs and prepping me for the big one was more than I could bear. But I loved Daniel and wanted it to be right—perfect, even.

I pressed my thin legs down as far as they could go and gripped the sheet until my nails sank deep into my palms. The hard hot stick massaged every inch of me, making my coarse curlies clump together. I'd been told to take slow deep breaths and concentrate on something pleasant, but I didn't know how I was supposed to do that when my legs were soon gonna be pushed behind my head and my cheeks spread as far apart as they could go.

I forced my eyelids together and felt my body rise out of itself. I hovered over Hannah Marie Love and watched the petite girl with the big green eyes and abnormally big feet hold on for dear life. Her weaved wavy hair, which hung past the middle of her back, was damp, and her skin, normally a honey wheat hue with olive undertones, was now a ghostly pale pink. She bit down on her bottom lip and sucked in the oxygen from the tiny room and—

Yank!

The frail Russian woman snatched the waxy cloth from my outer lips, pulling with it every pubic hair I owned, instantly reuniting me with my body.

"Hooolllyyy Ssshhhiiit!" I screamed. Was she serious? "Are you serious?!"

Olga looked up at me and scowled, and I grew even more afraid. My eyes welled with tears, and I looked down at the strip of naked red skin between my legs. Who was I kidding?

"Wait. Wait!" I begged as she pressed the cloth against the area just below my bum. "Ahhh!" I yelped out again as she snatched away the hairy fabric. My eyes bulged so much that even Olga would understand why the kids in school had called me Bug.

Who the hell could get used to this? I'd waited twenty-eight years for this bitch of a Brazilian and could have waited another forever. The only reason I was even going through this hairy hell was that I'd wanted to do something special, different—something surprisingly spicy for the night Daniel and I were going to christen our first place together.

He had been on the road since we'd closed on our condo, and we hadn't had a chance to baptize it properly. Tonight he'd finally be flying home, and I wanted to surprise him by going that extra mile to give him a smooth landing strip for his ride in. But—"Aaahhh!" This was ridiculous. Nobody should be back there.

I TOOK A SIP OF SHIRAZ AND LOOKED AT THE CLOCK. 9:45 P.M. DANIEL WOULD BE walking through the door at any second and I still needed to jump in the shower and wash this tangled weave. After the nightmarish snatch wax, I'd stopped and picked up some Herbal Essences because he loved the way it smelled. He'd bury his nose in my hair and inhale the cheap shampoo just before grabbing my ass a little tighter and pulling me a little closer. And I'd be counting on *that* a little later.

I took another sip from the goblet and thought about how much I hated when he worked late like this. But his new position mandated that his girlfriend be extremely understanding—it was in the damn job description! Daniel had been trying to make the best impression on his new boss and colleagues since his transfer to Chicago from New York two weeks ago. And even though I was still trying to settle in and get everything situated, he'd hit the ground running as usual.

He'd called earlier to tease me about the "little surprise" he said he'd be bringing home. I'd taken a minute out of my own hectic day to pick up a little something for him, as well. After leaving Whole Foods on Huron with the shampoo and bottles of vino, I'd pulled over in front of Gucci on North Michigan and handed the valet the keys to my baby—a very yummy platinum-silver Range Rover with a peanut-butter leather interior. I'd hated giving my keys to pimple-faced strangers in red polyester vests ever since that infamous scene in *Ferris Bueller,* but today time just wasn't on my side. I'd wanted to stay on schedule, so I ran in and found the fabbest tie they had—in less than ten. Gucci had always been Daniel's favorite, and I figured he deserved a nice pick-me-up. He'd been working so hard to prove to everyone that he deserved that big promotion: Daniel Goldman, Senior Vice President of Finance at American Express. It was his biggest accomplishment to date and he'd taken to sleeping with his new business cards under his pillow. The only person happier was my Nana.

I refilled my glass, glad that I'd taken the time to pick him up the little love token. I floated through the dining room to the living room and over to the balcony of our new duplex and opened the French doors. I envisioned all the sun worshipers who would swarm Oak Street Beach in just a few months and the nightly Navy Pier fireworks parade that would take flight in the summer sky. But the March wind taunted me and quickly snapped me back into reality, reminding me where I was: the Windy City in winter. I promptly shut the doors, admiring the expansive view through the frosted windowpanes before making my way to the shower.

Daniel and I had closed on a three-thousand-square-foot penthouse in one of the hottest buildings in downtown Chicago's Gold Coast overlooking Lake Shore Drive. Everything about it screamed SEXY. I got goose pimples fantasizing about what our life was going to be like. Suddenly I couldn't wait for him to get home.

Everything was so perfect. I had the perfect job; I was reunited with the perfect friends, in love with the perfect man, living in the perfect condo, slinging the *most* perfect weave. It just didn't get any better than this!

I WAS DETANGLING MY HAIR AS FAST AS I COULD, MY ANTICIPATION GROWING BY the second. All I wanted to do was look into Daniel's hypnotic hazel eyes. I still hadn't seen a woman with lashes as long and thick as his—not without a little enhancement from MAC, that is. I took another sip of the watery wine from the goblet I'd brought into the shower and thought about how happy I was to have moved back to my hometown with the man of everybody's dreams.

Daniel had been the love of my life for three years, ever since I'd been struggling to make rent in a "charming" (read: matchbox) alcove studio in an overpriced Brooklyn brownstone. When we met, I was working in the city and had recently been promoted to junior product manager at Tru Records, where I was assigned a project with one of our baby acts, Minx. The label was prepping Minx to go into heavy rotation on most urban stations in the top ten markets, and she was a definite label priority, especially for my boss, Kimber.

I'd been running late to a photo shoot with Vibe, and I knew Trent, the shoot stylist, was gonna kill me. He'd messengered over this killer two-piece Chanel tracksuit for Minx and a pair of fantastically fab Jimmy Choo stilettos. I couldn't believe I was running late. It was one of the most important shoots for Tru that fiscal quarter, and I couldn't afford to screw it up. And even though Kimber and I had developed a great working relationship over those past two years, I knew she wasn't playing around with that particular project. It was also a great opportunity for me to shine. I had schmoozed, boozed, and paid my dues and was next in line for an executive marketing spot. The department had to make a lot happen with little monetary action, and Kimber had not been shy about expressing that very sentiment in our marketing management meeting earlier that day. She was gonna have my head if I was the sole cause of our department going over budget. Every second I was late would come out of our wallet and—the way Kimber had been talking lately—out of my paycheck.

Even though I had four bags, including a garment bag and my Marc Jacobs clutch in my hands, I still thought it would be faster to hoof it to the photo shoot rather than try and catch a cab during rush hour in midtown Manhattan on a midday Thursday in mid-July. Running late, yes, but not running *crazy*. I must've been in a daze because I could have sworn the light had turned green and the little white stick figure that signals you to cross had given me the go-ahead. I stepped down into the oncoming traffic and felt an arm grab me around my waist and knock all the bags out of my hands, except the Jimmy Choo shoes and the MJ clutch, of course.

"What the fuck!" was all I could manage before I turned around and got lost in his eyes. "You had me at hello," I heard myself say. (OK, truth? Yes, I really did utter that Velveeta cheesy line aloud!)

"Here, let me help you with that," he said, laughing.

He handed me his beige Coach briefcase and bent down and gathered all my crap, or rather Chanel, and handed it back to me. His shoes were Armani; his dark blue suit, Gucci; and his camel-colored shirt that complemented his bronzed freshly tanned skin, Pink. He asked me to dinner in what must've been an effort to calm my nerves, and I telepathically asked him to be my baby's daddy.

We dated casually for a couple of months before things heated up and I moved into his duplex Noho loft on Bleecker and Greene (trust-fund baby!). I was in no hurry to give up my 550-square-foot junior one-bedroom in Brooklyn—but it just made sense. At least that's what I told Nana when she realized the phone had been disconnected and deduced that I didn't live there anymore.

Daniel and I couldn't get enough of each other. He frequently traveled for his job with AmEx, and I was off to one city or another, living out of a shoddy suitcase for video shoots, touring, or baby-sitting different arrogant artists on the road. And whenever we found time to be together, we cherished it like the last Oreo cookie during a munchies binge.

Initially, I was very skeptical. Dating in New York City is the biggest joke. It's notorious for being nothing more than a hobby for successful young eligible men. And I found out that Daniel was just that—successful, young, and very eligible, not to mention *über*-fine. He was the managing director of finance at AmEx and had been with the company even before he'd decided to go to B-school and get his MBA from Harvard. I wasn't doing half bad myself. I'd been in Stern's evening MBA program at NYU and had graduated at the top of my class from Yale. But regardless of my credentials, the City was running over with successful, beautiful, bony women willing to do whatever a man like him wanted for little or nothing in return. So what would make this situation any different? Why on earth would he want to leave his augmented playground for a set of Baby Bs?

Over time, my skepticism dwindled as I realized that Daniel and I had multiple layers of random stuff in common. Chicago had been home to us both, and we'd actually attended rival high schools. Over

Chinese take-out one night, we discovered that I'd been on the JV cheerleading squad for the basketball team that had tried to crush his dreams of league MVP for three consecutive years. Our schools had been in the same North Side district. We realized that we'd even caught the same bus home from school and laughed at the possibility of having sat next to each other.

It was always so comfortable and easy when we were together. When he was ready to kick back and watch the game, he'd lift all hundred and twenty pounds of me on top of him and settle into his cushy dark chocolate leather couch. He'd wrap his arm around my waist and rub my back with his left hand, flipping the channels on the remote with his right. With my head against his chest, I could hear his heartbeat, and right around the third quarter, my eyes would get heavy and I'd drift off to sleep. He was the perfect lullaby.

"Baby, I got you something," I mumbled through the pasty gel in my mouth.

Through the soaked towel wrapped around my head, I heard the bathroom door open. I could never get enough of his scent. Issey Miyake. It kept me famished and wanting more.

"I really missed you, sweetie. But the twins came over to keep me company and help with the last of the unpacking."

My head was buried deep in the sink with my electric toothbrush, but the rest of my bare body was covered with him. He stood behind me, wrapped his hand around my neck, and pulled me out of the sink in one swift snap.

"Baby, let me finish brushing my teeth."

I could've been talking to the wall, because before I knew it, we were the after-hours X-rated Cirque du Soleil—and I was wet all over again. I wiped the steamy mirror, revealing parts of his sexy bald head and goatee, and it wasn't long before I couldn't take it anymore. I slid away and led him into the master bedroom, where he pushed me down onto the bed and ripped his wet shirt off, kicking his pleated pants to the floor.

My legs were spread in the air—this time freely and willingly—and my hands cupped his smooth head as he spelled out the alphabet at varying speeds with his tongue between my thighs. When he was done with the letter Z, he slid his slippery fingers from inside me and ran them across the silky bare lips of my waxed skin before landing his tongue on his newly designed runway strip.

I choked on the six-hundred-thread-count Egyptian cotton sheets, whispering between breaths, "Damn, I missed you so much. I'm on fire—can't take it anymore—need to feel you inside me right now." He stood, and my entire body pulsated. Even before he touched me, I began to shake.

We made sweet *in love* love before we began to fuck. My eyes were closed, my head was spinning, and I was almost at my breaking point when I softly moaned, "Yes, yes, yes." I pierced his skin with my fingernails and lazily opened my eyes. A 4k princess-cut diamond ring was lodged between his forefinger and his thumb, sparkling down at me.

I screamed even louder. "YES! YES! YES!"

5

THERE ARE JUST NO WORDS. I DON'T KNOW HOW IT CAN GET ANY BETTER THAN that. We cuddled in a blanket on the oversized sheepskin rug in front of the fireplace with the balcony doors slightly ajar, and gazed out at Lake Michigan. Daniel stood up and grabbed his wineglass. I loved him in those Calvin Klein boxer briefs. Hell, I loved him in a snowsuit.

"Babe, I'm going downstairs. Want more wine?" He spoke softly. The baritone whisper was the intro to the first single on the sound track of my life. I was in a daze but must've said yes, because he was back in what seemed like seconds, bending over me with his new blue-and-white striped tie dangling from his neck, accentuating his strong, perfectly developed pecs.

"Where do you want me to put this?"

I took the glass from him, grabbed his arm, and pulled it closer to my chest, kissing him from wrist to elbow. "You have made me the happiest girl in the world." I sighed deeply. "I'm gonna go call Nana."

"Wait till tomorrow. Let's enjoy our news tonight—just you and me." He pulled me into him and softly kissed my temples. "We have all night, but I do have bad news about tomorrow. I've gotta go out of town first thing. It's last-minute, I know, but I can't get out of it. I really need to be in Atlanta for the southeast regional meeting. Baron just isn't strong enough to handle it alone yet. It's only an overnighter, and now you have four new carats to keep you company while I'm away."

I looked down at the ring, which took up almost half of my finger. "Nothing can take the place of you. But I understand. I'll be right here when you get back." I looked around the room. "I think I'm gonna have the interior designer come over to view the space tomorrow. I'll invite Nana and surprise her. She's been dying to get her little hands dirty decorating this place—all three thousand square feet of it." I looked down at my righteous rock. "But she won't be ready for *this*." I squeezed his arm that was holding me tightly. "I really do love you, Daniel."

"I know, babe. I love you too."

I watched the fire slowly die out before I walked back through the bedroom and slid into bed to cuddle next to him. I could hear his heart and feel its beat, and his heavy breathing always let me know he was sleeping peacefully. I took a deep breath, closed my eyes, and smiled, thinking that I must've done something right.

"And now I lay me down to sleep," I whispered. "I pray the Lord my soul to keep. If I should die before I wake, I pray the Lord my soul to take. God bless . . . Daniel."

6

I STUMBLED INTO THE BOTTOM OF THE BED AND OPENED MY EYES. THE PHONE RANG again. I was half asleep, walking toward the cordless on the other side of the room. It must've been on its third ring before I realized where I was and exactly what I was doing. Between Daniel's welcome-home surprise and the bottles of Shiraz, my body was beyond exhausted. I reached for my Versace specs and looked at the clock: 4:21 a.m.

"Hello. Hello?"

"Good morning. Is Daniel available?"

I looked at the clock again: 4:22 a.m. I pinched myself. *Ow.* I glanced across the room at Daniel. He hadn't moved an inch.

"Who's calling?"

"Is Daniel available?"

"Who the hell is calling?" I snapped.

"Oh, sorry; this is Shannon, his girlfriend."

My fingers went numb and I dropped the phone. I reached down to grab it. I hadn't taken a breath since her last word and still couldn't find my air. Where was my goddamn air?!

"His what?!" Found it.

I grabbed the satin periwinkle robe that matched my gown and took the phone out of the room.

"His girlfriend. You must be his sister, Hannah. Look, I have to get to work, but I wanted to tell him that I won't be able to pick him up from the airport later today. I'll be in ongoing meetings, but I'll send a car for him. Please let him know that the driver will pick him up in front of baggage claim, as usual. Sorry if I woke you, sweetie. He told me you were a light sleeper. He never keeps his cell on at night, and I didn't want to risk him not getting the message. Thanks so much."

The walls were closing in on me. A fire was ignited in my stomach, and my feet and legs began to shake involuntarily. I balanced myself against the hallway wall and slowly slid to the floor, finally stabilizing myself on the unscathed hardwood.

"His what?! I'm sorry; did you just say that you're his girlfriend? What do you mean—*as usual*? The car will pick him up where exactly—*as usual*? What city are you in? *I'm* his fucking girlfriend. No, I'M HIS FUCKING FIAAANNNCCCÉ. What sister? Daniel doesn't have a fucking sister, and I am not a light fucking sleeper. Who the fuck is this? *As usual*? WHAT THE FUCK IS GOING ON?!!!!"

What seemed like two lifetimes was a phone conversation that lasted roughly two hours. She'd been his girlfriend on and off for the past five years. Shannon. That was her name. Shannon Montgomery. Shannon was an airline executive in Atlanta. Shannon said she usually saw him twice a month. Shannon was white. Shannon was madly in love with him. So was Fisher, their two-year-old son.

Shannon was crying very hard toward the end of the conversation. The rest of my body had caught up with my fingers and had gone numb. "But we are his family" was all I'd heard Shannon say, and what had been the brightest day of my life was suddenly murdered pitch-black.

I watched myself descend into a deep dark hole with threatening velocity. I heard nothing but piercing silence. It was loud. I couldn't make it stop. I didn't want to. I opened the frosty doors and walked to the edge of the balcony off the master bedroom and looked down—all the way down. Just how long would it be before I hit bottom? Would I make it? Would this kill me?

I closed my eyes and saw my team at Tru Records hugging both Daniel and me at my "You rock, girl—we'll all miss you" goodbye party on the rooftop at the Peninsula Hotel. They'd rented out the lavish lounge, and it was by far the hottest going-away party I'd ever been to—the "girl, you missed it" soiree of the season. There had been so much love in that room. Kimber was quite proud of me for taking the junior vice-president of marketing position with RockStar Records. She'd said that even though I was young, they couldn't have picked a better person to roll out the label in the Chicago market. Secretly, I wanted to be just as good as she was, if not better. I knew I was ready, she'd trained me well, but I never thought I would've been able to do it on my own. The big move back home was supposed to be exciting and thrilling because Daniel was by my side. I hadn't doubted myself since he'd come into my life. He wouldn't let me. He was my best friend and biggest supporter through business school, through two promotions at Tru Records, and with my new gig at RockStar.

And just like that—he was gone.

FIRST QUARTER

7

"BRITTANY ALEXIS LEE, TAKE THOSE GODDAMN MANOLO BLAHNIKS OFF. I DON'T care *whose* name is stitched into them; if you scratch up my brand-new hardwood floors, you'll forever be suspended from the Brats circle," I warned, watching her rock out in the mirror and fall even deeper in love with herself.

I looked across my huge new living room at all the boxes that had finally been resorted and repacked. After Daniel got on the plane and disappeared into the ex-love-of-my-effin'-life abyss, there was still the monumental matter of all our shared memories and accompanying mementos that required attention—three months later! Somehow, I'd managed to completely immerse myself in my work instead of taking the time to throw out all his toxic shit the day he left to be with his "family." Attempting to avoid the confrontation of a long, drawn-out fight or a crashing crying spell, today was the day I'd asked two of his boys to come by and pick up what was left of his belongings that I hadn't already designated to the Salvation Army or hurled down the incinerator whenever the urge had struck over the past twelve weeks, two days, nine hours, and fifteen minutes.

In the beginning, I'd cried for what seemed like an eternity, but I managed to find the strength from somewhere deep down to keep waking up each morning. The absolute shitty part was that once I woke up, I wanted to roll over and throw up. And several mornings I did just that. But I was never alone. Following a three-way phone call that fateful morning after, the Brats had rushed in like a pack of wolves sniffing out their prey. Ready to devour, they came with bats, canes, and even a spatula but were disappointed to find that their intended victim was already playing house in *Hot*lanta. But it was always reassuring to know that if nothing else, I could always depend on my girls.

It had been ten years since our high school graduation when we'd committed to remaining "the best of friends till the end." That day our hair had been braided in long beaded cornrows, and we'd cocked our graduation caps to the side. Brittany had held up two fingers behind her twin sister's head, and without ever parting her lips, Kennedy had smiled perfectly, being ever so careful not to expose her shiny new braces.

"OK, Brats, say cheese," I'd heard my Nana yell.

"Moneeey!" we all screamed, understanding the price point of couture at an early age.

In the beginning, we'd been nicknamed The Brats by the kids in junior high because we were misfits, constantly being sent off to the principal's office for gossiping or passing notes, but usually finding a convenient detour while en route and rarely making it to his disciplinary den. We were often dogged by the other children; the sad truth was that we were all rejects and had found simple solace in each other. Brittany and Kennedy Lee were fraternal twins, half Korean and half black, and were teased terribly because of their pasty yellow skin and slanted eyes. Brittany, however, carried the additional chubby, chunky, thick and hefty, big-boned burden of being the obviously overweight one. And I was tragically a bifocaled, biracial, Proactiv infomercial waiting to happen. We'd been through the hurt together and understood one another's pain in ways no one else could.

I'll never forget when fate blew me a smooch one rainy Sunday when Nana and I were shopping for Trapper Keepers and pocket protectors for my very first day in my new school. I was insisting to Nana that no one worth their Jody Watley leg warmers would be caught dead sporting a pocket protector when I heard a raspy voice behind me politely concur. It was a rail-thin girl who looked cool enough to be spearheading the MTV phenomenon herself. She took the coconut-colored pocket protector from Nana and handed me a sleek metallic purple pencil case. The girl standing next to her winked and shoved a Twizzler into her mouth. After Nana finally agreed, I turned to thank my personal shopper, but she and her Twizzlered twin were squishing off in their golashes. The next morning I rushed out of my apartment with my purple Trapper Keeper and matching pencil case tucked away in my Hello Kitty backpack and nervously stepped onto the elevator into the morning aroma of fresh Folger's and red licorice. I peeked behind the trio of nannies monopolizing the close quarters to find my MTV vixen and her twin sister huddled in the corner—smiling. The licorice lover reached into her bag and offered me some of her sweet stash. I accepted.

Living in the same high-rise condo with the twins in junior high made my transition into luxe living an awesome one. Nana and I had just moved into the yuppified Lincoln Park area just outside of downtown Chicago, and I'd quickly bonded over difficult days and turbulent times with my new Best Friends Forever.

On a completely separate sloshy Sunday, Brittany and Kennedy found their anorexic mother routinely doubled over next to her bed in an alcohol- and pill-induced coma. They took the elevator down to my a.p.t. and camped out in my brand-new room in the brand-new tent that my brand-new stepfather had pitched for us. Nana made us ginger tea and tuna sandwiches with the crusts cut off, and we dished to each other and lunched.

It wasn't until that particular episode that I finally opened up to them about my old covert life in Englewood, one of the scariest neighborhoods in Chicago. To the tune of the heavy rain pounding against the windowpanes and only the glow from the three industrial-sized flashlights shining through the vinyl tent, they listened intently, still in disbelief that only a few months prior, I'd called that war zone home. Nana, the only mom I'd ever known, had raised me after my biological mother—who was only fifteen years old at the time—died during childbirth. She'd explained that my mother had swooned over the janitor at her school and had made the irresponsible decision to drop her knickers and "bed" him behind the bleachers. My green eyes, frizzy hair, and olive skin were still the only remnants of his Caucasian presence in my life. Nana, on the other hand, was a constant discerning influence and had worked three jobs to keep the two-room apartment with its leaky roof over our heads. And as my newly inducted B.F.F.s struggled to grasp the concept of Oodles of Noodles, I clicked my heels three times and tried to forget all the lunches and dinners when I'd reluctantly sucked them down.

But that all changed when Nana met and fell in love with her boss, Roman (undisputed heavyweight diner franchise king), at her downtown graveyard waitressing gig. After they married—the Evanses met the Jeffersons—we moved on up to trendy Lincoln Park to finally enjoy the Good Times. And even though the Brats couldn't conceive of the kind of poverty I described, they never judged me; rather, they accepted me, with all my insecurities and secrets, and have loved me ever since.

After that first JH semester together, we never cared what the kids at school said or thought about us. We couldn't relate to them anyway; we were studying the pages of *Vogue* and counting calories while they were sporting Cross Colors with Swatch watches and begging the cafeteria lady for that extra Klondike bar.

Graduation inevitably came, and we all went our separate ways for undergrad. I was in New Haven at Yale, Brittany was in Evanston at Northwestern, and Kennedy was in Cali at Berkeley. But no matter how many zillions of miles were between us, we never went too long without each other. Brittany always made a particular point to get us on three-way every Sunday since our first week away at college. It was the only day we could make long-distance calls and pay local rates, so it became our ritual: the day the Lord was resting, we were on the phone talking shit. "OK, ready? All bitches accounted for?" And that's how Britt would start every Sunday call. But before she could get the last words out, we were off and running—praying the Lord wasn't listening.

These days, the Lord was not only listening but apparently sprinkling a little fairy dust my way. Just that past week, I'd gotten a phone call from Daniel's overly apologetic mother, insisting that she'd worked it out with him so that I could permanently keep the duplex *and* the furniture. He'd paid for most of the penthouse when we'd closed on it, and she agreed that the least he could do was let me take over the minimal mortgage. I didn't see an issue with that. Hell, I was finally beginning to get used to seeing something/anything other than the inside of my toilet bowl.

Earlier in the afternoon, Britt had bolted through the door with the new deed to the property. I was officially on my own, and the deed signified the end of the Daniel Goldman chapter. Now it was time to start an entirely new book. No tears were shed, but toasts were made to "Partying Like Superstars, Drinking Like Rockstars, and Fucking like Pornstars!"

BRITTANY BUMPED UP THE MUSIC ON THE BOSE STEREO, WHICH WAS BALANCED ON top of one of the empty cardboard boxes marked "Salvation Army," breaking me out of my reverie. She snapped her fingers to the beat and stared at her flawless reflection in the mirror. Her canary-gold Chloe capris complemented her freshly facialed skin and hung nicely off her size 14 StairMastered ass. She smiled at the thick voluptuous woman looking back at her and breathed a deep sigh of adoration. I don't think she ever noticed that the mirror was cracked straight down the middle.

"Brittany, please *please* take those Manolos off. I'm begging you."

I had to admit they were the sickest shoes I'd seen all season. Gold embroidery was stitched into the rose-pink leather ankle strap, which was long enough to wrap twice around her long curvy legs.

"Stop hating on the thousand-dollar floors. Hardwood is your friend," I advised. I tried my best to avoid succumbing to their allure, but it was just too damn powerful. "OK, fine, where'd you get them anyway?"

I hadn't seen the fierce floor-scratchers on the runways or in the boutiques either. She was always good for that. The rumor was that she had an Italian midget underground shoe dealer buried deep inside her payroll.

"Give it a rest," Britt said, clearly ignoring my devotion to the unscathed floors. "Let's not forget that I'm the one who sold you this badass boudoir anyway."

Brittany Alexis Lee was one of the most sought-after residential real estate tycoons in the region. She only dealt with gold that she knew she could flip to platinum. And this place had been no different—though we'd only paid in silver. She was the best in the Midwest and was quickly becoming a contender on the East Coast.

"Bitch, don't scratch up my floors! Kennedy, tell her not to fuck up my floors," I implored, beginning to get irate.

Britt tossed her long chestnut-brown hair over her left shoulder, winked at me, and shot Kennedy an evil look before eyeing the floor and bending down to slowly, deliberately dance her left index finger across its surface. And like a proud mother, she smiled. When it came to her properties, the girl was on fire. Her instincts were impeccable. She had a flair for both beautiful real estate and undeniably beautiful men. Just the previous month, Kennedy had e-mailed me a picture of Britt on one of her "we fucked on the beach till the sun came up" weekend getaways. She was laid out on a seventy-five-foot yacht in the middle of the Gulf of Mexico in a gorgeous tangerine two-piece BCBG tankini. Her asymmetrical bangs had been perfectly cut and hung just above her high cheekbones on both sides of her face. She was being oiled down by some chocolate hottie, and her signature sexy eye slant was caught on film as she smiled mischievously at the camera. She was a self-proclaimed lover—of men, refined spirits, well-crafted shoes, and rich, decadent foods. She'd been approached by three reputable photogs three times in her life to test shoot for various plus-size mags and had silenced each one in a "you-should-be-so-lucky" huff. Her theory was that she was simply too hot to be put in anybody's categorical box, no matter how BIG it was.

Tonight she'd been doing more sipping on her vodka than organizing boxes for Daniel's definitive dismissal. She slapped her bootylicious rump and dropped her martini glass, nipping her finger and causing blood to trickle to the floor. And like a well-rehearsed ballet, Kennedy grand-jetéd over to the first-aid kit on top of the box marked "Asshole's Shit" and assembled the tools to wrap her other half's swollen finger.

As always, Britt's French mani matched her French pedi, and the tiny gold rhinestones on both pudgy pinkies subtly set off her canary-gold two-piece Couture casual set. Her soft hair was tousled and frizzy, and hung down her back, her bangs were haphazardly tucked behind her ears, and the tiny Band-Aid now wrapped around her pinky was the only imperfect accessory to her ensemble.

I got up to make my way into the kitchen, tapped Kennedy on the shoulder, and motioned for her size two, five-foot-six frame to follow. I buried my head in the fridge and rocked out to Pharell's quadruple platinum track blasting from the Bose.

"Bug, do I look fat?" I heard Kennedy ask over the refrigerator buzz.

I pulled my head away from the cheese, put the glass of vino down, and tried incredibly hard to swallow—careful not to spit the wine all over the ivory marble kitchen floor. There was absolute terror in Kennedy's eyes as she fearfully studied her curvaceous sister juking in the mirror. Kennedy couldn't have weighed more than a-buck-point-five. I could see my best friend's chest bones and honestly thought she was starting to look a little like Whitney on that godforsaken Michael Jackson tribute special.

Without missing a beat, Brittany yelled from the living room, "Shut up, bitch; have a Twinkie," just as she'd been ruthlessly advising Kennedy since puberty when she first began obsessing over her weight.

As the song ended, Britt turned away from the mirror and switched over to the kitchen. She put her left arm around her sister's waify waist and pulled her near and with the drink she'd just snatched from Kennedy's hand raised her glass for a toast. Her voice was soft but emphatic. "Y'all know what? We really are some bad bitches—especially now that we're *all*, as Outkast put it, keeping it 'so fresh and so clean.' "

I took a deep breath and fanned between my legs. Earlier that morning, as a tingly tribute to my new life, I'd had my second lesbian-istic session with Olga. "I'll toast to that." Truth be told, I actually liked the sheer sleek coochie-coif I was now sporting.

Empty-handed, Kennedy laughed. "And to Hannah-Bug and her clean cat being back home in Chicago where they *both* belong. And no worries; we'll be right here with you on this next leg of your fabulous journey."

I had to admit, we were quite fab. We all looked damn good for twenty-eight; we were young, educated, and hot. Britt and I both had MBAs, and although Kennedy had not gone on to complete her residency, she'd relentlessly finished med school. We were justification for higher education!

"OK, ready?" Britt queried, after taking a deep breath. "All bitches accounted for?" she rallied as we giggled like tipsy teenagers. I took a sip from my glass before handing it to Kennedy so we could *all* drink to that. I couldn't have asked for better friends, and this time I certainly hoped the Lord was listening.

Within seconds, Britt mumbled something to Kennedy about needing to see which ballers were in town, and before I could get to my last gulp of wine, they'd grabbed their Louis bags, kissed me on the cheek, and headed for the door.

"So glad to see you're doing better, Bug," Kennedy said, doubling back to kiss my cheek again.

"I'm glad your ass is gettin' right too, girlie. And now that you've put some wax to those cracks," she said, on her way to the door, "always remember"—she schooled as she headed for the hall closet instead—"that unless a man's name is George, he don't wanna be swinging through that jungle you had sproutin' all up and through. Trust!"

She rifled through the wooden hangers for her coat before reaching into her inside pocket and pulling out a red licorice twist. She bit off the tip of the Twizzler and winked before throwing the Prada trench over her shoulder.

"Want one?" she offered, reaching into her bag for another sweet treat. And again, I accepted.

"Just give me five more minutes, Nana." In my sleep, I could feel the small soft hands nudging at my shoulders.

"Bug, you're gonna be late for work. It's going on nine."

My eyes shot open at the purr of my Kennedy's voice. "Shit. I have to chair the meeting this morning before the luncheon. Where's the phone?"

I reached for my specs. 8:35 a.m. Even though I probably had more than enough time to get to the office, which was less than a mile away, rushing had never been my speed of choice.

I dialed the office even though I knew my assistant, Cobra, had everything in order. I left him a speedy garbled message, panicking at the thought of being late. I'd been fighting that demon since I'd learned to set the alarm clock.

"Now, here's your Venti soy extra caramel, caramel macchiato with whipped," Kennedy said, smiling, showing off her perfectly straight teeth. She was still in her running shorts and fitted Cal baby tee.

I pushed the strawberry Frette sheets back and stared at the floor. "I promise, I'm gonna get up tomorrow and run with you. I just haven't been sleeping well this week. I'll be better once Rain's budget is in and I've had a chance to see the revisions that were made to the video treatment."

"No worries. You know I'd love for you to join me, but there's just something about being alone out there at dawn with the sunrise, the water, and the waves. It all makes for such a spiritual exercise," she zenned, situating herself on the floor.

I stepped over her. She was laid out prepping for her three-hundred-crunch postworkout morning routine.

"Besides, we may not be able to get up that early tomorrow. We're supposed to be going out tonight—or did you forget?"

"No, no. I'm gonna try and get out of the office a little early and meet you at Barney's for some preliminary shopping."

Kennedy usually had auditions or castings lined up on Fridays. Lately she'd been making the rounds on calls for reality shows even though she secretly thought most of them were corny. She was currently in a national ad for Garnier Fructis conditioner that had started running the past week, and she was up for a national Baby Phat spot. Things were starting to pick up for her and finally go the way she wanted. After med school, she'd decided not to take the residency offer from the University of Chicago after her shrink told her that her ulcer was not due to her academic workload but to her unhappiness about her current career choice. Kennedy had sulked for weeks before deciding to end it all, including her two-year relationship with her "sorry,

Honey, my godlike work comes first" boyfriend, Ryan, who just happened to be the head of surgery at the university hospital.

"What time's your first audition?" I yelled over the buzzing of my
Sonic toothbrush before turning on the shower and reaching under
the sink for the Herbal Essences. *On second thought, Paul Mitchell is more
my speed now,* I thought, tossing the three unopened bottles of discounted shampoo and conditioner into the trash.

"One o'clock. But I need to pick up my new comp cards before then,
and I wanna be here when Gianni comes by with the samples for your
throw pillows."

"Thanks, Sweets; you've been amazing. I don't know what I
would've done without you these past months."

I glanced at the Movado. It was already nine thirty, and I was
standing at the front door panting, trying to squeeze my foot into the
hot-pink four-inch Mary Janes. I couldn't shake the feeling that I was
forgetting something. Anxiety was knocking, and sweat was starting
to bead under my arms and behind my knees. Ew! Kennedy stood
against the island and dangled my BlackBerry in front of me. Sigh.
What would I do without her? She'd basically moved in and claimed
one of the guest bedrooms downstairs as her own, and I'd never seen
the upside in reminding her that she technically still lived with and
paid rent to Britt for their four-bedroom loft in the West Loop.

I tried Cobra again at the office. Voice mail. I'd lucked out the day
the young-looking Puerto Rican with the freakish pinkish blond hair
came in to interview for the assistant's position. In the beginning, it
took a while to get used to his ever-changing hair colors and his
many tattoos, but over time, it had all grown on me. Secretly, I thought
some of the permanent art was even kinda cool, but in a very new-
millennium sort of way. The snake (an homage to his namesake)
wrapped around his neck, though—well, let's just say his winning
smile and enthusiasm had more than compensated for his twenty-
year-old punk-rock approach to life.

I had to admit that he'd been very good for me. And even though
our eight-year age difference hadn't been an issue for him, sometimes
I still had to close the door for some of our gab sessions. Other folks
didn't need to hear some of the things that came out of his mouth. Like
his commentary on the Daniel situation, ". . . and, girl, any man that

stays gone that much on the road needs to have his dirty drawers inspected when he comes home—before they even make it *out* of the suitcase. Honey, yes, he had the finances and he showed you the romance, but never ever *never* trust that kind of back-to-back *dis*-tance. Remember, Bosslady, recovery from a cheating man is about the sand, a tan, and a brand-new man. Ooooh-kay?"

Cobra just had a way of getting straight to the point and punctuating it with a neighborhood neck roll and a pout. He'd seen me get teary a couple of times at my desk after the big breakup and had assumed correctly. And on many days, he'd been just what the doctor ordered.

"Just remember, you are the prize, OK . . . ?" Then he'd smile cunningly and bat his dark brown eyes, his lime-green contact lenses always a nanosecond behind.

"Don't forget your lunch," Kennedy reminded me, turning around to hand me a Wonder Woman lunchbox. I took it and remembered the night a few months earlier when I was still enrolled in Remedial Heartbreak Hell 101, and my girls and I had stayed in (again) to watch the *Sex and the City* finale on TiVo for the eleventh time. Kennedy had handed me a wrapped gift, and I'd opened it to find the vintage Wonder Woman lunchbox. They said she would be my strength in my moments of angst when they couldn't be around.

"Have a great day, call me around noon, and play nice with the other children," Kennedy said in her most nurturing tone.

I opened the door as my cell was going off. I knew it had to be Cobra.

Caller ID: Brittany.

"Hey Britt. On my way to the car. Almost running late," I explained.

"You're always *almost* running late. Did Kennedy fix your breakfast?"

"She packed it in with my lunch," I said loud enough for Kennedy to hear.

"And your Starbucks," Kennedy yelled after me as I was heading toward the elevator, aware of Britts's routine line of questioning.

"Yes, and she picked up my morning coffee. Thank God, cuz I was a wreck. And to think I said I was gonna do that Pilates class with you. I could barely get out of bed."

"Wanna puke this morning?" she asked, delicately.

"Girl, please, I haven't felt the physical pains of heartache in weeks. Besides, all I have to do is look around the house—or better yet, open the French doors and check out the view. It's got my name written all over it—literally."

"Or watch the Big O on one of those phat plasmas," she added, laughing.

I was very aware of the recovery/grieving process and had no qualms about going through its respective stages, but the truth of the matter was that after three months of it, three words summed it all up perfectly, "C'est la vie, asshole." OK, so four words.

I balanced the phone with my shoulder, looked for the keys to the Range, and blew Kennedy a kiss before getting on the elevator. She was still standing at the door like she did every morning. She'd probably go outside on the balcony and watch for my truck to pull out of the driveway before heading for the shower.

"No, I didn't forget about tonight. Getting on the elevator, we might get cut off. Hold on a sec; that's my other line. Probably Cobra," I told her.

"No, wait. What's this about you and Kennedy running over to Barney's?" Britt questioned.

"Hey, let me just click over and see what he needs," I insisted.

"But I just wanted to know what time you all were gonna try and meet up, cuz I need to pick up a couple of things on Oak Street anyway. I'll be done showing this property by then and will be on my way back toward the Gold Coast. So when do you think—"

"Brittany! Just give me one sec," I demanded.

"Fine. Whatev! I've gotta run anyway."

"OK, love you. I'll call you when Rain gets to the office for the luncheon," I said, attempting the ultimate pacification.

"Ooh yeah, Rain! Now don't forget to get an autographed picture for me. And try and find out if she had her tits done. I'm not kidding; I simply *have* to know," Britt begged.

"Goodbye, Britt. Oh wait, quick question—"

"Gotta go now," she snorted. "Outie!"

"Hello? Hellooo!" *Seriously?!* I thought, and snapped my cell shut.

9

I TRIED COBRA AGAIN AT THE OFFICE.

"Morning, Bosslady," he greeted me in his usual chipper voice.

"Yes it is, isn't it? It looks like He woke me up again, and for that I thank Him," I testified as I hopped into the Rover and headed toward the 900 North building on Michigan Avenue.

"That makes two of us."

"You know the drill; give me a quick rundown."

"OK," Cobra said, and took a deep breath. "The copies have been made, the conference room has been set up, and the limo will be at O'Hare ten minutes before Rain's plane is scheduled to touch down. It'll also be available to take her to the station after the luncheon and then back to the W on Lake Shore. I put in a call to Joshua at the radio station. His assistant is gonna get back to me about Rain's interview once she gets a chance to look at his schedule, and the caterer will be here in one hour to set up."

"You rock! See you in five," I said, and hung up the phone to switch on the radio, feeling appreciative that Cobra was on my team.

"... so if you think you've got what it takes to be a Diamond Doll, one of the super-sexy cheerleaders for the Chicago Diamonds—no, not the Bulls, our other winning Chicago ball team—send in your application with a picture. You can call and request one or just download it from their website: www.chicagodiamonddolls.com. Yo, that happens to be one of my favorite reasons to go to the games, guys. No offense to Max Knight and his crew; they definitely do their thing. But come on now, you have to admit, those girls are fine. All right, stay tuned, y'all, because in a couple of hours we're gonna have a very special guest in the studio for the afternoon drive. That's right— Rain is gonna be joinin' us to talk about her new album. I know y'all saw her all up in the video with Kanye. She did that joint wit him last year. She's even hotter now, if you can believe that. I saw her at Diddy's party a couple months ago. Whew. She's also gonna let us know where her sexy debut video *is gonna be shot. Cross your fingers and pray it's Chicago. Now, come on, brothers, that's one honey that would surely make the cut with the Diamond Dolls. She wouldn't even have to audition. She could cheer for me any day, if you know what I mean. It's sooo hot in here!!! Coming up next . . ."*

10

I TYPED IN THE URL: WWW.CHICAGODIAMONDDOLLS.COM. WELL, I'D ALWAYS been curious. Plus this would be a great distraction—something to keep my mind from straying back into hazardous territory. Dr. Ivy, my shrink, had strongly urged me to find a hobby to serve as reinforcement for our mutually agreed-upon pact: no men, just Hannah! Besides dancing since I was eleven, I knew I still had the moves and I'd kept my body tight, so why not—

"Yes, Cobra," I said, minimizing the screen as he knocked on the door to my office.

"I just wanted to say that you look quite fab today and that you ran a great meeting this morning," he said, flashing his semistained coffee-colored teeth.

"Why, thank you."

I'd settled on a Dolce & Gabbana camel cotton stretch lightweight trench coat–inspired suit. It was just right for this beautiful May morning, and it added the perfect balance of chic sophistication and urban appeal for the morning meeting. I'd even made a point to accentuate with cinnamon-tinted Christian Dior sunspecs.

"So, I guess that's my cue to say that you coordinated a wonderful luncheon," I bit, wiggling my pencil at him.

"Well, you didn't have to say wonderful, but—"

"Is Rain ready to head over to the station?"

"Uh, yeah, she's coming out of Eli's office now," he said, straining his neck around the corner to get a glance down the hall toward the boss's door.

Elijah Strong, the senior vice president of RockStar Records, was scheduled to work out of the Chicago branch for only one year before turning the office over to me and heading back to Nationals in New York. He'd been a big supporter of mine since negotiations in New York when discussions surrounding my age and ability to handle my position got heated. He'd also been young when he got into the music game and had worked his way up the ranks quickly, starting out on various street teams before moving around to different labels and eventually holding down the SVP position at RockStar. At thirty-six, he knew the game inside and out, and was one of the most connected and influential men in the industry, frequenting only the most exclusive parties and dining with the celebrity elite. Aside from the fact that he really understood this business, I knew I was lucky to have him in my corner. Since the beginning I'd found him powerfully intriguing, and from the moment we'd met at an industry event in Soho, we'd clicked. Our relationship had been pretty easy, and though we had very different educational backgrounds and working styles, we'd immediately found ourselves in a good rhythm and flow at RockStar.

"Great; tell Rain that we're going over to the station now." I got up and grabbed my suit jacket and tote.

"We?" Cobra asked in a surprised tone.

"Uh-huh, grab your sweater. You earned it. Great luncheon," I said, and headed down the hall.

"But what about the phones?"

"That's why we have voice mail, cell phones, two-ways, Sidekicks, BlackBerries, Treos, old school pagers . . ."

11

I REALLY COULDN'T TELL WHETHER THEY WERE REAL OR NOT. THEY SEEMED TO bounce nicely enough and didn't appear hard, rippled, or abnormal in any sort of way. Damn that Brittany.

"So, how'd you like growing up in Philly, girl?" I heard Cobra ask Rain. He was sitting with his legs crossed, dangling his hot-pink All Stars in the backseat of the limo. I was gonna kill Britt for making me sit here and assess this girl's breasts.

Rain was a cross between Beyoncé and Pamela Anderson. She was the most marketable new artist on the scene, and we couldn't seem to generate better PR than when she simply walked down the street. Star quality—she had it oozing out of her perky pores.

As usual, the Magnificent Mile was packed with people. Rain lowered the window just enough for the tourists to catch a glimpse of her crisscross Lola hat cocked down over her Gucci studded aviator glasses. She took out her tube of ooh baby lipgloss and, like a pro without a compact, retouched. Her features were perfectly symmetrical, and her pouty lips could have made a crappy Carmex ad sexy. And I knew for a fact that those shades were not easy to pull off. I'd argued with the saleswoman at the sunglasses counter in Bloomies the past weekend for half an hour about the fact that my nose didn't have a strong enough bridge to hold them up without my face looking like the glasses were wearing me.

"Now remember, Rain, we're just gonna tease the hell out of them about the video. Just don't answer anything definitively. We haven't gotten the rubber stamp on the budget yet," I told her as we pulled up to the radio station.

The window was still down, and her long fiery reddish-blonde hair was blowing in the wind. At first I thought the dumbfounded look over her shades was because she couldn't make out what I was saying over the forty-five-mile-an-hour breeze blowing in her ear.

"We'll just tease them a little, OK?"

"Sure, Hannah. You're the boss. I've got no problem flirting with 'em."

"No, hon, I don't mean tease in the literal sense. I mean about the video. You know—never mind. Maybe we should just stick to saying that it's gonna be really hot," I suggested.

"Whatever you say, Hannah." She shot me a nervous grin, still managing to look like she deserved to be on the cover of *King*—every month.

I looked over at Cobra, who had put his hand on top of hers. He stared blankly at her for a couple of seconds, then leaned in closer and said, "I like your shades, girl."

12

I STOOD OUTSIDE THE RADIO STUDIO NEXT TO THE BATTERED BLUE COUCH IN THE waiting area and anxiously flipped through Rain's press kit for the third time. It appeared that her bio, which was supposed to be in the folder, was missing. It would be a great day when electronic press kits became standard PR support, but today just wasn't that day, so I carefully looked through each document in the folder again. I was sure Cobra had put it in there.

"OK, Sam, don't leave me hanging tonight," I heard a velvety voice warn outside the studio.

My head was still buried in the papers when the folder was abruptly knocked from my hands and everything flew everywhere.

"Shit," I fumed, and watched the elusive bio slide under the big behemoth of a couch.

"Oh, excuse me. I didn't mean to almost knock you over. I need to watch where I'm going," that same smooth voice said through a cloud of arresting cologne.

I chased the bio, now hidden halfway under the dusty death trap, and knelt down to the floor, preparing to go one on one with it. My oversized training bra inched up halfway over my breasts as I stretched my arm under the spiky sofa springs and struggled to pull the stubborn paper out with my index finger. I was laid out, facedown with my cheek smashed into the parquet floor, when a dustball nestled comfortably among my nose hairs and—and—and—my face jerked from the floor and smacked back down against it as I sneezed involuntarily and watched as the paper caught the spray of fluids, all over Rain's name.

I glanced up at the tall stranger, wishing he'd rescue me, but instead he walked away, taking with him the deepest deadliest dimples hidden under a crisp white fitted baseball cap.

"No worries. I'm not really paying attention to what's in front of me," I muttered, mostly to myself, as I sat up and tried to discreetly sanitize the papers that were overflowing in my arms.

"You should start. You just might miss something."

Grabbing the rest of the documents, I stood up and adjusted my bra just in time to catch another glimpse of the most perfect ass in a perfect pair of dark denim Seven jeans.

Real smooth, Cheese, I thought to myself.

"Come on in, Rain," Sam Sylk, one of the station's radio personalities, said in our direction as Cobra eyed me suspiciously and took the press kit, effortlessly arranging the papers in order.

"It's so nice to finally meet you. I'm Sam Sylk, the afternoon drive host here at Chi-town's most listened-to radio station." Sam extended his hand to Rain. "Welcome. You're as gorgeous as they say you are." He wiped his forehead and turned toward me. "Hey Hannah, how's my favorite hype-master?" he asked, and put his arm around my shoulder.

"Hey, Sam, this is Rain," I said, picking the family of natty dustballs from my armpit.

"Yep, we just covered that. You OK today?"

Cobra extended his hand. "Hey, I'm Cobra, her assistant. She's fine. I've just been driving her nuts," he said and handed Sam the germy PR kit.

Sam shook Cobra's hand and shrugged before turning back around to Rain. Looking at her intensely, he went into instruction mode. "OK, this is how it's gonna go down," he began, and all I heard was "blah blah blah blah blah blah blah blah . . . and we'll finish up and have you do a couple of drops for the station. Sound good?"

I could feel Rain looking at me as if she had no idea what he'd just said. She wasn't the only one riding the short bus today.

"Sounds great, Sam," I said instinctively, and grabbed Rain's hand.

I scooted closer to her and patted her on the back to let her know I'd be next to her through the entire interview. Sam gave each of us headphones before taking a seat in front of his mike. Rain watched him fidget with the buttons and knobs in front of him like a deer caught in his Oldsmobile headlights. I took a deep breath, crossed my fingers, and hoped for the best. Cobra stared blankly at her for a couple of seconds, then leaned in closer again and said, "Did I tell you that I really like your shades, girl?"

13

"I'M OUTTA HERE, ELI. HAVE A GREAT WEEKEND."

"You leaving me already? How'd everything go with Rain down at the station?"

"Like butter. She sounded great and Sam really liked her, so he made a special effort to ensure that she came across well to his listeners. We're gonna need to get her some coaching, though. But, overall, she did a good job, especially to not have had any coaching at all."

"That's what's up. I wasn't worried; you're hot. Rain told me at the luncheon that she feels real good around you. It's just your way. I want you to know that I really appreciate you always bein' so on point. All right, handle that then, media coaching, interview tips—whatever she needs. Good looking out."

"Thanks, Eli, but you don't have to—"

"Close the door."

I reached behind me and pushed the door shut without taking my eyes off him. I hoped he meant for me to close the door while I was still *in* the room. I dared not ask; he'd have to tell me differently. Warily, I watched him shoot an e-mail off to the label gods, realizing that he was completely captivating. I was mesmerized. I'd always revered powerful men.

Eli leaned back in his cognac-colored leather executive chair and folded his hands across his chest.

"I got something for you. Now you know I really fought hard to bring you onboard. And you haven't disappointed me, particularly with the personal shit you just went through these past couple of months. I was checking for you to see how you'd handle yourself. You worked it out, and I'm not mad at your game."

He pushed his chair back and walked around the desk, nonchalantly neglecting to tuck his black button-down Sean John shirt into his loose-fitting jeans. I couldn't help but notice that his wardrobe choices always framed his six-foot-two build exceptionally well. He had a small scar just above his eyelid that he said he'd gotten in a basketball game. Somehow I never believed him; it smelled a little prisony putrid to me. He was rugged and still a little rough around the edges, in an ultrasmooth sort of way. Sexy described him best—his walk, his bravado, and especially his East Coast twang. The girls around the office would ask him to repeat himself just to hear the way he said words like *"tawk"* (talk), *"cawr"* (car), and *"cawl"* (call). He'd generally oblige before shaking his head and shoving his hands deep into his pockets. He'd grin, they'd coo, and he'd walk away, always adjusting his starched collar as he moved. He was an impeccable dresser and knew how to flip it—from Morning Meeting Mondays to Casually Cool Fridays and every day in between.

Just as his BlackBerry beeped, I felt my cell vibrate in my tote (that made me giggle). He reached into the inside pocket of his charcoal jacket and pulled out a little blue box and a red envelope.

"Don't open this in front of me," he said, and smiled, licking his lips at the same time.

I reached into my bag and grabbed the phone after it vibrated again (still funny the second time). I'd have to call Britt back later.

I looked up at Eli, never having noticed before now just how sexy his lips actually were. Even though his teeth weren't perfectly straight, I wouldn't have changed a thing about them.

"I don't know what to say," I muttered.

"Thanks usually works."

"Yes, of course. Thanks."

"Your game is tight, and that's what's up."

"Yeah, but you didn't have to—"

Eli had already walked back around to his chair and was deep into his text messaging.

"Have a great weekend. See you Monday."

"OK, it's a date." Shit. "I meant—"

"No, no dates this weekend for me. Just gonna hit the gym whenever I get outta here, and then I'll probably grab some grub and take it in with me." He looked up at me and paused, then continued. "I'm coming back into the office tomorrow, though. I missed Freddie's Fresh Fade Fridays at the salon today, so I'll probably have him come in and gimme a cut and a tight lining tomorrow while I'm checking out some of Rain's interview footage. Cameran can put a digital kit together on Monday; we're gonna put her press package on CD. She's fuckin' hot, her voice is sweet, and we've gotta get her Grammy-ready right now! She should be on that stage accepting at least two golden joints in February. The marketplace hasn't seen anything like her in a long time. Imagine if Carmen Elektra could sing or if motherfuckers actually *liked* Mariah Carey. We struck gold with Shortie, and I wanna do her justice. She needs to come out blazin'. You know, really max her potential and leverage her talent."

"You always know exactly what the market needs."

"Yeah, well, that's my job. But the key is to surround myself with other people who get it too; know what I mean? That's why your lil ass is right down the hall."

I slid my left hand behind my back and over my skirt, and rested it on my ass. *Lil?*

Heart-pounding silence.

I stared at the "Wound from Oz" beneath his brow while he eyed my apricot lace minibra.

My phone beeped. Britt left a message. I looked down at the little blue box and the envelope in my hands and glanced at Eli sitting behind his desk with his cell already at his ear and his BlackBerry on top of three composite sheets.

I cleared my throat. "OK, so, see you Monday."

"That's my girl," I heard him call out at me. I was halfway down the hall before I turned around and looked back at him already engrossed in two other conversations. His girl?

14

It was nearing 6 p.m. and I'd been circling around Oak Street and Rush for a good ten minutes. I hated looking for parking, but valet was simply not an option.

Pouting, Kennedy sat outside the Starbucks under one of the green-and-white canvas umbrellas, puffing on a skinny Capri ciggy as if the little cancer stick was holding back terrorist information. After pulling in next to a hydrant, I plopped down at the green wrought-iron table to join her.

"Is it really that bad, Sweets?" I asked, and changed the ring settings on my cell just before it rang. Brittany. "Hey girl, where you at?"

"Car. Left you a message twenty minutes ago. But, whatev! I've been circling around Michigan and Oak, but with all this traffic—"

"Why didn't you just drop the car at my place and walk?"

"What! And chance ruining my Yves Saint Laurent peek-toe patent-leather pumps? Don't think so."

"Of course. What was I thinking? We'll be at the Starbucks across the street from Barney's."

"K, chickie. Outie!"

I looked over at Kennedy, who hadn't looked away from her cup of joe. Her Venti nonfat latte, sans the foam, was getting dizzy as she spun the cup round and round in her tiny hands.

"Talk to me, mama. How'd the audition go? Not so good?"

It rang again.

"Where you at?" I instinctively said into the cell again, but I heard Britt screaming before I could even put it to my ear.

"What the hell is up with all this traffic today? I mean, I know it's Friday, but damn! I'm on Division and State now, and you'd think they were giving away free invites to see Jay and B. get married. Now that's one wedding I would just *have* to be at. Do you think she'd wear Vera or Versace? Cuz I think—"

"Britt, honey, please!"

"K. Breathe," she zenned to herself as she took in tons of air. "Now, where you at again?" she asked, this time with the calm of a yoga nut.

After dishing the coordinates, I reached over and grabbed Kennedy's smoking fingers. She was already on her second cig. I suffocated it with one of my Mary Janes.

"Now, what happened?" I pleaded for her to come clean.

Her foot was shaking back and forth, and she was twirling the end of her hair with her free hand. Even in her moments of angst, Kennedy looked fierce. Rocking her favorite rose Ella Moss Venus mini and Miss Sixty Counting Crow black tee, her pouty mouth and symmetrically high cheekbones would have appealed to any fashion editor.

"I guess the audition went fine. I mean, I *guess* it was going fine and I *guess* one of the producers was flirting and I *guess* I didn't really mind until he tried to touch me. I dunno—I kinda freaked. It's just not that important to me to compromise myself that way, and sometimes I think it should be, you know? Girls do it all the time."

I pulled her hand away from her hair and held it firmly in mine. Like her twin, Kennedy opted for short square French manis when she had to prep for auditions and castings. It always looked sleek on her lanky fingers, and Roxy, her agent, even sent her on calls for specialty hand parts from time to time.

"Listen, Sweets, you should be proud of yourself for that. If it doesn't work out, then it just wasn't for you. You've got to pick your battles. You're talented and beautiful. Don't let anyone take that away from you. They're men—young, dumb, and full of cum!" With her complete attention, I continued. "Now, if you need a pity party, I'll coordinate it. But don't party too hard, cuz we've got some shopping to do."

I could see the corners of her mouth begin to turn up into a smile just as I heard Britt's high-pitched voice trailing from the street. She'd pulled over and was leaning out her window chatting up a police officer who was beelining for my truck. But in the next couple of seconds, she'd worked her mojo and the officer split, heading in the opposite direction. Britt flashed her recently Zoomed pearly whites at us, tossed her hair over her left shoulder, and sped away in her cherry-red Porsche.

"And can you believe that Brittany Lee would rather ditch gas driving around in traffic than get her high-heeled, high-profilin' ass out and walk?" I implored, easing the green ashtray away from Kennedy's fidgety fingers. Bending down to put the butt-holder on the ground, I spied Brittany Lee center stage while everyone around us stalked her slithering toward us. Her red Carlos Falchi doctor's bag was thrown haphazardly over the shoulder of her crisp white Tahari pin-striped suit as she catwalked in her candy-red YSL patent-leather peek-toe slingback stilettos. I saw a couple of blonde women point, gawk, and coo—but this was nothing new; Britt always looked as if she'd just come from a plus-size photo shoot and was ready to lunch with the best of them. She removed her Chanel sunglasses with her right hand and flipped her wavy hair over her shoulder with her left. Kennedy and I looked at each other and each held up eight fingers, yelling in unison, "Eight! Eight! We give it an eight!"

"Now come on, chickies, is that the best you can do—an eight? I'm good for at least a nine. I even got our friendly neighborhood police-man to admire Bug's SUV instead of ticketing it," she said as she glanced over her shoulder at the officer, who was now leaning against her car yapping away on his phone. "I deserve an extra point on GP for that alone," she said, and took Kennedy's coffee cup out of her hand.

Britt placed her arm candy in the chair and propped her heel next to it, directing our immediate attention to her feet. I had to admit—her YSLs rocked! and were completely undeserving of the harsh concrete punishment of even one city block.

"Hey chick," I said.

"Don't 'hey chick' me." She wiggled her feet in the air. "Just look at these. They're priceless." She took in a long deep breath. "I heart them." She blew a smooch toward her toes and finally came up for air. "Now you know they warrant a chauffeur, both of them," she argued, then grabbed my bag and began hunting through it with precision.

"What're you doing?" I asked, holding back laughter.

"I'm looking for my autographed picture of Rain that I just know you didn't forget." She tossed my files around and suddenly slowed her foraging through my tote. "But, wait, what's this? What have we here?" she asked as she pulled out the rectangular box.

"I, I honestly don't know what it is," I stammered, looking away.

"You mean it just appeared in your bag, and you've never seen it before?" She tapped her nails on the tabletop. "I expect better from you. You know you simply can't bullshit a bullshitter!"

"Elijah gave it to me as a 'welcome to the team' token. I haven't had a chance to open it yet."

Britt stared at the box for a moment. "Well, well, well. That explains it: the long hours at the office, the extreme work-week fatigue, and the quicker-than-most recovery and checkout from Heartbreak Hotel."

"Elijah, huh?" Kennedy quizzed, narrowing her lids.

"No, it was more of a *company* gesture," I corrected as I turned away again to look at the people passing behind Britt.

"Are you sure about—"

My attention veered as everything around me faded to black while I zoomed in on the washed-out back pockets of a tall stranger in a white baseball cap who was crossing the street in the distance at the congested corner. Spotlighted in Technicolor, he moved in slow motion, walking and talking on his cell. I held my breath, watching the stranger laugh, wanting nothing more than to be the lucky person on the other end of that call. The way he moved made me wonder if there was any room for *me* in his dark denim five-pocket jeans. Everything else remained in freeze-frame as I zeroed in on the quite-spectacular stagger of his swagger . . . just before he disappeared around the corner.

"Hellooo? Am I talking to myself?" Britt interrupted.

I blinked, and the world around me gradually took shape again, filling in with color. "Huh?" I hesitated, turning to Britt.

I was stuck. I eyed Kennedy, but even my wing-chick stood me up.

"Hannah, the little box says Bailey Banks & Biddle. That's simply not a welcome memento. What the hell are you waiting for? Open it already!"

So there we sat—the three of us, huddled over the tiny box beneath a wobbly umbrella, breathing deeply. I slid the mysterious box open and ogled the goods. And there it was: an 18-carat white-gold diamond tennis bracelet sat motionless, watching us just as intensely as we were watching it.

15

WHY IS IT THAT WHENEVER A WHITE WOMAN IS WEARING EXTRA HAIR ON HER head that clearly isn't growing out of her own scalp, she has "hair extensions," but as soon as a "sista" attaches and secures the wefted tracks, it's a "weave"?

I could see Halle Berry posing perfectly on the cover of the *Cosmo* that was neatly situated on the coffee table as soon as I poked my head into the outer waiting area of Dr. Ivy's office. Being casually careful not to look around the room, I headed straight for the lemony-yellow armchair positioned directly diagonally to her inner office door. Puma was the name I'd given the purple-and-black-striped flame angel in the miniaquarium four weeks ago when I'd had my first visit with the highly recommended head shrink. Since that initial encounter, Puma had seemed to understand my anxiety-ridden struggle and had given a welcome wave with his fish tail.

I coolly crossed my legs and got *un*-comfortable in the chair, apprehensively flipping through the very old issue of *Cosmo*. Since *Catwoman* (ew!), Halle had kept her hair long and wavy, and looked fab with her extensions/weave. (If the woman wearing the hair is mixed, what do you call it then?)

I breathed in deeply. Sitting in the shrink's waiting ward was already intimidating enough, but then *Cosmo* only worsened the daunting experience by pitilessly pointing out every additional imperfection I didn't already realize I had. I looked down at my foot, which was shaking incessantly, bordering on a conniption, before turning the page of the juicy mag anyway.

Movado check: 3:33 p.m. Dr. Ivy was already three minutes late for our session, and I knew that would put me into the next half hour on my parking meter. Heart pounding. Puma swam back around the coral, and Halle looked up at me from the pages on my lap, both daring me to leave. I eyed Dr. Ivy's door intently and contemplated an escape route. Beating louder. The door swung open. Shit!

I surrendered and closed the *Cosmo*, flattening both Halle and her *extensioned* weave.

"Hannah, you can come in now. Sorry for the delay. I hope this doesn't inconvenience you in any way."

"No, no, it's no problem!" I lied.

I tapped at the fish tank and glared at Puma before taking baby steps into the warm office. The walls were painted a soft tangerine, and the thick, oatmeal-colored Berber carpet balanced them nicely. Each week when Dr. Ivy opened the door, the room welcomed me in with what felt like an overdue hug from an old fat friend.

"Have a seat. Get comfortable."

I walked over to the plush leather sofa in front of the bay window, which served as an oversized frame for Chicago's latest developmental gem: Millennium Park.

Dr. Ivy sat across from me, with only a russet leather ottoman between us. She was a slender brown-skinned woman with long legs. Her jet-black chopped wavy hair was tapered meticulously at the base of her neck. Her curvy body, keen features, and sense of style just didn't resemble anything I'd ever imagined a clinical psychologist would look like. The first day I looked at her I strongly thought that she could've easily been an extra on any episode of *Baywatch*.

Her clipboard never left her hands as she periodically jotted down a sentence or two; it was the only thing that ever reminded me that we were actually having a session. Other than that, our time together was always comfortable—sometimes friendly, even. During our very first meeting, I'd opened up and was decidedly disappointed when our time together was over.

"Hannah, please—have a seat."

"Yes, of course," I agreed, leaning as far into the corner of the sofa as possible.

"So, how was your week?"

I took a deep breath. "Much better. This one was definitely much better than the last. Definitely."

"What about your anxiety? Any sudden attacks—panic attacks, anxiety attacks—"

"No. Nothing out of the ordinary."

"Very good. That's what the process is all about, getting you where you need to be again. Now, have you given any more thought to what we discussed in regards to your taking up a new hobby, one that will allow you to focus only on Hannah?"

"Well, actually I've been giving it some very serious thought, and I think I've finally made a decision."

"Please, tell me more," she said, leaning in.

I cleared my throat and hoped she wouldn't think I'd lost my mind. "OK, well . . . ever since I was a little girl I always wondered what it would be like to be one of the cheerleaders for the Chicago Diamonds—you know, a Diamond Doll. Grandpa Red, my Nana's dad, used to sit me in front of the nineteen-inch black-and-white in the kitchen and explain the different elements of the game, but I'd watch just to catch a glimpse of the cheerleaders under the basket or on the court just before they'd go to commercial."

I looked at Dr. Ivy and searched for some sort of reaction.

Nothing.

"Well, I never followed the game and still can't tell you any of the players on the team, but I always told him I was gonna be out there one day performing during somebody's halftime." I searched her face again.

Nothing.

"So, before I left for college, I promised myself that if I ever moved back and was still in good shape, I'd try out for the team. Now, of course I didn't think I'd be twenty-eight, more like twenty-one, but I've been thinking that now is as good a time as any to take that chance and see what happens. You know, take a chance on me and do what we've been talking about: stop dating for a while and do something just for Hannah."

"Interesting. I think that's quite an undertaking and a very dedicated thing to do. But I was thinking more along the lines of a pottery class."

I watched her jot down a line on her clipboard.

"What about the time commitment and your job? Have you given that any thought? I'm sure it's a huge commitment."

I folded my hands tightly in my lap.

"I know. I was thinking about that, and you're right: it is a serious time commitment. They practice twice a week and perform at all the home games during the season, not to mention all the other promotional engagements. But Cobra's been doing a great job these past couple of months, and I was thinking that if necessary, I always have the option to hire an intern."

"So you've given this some serious thought. I see. When do you have to make a final decision? Don't they start the audition process sometime in the summer?"

"The applications have to be postmarked by the end of the week."

"This week?"

"Uh-huh. But I can download everything and still meet the deadline; I just have to make a decision—right now! They want a picture and some references. And then there's still no guarantee that they'll even ask to see me. Last year out of twenty-five hundred girls who sent in applications, they only invited two hundred to come in for the closed audition."

As I talked my heart was racing at NASCAR speed.

"Well, it sounds like you've already made up your mind. I guess I'd better get my season tickets now."

"But I haven't made the team yet."

"Uh-huh," she said, laughing to herself. "Just let me know if they offer a discounted rate for therapists."

16

I'D KICKED MY NORMAL SORRY-ASS-BARELY-THERE WORKOUT ROUTINE INTO HIGH gear and had packed in as many dance classes as possible in the evenings and on weekends. Over the past two weeks, my workouts had been getting increasingly more intense, and my trainer, Mecca, refused to cut me any slack. He had me on a cardio/strength combo that consisted of treadmill and elliptical machine work followed by light weights at high reps. The agony!

Handing off my car keys to Dallas, the valet/doorman, I opened my mailbox and began sorting. Besides the usual bills and junk mail, there was a thick white envelope with an unfamiliar return address. I got on the elevator and pressed for the penthouse. It headed for the parking garage instead, but I was too tired to care. A handful of people got on while I wrestled with the envelope, managing to pull the folded letter out intact. I'd been staring at the return address when the doors opened on the twenty-fourth floor. My right leg had finally stopped throbbing from the murderous squats and was now starting to spasm. I took a slow deep breath and shuddered at the seductively familiar smell in the tight enclosed space. I couldn't pinpoint exactly where I'd been introduced to this olfactory friend, but there was no denying the strong commitment my senses had already made to it.

Peeking slightly over the letter, I saw the back of a tall man. Doing a quick once-over of the elevator, I realized that it had cleared, leaving only the two of us. I glanced up over his shoulders: a nice-enough neck. On to his head: a fitted white cap. Holding my breath wasn't going to help me become invisible, but I did it anyway as I pulled the letter back over my bugged eyes. I wished I'd showered at the gym— not that I ever do. I tried to smooth down the edges of my hair, check for body odor, and disappear into the corner of the elevator. He, on the other hand, smelled familiarly delish and made me almost want to say "hello" and to hell with my B.O. But before my eyes could take in any more of him, he shifted his weight to turn around, and I immediately reshifted my focus to the 12-point font.

Dear Hannah Love,

Congratulations on being selected to attend the Chicago Diamond Dolls auditions.

"Ohmigod!" I gasped, even as the pair of eyes peered down at me, burning holes through the letter. He cleared his throat, and I shut my eyes until the doors opened again on the thirtieth floor, where he got off.

I strangled the paper with my fingernails before quickly resuscitating it.

We are happy to inform you that out of 2,243 applicants from the Chicagoland area you have been chosen to be one of the 200 attendees at this year's first round of auditions. The first round will take place Saturday, June 12th, at the Chicago Stadium and will begin promptly at 9 a.m. You can expect the audition to last the entire day, so plan on being at the Chicago Stadium until 6 p.m. You will need to bring a lunch and snacks. We will provide beverages.

Please wear a leotard and flesh-colored pantyhose/stockings or tights, black soft-soled dance shoes or sneakers, and full makeup and hair.

If you advance to the second round, you will participate in a three-day minicamp the following week, which will culminate in the selection of the Chicago Diamond Dolls team. All candidates will be judged on physical appearance, dance ability, and attitude. You will have an opportunity to showcase your freestyle dance skills as well as technique. Last, you will be put through a series of interviews with an esteemed panel of judges.

Enclosed please find a parking permit for Saturday, June 12th. This permit is good for the scheduled hours of the audition only. Please park in the east lot adjacent to the Michael Jordan statue.

Be aware that these auditions are closed to the public. No media or photographs are allowed except those taken by Diamond Dolls staff. If you have any additional questions, please contact Nikki at 1-800-CHI-DOLL.

Best of luck,

Nikki Tyler
Chicago Diamond Dolls
Coach

I stared at the letter and could hear Grandpa Red's words resonating in my head: *Baby girl, somebody's gotta win; why not you?*

Later that night, I was finally able to get into the Jacuzzi to soak, reflect, and visualize. I closed my eyes and tried to envision myself hitting every move of their routine. My toe touches and Chinese splits were now up to par, thanks to Mecca's ruthless stretching sessions. I zenned out and envisioned landing all the double and triple pirouettes I'd been practicing, but instead I disappeared into a kaleidoscoped zone of perfect asses, broad shoulders, and a myriad of white baseball caps. And it didn't really matter how much almond bath gel or sweet aloe vera oil had been doused into the bubbling bathwater. All I could smell was him.

17

THE GLARING SUN FORCED ME OUT OF BED. I STUMBLED OVER TO THE BALCONY, pained from my workout hangover, and opened the French doors. The sun lit up the glassy waters of Lake Michigan far beyond the horizon. I watched the lake glisten like a sea of sapphire jewels before stepping out into the morning air and wrapping myself in its silky embrace. I watched the runners enjoying their sunrise workout on the Drive and felt myself begin to tense. Mecca had strongly suggested that I refrain from exercising today. "The day before the big audition should be spent relaxing, meditating, and stretching," he'd said. I closed my eyes and thanked God for absolutely everything before attempting to visualize the panel of judges.

"Oh good, you're up."

I spun around and saw Kennedy standing in the doorway, already sweaty from her morning workout.

"It looks that way, doesn't it?"

"I need you to come downstairs and take a look at something for me."

"What's wrong?"

"Nothing. I just need your opinion on something."

I followed her down the spiral staircase, through the living room, and into the kitchen.

"Surprise!"

Britt and Kennedy were standing next to the island with balloons and little bears outfitted in cheerleading uniforms with "B-R-A-T-S" spelled out on the back.

"You didn't think we were gonna let you go through the day without wishing you good luck, did you?" Kennedy asked, waving one of the bears back and forth like a pom-pom.

"You guys rock! You didn't have to go through all this. My audition isn't even until tomorrow."

"Yeah, but we know your ass has to get up early tomorrow morning and do your zen thing. Plus Mecca would kill us if we had you out tonight trying to celebrate. You'll need your rest if you're gonna compete with all those bitches that've been training since last year," Britt declared. She grabbed one of the big gold balloons and handed it to me. "You're gonna work it out tomorrow. And don't forget to pack your snacks in your superhero lunchbox. That way, we'll be with you all day. Kennedy, make sure—"

"Already got it covered. I'm packing her lunch myself. Now, Hannah-Bug, you didn't think we were gonna let you face one of the biggest challenges of your life without us cheering you on, did you? *We* don't have to audition to be your cheerleaders."

I walked over to the two of them and kissed each one on the cheek, realizing that this was one of those moments I'd already thanked Him for this morning.

Britt coughed and inched away. "I love you and everything, girl, but don't smear my foundation. MAC says this shit is kissable, but I don't have time to be testing it out. Now a sister has to get to work," she said and grabbed her Coach briefcase. "I have to show a hot spot to a hottie in Water Tower in an hour. That gives me time to grab a latte and wash down those three mimosas I had with my masseur this morning."

Kennedy and I stopped and looked at Britt, who was on her way out the door.

"What? Don't look at me like that. A sister has to handle business before she can handle *business*. Don't hate, cuz he doesn't discriminate. He'll rub y'all down too in all the right places. Why y'all trippin' anyway; you know I don't mind sharing." She blew kisses in the air and switched off to the elevator.

Kennedy waved to her sister and stood by the door. "Do you need me to help you with anything, Bug? I'm free till the afternoon."

"No, Sweets, I've got it all covered." I grabbed my balloons and headed toward the stairs. "I'm just gonna head to the office and look over more footage from Rain's video shoot. Besides, I really don't wanna spend all day today focusing on tomorrow."

"If you change your mind and you need some help, call me on my cell. I'm going for a run on the beach."

"Didn't you just come from working out?" I shouted over the banister.

"Sort of. I did a couple of miles on the treadmill, but that doesn't compare to a morning beach run on a perfect day. Plus, I just ate a bagel and need to burn it off. I'm feeling bloated and pudgy anyway."

"What! You can't be serious. Kennedy, honey, wait a second—"

"No worries. I'm fine. Trust me."

"Kennedy?!" I ran down the stairs.

"Call me if you need anything. I have a casting for a Phillip Morris antismoking spot later. They're casting ex-smokers in an ad for their print campaign."

"But your ass still smokes."

"Yeah, and Phillip Morris still sells cigarettes."

18

I'D GIVEN COBRA THE DAY OFF. PERIODICALLY, I LIKE TO REWARD HIM FOR ALL THE weight he pulls around here. But when I walked into my office he was standing behind my desk arranging a big bouquet of white calla lilies.

"What're you doing here? I gave you the day off."

"I know. I'm not staying," he informed me with his left hand on his hip and his other making whirly motions in the air, "but I wanted to bring you flowers and tell you in person that no matter what happens tomorrow, I'm proud to have you as my boss. And when I grow up, I wanna be just like you, Bosslady."

I didn't know what to say. I walked over to him, picked up the vase, and situated it on the antique credenza behind my desk. Slightly choked up, I turned back around with my arms extended to give Cobra a much-deserved hug but found Eli standing there instead.

"Well, it's good to see you too, Hannah." He smiled his crooked yet winning smile.

"I . . . I . . . was . . ." I looked around for Cobra, who'd mysteriously disappeared. Eli moved in closer and put his arms around my waist. For half a second, I went limp, unsure of an appropriate response.

"Those are very beautiful flowers. What's the occasion?" he whispered in my ear, gently pulling me close to him. I pulled away and cleared my throat, straightening my red pencil skirt and brushing my bangs from my forehead. He put his left hand into his Armani jeans and with his right forefinger tucked the loose ends of my hair behind my ear.

The pounding of my heart was louder than a Rob Base drum line. I could see Cobra's cheek inching its way around the door as he was trying to sneak a peek. Without taking his eyes away from me, Eli walked back around my desk and kicked the door shut with his left foot.

I fell into my seat.

"Well, um, those were a good-luck gesture from Cobra," I said, gesturing toward the flowers. "Big day tomorrow."

"Yeah, I heard. Auditions, right? That's what's up. Now I couldn't let your big day go by without wishing my favorite girl good luck, could I?"

"You couldn't?" I asked, sitting motionless in the chair, unaware of what my expression might say. Eli reached into his blazer pocket and pulled out a small blue box. I recognized both the box and the infamous creamy white ribbon. Tiffany. He walked back over to my chair, bent down, and tenderly kissed my forehead.

"Good luck tomorrow, Angel."

By the time I'd snapped out of it and could prepare something to say, he was halfway down the hall with his cell to his ear, texting away on his BlackBerry.

I looked down at the little blue box on top of a videotape of unedited footage, then grabbed both the tape and the blue box and ran out of my own office. I was almost past Cobra's empty desk when I heard Eli call my name from the opposite end of the hall.

"Yes?" I responded, realizing my voice was quivering even though I hadn't done anything wrong—or had I?

"Get a fuckin' intern!"

"But—" I stammered, turning around to address his directive. He was already in his office, with the door closing behind him. I looked over at Cameran, his ever-present assistant, who was wearing an irresponsibly short skirt. Her forced smile made me want to hide the little blue box behind my back.

"OK," I squealed to the closed door and headed for my car.

When I finally arrived home and pulled into the driveway, Dallas came out of the building with a crisp white envelope in his hand. We made an even exchange: my keys for the envelope.

"Who's this from?"

"Not sure. When I came in this morning, it was sitting next to the phone. There was a note attached that read 'For the woman in the penthouse.' And you're the only woman who fit the description he gave me in the penthouse."

"Thanks, D," I said and slipped the envelope into my Capezio bag along with the new dance shoes I'd just purchased.

When I locked the door I realized Kennedy wasn't home yet. I couldn't wait any longer. Dumping the contents of my tote onto the floor, I held the square blue box from Eli in my hands before wrapping the ribbon around my finger a couple times. I imagined what could be inside before slowly opening it to see. There was the most beautiful platinum diamond lariat necklace with brilliant, round pavé diamonds in the shape of a star that dangled weightily from the clasp. The necklace took my breath away. The diamonds were absolutely yummy! Ohmigod! What did this mean? Why did he—

A small card peeked up at me from beneath the necklace. I pulled it out and read aloud: "Dazzle them like the star I know you are."

19

THE NEXT MORNING WASN'T NEARLY AS BEAUTIFUL AS THE ONE BEFORE. THE SUN was playing hide and seek with the runners out for their sunrise jog. I stretched, closed the balcony doors, and took the quickest shower of all time. I didn't want to invite any anxiety into my morning. I'd done my visualizations and deep breathing, and it was time to move full speed ahead.

I threw on my BCBG eggshell-white jogging suit and the matching white terry flip-flops. Seated at the vanity, I took my time with my makeup and focused on evenly applying the lengthy lashes just before packing my bag. I tried hard not to forget anything important or required. Leotard: check! Hosiery: check! Makeup: check! I even packed an extra curling iron in case the one I always used decided to break. There was no sense in relying on my competition to help me with anything. I'd watched enough reality shows to know better.

Myoki, weavestress extraordinaire, had worked her magic and had given me a tight (ouch!) body-wave weave. It was meticulously triple layered and stopped just past the middle of my back. When I swung my head, the hair gloriously followed. She'd left out enough for low bangs that fell just below my eyes and enough at the top so the blend was perfectly undetectable. Determined to make both the horse it came from and the judges happy, I planned on doing a quick straighten and curl just before my number was called. I'd need perfect hair to compensate for the lack of dexterity in my high-kick area. The Rockettes were still on my shit list for popularizing those dreadful moves.

"Hannah, come downstairs so you can eat something. You need to at least put something in your stomach before you leave. Now come on. You can't afford to be late today."

I knew Kennedy was right, but my nerves were already starting to get the best of me. I started to wonder: what on earth made me think I could pull this off after conditioning and training for only three weeks?

Most of these women had been training for the past year—some even longer, I suspected. Was I too old for this? Had my time already passed? Would I be going up against twenty-one-year-olds, fresh out of undergrad and sent straight to compete from their collegiate teams? I sat on the edge of the bed and put my head in my hands, letting the built-up anxiety get the best of me. Suddenly this all seemed far too foolish to pursue.

"Don't you dare get cold feet now! Your ass better be sitting there with your head in your hands praying to God and thanking Him for giving you the courage to go after something you've always wanted to do. Hannah-Bug, do you hear me talking to you?"

I looked up at her, and a single tear fell from my left eye. "Yeah, Sweets, I hear you. But what in God's name makes me think I can go out there and pull this off? What if I'm not good enough?"

Kennedy walked over to the bed, took my hands in hers, and knelt down in front of me. "You're better than good, and you owe it to yourself to see just *how* good. This is the first time since we were in high school, when you decided to run for senior class president, that you've taken a chance on yourself. Everything has always come so easy for you—school, grades, even work. But running for president was something you were actually nervous about. I still remember when you leaned against my locker on Election Day and said, "What if I don't win?" Do you remember what I told you that day? I told you that by taking a chance on yourself and just putting yourself out there, you'd already won."

"I remember that." Breaking a smile for the first time all morning, I wiped away the three tears that had finally decided to drop from both eyes and asked, "Who knew that I'd win by a 75 percent landslide?"

"I did," Kennedy said. She grabbed me by the head and pulled me in for a Sweet's bear hug—the kind that only a best friend can give. "Race you downstairs for a bagel," she challenged, and was gone before I could contest.

Rain or shine, I was in it to win it. We sat on the balcony outside of the living room, downing fresh fruit slices, bagels, and OJ.

"I'm getting more juice," Kennedy said, and headed back into the kitchen.

"Hey, grab my jazz shoes out of that bag. They should still be in the shoebox. I need to make sure they get stretched out."

Pushing the bagels aside, I popped a slice of watermelon into my mouth and looked up at the sky. I had to remember to bring my umbrella. The temp was cool, but the sun seemed perplexed about whether or not she was going to fight the good fight and come out shining.

"Bug?"

I looked up at Kennedy, who was standing in the doorway with her hand on her hip.

"What's this?" she asked, holding up the envelope Dallas had given me the night before.

"Not sure. Dallas gave it to me."

"It looks mysterious. 'For the woman in the penthouse?' What is it?"

I reached up and snatched the envelope from her hands. "Let's see." I opened it and quickly realized it was a card with a picture of a raised shiny silver question mark on the outside. I opened it and read aloud,

QUESTION: Are you finally beginning to pay attention to what's in front of you? I would really hate for you to miss something.

I sat still for a second and became one with the words on the card. They were familiar. Frantically, I went through my mental Rolodex and searched for some kind of connection. My search landed me back at the radio station, outside the studio, laid out, flat on the floor, reaching under a dusty ratty couch.

"Bug, what the hell is Dallas talking about?"

"I don't think this is from Dallas."

"Fill me in, cuz none of this is making any sense to me." She sat back in the lounge chair and tossed the napkin onto her plate.

I looked at my watch. The Movado warned: seven-thirty! Time hadn't betrayed me yet, but I had to get moving if I was gonna have time to get to the stadium, stretch, and decompress my nerves before the clock struck nine.

"I'm not sure myself, Sweets. I'll give Dallas a call when I get back, and we can get to the bottom of this together."

"You swear? Cuz girl, you know my life is only as juicy as a phone call from Roxy about a callback for a cancer stick ad."

"Pinky swear," I promised, and grabbed another slice of watermelon before getting up from the table and gathering all my crap.

"You look amazing. MAC would be proud—especially love the lashes. Don't forget your lunch, Wonder Woman."

"Thanks, Sweets, for everything!"

She swung the door open and threw her arms around me. I returned the massive hug and was out the door, rummaging through my white-striped Adidas gym bag in search of my cell. It had been ringing for a couple seconds and I knew exactly who it was before I flipped it open. "Hello."

"Where you at?" I heard Britt's voice on the other end.

"Hey chickie. Where do you think? I'm on my way to the elevator, still desperately trying to stay on schedule."

"Well, I don't wanna keep you," she continued. "Just wanted to give you a call and wish you the very best of luck. I know you're going to kick major ass. Between your zen shit and your fresh weave, Kennedy says you're ready for whatever. I love you, bitch, and I'll be thinking of you all day," she said, and paused for a moment. "Oh, and tell Shepherd Hunt I've got something real special for him," she purred.

"Who?" I quizzed.

"Shepherd Hunt. He's only the best player on the team right now," she explained, trying to school me. "Point guard. Number 27. But then don't sleep on Max Knight either," she continued, correcting herself. "He's the hottest and the most eligible player in the league."

"Must mean good contract," I figured aloud. "Listen, I'm trying out to be a cheerleader, not a ballplayer. And, Britt, he ain't checking for whatever you're offering."

"I happen to have a great house in North Shore that would be perfect for him. Get your mind out of the gutter."

I took the phone from my ear and stared at it, thinking for a sec that now would be a good time to introduce her to the dial tone.

"No, seriously, Bug, Kennedy and I will be at the house later tonight. You got Wonder Woman?"

"Yep. But I'm anxious anyway."

"That's normal," she quickly responded. "All that matters now is that you go in there with your game face on and show them the star that we already know you are."

I flipped the phone shut and stepped into the elevator, hoping I could live up to everyone's starry expectations.

20

BEFORE THE ELEVATOR DOORS EVEN CLOSED, I REALIZED THAT I WAS IN OVERDRIVE: my fingers were going numb, and my body was overheating. So there I stood, flapping my arms like a version of the funky chicken in the middle of the elevator, desperately attempting to cool down, when the doors opened on the thirtieth floor (oh, but yes). And just like that, we were standing face-to-face, looking directly at each other!

It was him—right there, in his fabulous flesh: broad shoulders, perfect ass, and crisp white baseball cap, looking at me look at him. And in that instant it all came together: the radio station bully, the spotlighted Technicolor pedestrian, and the elevator phantom—all one and the same! All I had to do was kill the funky chicken and keep my cool. He was standing so close to me that I could still smell the soap beneath his familiar cologne.

I stared at his white Nike T-shirt, which was fitted just enough to show off the curves of his muscles. And when I thought it couldn't get any worse, he smiled. There was no denying that his dimples were possibly more dangerous than his muscular bronzed legs under the long nylon and mesh Nike shorts. (Mental note: buy stock in Nike.) That's when things got fatal—he spoke! The words lingered in the air long enough for me to brim over with anticipation before they reached my ears.

"Good morning, Hannah."

Ahhh! His velvety deep voice was accented with Southern texture.

I held on tightly. How the hell did he know my name? I pinched my thigh with my thumb and index finger to make sure this was really happening.

"Ow!"

"What's wrong?" he asked, staring into my eyes.

I didn't want to give off my normal whacked weirdo vibe, so I just stood there in the middle of the elevator, rocking back and forth in my flip-flops, hoping he couldn't tell where my real lashes stopped and the fake ones began.

"Um, hey," I finally said. I couldn't think of anything better than that? Who says "hey" to a man who's been subtly stalking her subconscious?

"How are you?" he asked. His voice was filled with a perfect blend of testosterone and tenderness.

I took a moment and cleared my throat. "Fine. Um, how'd you know my name?" I asked delicately.

"Well, I'm on this new kick where I'm trying to pay really close attention to what's in front of me."

"Oh," I said, after a long, drawn-out pause. I really needed to do better with the whole vocabulary/communication thing.

"And I called the concierge at the front desk and asked."

For a second I was relieved that he seemed a little uneasy and maybe even human. Then that second passed.

"Oh," I said again, this time laughing nervously, thinking that this had to be the longest elevator ride to the lobby in the history of elevator rides to lobbies!

"Where are you off to so early on a Saturday?" he asked, staring at my mouth.

I closed my eyes, imagining this incredibly sexy man stepping out of the shower wearing only a towel knotted at his side, with soapsuds settled in the chiseled crevices of his back. I envisioned the towel dropping to the floor and—

"Wait; you don't have to answer that if you don't want. I didn't mean to be rude by getting in your business. It's just that it's early, and you—"

"What? What'd you say?"

"I asked where you were going so early on a Saturday morning, but you don't have to—"

"To the Chicago Stadium," I blurted out, happy to have something to say besides "oh" and "um."

He looked at me blankly and turned to face forward. Was it my turn to say something now? Was the ball in my court? Was the game over? Did I lose?

"Well, have a good day, Hannah."

We finally touched down, and he was the first to get off. The doors started to close before I realized this was my stop too.

He turned around to face me and flashed a smile that would have made my panties moist, had I been wearing any.

"By the way, you look really good in white."

"Thanks," I murmured, in a barely audible tone.

Instinctively, I looked down to give myself a once-over and set the model-like smile I was preparing to shoot back at him. But when I looked up, I was shooting my killer grin directly at Nyo, the seventy-one-year-old Vietnamese morning doorman.

"Morning, Nyo," I managed, completely consumed with embarrassment.

"Good morning, Ms. Hannah. Would you like me to bring your car around?"

"Yes, please." I took a seat in the lobby to pull myself together and handed the keys to Nyo, who flirtatiously returned his best half-toothed grin my way.

SECOND QUARTER

21

I RODE IN SILENCE ALL THE WAY TO THE STADIUM BEFORE FINALLY PULLING AROUND into the designated lot. Passing the parking attendant my permit, I so desperately wanted to ask for the inside scoop: how many girls had actually sucked it up and shown up? How many of that bunch were cute, gorgeous, stunning? How many had done this before? Could I have been lucky enough to audition the one year when everyone else competing against me was fucking huge?

The SUV quieted to a barely audible buzz. "Somebody's gotta win, baby girl; why *not* you?" was what Grandpa Red had said on the phone the night I'd applied for that high school scholarship. I didn't know I had the goods until he knocked on my bedroom door and handed me the coveted congratulatory letter. That was the first time I'd ever seen him cry.

I slammed the car door and took a deep breath. Kennedy had told me to take a chance on myself. "No worries," she'd said. "You've already won."

The walk to Gate 4 scored a scene from *A Spike Lee Joint*. Gliding along, never feeling my feet touch the ground, I passed the Michael Jordan statue and threw up the black power fist. The sign read Diamond Dolls Auditions. A middle-aged pasty-white woman with short graying hair asked to see my ID. Everything about her screamed AVERAGE! and she reeked of one-dimensional Midwestern blah. Trying to guard against her energy and remain in my zone, I took the number she handed me, 108, and proceeded down the hall and around the corner.

Gold carpet lined the hallways, and the walls were adorned with pictures of Chicago sports legends. I looked to my left and saw Walter Payton posing with a younger Michael Jordan. To my right was Scottie Pippen dunking a basketball with a legion of open-mouthed fans gasping in amazement. The rows of glossy autographed photographs were framed between thick sheets of Plexiglas and mounted above several small light boxes—the perfect aesthetic tribute to the sports-loving town, I thought.

After taking another right and downing a flight of stairs that led me into one of the press rooms with a couple hundred other girls, I nervously took a seat along the wall next to a girl who resembled a younger Katie Holmes. And though initially she looked harmless enough, after a few seconds she leaned into her chair and began attacking her nails.

"Hi. I'm Minnow."

I looked over at the younger Katie and broke a smile. "Hi, Minnow, I'm Hannah."

"I've tried out three years in a row. This makes year number four," she rambled on robotically, with her fingers still in her mouth.

"Wow!" I exclaimed before catching myself. "Year number four, huh?"

"Your first time?"

"Yep. My first."

"Well, I can tell you that it will go really fast once they get started," she explained, scanning the room. "I recognize quite a few of the girls who've done this before. So, like, in about fifteen minutes, all the veterans will stroll in and huddle together next to the door, survey the room, then rate everyone. They audition mostly so the judges can see if they're still skinny enough to keep their spot."

Somehow I wasn't quite prepared for all that she'd just dished. Mecca would have suggested I cop a squat on the floor and begin stretching to remain focused. To hell with that—I wanted to know more, and seeing how Minnow had already done this *several* times, she was just the one to probe. But before I could begin my inquisition, a gorgeous woman bolted into the room and commanded everyone's attention. I figured this would be an appropriate time to slide to the floor and begin an easy stretch while listening to her directives.

She was dressed in a Diamond Dolls gold-and-white Nike warm-up suit with a big Diamond patch over the heart. Five foot seven with light brown hair, chunky blonde streaks, and an imperfectly perfect mole just under her plumped bottom lip, she was trés fabulous.

"Attention. Attention!" The perky Doll clapped her hands together. "My name is Nikki Tyler—that's Nikki, or Coach, or Coach Nikki to you. I'm the head coach of the Chicago Diamond Dolls," she greeted in a slightly pitchy voice. "Let me just say it's a real pleasure to have you here at the home of the Blackhawks, the Bulls, and the Diamonds. We welcome you. Now, I assume everyone knows what they should be wearing and . . . blah, blah, blah."

She bounced out of the room with a sincere enough "Good luck!" and all the girls jumped up and started fussing over themselves; hair spray, makeup brushes, and long/short/stubby/stocky/skinny legs took to the air. My calm was being de-zenned by my nerves, and I contemplated calling Kennedy as others rang their mothers, boyfriends, and even children. As soon as Minnow began chatting up someone else, I tiptoed toward a corner in the back of the room and set up shop under a table.

Creating a makeshift changing space turned out to be the easy part; the deafening challenge was listening to 'Mitzi' and 'Bitzi' a few curling irons away. They were two mid-twenties bottled blondes who'd clearly been down this road before. I easily deduced that one of their roadblocks may have been the seriously overdone bright blue eye shadow topping off just under their brows, circa 1988. No sooner had I leaned in closer than I detected their pickup truck–heavy Midwestern valley drawl. Yikes!

When I couldn't take it anymore, I dug deep into my bag like a hype scrambling for a pipe. It was past time for me and Jay-Z to take a hit.

Continuing to stretch, I rocked out to my favorite track, taking my time to assess the competition from my cozy corner office. But when the veterans made their grand entrance, I had to put Jigga on pause.

Ray Charles couldn't have missed them. The seas parted as they each came slinking into the room, sporting the exact same gold-and-white warm-up suit as Nikki. Their arm candy was oversized gold-and-white embroidered Chicago Diamond Dolls duffel bags. The room quieted to a hush, and two hundred voices whispered into their cell phones simultaneously: "I'll call you back."

Within a matter of seconds the vets had sized up each wannabe before situating themselves into a huddle by the door to begin their private critique session. I glanced over at Minnow, who winked and dutifully delivered an "I told you so" nod.

As soon as I spied them glancing my way I knew I was up for review. Instinctively, I sucked in my stomach and pushed back my shoulders. I'd hoped to be a serious contender weighing in at a hundred and twenty-two pounds, size 4.

The veterans wore their confidence almost as well as their warm-up suits. Turning away as if their superiority scene had left me unfazed, I thought to myself: *Who am I kidding? I want both the warm-up set* and *the matching oversized gold-and-white duffel with the plush Diamond patch on either side.*

This was getting pretty serious; I'd brought clothes and accessories into the equation!

22

BEFORE WE COULD EVER CONCEIVE OF BECOMING D-O-L-L-S, WE BECAME G-O-A-T-S: two hundred of us herded onto the court in front of the industry judges. There were seven of them, spread out across the full length of the floor along the sidelines. Positioning myself in front of the other wannabes, I stood directly in view of the two judges on the far right. Though they were the only two I could clearly make out, one thing was certain: if I could see them, they could certainly see me. Kennedy had dished audition tips, and her strategies were already paying off.

A frenetic pace ensued, and I picked up as many steps as I could before Coach spiked the volume and motioned to an obnoxiously young-looking girl standing next to an enormous sound system. Shortstuff couldn't have been more than thirteen years old and looked like a mini-Nikki: warm-up suit, highlights, dancer stance, miniature mole, and all. She knew all the moves and exuded confidence as she worked it out like a prepubescent video vixen.

"This time, everyone with the music," Coach instructed as J-Lo screeched from the speakers.

Minnow was right. Before I knew it we were back in the holding cell waiting for our group to be called to perform for the judges. Each of us had sliced out a little piece of the room to rehearse, talk, eat, and even snore. I pulled out my iPod and searched frantically through my playlist for J-Lo, making a mental note to give Kennedy a big smooch for the file-sharing.

"Group 3." Heart pounding.

I shut my eyes and felt Sly slide me five to the intro of the *Rocky* theme: track number 7 from the sound track of my life! I walked through the tunnel and onto the court with the other thirty-nine goats and—

I froze!

Chills crept up my spine. Crippled by the enormousness of the stadium, I was simply unable to move. The other goats flocked to their positions and, without hesitation, hit their mark. I heard cheering, chanting, and screaming from the balconies as strobe lights danced through the countless rows of fans: toddlers on laps, middle-aged bald guys, international celebrities, inebriated frat boys, gorgeous groupie girls—and a commanding cheerleading squad pumping up the crowd in the middle of it all.

I thought of all the phenom athletes who'd stood right where I was now, beneath this very basket. I thought of what Grandpa Red would've given to have swapped his spot in front of the nineteen-inch set in our minikitchen for any seat behind that very rim.

"Number 108, we're waiting. You ready?"

A sweet calm came over me.

"Sorry. Yes, I am now." I looked around the court at the blurred faces staring back at me and explained: "It's a real honor to be here, in this place. It's my grandfather—I mean, he would've been very proud."

Out of the corner of my eye I saw one of the judges write something down, and I wondered if I'd just blown it.

Our group was spread out across the court in two lines of twenty. I was the last girl on the far right in the same corner where I'd learned the routine. Another Kennedy cue: stick with what's familiar. Coach twirled through the logistics, and before I knew it, the music was echoing throughout the dome. I slipped into a dance trance and hit every step, adding an extra pop at the hook. I didn't really mean to cheese that much, but something settled inside me and exploded. Once or twice I even focused in on the two judges in front of me and, per Kennedy, tried to make a connection.

Back in the holding cell, I stretched out on the floor in my corner and opened my lunchbox to see what special treats Sweets had packed. I was in the middle of peeling a very *orange* orange when Nikki sprinted into the room to make the first cut.

Deafening silence! You could have heard a pom-pom drop.

"If I call your number, congratulations; you've been chosen to remain with us for the afternoon and participate in the second half of today's auditions. Please move to the side of the room so everyone else can gather their belongings and leave. Thanks again. You were all talented and wonderful and—"

Minnow really wasn't kidding. Everything was happening so fast; the only thing I could think to do was cross my fingers and toes while keeping my eyes closed.

". . . Number 13, Number 74, Number 3, NUMBER 108 . . ."

My heart raced, and the room shocked a pulse again. Hair was flying in the air as the chosen ones screamed and jumped around. I searched the room for Minnow. Everything slowed just as she appeared from behind one chubby girl's back and over a remarkably tall girl's head, beaming, with two thumbs up. I took a steady breath and was relieved to see that we'd be around together for at least one more round.

23

AND THEN THERE WERE A HUNDRED GOATS.

The room looked bigger already. Coach didn't waste any time somersaulting into our quarters to call out the next numbers for the freestyle round—or what I liked to call The Sooouuulll Train Line.

"This round will run a little differently. If I call your number after your group performs, please step to the side. If I don't, you can gather your belongings and leave. Freestyle is extremely important; we need good dancers. We can't have you standing around at the end of the routine biting your nails."

My number was summoned to be in the first group of twenty pulled out onto the court. Standing in my usual spot under the basket, ready for my close-up with Don Cornelius, I exhaled. This was the fun part. Minnow obviously didn't share my sentiments, I thought when I looked up to see her gnawing at her nails ferociously.

"Minnow, you've gotta calm down. This should be the fun part," I whispered just before the music sounded.

"You don't understand. This is where I get eliminated every year. I don't have any rhythm."

"Neither does Taylor Hicks."

She looked at me blankly, and when Shortstuff turned on the music, Minnow slipped into convulsions. For a moment I believed this mission might be unsalvageable. Nevertheless, I danced over to her and stared her in the eye, without missing a beat. By the grace of God, she relaxed and found a haven *between* the beats, if not quite *on* them. At least I knew she could *hear* them. It was a start.

Coach was on perk alert as she vigorously moved through the twenty of us, showing us up with her boundless enthusiasm. As she approached our end of the court I grabbed Minnow's hand so we could dance together. Even though we looked rather silly, we remained composed. Coach chuckled before bouncing on.

"Ohmigod! I don't know how to thank you enough. I know I still looked like a maniac, but I totally appreciate you going out on a limb and helping me out. Nobody's ever done anything like that for me before."

It was the longest I'd seen Minnow go without gnashing her nails into her teeth.

"No worries. You just needed to look like you were having fun out there," I said as we walked over to the sidelines while the judges tallied scores. "I'll teach you how to actually *dance* another time."

"No, you don't understand."

"I think I do."

"I just know I'm going to get cut. After four years, they know this is my weak spot. Look at the other girls—they know it too."

I glanced over at the giggling goats in our group. Some of them had formed a huddle and were looking over at the two of us and laughing. I recognized the ringleader as one of the bitchy chicks from my dance class. It was like junior high all over again.

I grabbed her hand. "Don't let them get in your head. You came to win."

"OK, ladies, if I call your number, please remain on the court. If I don't, please go back to the press room and grab your things on your way out. We appreciate your enthusiasm, but unfortunately—"

I looked down at the number pinned on Minnow's green leotard: lucky Number 13—just wrong on so many levels! I figured I'd designate the crossed fingers on my left hand for her.

"Number 87, Number 46, Number 22, Number 4, Number 108, Number 9, and lucky Number 13 . . ."

Minnow's hands covered her mouth as she stood still, tears welling in her eyes.

"Congratulations, Number 13," Nikki said, and winked at Minnow as she dashed past the two of us.

"I can't believe it. I just can't believe it. I actually made it past freestyle. Hannah, we did it. You totally rescued me out there."

"No need to thank me. I told you, Soul Patrol has nothing on you, and even Ms. Spears-Federline had better watch out. Everyone knows she stole her moves from Janet anyway. Now c'mon, let's eat."

True to form, Nikki didn't waste a nanosecond after lunch. It was time for interviews, and each goat was to be called in individually to answer questions from the panel of judges. Minnow didn't have the Cliff Notes for this round so we'd both be flying blind.

I retouched my makeup, brushed my hair, and stretched my tired muscles. I took a tally of the room and noticed that the veterans were less focused on the wannabes and more concerned with themselves now. Sixty-one girls remained, including the vets, Minnow, myself, and the obnoxious diva from my hip-hop dance class.

"Number 108, you're up first."

"Huh?" *First? No, really. First?*

"Good luck in there, even though you don't need it. You're so in," Minnow whispered.

I tried to keep up with Nikki as she led me through the tunnel and onto the court. There wasn't anything to really be nervous about, I thought. Just like interviewing. I'd have to take a second to think about the question, compose myself, and be sure to make eye contact while answering. No worries, right? Piece-o-cake.

She directed me to the middle of the floor, where I had an unobstructed panoramic view of the stadium. In that great space, I quietly realized that it was just me and a little girl's dream.

"This is Number 108, Hannah Love," Nikki informed the judges. "Each of the judges will introduce themselves so you'll have some idea who you're talking to," she informed me.

A woman on the far left began. I smiled and listened, being careful to maintain eye contact. She muttered something about handling the PR for the Chicago Diamonds franchise. I nodded and tried to hold a comfortable stance, feeling very self-conscious out there on the massive court alone. The next judge began to introduce himself, and a knot immediately formed in the pit of my stomach.

"I'm Maximillien Knight. This will be my fifth year playing for the Chicago Diamonds."

The seats in the mezzanine began to run together, and I couldn't feel my fingers. Where were my goddamn fingers! It was the perfect ass, broad shoulders, and fitted white baseball cap—for the second time today. He'd been sitting at the far left end of the judge's table (sans the baseball cap), and I hadn't been able to see that far down the court all day. *Breathe.* I cleared my throat, and saliva skidded down the wrong pipe. I coughed. I choked.

"Excuse me," I pleaded, heaving, gasping for air.

"Are you OK?" Nikki asked. She ran over and patted me on the back, whispering, "Are you OK, hon? Do you need some water? You're turning red."

Hell no, I'm not OK. Fuck the water; I wanna get outta here.

"I'm, I'm fine. I just—"

I bent over and put my hands on my knees and tried to reopen my chest cavity. How unsexy would it be to pass out in the middle of this interview? Kennedy didn't school me about this part of the process. Shortstuff hurried over with a Styrofoam cup half filled with water. I took a few sips and strained a smile between gulps.

"Please excuse me. I'm OK, just swallowed the wrong way."

Vel-vee-ta! Who friggin' swallows the wrong way?

"Please continue," I said.

I stood up straight, handed Shortstuff the cup, and exhaled. Realizing I was fidgeting with my hands, I put them behind my back and focused in on his gorgeous smile. I hoped he wasn't enjoying this. He could've said *something* in the elevator this morning—something, anything. Maybe he was just evil.

"I do believe that dance ability and appearance are important, but I'm really looking for a woman who has great energy—a certain je ne sais quois. The players appreciate it when we're on the court hustling, and the energy coming from our cheerleaders is, well, undeniably dynamic."

Was he serious? "Undeniably dynamic" my ass! I wanted to jump over that table and choke the shit out of him.

The rest of the judges introduced themselves, but I didn't hear a thing they said. Nikki asked me a couple of questions, and I answered them as honestly as possible, trying not to appear too shaken. I told them where I worked and that sweet little story about Grandpa Red and the goddamn nineteen-inch kitchen TV!

"Thanks so much, number 108," I heard Nikki finally say, and I followed her toward the tunnel back to the media room. When I reached the hallway, I looked back at the judges' table in disbelief. Maximillien, who was watching me intently, smiled that winning smile, and our eyes locked for a stolen moment.

Asshole!

24

"SO HOW'D IT GO? WHAT'D THEY ASK YOU? WHAT'D YOU SAY? WHAT DO YOU DO next?" Minnow probed, shaking her hands.

I didn't know what to tell her. I couldn't believe what had just happened myself, and I wasn't ready to try and explain it to her. I needed to ring Kennedy.

"The panel of judges introduces themselves, and then Nikki asks you a few questions. Just be yourself and you'll do fine. Oh yeah, and try and be dynamic," I said, and rolled my eyes.

Sitting under the table, I realized that it was completely out of my hands now. I should've been able to relax, but the big mean man in my dreams was deciding the fate of my little girl's dreams.

Finally, Nikki came in to get the last girl, and all the girls in the room slowly started to clean their areas, change their clothes, and pack their bags. I wanted to be confident, but I kept replaying the entire day in my head, wondering what my elevator buddy thought about it all. Maximillien. If only he'd said something. Part of me wanted to be mad, but I couldn't decide at what exactly.

"OK, ladies, this concludes our time together. I can't express to you how much we all appreciate you being here with us today for the first round of the Chicago Diamond Dolls auditions. Your interest and enthusiasm have been unmatched. If I call your number, please come forward and take one of the packets on the table labeled "Diamond Dolls Candidate" with you on your way out. This details everything you'll need to know for the minicamp next week, as well as a number to call should you have any additional questions. It's going to be a very exciting year, due partly to you. So without further delay: Number 76, Number 64, Number 154, Number 5, Number 101, Number 108, Number 3, Number 119, Number 13."

Minnow threw her arms in the air, thanking God or Buddha or whoever. I wanted to completely share in her joy, but I was stuck between elation and pissed-offedness. My thoughts, a mixture of anger and joy, continued to drift back to Maximillien. I needed to get out of there and clear my head; the Brats weren't going to believe this one.

I pushed open the door to Gate 4 and headed for my SUV. The keys were buried in my bag. I rummaged through all the compartments to find them while unsuccessfully trying to walk and run at the same time.

"Hannah, wait a second," I heard Maximillien's voice call out from behind me.

Was he serious?!

"Can I talk to you for a minute? Please?" he asked, jogging toward me.

I didn't know whether to break for the SUV or stand in the middle of the parking lot and let him explain why he had let me almost choke to death as a result of his little nondisclosure. I slowed my brisk walk to an easy stride.

"Hannah. Hey. Congratulations. You were great today," he said, finally catching up to me.

He was wearing his white baseball cap now and had a gold-and-white Diamonds duffel bag hanging over his shoulder. He looked even more amazing than he had just one hour ago.

"Thanks. Maximillien, is it?" I asked, crossing my arms.

"Yeah, but please, call me Max; all my friends do," he pleaded with eyes that made me think about rescinding the sassy attitude.

"Well, Maximillien, I'm not your friend. And if I were, I'd certainly have to dissolve this friendship after what you just pulled in there."

"Hannah, please, let me explain."

"No, there's nothing to explain. I've gotta go. I need to be somewhere," I said, and started toward my SUV again.

"Please. I don't know what else to say. I didn't mean to upset you."

"Well, I'm not sure how you thought that was gonna make me feel. I mean, I almost choked on my phlegm in there, in the middle of my interview, in the middle of the court, in the middle of the stadium. I could've blown it all."

"No, you were perfect. I loved you from the very beginning," he said warmly.

I stopped in my tracks. Suddenly that knot had resurrected in my stomach, and I couldn't feel my fingers. There must be something I can take for that problem, I thought, looking up at him.

"I mean, you were amazing today, from the minute you came out there and froze, to what you said about your grandfather, to helping out number 13 with that crazy dance—and your eloquent answers. I loved it. And you're so beautiful, your eyes—"

He reached out his right hand and touched my cheek and smiled.

I turned away. "I really, um, have to go."

"Let me take you to dinner. I know you must be starving by now." He reached for my shoulder. "That whole process is kind of grueling. I'll treat you. Wherever you want to go, it's on me. Shaw's or Houston's or Gibson's or—just tell me where, and I'll take you there. It's the least I can do."

"Well, Maximillien, I have my own transportation, and I don't need you to take me anywhere. Besides, Houston's shut down forever ago and I have a taste for chicken—some good ol' greasy Harold's Chicken."

"Sounds good. Let's go. I'll follow you."

For a few seconds, there was no one else in the parking lot except the two of us. I had to make a decision and had no idea which way I was leaning. The SUV was a couple paces away, so I headed in that direction without giving him an answer.

"Hannah, please. I'm serious. I feel really bad about all of this and would just like to talk to you."

"We're talking now," I said over my left shoulder. I really wanted to sit across a table from him and watch him beg, but the Brats were back at the house waiting, and the ringing in my bag was probably them.

"Hello," I said, flustered.

"Hey chickie, where you at?" Kennedy questioned.

"Still at the stadium, in the parking lot."

"How'd everything go? Are we moving on to the next round?"

"Yes, we're going to minicamp."

"Right on!" Kennedy screamed into the phone. "We're moving on to the next round," she screamed. "So what's wrong? Why so blue, Panda Bear?"

"Everything's fine."

"Yeah, no. I know you better than that. What's going on? Are you on your way in? We're here waiting for you."

I looked up at Maximillien, who had his hands pressed together, mouthing the word *please* over and over.

"I'll be home a little later. Just wait; I have to make a stop first. I'll explain when I get there. I'm fine, though."

"OK, Burger Queen, have it your way," Kennedy spouted, screaming as she hung up.

Maximillien grinned, and I instantly felt as if I'd given up some of my Spice Girl power.

"Good; now let's go get you some chicken. I'll follow you, but I need a ride back over to the player's lot. I just need to grab my car."

"You're on a roll with the requests tonight. Get in."

I got into the Rover and tossed my bag behind the seat. As Maximillien closed the door on the passenger's side my poor heart was trying to keep up with its own insanely fast beat. Out of the corner of my eye, I watched him let the seat back to get comfortable.

He looked around. "Nice. Now I know where you live, what you do, *and* what you drive."

"In a minute I'll be able to say the same. So why do I still feel like you have this unfair advantage? Maybe it has something to do with the fact that you are my judge! That's pretty damn unbalanced."

I drove around to the player's gate and into the separate lot just as all the other goats were beginning to file out of the stadium. He got out, adjusted his bag on his shoulder, and rested his left hand on the top of the car. I watched him lean back into the passenger seat and stare into my eyes.

"I'm going to try and change that right now," he said convincingly, and bit down on his lower lip before closing the door.

25

I PUT THE CAR IN PARK AND WAITED. BOTH MY HANDS WERE WRAPPED AROUND the steering wheel, and I didn't know what to think about first. *What am I doing? This could get really dangerous; he was a judge, for crying out loud! But we're only going to Harold's Chicken Shack. It's not like anything could happen there; just going for some friendly fried chicken.*

I gripped the steering wheel and watched him pull his silver Mercedes SL500 convertible out of the underground garage.

Throwing caution to the wind, I shrugged and took off for a four-piece mild chicken dinner with salt, pepper, and extra barbeque sauce.

When we pulled up in front of the chicken joint, Maximillien stepped out of his car and was immediately mobbed by two men who'd been stalking him as he parked. "Hey Max—what's up, man? Can we get an autograph from you? Man, my son would love that."

After signing various scraps of paper, Max jogged across the street to meet me. "I've gotta go, guys. My friend will kill me if I don't feed her soon," he yelled over his shoulder.

"Thanks, man. Kick ass this season. You're the best," they buzzed, still staring at him in complete reverence as he led me down the street.

"Sorry about that. They get mad if you blow them off. They feel like they know me. You know, they read about us all the time and watch us in their living rooms. It can't really get any more intimate than that, when you think about it, you know?"

"Makes sense. So are you really *that* good?" I asked as we walked the few steps to the take-out joint.

"Well, I like to think I'm *that* good, and I've been playing for the team long enough for everyone here to know me—well, almost everyone." He looked down at me and laughed.

"Look, let's get this straight right now," I said, grabbing his arm and turning him toward me. "I've heard your name before; who hasn't? But I wouldn't have been able to put a face with it. I haven't seen a basketball game since college. And I don't know about you, but since I got my first job out of college, I've religiously put in twelve-hour work days. Then when I moved to New York to work at Tru Records I slept on the floor in my cubicle *slash* closet on more than one occasion to get the job done. And for the year and a half I squeezed in night school full-time, I didn't even know *where* my remote control was. So if your picture wasn't in *The Fundamental Elements of Marketing* or *Introduction to Microeconomics*, please forgive me for not recognizing your infamous face." I shoved my hands into my hoodie.

Max took a step back. "I didn't mean—"

"Now, because not *all* tall black men are ballplayers, I'd never assume. So, if I'd known who you were—you know, introducing yourself on the elevator or maybe telling me that you were going to the stadium too—it's quite possible that I wouldn't have made a complete ass of myself out there today. I mean, they were one heave away from calling the paramedics. Did you *see* Coach's face?"

"Again, Hannah, I'm really sorry about that. But just for one minute, try and put yourself in my shoes. What was I supposed to do? I mean really? I didn't know you either—and, well, what if you'd sucked?"

I thought carefully about that scenario. "OK, I'll give you that, but it was still shady," I argued as he put his arm on my shoulder and directed me to the door that he was holding open.

"You actually slept on the floor?"

"What? You didn't?"

After standing in line for what seemed like forever, I got to the counter and could feel my stomach coiling. I was unsure if it was from the hunger pains or this six-foot-five phenom pleading with me for forgiveness. I gave the woman in the black hairnet my order before realizing that she hadn't heard a word I'd said. She was mesmerized by Maximillien, along with everyone else in the restaurant who'd crowded around him, vying for autographs. This really wasn't the best plan after all.

After he'd Hancocked several pieces of paper torn from the chicken menus and made small talk with everyone, our food was finally ready. He paid for it and grabbed my hand, leading me out the front door.

"Truce?" he offered, looking down at my hand in his.

"Why fight it? I'm sure you get whatever you want anyway."

I struggled to ignore the fact that my hand had settled into his and my goddamn fingers had gone numb—again!

"Sorry about that in there. I thought it'd be better if we got this to go."

"And go where, exactly?"

"It's such a beautiful night. Get in; I know the perfect spot."

I stood in the middle of the street next to his car and eyed him suspiciously with one hand on my hip and the other on my chin.

"I promise, I'll bring you back to your car as soon as we're done eating. Trust me; I don't wanna get in any more trouble with you—not tonight, or any other night for that matter. Get in. Take a chance on me," he said smoothly.

After grave consideration, I gave in. It was only chicken—and he was right; it was an amazing night. The moon was almost full, the stars blanketed the sky, and as vintage Brian McKnight crooned from the speakers we coasted in the cape of this Supercity. The wind blew through my hair and I vibed to the music, counting the rows of yachts docked in the harbor along Lake Shore Drive. The Field Museum was just ahead, but he turned into the Grant Park complex and parked next to the Shedd Aquarium. Before I could unfasten my seat belt, he'd gotten out and grabbed a blanket from the back.

"Come on, let's go. You've gotta be starving. Just a couple more seconds," he assured me, opening my car door.

"Where are we going?" I asked, trying to avoid getting my white cloth flip-flops dirty.

"Right over here."

He took the big bag of chicken from my arms and grabbed my hand, pulling me across the street. We walked down a hill and into a secluded sandy nook close to the water, where he opened the blanket and set up shop.

"Close your eyes," he whispered with authority into my ear, causing little pricklies to pop up around my lobe. "Trust me."

I could feel him standing close behind me when he shifted my body around.

I felt the back of his hand touch my cheek.

"Don't open them yet."

I obeyed, balling my fists and trying hard to calm the stomping of my heart.

Max grabbed my hands and gently pulled at my tense fingers until he was rubbing the inside of my palms with his.

"OK, you can open them now," he allowed.

I was looking past the still waters and the shore directly into the pristine skyline.

"It's perfect," I said.

"I'm glad you get it."

I looked out over Lake Michigan, just steps away from where we were standing. In the near distance the Sears Tower, the John Hancock building, and the Navy pier could be seen, and all the tall, commanding buildings in between. The Ferris wheel on the pier was covered in lights, adding regal character to the majesty that is Chicago's broad shoulders.

"I'm not hungry anymore," I said.

"If you don't want to eat, you don't have to. You don't have to do anything you don't want to do."

I could still feel him close behind me and wondered about all the things that I *did* want to do. Instead, I inched away and took a seat on the blanket, secretly cherishing the scene he'd set.

Maximillien sat across from me, with only the warm chicken between us.

"Let's work on balancing that scale now," he said, and took off his white cap, being careful to set it as far away from the chicken as possible. He ran his fingers through his curly mess of hair, then scratched at his perfectly lined five o'clock shadow. He stretched out on his side and leaned forward on one of his tattooed forearms, which were decorated with various tribal symbols under a rising phoenix. "Now, what would you like to know about me? You already know where I live, you know what I do for a living, and you know what kind of car I drive—well one of my cars." The corners of his mouth turned up, and he looked down at the blanket.

"Hmmm, I dunno. For starters, I guess, what made you want to play basketball?"

"Truth? Well, I've always been good at it, always enjoyed it, and even though people pushed me in that direction, I really needed it."

"Was there ever anything else you thought about doing?"

"No, not really."

"Nothing?"

"Well, if I didn't make it in the league, I guess I would've probably wanted to be a professor."

"Really? I didn't expect that. What would you have professed?"

He chuckled. "I'd have been into literature or poetry or psychology—something along those lines."

"Poetry or psychology?"

"Yeah. I love to read and write poetry, and I majored in psych in college, and they both still get me going. See, on one hand, I love the beauty of words, and on the other, I think it's interesting how our behavior is rooted in so many layers of social and genetic history." He watched me watch him for a few seconds. "We're not all dumb jocks." He laughed and nudged my arm.

I was impressed. I looked out at the cars racing behind him on the Drive and got lost. Their headlights, coupled with the lights from all the buildings, were the perfect backdrop for his close-up. He was talking about Chicago finally feeling like home when I stopped staring at him and tuned back in.

"So, do you wanna recite some of your poetry?"

"Right now? Right here?"

"Uh-huh. Why not?"

He gazed out at the water. "Nope."

"No?"

"Nope. But maybe one day—soon."

"OK," I said, comfortably pressing on. "Well, would you like to make this your permanent home? Chicago?"

"I'm open to whatever life brings me. Not really set on any one place, kind of going with the flow right now. What about you? Are you gonna stay in the Windy City and settle down with the husband, the kids, and the white picket fence?" He leaned back on the blanket and looked up at the sky.

I was taken aback by that question and looked down at his fingers, which were barely touching mine. My eyes caught his and locked for the second time today. This time I was in no rush to break the connection. A chill shot up my spine.

"Are you OK? You getting cold?" he asked, and sat up to move nearer to me. I watched him without protest. He inched closer until he'd situated himself behind me with his legs enclosing my body in his. He rubbed my arms with his hands and rested his chin on my shoulder.

"Is this better?" he whispered in my ear, brushing my neck with his lips.

"Uh-huh," I responded, and closed my eyes, picturing the scene in my head. He kissed my neck gently, barely making contact with my skin. Then he kissed it again.

"Is that better?"

"Uh-huh."

"So, are you?"

"Huh?" I asked, still with my eyes closed.

"Going to settle down here and start a family?"

"Oh, I—I don't know."

"Do you even want to have a family?"

"Yes," I responded, opening my eyes. "I want a family, but I really want to find the right person to have one with. I want it to be forever. That probably sounds silly and a little old school to still think that forever is possible, but that's what I want."

"No, not silly at all. Keep going; I'm listening."

"Well, I was lucky enough to have a stepfather who came into my life when I was eleven. He took good care of us. But my Nana and I went for a long time without that kind of completeness, and I watched her hurt for so many years before they found each other. So, I'm not rushing the family thing, but I would love to have it one day."

He ran his fingers down the outside of my right arm.

"I actually know what you mean. Home is wherever your family is. I never really had a home growing up. I bounced from place to place when I was little," he said, and started making tiny circles with his index finger on the blanket. "Me and my little brother and sister were foster kids in Louisiana, and we got caught up in the system."

"Really?" I asked, gently.

"Yeah. Basketball was my way out, and even though I was a pretty decent student, I counted on basketball to get us all out of that life and away from New Orleans. We got separated a few times, but I swore that one day I'd make sure we were together again, the way a family is supposed to be."

"And what about now? Where are they?" I turned around to face him and watched as he pulled up single sprouts of grass from the sand.

"Well, my little brother, Noah, is in law school at Penn, and my baby sister, Cree, is raising my niece, Zoey. I take care of them all. They're all I have, and we've gotten through this thing together. None of us are bitter, though, and that's what I'm most proud of. I never wanted our lives to be dictated by our struggles. No matter how much we suffered or how many times the system split us up, we still had each other. They couldn't take that from us. And now, well, they know that I'm always gonna do my best to make up for the hard times. So, my home is wherever they are." He held out his arm, which had been gently wrapped around me, and pointed to the three tribal symbols extending down his forearm. "This one is Noah, this one is Cree, and this slightly smaller one is little Zoey," he explained, reaching for my left hand to trace my fingertips over each character. "This bigger one beneath the rising phoenix is me," he continued, raising the sleeve on his T-shirt and placing the palm of my hand over the phoenix on his biceps. "That symbolizes hope—eternal, undying, and immortal."

I didn't know what to say, so I said nothing as I contemplated the unexpected layers of this man that I was seeing for the very first time.

Maximillien kissed my cheek and reached down to grab a cold chicken wing and playfully force it into my mouth. When I laughed, my eyes played hide-and-seek with his dimples and I accidentally smeared the thick sauce all over my white BCBG hoodie—and I couldn't have cared less.

"Now you look good in red *and* white," he teased, and tried to wipe it off, only making it worse.

WE TALKED FOR WHAT SEEMED LIKE HOURS ABOUT HIS LIFE, MY LIFE, AND WHY I wanted to be a cheerleader. He told me that he wouldn't be judging any more of the competition and that he thought I was talented and had what it took to make the squad. We talked about my job and where I wanted to take my career, and he elaborated on the symbolism behind some of the body art on his other arm.

"Right now, my favorite is this cross encircled by the four rings of fire." He smoothed my hand over it lightly. "It's expressing the transformation that ordinary human beings have to undergo before entering the sacred territory within. The four rings I'm responsible for are—"

"You, Noah, Cree, and Little Zoey," I finished.

"Ah, somebody's been listening." He smiled at me and leaned even closer, breathing into my neck.

"Uh-huh."

Then we sat in silence for a while, and the silence was a conversation of its own.

"So, Hannah, I should probably ask if you have a boyfriend now."

"Why should you *probably* ask me that?"

"Because I'm dying to kiss you and I wouldn't want to step on anyone's toes. That's the Creole gentleman in me," he confessed with a more pronounced, alluring drawl than usual.

I'd turned back toward the water and could feel him smiling behind me. I was at a loss for words.

"Well, I guess the answer to that would be that, I'm, uh, single."

"I detect some hesitancy. How much guessing did you have to do to come up with that answer?"

"Well, I'm not dating anyone right now, and I've kind of sworn off men for the time being."

"Interesting. And why is that?" He leaned back on his forearms.

"Let's just say that I needed some time to focus on me and check in with where I was. Making the team is really important to me, my job is crazy right now, and my biggest obligation at work is Rain. It just isn't the best time for me to get involved with anyone—that's all."

"I see," he said, as if he were trying to assess the honesty of my response.

"What about you, Maximillien? Do you have someone serious in your life right now?" I asked, suddenly feeling anxious about his reply.

"Nope. No one serious in my life right now either, besides Cree and little Zoey. But don't get me wrong, I do date."

"Do you date *a lot?*" I pressed, this time even more nervous about his response.

"If we're being honest here . . . sometimes, yes. But it's difficult. I'm raising little Zoey with Cree, and that takes more time than you would think. Then, of course, my basketball schedule is crazy, and I'm always on the road. Plus, I have to be very careful about the women I let into my life. Between the stalkers, the gold diggers, and the plain old crazies, dating can get to be quite challenging for a baller. I'm not opposed to having a girl, but with everything I've got going on, it's a lot to ask of someone. Money would never be an issue, and I would give her the world, but she'd have to be very special to be able to handle all of the idiosyncrasies that are my life." He touched me behind my ear and gently moved his finger along my hairline and down the nape of my neck. "I'm not naïve, I know it won't be easy, but like I said before, I'm just going with the flow. Things will work themselves out. I have a lot of faith, and I've never stopped believing in the power of hope. Hope is a powerful, beautiful thing, Hannah."

He leaned over my shoulder to kiss me softly on my cheek, and then turned me around until I was facing him.

"Hey, I had a really nice time with you tonight. Thanks for having dinner with me. And thank you for trusting me. See, I'm pretty harmless." He ran his hand across the back of his neck.

"I don't know about that."

"Can I tell you a secret?" he asked, staring into my eyes.

"I guess."

"I've wanted to meet you ever since I saw you sprawled out on the floor at the radio station in those very pink shoes."

"Oh my God." I winced, and pounded my forehead with the inside of my wrists.

He grabbed both my wrists in his huge hand and lowered them from my face, then stroked my cheek with the back of his fingers. "And since I saw you with your crew at Starbucks, and hiding in the elevator—"

With each word, my eyes grew bigger and I wrinkled my eyebrows until they touched my eyelids.

"—behind your mail. Hey—" he stopped, and locked his fingers with mine. "I'm drawn to you. There's definitely something about you."

"Do you think I'm . . . dynamic?"

"Yes, darlin'. I think you are *undeniably* dynamic."

I looked into his dark eyes and saw what looked like home to me.

With his right hand he grabbed the back of my neck and kissed my forehead. He kissed my left cheek. He kissed the tip of my nose. He kissed my right cheek and my chin. I opened my eyes and watched intently as he licked his lips and bit down on his bottom one. "I really want to kiss you right now."

"You've been kissing me all night," I murmured, caught in a suffocating haze.

"No, I want to kiss you. I want to *really* kiss you. I want to explore your soul with my tongue and introduce you to the rhythm of mine. I want to grab your hair and pull your head back and suck your neck, slowly making my way up to your lips. I want to lick the outline of your mouth with my tongue and kiss you so sweetly deep that I can't come up for air—not because I don't want to, but because I don't need to."

Oh.

"So, what's wrong?" I asked innocently, trying hard not to sound desperate.

"I think we better go. I have to get you back to your car, and I know your body has got to be exhausted from your long day of stress."

He had no idea what my body was going through. He leaned back and held my face in his hands. He studied it closely, paying careful attention to my eyes and my lips before he released me into a deep, heavy sigh.

"Sit here and enjoy the night while I bring the car around and get this stuff loaded in."

Instead, I stood up and put my hands into the minipockets of my hoodie, which now smelled like a chicken pit. The city was on fire tonight, and I'd gotten burned.

He walked up behind me, bent down, and wrapped his arms around my waist. We both gazed out over the water into the light of the night.

"It's not quite as captivating as you are, but it does come close," he charmed.

"Thank you, Maximillien." I thought to myself that I could get used to this. "So what now? What happens next?"

"I don't know. Like I said, my life is really crazy, Hannah. I will say that this was the best night I've had in a long time. The good thing is, I know where you live," he said, and squeezed me gently around the waist.

For the first time, I turned around and reached way up on my tip-toes to wrap my arms around his neck and return the embrace. He lifted me into him, and I completely let go of myself to squeeze him tightly and expose my needs.

On the way back to get my car, we didn't speak. Our intertwined fingers made lengthy conversation as they massaged each other until I couldn't tell where his fingers stopped and mine began. The evening air was intoxicating, and by the time I got to my car, I was drunk from it all.

"Hannah, you have to promise me one thing," he said, as he opened my car door.

"What's that?"

"Promise me that you'll pay close attention to what's in front of you from now on. The one thing I can't afford is for you, or even worse, for us, to miss anything. I just found you, darlin'."

"My radar is up and active." I followed him to my car and reached into my bag for the keys. Once inside, I let the window down and looked into his eyes one last time to take a mental snapshot. "Now, you promise me something."

"Anything," he agreed.

"Promise me you'll get home safely."

"Done. I have to make a quick stop and check on Zoey, but that won't take long."

"OK."

"Let me see your hand."

"What?"

"Your hand. Let me see your hand. Don't get all shy on me now. Give me your damn hand."

I stuck my hand out the window, and he grabbed it and turned it over to scribble down a phone number.

"Keep this close to you. It's the number to my private twenty-four-hour access line. If you ever need anything, and I mean anything, give me a call. You know: shoes, cars, feminine products—whatever."

I laughed, and with my superhuman powers tried to freeze-frame this moment.

"Will do," I said.

"Plus, you know where I live—or at least one of the places I live."

"That's right, the thirtieth floor."

"Not quite. I own the thirtieth, thirty-first, and thirty-second floors." He took my hand and kissed it lightly. "Now, goodnight, my little dancing doll."

"Goodnight, Max."

"Right—Max." His deep dimples bore holes into his cheeks as he smiled the biggest smile I'd seen all night. He nodded his head and threw his arms in the air. "Welcome to my world."

And with that, he hopped into his hot rod, turned the corner, and was off into the city's night.

26

"I DON'T KNOW WHAT'S HOTTER, YOU GOING TO CAMP OR THAT RIDICULOUSLY spicy night you just had with Max Knight," Kennedy pondered as she pulled the comforter up to her mouth and stared blankly at the flat screen. "I mean, you and Daniel were sweet, but this is Cinemax."

"I know. The whole ride home I went over every single detail in my head, trying not to forget a thing. I even tried to remember exactly how many inches his fingertips were from mine on the blanket." I pulled the other half of the covers up to my mouth and let the muted plasma watch me.

We sat in my bed with a quarter-eaten box of cold Giordano's stuffed pizza between us. Even though I'd called on my way in, when I charged through the front door Britt was M.I.A., with the leftover promise of stopping by my job to get the 411 on the thirty-five-million-dollar-man the next day.

"So, what does this mean for us? Are we gonna call him? Are we gonna see him again?" Kennedy's tone was monotonous and her body frozen. Neither of us had moved a muscle or blinked a lid since I'd gotten to the part about him standing provocatively close behind me on the shore with the skyline in the distance.

"I don't know. I mean, I can't right now. I need to focus and concentrate on making the team. Dr. Ivy would kill me if she knew I was pursuing him," I said, finally breaking my staring contest with Jimmy Kimmel. "Besides, he's a ballplayer. He probably has a truckload of girls all over him. He practically admitted it; he even *told* me he's dating—a lot. Probably exhausting chicks from the muffler of his SL500 right now."

"Good point."

"But Sweets, he was my perfection: incredibly fine, talented, smart, sensitive—and his tattoos almost made me cry."

"Made you cry?"

"You had to be there."

"And you don't think that's worth squashing the pact with the quack? I don't know, Bug," she argued, dropping the comforter and crossing her arms.

"It's more than just a pact with the quack. This is supposed to be a shot for me to get to know Hannah. I haven't been single since sophomore year in high school. First there was Ronnie, then Bobby, then Ricky and Mike. The only one missing was Ralph."

Kennedy choked, trying to hold back laughter.

"Then Daniel. Oh God. *Daniel.* I don't even know how to begin trusting a man again. And a ballplayer at that? No dice. Just think about it; do you know how long it's been since Hannah did Hannah?"

"Well, let's see." Kennedy furrowed her brows and looked down at her fingers.

"Thirteen years!"

"Damn!" she blurted.

"Exactly. *Damn.*" I concurred. "I need this time to get to know me."

"So, how are you gonna get him out of your head?"

"I'm not. I already know it. I'm just not."

"Damn," she hushed, putting her arm around my shoulder.

"Damn," I concurred.

27

ANXIOUSLY, I OPENED THE DOOR TO DR. IVY'S OFFICE, DESPERATELY NEEDING TO talk to her and gain some clarity. Puma swam through the coral and seemed to nod when I glanced at the fish and took a seat in the yellow chair. Halle was still on that same *Cosmo* cover, looking fresh and ravishing. She'd been the recent inspiration for the extra wave in my weave. I crossed my legs, nervously kicking my right leg back and forth in the air as I flipped through the same goddamn girly mag, not giving any particular page consideration. With everything going on the past couple of days, I needed to process and focus, especially with three grueling days of minicamp ahead of me.

By my Movado, it was already 3:33 p.m. What was it with her and those extra three minutes?

The door swung open.

"Come on in, Hannah."

"Oh, already?" I got up and tapped Puma's tank on my way in. He flicked his tail and disappeared behind a huge purple rock next to his coral.

"Have a seat. I must say that I've been looking forward to this session. Tell me, how did everything go this past weekend?"

"Well, I made it past the first cut. Minicamp starts tomorrow."

"Congratulations; that's wonderful. You must be so excited."

"Yes, I really am. It was a surreal experience, to say the least."

"That's great, Hannah. That feeling is exactly what I wanted you to have," she said, and emphatically hit me on the knee with her fist. "This will be very healthy for you. Focusing only on you without any distractions will give you a real opportunity to learn more about who Hannah is as an individual and not as part of a couple."

My foot was shaking a million miles a minute, and I almost kicked her in the head with my pea-green Manolo Blahnik's, which matched my green-and-pink silk satin ruffled mini.

"How do you feel about what you are about to encounter?"

My mind raced with thoughts of Max and Eli and—

"Well, Dr. Ivy, that's all kind of what I need to talk to you about. What I am actually getting ready to encounter is a little different than what we initially had in mind."

"What do you mean?"

I went on to tell her about the past Friday at the office with Elijah and the second gift, which seemed to intrigue her. I figured if that piqued her interest, the doozy I was about to drop would surely send her toppling over.

When I was done dishing all the dirty details from Saturday's tryst, she sat back in her chair, adjusted her glasses, and scribbled down a couple of notes. There was a box of Puffs in the middle of the ottoman, and she reached for it after taking a long deliberate breath. I wasn't sure if she was going to blow or cry.

"Well, Hannah, quite a bit of excitement over the last couple of days."

A bit!? Did she hear all that I'd just dished?

"How do you feel about all of that?"

"Honestly, I'm not really sure how I feel. I spent the greater part of yesterday shriveling up in the bathtub, trying to divine my innermost thoughts on the matter. Didn't come up with anything more than, well, I'm conflicted and confused! See, I thought Max was just a doll at first, totally gorgeous and nice to look at. But we had this amazing night, and I mean a-maaa-zing! It was like something out of a Meg Ryan movie, you know, the older ones, not like that boxer flick she did with Omar Epps. I mean, I really *felt* him; we totally connected. It was a perfect song. I don't think either one of us wanted it to end. He wouldn't even kiss me. Well, I mean really *kiss* me."

"So you wanted him to kiss you?"

"Huh?"

"You said he wouldn't even kiss you, intimating that you *wanted* him to kiss you."

"Well, of course I *wanted* him to kiss me. Did you hear that setup he had going on with the blanket, the stars, the moon, and all that shit?"

"I see," she said, allowing a grin to slip onto her lips. "Well, what about the decision we made about you not dating anyone right now and shifting your focus to something completely healthy and Hannah-oriented?"

"Seriously, I was thinking about that. I don't think I need to date anyone right now either. But a sista is wondering if a little distraction wrapped in that package wouldn't be so bad."

"Uh-huh." She scribbled more. "Well, you certainly can't allow this distraction to stop you from addressing whatever this thing is with Eli. It's obviously not sitting well with you, and for good reason."

"I know, I know. You're right, it's just that he's my boss, and I don't want to injure the relationship that we already have by being presumptuous or saying the wrong thing."

"And exactly what kind of relationship do you two have? The lack of definition regarding the relationship seems to be injuring the integrity of it already, don't you think?"

"Truthfully, I was kinda hoping it would just work itself out."

"Uh-huh," she said, and wrote down a few more notes. "You need to have a conversation with him and get it all out in the open, Hannah. Those were some gifts—a tennis bracelet and a diamond necklace?"

"I know, I know," I whined again.

"Well, those generally aren't the kinds of gifts one gives with absolutely no meaning behind them. You see where I'm going with this?"

"Yes. You're right, and I know it. It's just—"

"How do you really feel about him, anyway?"

"I respect him a lot. He's damn good at what he does, and I'm lucky to be able to work with him and learn from him. Besides, he went to bat for me and really fought so that I could be brought on at the label in the VP position. I mean, I don't know too many junior vice presidents my age who have—"

"I get all of that, Hannah. But how do you *feel* about him?"

"I think he's sexy and smooth—and hell, I don't know. Sometimes he scares me and makes my heart beat fast and I get all sixth-grade nervous around him."

"Is that because he's your boss, or is there something else there?"

"I don't know. I'm really not sure."

How much was I paying her?

"Fair enough. Let's keep that on the radar and assess it more after you've had an opportunity to clear some of this up with him. Not only do you have to work together, but he's your superior. I want you to tell me all about it next week. And good luck with minicamp. I'm sure you're going to do an amazing job."

Was that it? What about my extra three minutes?

WITHOUT EVEN CHANGING MY CLOTHES WHEN I GOT HOME, I DECIDED INSTEAD TO get ready for my big day tomorrow. *Entertainment Tonight* was blaring from the TV in the bedroom, where I was packing all the essentials. I was on my way downstairs wondering what kind of goodies we had that could be thrown together in a salad when I heard a knock on the door. Kennedy was still at the Athletic Club. Their climbing wall was her favorite, so I knew not to expect her anytime soon; Mondays were her wall day.

"One second," I yelled, making my way to the keyhole. A partial tattoo of an angel's wings under a red cotton shirt and a deep dimple greeted me. Max!

I turned away from the door and then back around to the door and then away from it again. Shit. What was he doing here?! I smoothed down the ruffles in my mini, threw my hair over my right shoulder, and opened the door.

"Uh, hi, Hannah," he said from behind five medium-sized white boxes in his arms.

I stood in the doorway and looked back at him and smiled, not saying a word.

"Hi. Can I come in, or can you take one or maybe two of these boxes out of my arms, please?"

"Oh yeah. Sorry," I said, and took all of them, stacking them on a small round table in the foyer. "What's all this? And what are you doing here?"

"Well, I'll be honest. I wanted to see you and I didn't have your number. And you never called me, so . . . I feel like so much time has gone by since I saw you last, even though I know it was just the other night." He stepped back and blushed like a schoolboy with a cute crush before letting out a deep breath. "You look great."

"Thanks. So do you." I returned the blush *and* the cute crush. "What is all of this?" I asked, eyeing the boxes.

"Open them and see for yourself." He rubbed his hands together.

"Come in, come in." I moved aside and motioned to him before closing the front door.

Facing Max in the hallway, next to the oversized mirror and small table, I tried to be cool, calm, and slightly collected. But each time I looked up at him, my stomach somersaulted, and I could feel the sensation in my fingers beginning to disappear. I looked anyway. He hadn't shaved and was wearing a red baseball cap that matched his red polo shirt and a pair of loose-fitting Diesel jeans.

"Well, are you going to open them or not?"

"Yes, of course," I said, clearing my throat and picking up the top box. I glanced at him and opened it slowly. There was a white BCBG two-piece cashmere jogging suit in the first box. I stared at it without looking back up at him.

"Open the other ones," he said, and took his hat off to run his fingers through his curls before slipping it back on.

I opened the second box and found an orange one. In the third box was a pink one, in the fourth a cream one, and in the fifth a black one. Shaking my head in disbelief, I looked over at Max, who was eagerly awaiting some sort of response. I stood and looked down at all the open boxes, then back up at him.

"Well, I know I ruined your white one the other night with the barbeque sauce, and I thought this was the least I could do to remedy that. I hope you like them."

"Max, you didn't have to do that, really. Besides, my jogging suit wasn't cashmere."

"It doesn't matter, and yes, I did. These are the best. I can't have you walking around in a stained jogging suit that smells like chicken grease and barbeque sauce. Definitely not the impression I'm trying to leave, darlin'." He cleared his throat. "But when I didn't know what your favorite color was, I just got them all. The saleswoman said that these were the most popular colors."

"Thank you. Thank you so much. You really didn't have to do that, but it was very sweet."

"So are you. Now, really, how're you doing? Are you ready for your big day tomorrow?"

"I guess. I don't really know what to expect, so I think I'm as ready as I'm ever going to be. I'm a little nervous, but that's normal, right?"

"You'll do fine." He stared at my lips. "Listen, I really had a good time with you the other night."

"Yeah, me, too."

We stood there, again in silence, studying each other.

"Well, I guess I better go," he finally blurted out. "I hope I didn't interrupt you. I just wanted you to have these in case you wanted to wear one. You looked so good in the one you were wearing Saturday. Plus, I really wanted to see you."

"I kind of wanted to see you too."

"So you *have* thought about me?" He bit down on his bottom lip.

"I didn't say that. I said I kind of wanted to see you too."

"OK, that'll do for now. I'm just glad you like your gifts, and I hope they fit. I figured you for a size four. You look about the same size as my sister before she had Zoey."

"They're perfect."

"Good. I was hoping you'd say that."

He turned back toward the door, opened it, and walked into the hallway. He came back in with five smaller shoeboxes and set them on the floor next to the table.

"Now, what's this?"

"Open them and see."

I bent down and grabbed the box on top. "You thought of everything, didn't you?" I said, pulling out a pair of white BCBG flip-flops just like the ones in my closet. I opened the other boxes and found all the colors to match the jogging suits. After putting the last shoebox down, I reached up to give him a hug, and his arms easily found my waist.

"Wow," I said in response to both the gifts and the touch of his arms wrapped tightly around me. The deep breath that followed was an automatic response to the way he smelled—simply delicious!

"It's the least I could do, and to know that my efforts made you smile like that makes it all worth it. I'm gonna go so you can get back to doing whatever you were doing. You'll be great tomorrow." He released me and walked back toward the door. "Have a good night, darlin'."

"You too. I'll have to figure out a way to repay you."

He shook his head and laughed.

"What?" I asked, but he just bent down to kiss me on the forehead before walking into the hallway.

I leaned against the door and watched him walk away. As if he could still feel me, he looked over his shoulder and smiled. I closed the door, pressed my palms and face against it, and wondered how many different smiles he had. So far, I'd counted four.

My thoughts lent themselves to Dr. Ivy's drivel. My foyer was filled with ten white boxes, and all I could do was lean against the door like an idiot and gawk at them. I'd like a sneak peek at Dr. Ivy's best defense.

"Are you still standing at the door, darlin'?" I heard Max ask, making me jump two feet into the air.

"Hannah?" he said, knocking softly.

I cleared my throat and untwisted my bra. "Yes," I answered meekly, and pulled at the door. His sneakers were planted firmly, and his hands were buried deep in his pockets.

"I was thinking that I know how you could repay me."

"What exactly did you have in mind?" I knew all kinds of ways *I* had in mind.

"Have you had dinner yet?"

And dinner wasn't one of them.

"No."

"Well, I was thinking that while you were getting ready for tomorrow I could make us dinner. I haven't eaten either, not since I finished at the gym."

"Uh, I, uh, I don't know. I—"

"Come on."

"Max, you've already done more than enough. It's not that I don't appreciate the offer, because I do, really. It's just that I should probably rest and focus. Probably couldn't do that with you here."

Judas Priest! I flat out didn't trust myself. As I was mulling over that reality he stepped up so close to me that breathing was no longer an option, either. I took a few quick short breaths, forgetting to blink.

"I understand."

I had to admit, I was a little disappointed. He'd given up without much of a fight.

"OK, how about you let me take you to camp tomorrow and bring you back after? I could be your chauffeur, you know, Driving Ms. Hannah."

He stood in the doorway and pantomimed putting on his seat belt, adjusting the mirrors, and maneuvering the steering wheel. My laughter broke the insane intensity.

"Why would you wanna do that? You don't have anything better to do?"

"Well, after I hit the gym, I'm going over to Rockwell for tutoring for a few hours, but after that—"

"Your math a little shaky?"

"Oh, you got jokes?" he mused, licking his lips. "Not me. Some of the foster kids at the center come in for a couple hours during the summer. And not math; we're in the middle of *Moby Dick*."

"Never read it."

He took my hands. "Maybe I'll tutor you through it. We can start after I pick you up tomorrow."

"OK, listen," I decided, pulling my hands away from him. "I have to be there at six, which means I need to leave home at four-thirty, four forty-five at the latest. I need to be there at least an hour early to change, mentally prepare, and get warmed up." I nervously twirled my hands in the air as I detailed my itinerary. "You really don't have to do this, you know."

"I know, but I wanna be the last person to wish you good luck and the first to find out how it went." He leaned against the door and crossed his arms stubbornly. "If you couldn't tell, darlin', I'm not going to take no for an answer."

I threw my hands in the air. He'd worn me down and won. "OK, Max. Meet me in the lobby at four-thirty. If you're late, I'll drive myself."

"See you tomorrow at four-thirty. Try and get some rest."

He turned the knob to the door and stood in the hallway, continuing to surprise me with unabashed resolve. I had to admit: this wasn't the man I thought would emerge from behind that baseball cap, with the big broad shoulders and the insanely perfect ass. He was stubborn and sweet, smart and gentle, funny and kind, silly and thoughtful and—

He pulled me into his body and bent down to kiss me on the cheek this time. Why did he keep doing that? The grin on my face began somewhere deep down in my gut and made its way up to my deprived lips. I came back inside and closed the door, wishing for another knock, but instead was summoned to the living room to answer the phone and listen to Nana chat me up while I prepared that salad.

29

"Take more than a second to think about it, Cobra. If you know of any-one who'd be both a good intern and a good fit here at RockStar, sched-ule them for an interview. You'll be working with them more than I will, so it should be someone you feel comfortable with—and that doesn't mean your best friend. Trust me: that can get messy," I ex-plained that morning before our weekly lunch meeting with the pro-motions and sales department.

"I understand, and I won't bring in my roommate or my homies from the block, Bosslady," Cobra assured me, as he grabbed his note-book, pen, and pink Lacoste sweater. "By the way, did you get a chance to look over Rain's video footage this weekend? I thought she looked so hot. That girl is on fire."

"That's it, Cobra! That's it!" I screamed. "That's what's needed to pull the whole piece together. That'll be the title of her video: *Rain on Fire*. Genius! It sums up the backstory perfectly. That might even be the theme of her entire project. I absolutely love it!" I raved, shutting my door as we headed for the conference room to meet with the other department heads. "And see where we are with getting Usher in the studio for the remix of *Rain on Me.*"

"Ooh, Usher, now he is my kind of—"

"Shut it, Cobra. You're focused, and you're taking notes right now. That's all!" I had him by the elbow, hightailing it down the long halogen-lit hallway.

"You smell that Italian sausage?" he asked, inhaling the spread he'd had catered in from Maggiano's. "For the life of me, I don't get folks who can't appreciate a nice long piece of sausage."

"Meat doesn't agree with everyone," I answered, ignoring his innuendo and pulling him past the oversized posters of label artists plastered on the walls. Loud music streamed from offices and cubicles, getting lost in translation as we hurried by.

"No meat?" he continued, "Their loss; more for me."

I shot him a sideways glance.

"And speaking of meat, Ms. Hannah, I noticed you haven't returned any of Eli's phone calls. What's up with that? That man ain't dumb; he knows you're dodging him. He asked me this morning if you were getting his messages. I couldn't lie, so I just told him that you'd been tied up all morning on a conference call with Rain's manager and the stylist for the XXL shoot. OK, so I lied. But he didn't buy that bullshit for one second. I'd advise you to handle your business, Bosslady. I recall a little blue box with a white ribbon from Tiffany's being handed to you last Friday. Now you know I'm not one to gossip, so you didn't hear it from me, but rumor has it that that's not the first little expensive box you've received from Mr. Elijah Strong," Cobra said, and switched off in his hot-pink cotton ribbed Enyce pants and white penny loafers.

"It's Tiffany! Ditch the 's.' And I can't have this conversation with you right now, but thanks for the assist," I called out to him, but to no avail.

I stood in the doorway of the room and fiddled with my fingers. "Now focus and smile, cuz you're on," I mumbled to myself and walked into the conference room later than usual to greet everyone else. Between hello hugs and smoochie kisses, I thought about the goddamn rumor mill and sighed—as if I needed anything else to worry about!

30

4:24 P.M.

I was convinced that I'd forgotten something. My Adidas bag felt a little lighter than it had on Saturday, and I was two grande cups of vanilla latte past being jittery. I double-checked everything—again! My toes beat on the bottom of my flip-flops to the rhythm of the thunderous three-story marble waterfall that had been recently built in the lofty waiting area of our building, which only made me have to pee. I compulsively rummaged through the bag. It appeared that all the essentials were there. Kennedy had packed my snacks, and I'd grabbed the lunchbox she'd left sitting on the island in the kitchen before she headed out to a photo shoot. Movado check: 4:25 p.m. It was still too early to decidedly drive myself—even though I was tempted to responsibly extinguish any emotional fires that could potentially arise from just sitting in a car next to Max. Still 4:25 p.m. I really did have to pee. Maybe I should have worn different shoes. I stared down at my new orange flip-flops, which matched the orange jogging suit Max had given me. I was hot. No, really *hot*. Maybe it was the cashmere. I still had to pee. It was definitely the cashmere. I needed some fresh air and a divine sign.

"Hey, Hannah, your driver is here, and the car is all gassed up and ready to go," Max said as he came bolting through the front door holding one single rose. "And this is for you. Just a little way to say good luck."

"Thank you," I said, smiling, glad I'd decided to wait for that sign.

I no longer had to pee.

"You look great. Ready to go?"

"Uh-huh." Nervously, I stood up, strategically pulling the clinging jogging pants from the crack of my ass.

"Do you have everything? Did you go over your list and check it twice?"

"Yes, and I still think you're a little naughty and a little bit nice."

"Ah, you're on your toes, despite the pressure. That's a good sign. You'll do just fine," he said, opening the passenger door for me. "Now, let's rock and roll. I think the lady is ready to dance."

There on the seat were two dozen long-stemmed red roses. I nuzzled my nose deep into their silky buds.

"Whoa, you've got your A game on tonight." I smiled.

"Well, the single rose is to wish you good luck. These twenty-four are just because you're so damn beautiful. One has absolutely nothing to do with the other, darlin'."

Max slid into the driver's seat, leaning over to kiss me on the cheek. Before I could even exhale, he'd gently rubbed the kiss into the apple of my cheek with his thumb. "Now, that'll be with you for the rest of the night," he said, and pulled off with the top dropped.

Noticing my knocking knees and the dense nail impressions I was embedding in his car's leathery center console, Max rubbed the back of my neck. "A little nervous?" he asked gently.

"Uh-huh."

"Don't be; you're going to do great," he said definitively, as we pulled up to the stadium. "I'll be right here when you get out at nine. Maybe you'll let me cook something for you while you tell me all about how you kicked butt." He got out and opened my door. "How's lasagna sound?" he asked, winking at me and handing me my bag.

I didn't answer but let the expression on my face be filled with maybes. I walked toward Gate 4, throwing up the black power fist again as I passed the Jordan statue before looking over my shoulder one last time. Max was leaning against his car, legs and arms crossed, smiling back at me.

I could hear a couple of the girls in the near distance, running and giggling. I recognized the two veterans from Saturday as they darted past and opened the door to Gate 4, not bothering to hold it for me.

"Hannah, Hannah."

Minnow snapped me out of my trance.

"Hey, Minnow, how's it going?"

"I'm good, but it looks like you're doing much better than me. Wasn't that Max Knight I just saw waving goodbye to you? Ohmigod! It was, wasn't it?"

"Huh?"

"That was Max Knight! I could spot him a million miles away. What gives?"

"What do you mean?" I stammered, caught off guard by the sudden interrogation. *Should I lie? Tell the truth? There was nothing to hide because there was nothing really going on. Right?*

"Come on, you know what I mean. What gives? Do you know him? Well, of course you know him. But how? Oh my God, that *was* Max Knight."

"Well, yeah. I mean, not really. I mean we're friends—I guess. I mean, he lives in my building."

"And he just happened to drop you off tonight? He was *only* one of the judges last Saturday. That's rather interesting. Come on, Hannah, we're like best friends. Fess up: is there something going on between you two? Oh my God, you're dating Max Knight." Her eyebrows shot up into her hairline as she put her hands up to her mouth and looked around as if she needed to spread the gospel.

"No, I'm not. And keep your voice down," I hushed. "We're really just friends. He was heading this way anyway and offered me a ride so I wouldn't have to worry about traffic—that's all!"

"Oh, Hannah, Max Knight is no chauffeur. He is only like *the* most eligible bachelor in Chicago *and* he was in *People*'s Most Beautiful People! Whoo!" she oozed, wiping her forehead. "But OK, I'll, like, take your word for it." She shook her head and grabbed my hand as we made our way through the hall and down the stairs to the floor level of the court.

"I believe you; really I do," she said, appearing to have given it more careful thought. "Now it's not my business, but if I were you, I'd keep that under wraps. It looks a little shady. He was our judge, for crying out loud. Anyone else might not be so understanding."

When we got down to the court we were directed to a smaller press room next to the locker rooms. My heart was speeding as I wondered who else might have glimpsed Max outside with me. I'd earned my spot on my own merit, but Minnow was right. I didn't want anyone else to get the wrong idea.

"Hannah," Minnow got my attention again. "Better be extra careful; you know the Golden Rule."

"What rule? What are you talking about?" I whispered, searching in my bag for my shoes until I realized I'd already taken them out, put them on, and double-laced them.

"The Golden NBA Rule that explicitly states that cheerleaders aren't supposed to date the players on their home team. It's only like the biggest rule—it's like rule Numero Uno. If a cheerleader gets caught dating a player, she gets kicked off the team immediately—no questions asked! It's like in some ancient Chinese cheerleading handbook. Everyone knows that."

What type of shit was that?! No one had ever told *me* that rule. Who made up that dumb-ass rule anyway? And what was the big-ass deal?

"Oh yeah. Right. That rule."

"Hannah, seriously, it's like an NBA rule that applies to every cheerleading team in the league, not just the Dolls." She lowered her voice. "I understand that you two are just friends and all, but it might not be interpreted that way by everyone else if you're spotted with him. Plus you're not even a rookie yet. We're like groveling groupies. You could blow your chances before you even make the team. And I really don't wanna go through this without you."

Jesus Christ Superstar!

I looked around the room and noticed that some of the goats were whispering to each other and had begun staring in my direction between stretches. This couldn't be good.

"Thanks for the heads-up, Minn, but there's nothing going on between me and Max. We're just friends, really."

"Well, I believe you. I wouldn't be mad at you if there was something going on, though. He's so damn dreamy."

I glanced around the room at the goats, who were now overtly whispering and pointing at me. Great, I thought. The shitty part of it all was that my life was actually devoid of the naughty pleasures caught in their wicked web of speculation.

Right?

31

"WELL, HELLO, LADIES. SO GOOD TO SEE YOU ALL AGAIN," NIKKI SAID AS SHE popped into the room in a beautiful black-and-gold nylon warm-up suit. It looked damn good on her, and I wanted one, now more than ever. My gassy stomach bubbled and tightened at the thought of my chances slipping through my feeling-less fingers. I fought through the anxiety to catch her words.

"More difficult . . . intense warm-up . . . splits . . . flexibility stretches . . ." I shook my head to clear it and focus.

"Congratulations, again, to all of you. You should be very proud of yourselves. We've selected forty-seven of you to participate in this year's minicamp. We are looking to bring in roughly fifteen new girls with the ten veterans we've tentatively asked back, based on Saturday's audition. They'll go through camp with you. We'll be watching them too; we reserve the right to retract all offers."

Why hadn't Max told me about the Rule? Surely he knew? Even if he didn't think it mattered—since there was really nothing going on between us—he could have at least broached the topic with me. I grabbed my phone from my bag and slipped into the hallway before I realized that I hadn't programmed his number into my cell. Shit! He was gonna pick me up tonight, and that simply couldn't happen. I had to find another ride. I dialed Britt.

"Hey chickie; where you at?"

"The stadium."

"That's what I thought. What's up? Everything OK?"

"Fuck no! I seem to have gotten myself into a slightly sticky situation, and I need a ride home tonight after camp."

"Where's your ride?"

"Long story. Can't explain right now. Can you be here at nine?"

"Of course. Relax. Big Mama to the rescue. It's two minutes from my place. I'll just send Julio home."

Julio?

"Who the hell is Julio?"

"Oh, he comes over every once in awhile to unclog my drains," she said in far too sexy a tone for me to continue with the inquiry. "I'll be there at nine."

"Thanks. And Britt, you absolutely can't be late!"

I gasped when I hung up the phone and turned around. The buff chick from the dance studio was leaning on the wall behind me with her arms folded across her chest.

"So—Hannah, right?"

"Uh-huh," I said, hiding the phone behind my back. "What's your name?" I faked a smile through tight lips.

"I'm Six. I've seen you in some of the classes over at the Dance Studio. You're pretty good."

"Thanks," I said, wondering how much of my conversation she'd heard.

She looked through me as if my hand had been exposed. She was a little taller than I was, about five seven, with a short bob and more acne on her face than anyone over sixteen should have. Covered with heaping mounds of foundation, her acne would probably be overlooked thanks to her rock-hard abs and double-D cups.

"So, Hannah, is it true what everyone is saying?"

"What's that?"

"That there's something going on between you and Max Knight?"

"No, Max and I have been friends for a long time. We're practically like family."

Family? Where the hell did that come from?

"Family? That's interesting, because one of the girls said she saw like a million roses in his car when you were getting out. Sister to sister, Hannah—you can tell me, girl. What's really going on?"

"Those weren't for me. He was on his way to pick up his date. Really, we're like family."

"Oh, OK. Sure. Family. If you say so—"

"I say so, Six. Now, do you mind if I get in there and start stretching."

"Sure, don't let me stop you; it's going to be a long K-N-I-G-H-T and I wouldn't want you to miss an opportunity to MAX it."

"Sister to sister, Six—Neutrogena Nightly Cleanser," I murmured under my breath as I left her in the dimly lit hallway, touching one of the pus-filled pimples on her butchy chin.

As I unloosened my ponytail and recurled a few sections of my hair I tried to formulate a plan. Minnow was already out on the court when I headed out to begin my preliminary stretching.

"You OK?"

"Yep. Great. Couldn't be better," I answered on automatic pilot.

"Look, I overheard them talking about saying something to Coach about you and Max."

My mind sped into overdrive.

"Just thought you should know."

"No worries, Minnow, it's fine. I can't be penalized because Max and I are friends. I'll deal with it, OK? Now come over here and stretch with me."

Right on schedule, Nikki addressed everyone promptly at 6 p.m. by frantically clapping her hands together. "OK, ladies, let's go. Before we get started, I'd like all of you to stand up and introduce yourselves to our judges. Some of them are new and haven't had the pleasure of meeting you yet. Say your number aloud, where you're from, how long you've been dancing, and what you do for a living. Let's start with you, Number 5."

I learned that Minnow was a kindergarten teacher and Six was an aerobics instructor and a trainer at a Bally's on the other side of the city. There were actually quite a few teachers in the group, some corporate sales people who worked for medium-sized manufacturing companies, and some grad students from Northwestern and DePaul. Quite an interesting mix of women and backgrounds, I thought to myself as I mentally prepared my thirty-second elevator speech.

"Yes, I'm Number 108, and my name is Hannah Marie Love. I've been dancing since I was eleven, and I work at RockStar Records," I told the panel of judges in my very best pageant-like voice, hoping never to have to do that again.

"Great, Hannah; what do you do at RockStar?" Nikki asked.

"I'm the junior vice-president of marketing, and I handle imaging and packaging the artists for the target consumer: everything from radio and tours to videos and in-stores," I said, unsure how that read to everyone.

A couple of quiet gasps traveled through the goats, and a master plan took its first breath, beginning to come to life.

Minnow's gape turned into a smile as she looked over at me. I winked back.

Following group stretches, we learned the new routine. Coach was right; it was definitely more difficult than the first. There were triple pirouettes and high kicks, a series of leaps, and a jump split at the end. Finally, an hour and a half into the night, we got a five-minute break, followed by another hour and a half of intense masochistic beatings—every lashing was high-impact, nonstop, and more brutal than the last.

"OK, ladies. That's a wrap for today. Tomorrow when you get here, start stretching right away. We'll go back over today's routine and learn another awesome one and do several kick lines. Then we'll have a little fun and finish with freestyle."

One of the goats was hovered over a tall garbage bin releasing her guts.

I raced to the holding cell to grab my bag and break before anyone else. I knew they'd be vying for a prime spot to see if Max would be my ride home. But Six and Elle, a little Latina wannabe, blocked the doorway just as I was running out.

"So, Hannah, you need a ride home?" Six asked, sitting into her hip with her arms folded over the high hills on her chest.

"No, but thanks."

"So, you work at RockStar, huh?" Elle probed. "Sooo, do you know Rain?"

"Yeah, she's a good friend of mine. She's coming back to Chicago to cut the remix for her single, *Rain on Me*, with Usher."

"Ohmigod! Ohmigod! You like, *know* Usher," Elle repeated, frantically.

Six stabbed her in the arm, and Elle shot her an evil look.

"Yeah, I know Usher. We're cool. I used to work with him a lot when I lived in New York."

"Ohmigod! You used to live in *New York?*" Six shrieked.

Checkmate.

"Yeah, when I worked for Tru Records."

"Ohmigod! You used to work for *Tru Records!?*" They chorused in harmony.

I always loved this game.

"Uh-huh."

"That's so hot," they continued.

"Yeah, it was definitely hot. I worked with Ashanti and Nelly and Minx. They're all great."

"Wow, so like—you actually—"

"Yep, I sure did, but you know what guys, we can totally talk about this tomorrow. I've really gotta go; my girl is outside waiting for me, and she has to get back home to her plumber."

"Yeah, of course, no problemo." Six moved aside, pushing Elle rather forcibly out of the way and into Ashton and Simone, two other groupies who'd been cackling with them earlier. "Let her by already!"

I bolted out the door and down the hall. Turning the corner, I looked over my shoulder. They were heavy in conversation about Tru and the celebrities I knew, topped off by a glorious Manhattan lifestyle they were envisioning. Once more, I thanked Kimber for the shot she'd given me. It just might have saved my ass this round, I thought as I ran up the stairs, taking two at a time.

My watch warned me: 9:01.

Max and Britt had both parked on Madison Street and were standing outside their cars, casually talking to each other. I motioned vehemently at Britt to haul ass as I jumped over the red door and into the passenger's seat of the convertible.

"Let's go, right now! Step on it!"

She started the car and took off as I watched Max trail behind in the rearview mirror.

"What the fuck was that all about?" she implored as we turned onto Ashland Street and headed for Highway 290.

"You wouldn't believe what I've been through today" was all I could spill until she pulled into my driveway.

I jumped out and grabbed my bag, choosing not to watch her dangle her keys in front of Dallas, who'd come out to meet us. She dropped them down her extra low-cut Michael Kors silk top as I pressed for the elevator.

"Hannah, wait. What's wrong? What's going on, darlin'? Why'd you leave like that?" Max was calling out from behind me. He'd left his door open with his car running in the driveway behind Britt's.

"I can't talk to you right now. Do you have any idea what happened to me tonight?" I yelled at him.

Dallas poked his head in the door. "Mr. Knight, would you like me to pull your car around to the garage, sir?"

"Please. Thanks, man," he replied without turning around. "What the hell is going on, Hannah? This is not fair. Talk to me," he pleaded. "What happened?"

Britt walked into the lobby and leaned against the front desk to listen closely.

"I really don't want to talk to you right now, Max." I forced the words out.

"Can you at least tell me what I did wrong? Let me fix it, whatever it is."

"Why didn't you just tell me? You should've at least warned me. I could've ruined my shot at making the team. You know how important this is to me."

"I seriously doubt that, darlin'. You're the best rookie candidate and even better than some of the veterans. All the judges agreed that you were," he said, his eyes begging for an explanation.

"They said that?"

"Yes." He moved closer to me.

"Well, that's not the point," I insisted, moving away. "You can't do this to me."

"What am I doing to you?"

Dallas walked through the front door and gave Britt and Max their keys before handing me the armful of roses.

"This. You can't do this," I said and pushed the flowers on him. "It'll ruin everything."

"Hannah, what are you talking about? These are for you."

"Yeah, and I can't enjoy any of it because those girls all wanna take my shot away from me. They were threatening to tell Coach about us, I mean about you and me. I mean—you know what I mean!"

"Please tell me what you're talking about. You can't seriously be telling me that I can't do nice things for you, can you?"

I pushed for the elevator again and stepped on as soon as the doors opened. Britt licked her lips at Dallas, who was watching the heated exchange like a Venus and Serena wet T-shirt match. Tiptoeing past Max, Britt whispered, "It was really nice to meet you."

I obsessively pushed for the penthouse until the doors started to close.

"Hannah, wait. Talk to me, darlin'."

"I can't see you anymore, Max. Just stay away from me, please," I begged as the shiny silver elevator doors closed in front of him. Britt put her arms around me, and two tiny teardrops fell from my eyes.

32

I THREW MY BAG AT THE WALL IN THE FOYER, KNOCKING OVER THE SMALL TABLE that had held Max's gift boxes just yesterday, then headed for the stairs.

"Hannah, what's going on?" I heard Kennedy question from the sofa in the living room. She was sipping Veuve and watching *Brown Sugar* on the plasma when I ran past, desperately trying to get to my room without interference.

"I don't know what the hell just happened, but it's major," Britt answered. "And did you know Max Knight lives in this building?"

"Yeah, and—?" Kennedy questioned.

"You knew that?" Britt asked, stopping her train of thought, then revving it up again. "Well, did you know that he is so into our little Hannah it's not even funny? And apparently if I got it right downstairs, he didn't tell her something he was supposed to that could've gotten her kicked out of camp."

"What!" Kennedy exclaimed. "What the hell are you talking about? How could he have gotten her eliminated?"

"I don't know all the details, but he was there to pick her up tonight, and she went all section 8 and had me come get her. I was talking to him outside the stadium, and apparently he really enjoyed the little quality time they've spent together. He's feeling our baby Bug, and I don't know all the details, like I said, but he fucked up."

I could hear the stilettos charging up the stairs before they barged into my room, one behind the other.

"Hannah, honey, what's going on?" Kennedy asked. "You can talk to us. What's this all about?"

I lay on the bed with my head in the pillow, crying quiet tears, trying to go over everything in my head.

Britt was easing her way out of the bedroom when Kennedy yelled out to her, "And bring my drink up here and pour Hannah one too. I know that's exactly where you're headed," Kennedy ordered.

"I think this warrants a drinky-poo—or two!" she yelled back, already at the bottom of the staircase.

"Bug, sit up and tell me what the hell happened."

I sat up and looked at Kennedy. I didn't know how to explain it when I was still trying to understand it myself. Britt came back upstairs with three glasses of champagne and a newly opened bottle barely balanced in her arms. I took a glass from her and swigged it down.

"Hit her again," Kennedy ordered. Britt refilled, I guzzled, and told them the entire story, blow by unbelievable blow.

"Damn. When we were waiting for you at the stadium, he told me that he'd been sitting out there in his car for an hour, just in case you got out early. He didn't want you to have to wait. Hannah, he said he didn't want you to have to wait for anyone. Then he mentioned something about lasagna?"

"It looks like you're feeling something too," Kennedy said.

"Kennedy, you didn't see the man downstairs in the lobby. He looked like somebody snatched his $35 million contract away from him," Britt said.

Kennedy put her arm around me, and I looked at both of them sitting on the bed beside me. Why did it have to be this way?

"I just can't see him anymore. I can't risk getting kicked off the team before I even make it. I mean, you should've seen those girls in there tonight—they were ruthless. If they find out that there is even the tiniest hint of something between me and Max, they'll eat me alive. I just can't risk it," I said, and fell back onto the pillow.

"Wow, this is some sad shit," Britt said, and poured herself another drink.

33

THE NEXT DAY I DROVE MYSELF TO WORK, FEELING EMPTY THE ENTIRE WAY. I'D been a total mess last night and wasn't able to repack my bag or even take off my lashes. I'd cried so hard that I woke up with both lids stuck together. The Brats put me to bed somewhere between an episode of *Frasier* and their third bottle of Veuve.

I spent most of the day at work avoiding Eli's calls, all twenty of them, and going over interview questions with Cobra for the intern candidates he'd scheduled. I made sure I was following up on everything Eli had thrown at me, just without making any direct contact. I'd gotten quite comfortable communicating with him electronically and figured he'd have to catch me to confront me.

"Ms. Hannah, you're gonna have to talk to him sooner or later," Cobra advised, giggling. "He's seriously on my ass."

I reprimanded him with a glare. This wasn't the best time for sarcasm.

"But of course I'll do whatever you need me to in the meantime. It's just that he calls so much I feel like he's stalking *me*. I still don't know why you won't talk to him. So, he bought you some frost. Big deal."

"You never told me how you found out about that."

"Sorry, Bosslady, but everyone knows. Old news. Tales from the water cooler—"

"Look, just follow up and make sure Rain's car is scheduled to pick her up on time for her coaching. She's got a slew of major interviews she's gotta be prepped for. *Seventeen, King, Elle Girl*—"

"Will do. Now, what about Eli?" he pressed, just before I slipped out the door.

"Who?"

. . .

I PULLED INTO THE STADIUM LOT AND PARKED IN DIRECT VIEW OF THE STATUE, needing to funnel some of Jordan's effervescence my way. I knew I had at least a few more Jedi mind tricks up my sleeve.

"So, do you really know all those famous people?" Minnow asked as we changed into our required attire.

"That depends on what you mean by *know*," I answered cryptically.

"Uh, so, about Max—" Minnow looked around surreptitiously.

I gave her a "go on" look.

"Well, after you left I heard one of the veterans telling this other vet, Pepper, that she was gonna make sure she didn't mess up with him again like she did last year. Mona. That's her name. Mona."

I stopped dead in the middle of the three-four count I was beginning to show her. What was that supposed to mean? "Huh? Which one is Mona? And what about universal Rule Numero Uno?"

"Mona's the one with the big fake boobs and the shoulder-length platinum-blonde hair. She's really skinny except, well, her boobs. Pepper's the Afro-American girl with the long curly sandy-brown hair. She's got the really big round cheeks. Her boobs look pretty fake to me, too, but it's harder to tell. I don't study them or anything, it's just that they're so—"

"So what! Tell me what happened!?" I moved in closer.

"Sorry. So, like, Pepper kept all asking Mona if she'd heard about Max dropping you off last night, and Mona kept all screaming at her, telling her that no matter how good you thought you were and even if you made the team, you weren't gonna take what was already hers."

"And you're just telling me this?" I smacked her on the shoulder gently. "I don't get it. What about the Rule, Minnow, the goddamn Rule?!"

"I know! I'm, like, just as shocked as you are—well, almost as shocked as you are," she said, giving me her signature shrug.

"Is that all?"

"Well, OK," Minnow continued, "so Pepper all apologized and told Mona that you were no match for her and that you were probably screwing—but she used the 'f' word—all those celebrities that you claimed to know. Then Mona said something about making your life a living hell if you took what she'd claimed as hers two seasons ago."

"What!" I didn't even know who these girls were, and they were already signing off on my Diamond Dolls tombstone.

"But I guess it really doesn't matter, cuz he's just like your uncle or cousin or whatever—right? Maybe you could like plan a dinner party or something and invite them both over and get this all worked out." She giggled.

"You're enjoying this way too much." I grabbed my towel. "I'll be back. I'm going to the bathroom." I left Minnow studiously going over the sixteen counts I'd just taught her.

This whole thing was turning into something I might actually have trouble micromanaging. These girls definitely weren't amateurs. They'd earned their veteran viper stripes.

I pushed open the door to the restroom and took refuge in the stall at the far end of the wall. The dizziness finally subsided after several intense long quiet breaths. I bent over, held on to my knees, and closed my eyes, trying to channel a zen state of mind. I was prepping to start a palm-trees-and-ocean-breezes visualization when I heard someone heaving biscuits a few stalls away. My eyes popped open. I pressed my eyeball against the cold metal and squinted, trying to catch a glimpse through the tiny slit in the stall door. Nothing. The mystery barfer proceeded to gag a couple more times and vomit. Determined, I peeked under the stall door. Pointless. We all wore the same damn shoes. Still, I resolved to make an ID. After all, at this point, all information was power. Me against the barf machine. Letting myself out of the stall, I opened the bathroom door and let it close on its own, standing perfectly still against the wall. The lock on the anonymous stall door turned. It squeaked open, and the suckered vomit vixen was exposed. A super-skinny platinum blonde with huge boobs and red watery eyes tipped around the corner to the sink as I reappeared from behind the bathroom door.

Yahtze!

"Are you OK?" I asked through a slick smile.

"Huh! Yeah, uh-huh, I'm fine," she said, startled, trying to return the smile.

"Are you sure? Do you want me to call someone? I could run and get Coach if you want. I'm sure she'd want to know you weren't feeling well."

"No, no, it's fine," she insisted, and washed her hands frantically.

"By the way, I'm Hannah."

"I know who you are," she said dryly, this time attempting no smile at all.

"OK, well, what's your name?"

"What?"

"Your name?"

"Mona."

"Right, and I know who you are. I'm just going to take it that we understand each other now," I said. "I wouldn't want Nikki to find out that your tummy is upset."

Mona dried her hands and looked at me hotly.

"Well," I eyed her. "You'll probably wanna pop a stick of gum in your mouth." I turned around, exhaled silently, and walked out.

I was scared shitless as I walked toward the tunnel. I hated confrontation almost as much as I hated spinach, but tonight I was prepared to be Popeye's bitch if it meant holding on to my coveted spot.

34

NIKKI STOOD FRONT AND CENTER IN THE MIDDLE OF THE COURT, DOING HER BEST to stand still before she broke out in fanatical hand claps. She was gorgeous in an all-gold Diamond Dolls warm-up suit, almost as gorgeous as the gold chain that hung from her neck with the gold charm that spelled out D-O-L-L-S in cursive. I knew I'd have to eat a lot of spinach if I ever planned on wearing that one day.

"I'll start by saying that you're beginning to see who has what it takes and who doesn't."

I looked over at Mona and Pepper, who were practicing voodoo on me. Nikki continued: "Now, that's nothing to be ashamed of; this just isn't for everyone, that's all. Today we're going to stretch out, learn a new routine, do some kick lines, and end with a little freestyling. So let's get started."

The night raced away with only a five-minute water break, where it appeared that most people were questioning their sanity. When it was time for the dreaded kick lines, I did my best to blend in inconspicuously, but it was clear that my kicks weren't cutting the mustard when I realized that most of my kick line could get their psycho-lypoed legs behind their Aquanetted heads!

Nikki bounced in front of me for an entire twenty-four counts that dragged on for-effin'-ever, and it took every inch of dignity and hamstring strength I had to muddle through it. She wrote down a score next to my name on her penalty pad before she finally moved on to the next section of kicking goats.

Minnow's weakness was up next.

"OK, Minnow, trust me; you've got this. Just remember what we went over earlier," I encouraged.

"Right. Right. Right. Wrong. Wrong. Wrong," she said, and shook her head. "What if I screw this up?"

"How many times have you auditioned, Minn?" I asked, and moved the flyaway hair from her eyes.

She jutted two nails into her mouth and began biting away. "This makes number four."

"My point exactly. You've made it farther than you have any of those other times. This is it. Time to work it out and show them all that you belong here," I said, with both my hands on her shoulders.

"You're right." She took her place on the court with three other girls.

I crossed my fingers behind my back and hoped for the best when Shortstuff cranked up the music. Missy Elliot yelled from the speakers, and Minnow moved stiffly to the beat.

"She's not as bad as she was on Saturday," I overheard one of the vets say.

"Come on, Skye, she still doesn't have a chance in hell."

"I'm not saying she does; I'm just saying she's not as bad as she was on Saturday. She's gotten better in the last four days and that's saying *something.*"

"Yeah, that she still sucks!"

"She's more on beat than I've ever seen her. And look at those moves. She's been practicing. I like that," Skye observed.

"Whatever! She's sooo not going to make this team. She's tried out like twenty times already. Can't she take a hint? We don't want her."

"Shut up, Katie. This is her fourth time. I like that. She believes in herself. Failure isn't her friend. She's got real heart."

I was smiling to myself and leaning back farther to hear more comments from the honey-roasted peanut gallery when I almost lost my balance. I looked down at the floor and studied my shoelace until it was my turn to make up for my high-kick debacle. Immediately, Missy got into my head, and I opened with a triple turn and followed with the strongest toe touch I'd ever hit, landing in a split. When I back-rolled out of that, somehow I tossed in a few Frankie Knuckles house moves that took me back to the days before house music was ever a mainstream club favorite. I was Fatima on meth!

"Hey, 108," Skye called as we finished and she walked toward us. "Now that's what I call getting into a zone."

Skye was about five eight and had very long blonde hair with dark blonde streaks. She was what you'd call one of the beautiful ones. Perfect teeth and nose, and her Angelina lips were near-natural.

"Thanks. Thanks a lot," I panted.

I felt relieved, hoping I'd compensated for the puny peewee high kicks.

"I'm Skye. I'm a five-year veteran."

"Impressive," I said, and extended my hand. "I mean—that's not my name. I mean, my name is Hannah, and that's really impressive—the five years, I mean."

Minnow stood on her tiptoes and cleared her throat.

"This is Minnow," I said.

Over Skye's shoulder I could see Mona, Pepper, and another veteran, Hilton, watching keenly as we all made nice.

"Glad to see you back again this year, Minnow. You're getting better. Keep it up," Skye advised.

"Ohmigod! Thanks," Minnow stammered, awestricken.

"And this is Katie; she's a four-year vet. She's kinda harsh, but she doesn't mean anything by it," Skye warned.

Katie looked almost exactly like Skye except that her eyes were brown and her hair was one sixteenth of a shade darker. She was thin, too, but it didn't look as if it came naturally for her. A couple more

Krispy Kremes could have pushed her over the sideline and gotten her Diamond Dolls necklace snatched.

"Whatever! Hannah, that was hot. And Minnow, well, keep practicing. You know, you can always try again next year."

"I will if I have to. I'll be back until they ask me to stop coming," Minnow said, oblivious to Katie's jab.

"Well, good luck, guys. I hope to work with you both this year," Skye said, and grabbed Katie by the arm.

With each passing night, I hearted that necklace more than anything. But first, I'd have to get through the mini-interview session the following night, and I was already dreading the inevitable inquisition.

35

THE JACUZZI WAS SCREAMING MY NAME. I SLID IN CAUTIOUSLY AND GOT COMfortable, adjusting the bath pillow beneath my head, trying to relax and rid myself of the evening's venom.

My thoughts immediately slipped back to that ethereal evening with Max, sitting on the blanket with his legs wrapped around me and his lips barely touching my neck. The expression on his face when he looked at me, the pitch in his voice when he called me "darlin"—it was all too titillating. I wasn't certain about too many things right now, but I knew that he had the softest touch when he ran the inside of his hand along the apple of my cheek and the warmest tone when he talked about his love for his family. He appreciated life like very few people I'd ever met, and being next to him in the silence of stolen moments was liberating. *Why me*, I thought, and buried my face under the bubbles.

Through the water I heard the phone ring.

"Yes, Dallas, what's going on?" I asked, wiping the suds from my eyes after squinting at the caller ID on the stand next to the tub.

"Hi, Hannah; hate to bother you, but you have a delivery downstairs. I'm the only one down here right now, but I could have someone bring it up to you," he offered.

"What is it?" I asked, trying to assess the urgency, not wanting to surrender my suds.

"I'm not sure. It's a package is all I can really see."

"OK, thanks; send it up."

I stood up and grabbed a towel, hating that I couldn't finish what my mind had started before tying the magenta La Perla satin wrap robe and heading downstairs.

"Coming!" I yelled at the buzzer, growing more agitated by the second as I dripped a Hansel and Gretel path back to the bathtub.

"These are for you, Ms. Love," the messenger said.

"Thanks so much," I nodded, taking the huge bouquet of flowers and the gift bag from the messenger.

I placed the Waterford crystal vase on the island and inspected the tropical bouquet: birds of paradise, lavender orchids, and African violets.

Seconds after I peeked into the bag, the wrapping paper was falling to the floor and I was looking at a first edition of *Moby Dick*.

My hands were shaking as I read the card inside the bouquet:

Hannah, please accept these beautiful tropical flowers and know that I'm sorry for upsetting you. Maybe one day you'll let me take you to the native island of each one so you can be surrounded by something as beautiful as you are to me.

I miss you, darlin'.

Enjoy.
Max

Now more than ever, I needed to talk to Max, but I had no idea what I wanted to say. There was a soft knock on the front door. I ran to open it.

"Hey, Angel. How's my favorite girl?" Eli greeted, and bent down to plant a kiss on my forehead.

Holy Shit, Batman!

While scanning his black Armani three-button suit, my eyes got stuck on the dozen red roses choking in his hand.

"Eli!" I tried to sound more surprised than disappointed. "What are you doing here?" I took the flowers and strategically placed them in front of my nipples, now erect and announcing themselves.

"I know, I know—this is unexpected. Don't trip; I slid your concierge a few C notes to let me up. I convinced him that I was your brother and that I wanted to surprise you."

"Eli, I'm an only child."

"Obviously *he* doesn't know that."

"Why on earth would you do that? And what are you doing here?" I asked again, this time not caring as much about how I sounded.

"I know you weren't expecting me, Angel, but I needed to see you. You won't take my calls, and you won't even pick up the phone to *return* my fuckin' calls. You keep texting me, ma, and I need to talk to you face-to-face. It's starting to drive me bananas. Besides, I really didn't want to do this at the office."

He was right about that; I hadn't been receptive to him, and we definitely did need to talk. I knew things couldn't go on the way they'd been going much longer, and the rumor mill had already started to spin out of control.

"Why didn't you call first?"

"Shit. Because you won't take my goddamn calls. I've called you at least twenty times in the last three days."

Twenty-nine.

"I know lil man told you; he had to. I've started harassing his ass, too."

I had to laugh at the thought of Cobra being driven into the ground with Eli's incessant pestering and his demanding tone. Cobra was being tested on so many fronts, and from the looks of it he was passing them all with flying pastel colors.

"I'm not mad at lil man. But are you goin' let me in or what?"

"Oh, yeah, sure. Come in," I said, and moved out of the way, closing the door behind him. I led him down the hallway past the kitchen and into the open living room. "Please, have a seat. I'm gonna go and put some clothes on. Can I get you something to drink?"

"Naw, I'm only staying a second. I know it was kind of fucked-up to just stop by unannounced, but, but—hell, I'll have that drink." He sat

down on the couch. "Bordeaux or Shiraz is cool; whichever you got."
He eyed the breathtaking bouquet on the island. "Those are hot."

I nodded. "Uh-huh. My Nana sent them to me."

I walked over to the island and put the roses down next to the vase,
wondering why I'd just lied. I grabbed a bottle of 1996 Bin 555 from
the Mission-style rack and frantically snatched two glasses. I needed
that drink more than Eli and couldn't get the bottle open fast enough.

"Damn, that's sexy—the view, I mean."

"I know," I quipped, sitting uncomfortably on the couch next to
him looking out over the calm water.

I usually take my time to enjoy the rich wine—its lingering oak and
spicy finish—but seeing as how this clearly wasn't one of those times,
I tipped my head back, and when I came up for air, my glass was empty.

"Excuse me."

As I got up to pour myself another I could feel my fingers beginning
to throb.

"Aren't you supposed to be in New York with Nigel and Emmanuele
for the quarterly review meeting? I know the president and CEO can't
be too happy with you bailing out on them two days before you were
scheduled to return," I said, putting the glass down and shaking my
hands as if they'd gotten caught in cobwebs.

"I just got off the plane. The trip got cut short cuz Nigel had to handle some family shit and Mannie took a meeting with big brass at Universal."

"About what? Are they talking mergers and acquisitions?" I asked,
immediately concerned about my fate at RockStar.

"No—well, I don't know. Mannie said it was just a meeting and he
would give us a briefing as soon as he could. But there's nothing for
you to worry about. I got you. I always got your back, ma," he said, and
I was reminded again of his seductive power and just why I found him
so damn intriguing.

He took a deep breath, inhaling the aroma of the wine before he
sipped. "So tell me, how are your tryouts going?"

"Pretty good. A couple of surprises have been thrown at me here
and there, but overall, things are progressing nicely," I said, walking
back over to the sofa, ready to get to the point. "Eli, I really want to

thank you for the beautiful necklace you gave me, and again for the tennis bracelet. I don't quite know what to think, but I'm very grateful. You really didn't have to do any of that."

"I know, and that's what I wanted to talk to you about. I never want you to get the wrong impression about me, Angel, and I realized that my shit hasn't really been on the up-and-up lately. The last thing I want to see happen is you get fucked up in the head and have it affect your attitude about me and the job," he said, and took another sip.

I followed suit and took a much bigger one. Where was he going with all of this? The wine was already calming me, and I sat back into the couch and pulled my robe tighter.

"I know I brought you on at RockStar, and I know I'm your boss and we have a very good thing going. We're a good team, and we really make shit happen around there. I'm happy with the rollout of Rock-Star Chicago and most of that is because your game is always so tight. But there is something I need you to understand. The truth of the matter is—" He stopped and cleared his throat and took his BlackBerry out of his suit pocket. "Gimme a second," he said, and began typing away.

I overfilled my lungs with O_2 and my mouth with 555, and anxiously awaited the clarity I'd been seeking for the last month or so.

"My bad," he said, as his cell started to ring. "I need to handle this." He put the phone to his ear and then got up from the couch and walked out onto the balcony. "I can't really talk right now. No, it's not a good time to go on about that shit. This is what the fuck I'm always sayin' to you. Lemme hit you back. I'm gonna have to hit you back," he snapped into the cell and looked back at me, not at all uncomfortable.

"Do you need some privacy?" I asked, getting up from the sofa and motioning to close the French doors behind him. He waved his hand and mouthed the word no, obviously unaware or completely indifferent that I could still hear him.

"No, it's not. It's nobody. Don't worry about that. Look, I'll hit you back in a minute," he said to the listener, and hung up the phone before walking back inside to sit down. But just as he set his cell on the coffee table, it rang again. I watched him either send the call to voicemail or silence the ringer.

"My bad, ma; that was, that was—"

"You were saying that you understood the situation at the office and you wanted me to know—"

"Right. Right. I really want you to know that despite the fact that I'm your boss, I'm still a man and I'm still affected, like everyone else, by what's around me. Truth be told, Angel, I really have some strong feelings for you. They've been developin' ever since Kimber introduced us that night in NY at Q-tip's jump-off at Table 50."

I took another gulp from my glass and looked at this very powerful, very sexy, very rich man and at the little droplets of sweat forming on his forehead. He was fidgeting with his fingers and had loosened the red-and-white striped Brioni satin tie around his neck.

"You are so smart and sharp—and damn, you're fine. I think about you more often than I should. Now I'm not really good at communicating my feelings and shit, but the gifts are my way of showing you how I feel. Take all of that and do what you want with it. Just know that I'm here should you want to explore this thing."

I sat still and felt my nipples harden again as I was either really starting to feel the wine or really starting to feel him—or maybe a bit of both.

"Check me if I'm wrong, but I think you feel something, too." He lowered his eyebrows and, in his usual overly confident way, touched my knee and licked his lips.

"I don't know how to answer that. You're my boss, and I've learned a lot from you. I like things the way they are, so I don't ever let myself really think about what else could happen," I said, trying to be as smooth as he always was.

"I feel you," he said, and cocked his head to the side.

After a few seconds had passed, he took the last sip from his glass, got up from the sofa, grabbed his cell from the table, and headed toward the front door.

"Well, there it is. I can't be mad at that at all. You're far too valuable, and I wouldn't want to fuck anything up. But now everything is on the table, and you know what's really good."

We stood still at the door. I held my empty wineglass firmly in my hand. The thought of feeling his lips against mine momentarily tempted me. I scratched my throat, tightened my robe, and looked into his eyes. His BlackBerry broke the silence.

"I'll holla at you tomorrow, Angel," he said as I reached for the door. Before I could open it all the way, he turned around and said in his best LL flow, "Know this, I'll still be thinking about you; that's not gonna stop. I'm a man, girl, and just the way you look right now, well—"

My lips had parted into a smile, somewhat reflexively but also partially because, shallow as it may sound, I was beyond flattered that one of the superstars in the industry found it so necessary to make a special trip to my place to tell me he was feeling me. Although I hadn't begun to figure out my feelings for him—if I even had any—I was glad things were out in the open.

I pulled at the door, it swung open, and I looked up into Max's eyes just as he was getting ready to knock. He had one hand in his pocket, a small paper bag in the other, and a very confused look on his face.

Eli looked at Max and back at me. His cell had started to vibrate, and he put it to his ear.

"I'm out," Eli said, and gave a 'what up' nod to Max before starting in on his phone conversation. Halfway down the hall something clicked, and he looked over his shoulder with a stunned expression before continuing on his way.

Standing in the doorway, in a robe, with an empty wineglass in my hand—and two very erect nipples—I felt my knees go weak. I didn't say a word. None worth saying came to mind. Max looked at me with sincere sadness, and I even thought I saw the corners of his mouth turn down into a tiny frown. He turned to leave but changed his mind.

"I just wanted to bring you the food for the flowers. They'll last longer if you feed them this once a day. That's all." He handed me the paper bag and walked away slowly. "I missed you, darlin'. But I get it now."

I stood there with the paper bag in my hand, watching him run his fingers through his disheveled hair and shake his head before he disappeared into the elevator.

I closed the door and leaned against it listlessly. There was absolutely no feeling left in my body. It had all been sucked out of me with one short goodbye. When my hands started to shake, I put the glass down next to the roses to keep it from shattering into tiny pieces—just like my heart. On automatic pilot, I separated Eli's roses, cut the stems, and put them into a vase. I carried the tropical flowers and the card up to my room and left the roses on the coffee table. Even though the water was only mildly warm in the tub, I got back in anyway. My crying spell started slowly but quickly hit a crescendo and echoed throughout the oversized master bathroom.

An hour later, I climbed into bed with *Moby Dick* and reread his note. This time I didn't shed a single tear. There were none left.

36

I PULLED INTO THE STADIUM LOT, STILL GROGGY FROM THE NIGHT BEFORE BUT DE-termined to finish what I'd started. This is what it all came down to, and I couldn't help but think about the sacrifices I'd already made. There was no room for error. I sat in the driver's seat for a while, going over my backup plans and envisioning the flow of the night's events.

Minnow was waiting for me next to the Jordan statue.

"Hey, what's up?" I said to her, throwing up my fist.

"Why do you do that every day?" she asked.

"You really wanna know?"

"Uh-huh."

"It's the black power fist. Militant groups used it as a symbol to rep-resent solidarity during the revolution—part of the whole civil rights movement."

"Whoa."

"Heavy, huh? Can you dig it?" I held out my hand for her to slide me five.

She slapped it. "OK, but why do you do that every day? Is it because Michael Jordan is Afro-American?"

I had to chuckle at her sincerity. "Black works for me. Few people still say Afro-American."

"OK, is it because he's black?" she asked, in a hushed voice.

"No. It's just my little way of genuflecting to the cause. Like Jordan, I'm willing to do whatever it takes to make it. It's more symbolic."

"Oh." She thought for a minute. "But what exactly is it symbolizing? The civil rights movement is over." She held the door to Gate 4 open for me.

"That depends on who you're talking to. Many people would disagree with that."

She listened closely, like one of her eager students.

"Perfect example—there aren't as many black Diamond Dolls as there should or could be. By me going out there and doing whatever it takes to make the team, maybe more little black girls will see that and be inspired to reach for that kind of goal, or one similar."

"But Michael Jordan was a great *basketball* player."

"True. But for so many young black kids, boys *and* girls, he was so much more than that. He took the game to the next level, and people all over the world wanted to be like Mike. But for the kids in the community—he was inspiration; he transcended basketball and symbolized success."

"I remember the Gatorade commercials."

"I want to be that for the young girls. I won't change the NBA cheerleading game, I know that, but I'll definitely do my part to make a difference and be inspiring to the little ones out there who look like me."

"Like the example I'm setting for my kids."

"Well, something like that. Listen, enough of the black history lesson; let's go claim our spots," I said as we walked through the Hall of Fame.

As we passed the pictures of Scottie Pippen, Dennis Rodman, and Bob Love on the wall my face lit up. "Them too, huh?" Minnow asked knowingly.

"Yeah, Minnow, them, too. They've all done their part, in one way or another."

37

WE OUTFITTED OURSELVES WITH OUR ARMOR: PANTYHOSE, BLACK LYCRA SHORTS, and dance shoes. The room was tense and only got worse when Mona walked in with Pepper and Hilton in tow. It was clear that she was the ringleader of their big-busted circus show. She stared at me with demon's rage, her eyes rolling into the back of her head.

"Well, ladies," said Nikki, "I'm sure you can see that our group has gotten smaller. We started out on Tuesday with forty-seven candidates and are now down to thirty-five." She laid out the night's schedule with more intensity and zeal than I'd seen before.

We got through the high-impact routines with ease, and Minnow doubly delivered before we were broken up into groups of five, only to repeat the routines over and over and over! Sweat was flying from every part of my body. I was losing steam and starting to feel desperately drained—a clear repercussion of last night's misguided rendezvous.

The clock struck, and it was time for freestyle, and the energy in the room sizzled. For once, Minnow seemed to feed off it all. She stood in the center of the court, in the middle of the diamond, and I just knew she was fighting the urge to thrust her nubby nails into her grill. She smeared her moist palms on the sides of her sweaty shorts and took short huffy breaths. I looked around at the goats, and all eyes were on the underdog. A wave of whispers went through the herd. I tried to telekinetically bestow "The Force" onto her when Shortstuff released the "play" button, and—to our Diamond Doll delight—it was the exact same music from last night! Apparently my psychic powers were far-reaching and had resonated deep within the sound machine. Minnow used the core sixteen counts that I'd taught her the night before and threw in several more of her own. I could tell she'd been practicing. (Insider Secret: Freestyle doesn't necessarily mean improvisation; it can be rehearsed, and no one has to know.) And drum roll, please, Minnow stepped up to the plate and definitely did her thing!

"Thanks, ladies," Nikki said. "We're going to take a break and ask you all to go back into the media room so we can begin private interviews. Number 21, we'll start with you."

I felt really good about Minnow's chances but was beginning to get a little concerned about my own interviews. When the door opened, Mona got up to talk to Coach before she called for the third girl.

"Hannah, come with me please," Nikki said.

Jesus, Nikki, and Mary!

This was it!

I breathed religiously, forcing myself to ignore Mona and her crew. I thought of all the hard physical work I'd done to get this far. Whatever was coming now, I had to be ready for it.

I followed Coach onto the court and sat in the wooden hot seat in front of a long table covered in gold linen. Four judges were smiling pleasantly at nothing in particular; three others shuffled score sheets in front of them. My butt jutted down into the wooden "electric chair." Unnerved, I shifted my ass cheeks, hoping that being zapped wasn't next on the agenda. The numbness was creeping from my fingers into my hands.

"So, Hannah, how have you enjoyed the audition process so far?" Nikki asked.

"It's been great. Amazing, even. The workouts were intense, and it was kind of like having the best trainer working with me—for free."

The panel laughed politely, and I took a deep breath, remembering to smile despite my intense nervousness.

"What would you say some of your weaknesses are when it comes to working on a team?"

Stealthily, I rubbed my numb fingers under the seat of the chair, trying to bring them back to life.

"Well, I really enjoy working in a team environment because it gives me more people to learn from as I grow. My weakness would be that sometimes I try too hard to learn from everyone when I should be focused on my direct superior or team leader."

I watched the judges take notes. That answer always gets 'em, I thought, my fingers beginning to prickle slightly.

The rest of her questions were more of the same team-oriented blah blah blahs, with varying assessment queries relative to my time-management skills on a perceived strengths-and-weaknesses barometer. Whatever!

"This next question is really important. Take a second and think about this if you need to." Nikki attempted to raise her Botoxed brow.

"How do you feel about people who break rules on a team? Do you think that's excusable, and if not, then what kind of penalty would you suggest they receive?" she asked without straining a muscle in her pageant-perfect face.

I looked at Nikki closely, wondering if she'd constructed that question especially for me.

"Well, I think rules are in place for a reason, and by breaking them you are blatantly disrespecting the team. So, no, I don't agree with breaking established rules, and I think that when someone intentionally sets off along that path of rebellion, they need to be penalized. I can't say what should happen to them; I guess it would depend on what they did, kind of like the punishment fitting the crime. In an organization like this, though, I'd imagine that there are clear penalties for various types of misconduct."

That was the dreaded question, and I'd navigated my way through it without being weighed down by the force of the kryptonite.

"Great, Hannah, thanks so much. You can head back now," she said as I got up from the wooden chair as gracefully as I could, given that my hands were nearly useless. I thanked them and never looked back.

After the last girl goat was done, Nikki surveyed the room and cleared her throat, smashing her hands together relentlessly. "OK, ladies, this is what we've all been waiting for. Out of over two thousand women, you've made it this far."

I crossed every part of my body that I didn't fear would get stuck.

"Skye P., Mona S., Simone K., Six B., Hannah L." That was me, that was me, that was me, I'm Hannah L.! Ka-ching! I felt a rush of heat swell through my body and rush out just as quickly when I looked over at Minnow, whose name still hadn't been called.

"Brooklyn P., Hilton K., and last, but certainly not least, after four consecutive years of auditioning for this team, it is my pleasure and my honor to welcome Minnow C. to the Chicago Diamond Dolls. Congratulations. I am very happy to be your coach. Now, come, rookies, and join me and the judges on the court for a little champagne."

Minnow was crying tears of disbelief and was being bombarded by most of the new rookies when I stepped back into my corner and thanked God for seeing me through what had been a tough fucking week (sorry, God). But somehow I had a sneaky feeling that this was just the beginning.

We stood on the cherished diamond in the middle of the court while uniformed waiters served us tall plastic glasses of champagne on round silver trays. I looked around at all the goats who'd made it and realized that none of the returning veterans had been cut.

A few feet from everyone else, Brooklyn stood off to the side in deep discussion with Nikki. She nodded in agreement to everything Coach was saying to her.

I'd learned over the past week that Brooklyn was also mixed—half black and half white. She was deeply religious and had auditioned against her boyfriend's and parents' wishes. She had long natural wavy hair, a killer smile, and tons of energy, but she was noticeably thicker than any of the other girls who'd been selected for the squad. She was one of those pecan mints who had been blessed with a black woman's ass and the thick thighs that would have made even the most trifling red-blooded man stop his car and propose. She was a Southern sweetie and had told us that she'd been homecoming queen at Howard University both her junior and senior years in undergrad—and I definitely understood why. She was a knockout.

"I wonder what Coach's saying to her," Brooklyn's friend Chloe commented as our stares veered off in their direction. "It can't be bad. She made the team, right? I'm sure it's no big deal."

Chloe was a Winona Ryder look-alike. The two of them teamed together were just as curious as Minnow and I probably looked. Chloe had short, silky, slightly wavy hair and keen foxy features. She'd told us that her parents were white and Puerto Rican. Chloe was adorably striking, in a polar opposite kind of way from Brooklyn.

"We'll find out when she comes back over. Sip up and don't let it worry you," I urged, even though I had a pretty good idea what Coach was telling her.

When Minnow finally pulled herself away from her doting new B.F.F.s, she blessed us with her signature shoulder shrug.

"Who knew?" she asked, hunching her shoulders up to her tiny ears.

"We did," Chloe and I chorused as Brooklyn joined our tête-à-tête.

"What did she say to you over there?" Chloe asked curiously.

"She said we're gonna have regular weigh-ins, and if I don't lose fifteen pounds before our first practice next month, I'll never see the court!"

"OK, well, you can do that, right?" Chloe asked.

"It's not that easy, honey. My family is thick. We're big-boned Southern dimes, and it's not a common thing for us to be walking around looking like Paris Hilton," she said in a slightly annoyed tone. "Hannah, you know what I'm saying, right?"

I had to admit I did know where she was coming from. I just didn't eat like that anymore. When I was younger and Nana didn't know any better, we ate whatever she brought home from the carb-infested diner. It wasn't until my stepfather introduced us to a different lifestyle that she was even able to afford better and learn *how* to do better for the two of us.

"I do understand, Brooklyn. But I can tell you that it's possible. At least you've got an extra month to do it the right way."

Nikki was exuberantly making the rounds to each cluster of newbies.

"Girls, I'm really proud of you all. You're what this team is about. You've all improved and are very deserving of your spots. And Minnow, you're our little star for the night." Coach clapped her very red hands together. "I was so proud to see you out there this year, and each night you just got better. Keep it up. Great job, everyone." Nikki applauded one last time for emphasis, before dashing into the next cluster.

We put our arms around each other and snickered like sassy preteen girls with brand-new shiny patent leather shoes and matching minipurses.

· · ·

THINGS SLOWLY STARTED TO WRAP UP, AND I FIGURED IT WAS A GOOD TIME TO head out to share the news with the Brats. They were at the house, sittin' on Dom, awaiting my arrival to get the celebration started. I hugged Minnow and told her I'd see her next month at our first practice.

"Hannah, I'll never forget you for this. You changed my life," she whispered into my ear.

I puckered and planted a quick smooch on her cheek and floated outside to the parking lot, raising my fist to Jordan all the way to my Ranger and singing aloud, "If I could be like Mike!"

HALFTIME

HALFTIME

38

I SLIPPED IN THE FRONT DOOR AND CREPT DOWN THE HALL. I COULD SEE MY GIRLS stretched out in the living room watching *America's Next Top Model* and making bets on who'd be eliminated tonight.

"So, who wants to pour a Chicago Diamond Dolls rookie a glass of champagne?" I yelled.

Britt and Kennedy screamed together and jumped up from the sofa.

"Congratulations, Hannah-Bug! So does this mean that we'll be able to come see you at all the games?" Kennedy asked.

"That's my bitch," Britt squealed. "Now can we break open the goddamn champagne?"

"Yes, yes, get it crackin'," I insisted, and was clobbered by Britt's other arm as she imprisoned me with a tight grateful embrace.

They opened the first bottle, which we went through like the Golden Girls on cheesecake. It wasn't long before we decided that it was time to head out for a stiffer drink and toast on the town.

I took a quick shower and threw on a short cream semisheer Diane

Von Furstenberg wrap dress, cut down the front and back with a little Dirty Girl body sparkle dabbed deep into my barely there cleavage.

"The brown or the pink ones?" Kennedy asked, chewing on a tofu bagel and posing in front of the fourteen-foot bedroom mirror. I turned around and eyed her closely.

"The brown ones." I pointed to my second-favorite clover-honey Henri Bendel stilettos. Although Kennedy was a size nine, when it came to the Bendels, an extra shoe pad always did the trick. I grabbed my old faithful lavender snakeskin Christian Louboutin clutch from the bed and headed downstairs.

"Hey rookie, fill me up," Britt ordered from the balcony outside. "I was thinking that maybe I need to call Dallas and ask him to bring up a couple more bottles," she said, comfortably laid out in the lounger, nodding her head to old-school Michael (pre-I've-completely-lost-my-mind-and-now-act-like-I-was-raised-by-crazy-cult-clowns) Jackson.

I joined them on the balcony, popped open the last bottle, and re-filled all glasses. It was a hot June evening, and everyone was out preparing to dance under the moon, which had found a commanding spot in the sky over the lake. I inhaled the aroma of the city, always so rich with flavor.

"Hey Dallas. Could you send a couple bottles of Dom up here when you get a free sec? Or better yet, could you bring them up yourself?" I heard Britt whispering into the phone.

She was definitely up to something. I could hear it in her voice. I eyed her suspiciously as I headed for the bathroom with Kennedy behind me.

"You must be going bananas, Bug! I mean you did it; not that we doubted you for a nanosecond," Kennedy said, breaking my stare. "Do you think Max has any idea that you made it?"

"I dunno." I shrugged. "I've been trying hard not to think about it. I mean, I wanted to tell him. He was so supportive and everything, but I know he doesn't wanna talk to me right now. He has to feel like I lied to him and was a complete and total shit. I feel so bad, Sweets. I mean if you could have seen his face when I opened the door and he saw Eli lurking there next to me and—"

"Don't think about that right now. All you have to do is explain what happened. I'm sure he'll understand."

"No, honey. Don't get me wrong; I'd love to explain what happened, but I think it might actually be better this way—at least for now. It's hard enough not being able to hang out with him, the way I want, you know. At least now he'll just leave it alone, and everyone will just forget about it."

"If you say so. I just think it'd be better if he knew the truth. You really don't think he'd understand?"

"I'm not sure. All I know is that the first time when I asked him to stay away, he still sent me flowers *and* he still came by. It's like he didn't take me seriously. This way, at least I have some control—no matter how much it burns."

"I guess." Kennedy relented.

"I'll take care of this," Britt slurred as she made a mad dash from the balcony to answer the knock at the front door.

"Hi, Dallas." She licked her lips and cheesed coyly.

I walked out of the bathroom and leaned against the island in the kitchen and prepared to catch the show.

Britt grabbed his hand and pulled him inside. "Come on in." Michael's 1982 "Human Nature" was playing in the background: "Why/why/does she do me this way?" Michael questioned from the Bose speakers.

I took the three bottles of champagne from his arms. "I brought you an extra one. Just in case," Dallas added.

"Thanks, Big D," Britt said. "Did you wanna join us for a drink?"

He looked around the room. "Uh, I don't know."

Britt moved in closer to him and rubbed her hands against his chest.

Dallas was a fiery Latin hottie, a beefier Benjamin Bratt with dark wavy hair and deep-set eyes. He was almost six feet two and built like a football player, even having been in the NFL draft a couple years ago. But after getting hurt he decided to go back to school to get a master's in industrial engineering. Working as a concierge, he'd said, gave him time to catch up on his studies when it was usually quiet—except, of course, when Britt was anywhere around.

He stepped away from her, but she immediately inched closer.

Kennedy laughed aloud. "Britt, what're you doing? He's a professional, you know." She shook her head and walked back over to the sofa to grab the remote.

Brittany ran her other hand along his bulging forearm, making it clear that she considered Dallas a different kind of professional, one who was now starting to bulge in other places.

He cleared his throat. "Maybe I will have just *one* drink, if it's OK with Hannah."

I looked over at Britt, who was giving me a pleading stare. I shrugged, popped open a bottle, and hopped on top of the island.

"Great," Britt gushed, snatching the bottle from me and grabbing a fresh flute before promptly taking Dallas's hand and pulling him into the guest room closest to the foyer. They pushed at the door, not shutting it all the way.

I hopped down from the island, popped another bottle, and refilled my glass. Kennedy motioned for more, and before obliging I detoured toward the guest room. As I prepared to peek in, the door slammed shut in my face. Kennedy, who'd settled on a VH-1 special about reality show has-beens, laughed as I plopped down next to her on the sofa.

"So where are we going, anyway?"

"I was thinking we could swing by the Signature Lounge in the John Hancock," I said, struggling to ward off the visual inspired by the crescendo of incessant moaning coming from the next room.

Minutes later Britt stumbled out, eyes red, hair pulled back into a sloppy ponytail. Dallas came out behind her, buttoning his shirt over his sculpted chest. Bending over Britt's neck, he bit it again.

"Well, Dallas, I guess you got your tip," I joked from the sofa.

Dallas adjusted himself as he walked to the door. "I should be tipping her," he quipped.

Britt smacked him on the ass and tucked a $100 bill into his back pocket. "You gave me a lot more than just your tip." She swayed a little and grabbed the door for balance. "When you get downstairs, could you tell the driver we're ready? He can bring the car around now."

Dallas tucked in his shirt as he walked toward the elevator. "Right away. Anything for you."

Britt caught us all staring at her from the couch. She tipped her glass before finishing what was left in it. "Aaah. Good times."

"I thought I was supposed to be the one celebrating."

"Don't hate. I keep telling you bitches none of my friends discriminate. There's plenty to go around."

"You're such a slut," Kennedy said, rolling her eyes and getting up from the sofa.

"No," she clarified. "I'm an equal opportunity provider."

39

HEADS TURNED THE MOMENT WE STEPPED ONTO THE NINETY-SIXTH FLOOR OF THE Hancock building.

"I'm nervous and excited about the season, you guys—all at the same time," I told them as the server meticulously placed our martinis on the table in front of the floor-to-ceiling window.

"Girl, you better enjoy that shit. You're gonna be out there cheering for your man," Britt teased.

"He's not my man," I retorted, feeling a small tinge of sadness.

"Get over it. He's not your man cuz you got busted standing in the doorway with Eli, wine breath, and erect nipples," she continued. "Kennedy filled me in on your little ménage-à-trois-gone-wrong." She took an extra-long sip from her glass before exhaling. "Now, Bug, you know I could've helped you out with those two fine men," Britt added, speaking loud enough to drown out the retro jazz band playing on the platform in the center of the room.

Kennedy winced. "Damn! Must you always be so, so, so—"

"Let it go, Sweets. In some sick twisted way she's right. I should have changed into sweats as soon as I let Eli in the door. Granted, I didn't know Max was coming over and, and, and—well, whatever! It's still my fault, and I know better. I just don't know what I was thinking," I admitted. "I must've gotten completely caught up."

"Just slip into his locker room after the game and make it up to him," Kennedy slyly suggested between giggles.

"One of the vets might already be in there with him. Really."

"Girl, you better fight for that fine ass, sexy ass, hard ass—"

"Brittany, she gets it! Do you ever shut that thing off?" Kennedy snapped, nodding toward Britt's crotch. "How in God's name are we so different? You were born three minutes before me, and I swear sometimes I wonder if one of us was switched at birth."

"Shut up, Annie. What you need is for the right man to work you out the right way one day—you know, rub you, lick you, sock it right to you, and, and then feed you a goddamn Twinkie!" Britt said, licking her lips.

"Oh my God, will you both please stop," I begged under my breath. "I have to go to the ladies' room. I'll be back."

"Want me to go with you?" Kennedy pleaded, holding back apparent anger.

"No!" I got up and grabbed my clutch. "Be right back." I eyed Brittany, taunting superiority. "You're pitiful. Get your shit together." I fumed, secretly smiling as I walked away from the table.

The restrooms were past the bar on the other side of the lounge. After washing my hands I checked my hair and retouched my pout before giving the attendant a tip. I'd heard that in several establishments they didn't get paid but were still required to give a percentage of their tips to management—plus she was an older black woman who reminded me of Nana. I couldn't knock her hustle.

Heading back to the table, I glanced over to the bar and tripped over absolutely nothing when I spotted Max drinking and talking with a strikingly exotic Mystic-tanned woman. He seemed completely engrossed, laughing between swigs of Corona while she seemed to be telling a highly entertaining story as she daintily sipped her wine.

Who the fuck was she?

My stomach gurgled. Then burned. My heart drumrolled faster and faster and—and I couldn't feel my goddamn fingers! I sucked in my stomach and stood up straight as if an imaginary string were being pulled from the top of my head.

Oh-my-God. He scouted me stalking them.

I watched him excuse himself and stroll toward me. What was he doing? I really didn't need to be outed in the middle of the Signature

Lounge with an audience packed with posh people. I readied myself for a verbal assault, determined not to tear up.

"Hi, Hannah, how are you?" he asked smoothly, bending down to kiss my cheek. He smelled as amazing as he looked.

"I, I—I'm fine; how are you?" My insides were sizzling, and I knew my hands had started to shake, even though I couldn't feel them.

"So, is there anything you wanna tell me?" he asked, sliding his hands into the pockets of his black Donna Karan pants.

"What? Oh, uh, about the other night, well, it wasn't—"

"No, that's not what I'm talking about. I just wanna know if you were able to make that little girl's dream come true."

"Huh?"

"Did you make the team?" he asked sincerely, pulling his right hand from his pocket to run it through his thick curls.

"Oh, right. Of course. Yes. Yes, I made it. My girls and I are here celebrating."

"I know."

"Oh, you saw us?" I raised my eyebrows and twitched.

"Well, yeah; I could never miss you." He cleared his throat. "You look great. But then you always do." He looked down at the floor. "Plus, I saw your friend—the one I met the other night. She was having an intimate moment," he said with a warm laugh before stopping to clear his throat. "Well, that's great, darlin'. Congratulations."

I wanted to ask him why he cared, but I was distracted when I glanced past him and spotted his companion at the bar, who was now staring so hard at me I thought her eyeballs would pop right out of her head.

"Listen, Max, I kind of want to explain what happened the other night. I mean—"

"It's fine, darlin'. It's just that I really wanted you to have the food for the flowers because they were so beautiful and I wanted them to last and—"

"They're very beautiful, and the book, *Moby-Dick*, was—"

"And I'm proud of you. I know how hard you worked for that spot on the squad. So, good luck with everything. I'll see you around," he said, and walked back over to the bar, sliding his hand across the back of his neck. He took his seat next to the woman and continued his conversation, leaving me standing there alone, dazed and choked up, in the middle of the goddamn floor! As the band warmed up for the second set, the saxophone blared right into my ear, making my eyes cross into my head and my knees buckle. I snapped out of my trance and stumbled back to the table.

"Hannah, ohmigod! That was Max," Kennedy said, helping me with my chair.

"Honey, she knows who that was," Britt retorted. "You all right?"

"Yeah, Bug; you look a little spooked," Kennedy observed.

"Dizzy," I corrected.

"Whatever. Who's the bitch he's talking to?" Britt demanded.

"I can't believe it. He was so sweet. So nice," I said, bewildered.

"So, rookie, what are you gonna do?" Brittany challenged me, finishing her martini.

Before I could answer, our server appeared with a bottle of 1964 Louis Roederer Cristal and placed it regally in a silver champagne bucket.

"Ladies, this is courtesy of Mr. Knight. Ms. Love, he would like for you to have this." The waiter handed me a small white card, nearly genuflecting. "Mr. Knight wants you to know that whatever you'd like this evening has already been taken care of—including all gratuities. Please enjoy." He bowed again before spinning around in an about-face.

"OK, now that's what I'm talking about," Britt said, and tried to snatch the card from my hand.

"Well, read it then. Don't you dare keep us in suspense like this."

"Give her a sec. The girl's hands haven't stopped shaking since she sat down," Kennedy said, and put her hand over mine. "You're really shaking, Bug. Are you sure you're OK? Drink some water."

"Fuck the water. Read the card." Britt was getting impatient. She snatched the card to read it.

"Congrats, darlin'. I'm proud of you. Enjoy your night. You deserve it. Max."

"Now that's some smooth shit," Britt said, fanning her face with the card. "I have always had a thing for that man, even before he got into the league, back when he played for LSU. He always had that sweet Southern sex appeal even back then," Britt said.

"Is that a tear in your eye?" Kennedy asked me.

"No, well—I don't know. What difference does it make? He's just happy for me. That's nice. Right?"

"Whatever. He just spent over a grand on your ass, and he's sitting over there with a bitch. You better stake your claim and at least thank the man," Britt urged.

"I don't think so. I'm not going over there with that woman sitting all up under him."

"She's not all up under him, Hannah—well, not exactly," Kennedy said.

"I'll just smile and wave."

"For a bottle of Cristal? Girl, please; I'll repay him properly if you won't—"

"Shut up, Britt-ny! Now is so not the time," Kennedy said.

"Fine; you're right. I can focus. I can do this." Britt cleared her throat. "Well, does anybody wanna toast with me to Hannah making the team?" she recovered.

We raised our drinks in the air. My hand was still trembling, and I had to laugh at myself, even though I couldn't find one damn thing funny. Truth was, he was still sitting there with another woman.

We clinked and sipped while Britt poured her second.

"What?" She looked at us and rolled her eyes. "Y'all bitches are crazy if you think I'm about to sit here and be cute with it. This shit is good—and expensive, just the way I like it."

I finally got up the nerve to turn around, smile, and thank him for everything. I shined my teeth with my tongue and plastered a much-practiced grin across my face and looked over to the bar.

BUT MAX WAS GONE.

40

"COBRA, CAN YOU COME IN HERE FOR A SECOND?" I YELLED FROM MY DESK.

"Right away, Bosslady." He swished in, wearing powder-blue moccasins and tan cords with excessive suede fringes dangling from his legs.

"Listen, I need you to reschedule the interviews with the interns today. I need to get out of here earlier than I thought."

"Sure thing. Anything else?"

"Yes, see what time Rain is scheduled to be at the *King* magazine shoot on Thursday. I have a huge meeting with Nigel and Mannie that day, so I won't be able to attend. Everything should be in order and should flow smoothly. Now, I've talked to Piper, the stylist for that shoot, and we've gone back and forth about what kinds of looks everyone could agree on for Rain. I've worked with Piper several times over the last couple of years, and she really does her thing, so I'm not too worried. I need you to get me Rain's itinerary and double-check everything—Cobra, I mean everything," I said, and looked him directly in the eye once he finally looked up from taking notes on his cotton-candy-pink pad.

"No problem. I'll get started on that right now."

"And . . . since I can't be there with her, you'll have to hold her hand most of that day."

"What? But the shoot is in New York."

"I know; I'm taking you with me."

"To New York City!?" He dropped his pen and pad and smushed his hands over his mouth.

"Are you serious? Are you totally serious?!" he exclaimed.

"I'm totally serious. Starting next month I won't be able to travel during the week at all. I have practice every Tuesday and Thursday for like, forever, and then there'll be games. So, I'm really gonna be looking to you to handle travel for a while. You can do it; I'm not worried at all. This will be a good opportunity for you to prove yourself around here—not that you haven't already proved yourself to me." I enjoyed his excitement and was glad to be the one to give him his first big opportunity.

"Ohmigod! This is one of the most amazing things that's ever happened to me," he said, and came around the desk to hug me.

"I knew you'd appreciate it. Now before you leave, I'll take you through everything, step by step. You'll be more than prepared by the time we get on that plane."

"Ohmigod! I know I keep saying that, but Oh-My-God!"

"I know; it's huge. So . . . get started. Rain's in the middle of her promo tour, and in the last week she's hit most of the primary markets. She'll be coming back from Miami, so get her confirmations from Spike. Let's make sure she makes her flight before anything else. With her single climbing *Billboard* we can't drop the ball!"

"No problem. I can totally handle it. I won't let you down, Hannah," said Cobra.

And I believed him.

"Thank you so much, Bosslady," he said, and shook my hand. "I've never been to New York."

"There's a first time for everything."

WHEN I LOOKED UP, ELI WAS STANDING IN MY DOOR WEARING THE CREEPIEST smile.

"That's really not a good look for you," I said, and turned away from my laptop, giving him my full attention.

"So . . . I see you know that cat, Max Knight," he started right in.

"Yes, I know that cat, Max Knight." I folded my hands on top of my desk.

"So, is that the reason why I got the brush-off the other night?"

"Close my door, Eli," I instructed.

"My bad," he said and shut it. "So what's up with that? Holla at me, girl," he continued as his cell began to vibrate.

"What're you talking about? What's up with what?"

"Well, first a cat has to congratulate you on doing your thing and making the team. I'm not surprised, but, congratulations. That's what's up," he said, and smiled a smile that I recognized.

"Thanks. I did my best. I'm just glad that it was good enough," I admitted.

"Now what's up with you and the super-baller?"

"Nothing. We're just friends."

"That wasn't a 'just friends' look on his face the other night," he observed, and sat in one of the khaki-colored leather chairs facing my desk.

"Swear. We're just friends. I think you may have misread his expression. He was dropping by to, to, to—"

"Right, that's just what I thought. He was dropping by to handle his business. Well, I can't be mad at that man; I still wanna put my bid in," he said, and licked his lips. "Seriously, if my man wants to play ball, he's not the only one that can dunk. I meant what I said the other night. I'm feeling you, and you're gonna understand that before this is all over. He got game—I got game. Maybe he took the lead this quarter, but all I need is one fast break and I'm going home with the trophy—and her name is Hannah." He stood up and leaned over my desk, inches from my face.

I had to admit it was titillating, and I'm sure he knew he had me right where he wanted—totally completely absolutely SQUISHY inside.

"I'll give him this one, though. That must be why your ass didn't come in on Thursday or Friday. He was handling his business that night, too, huh?"

"You're pitiful," I said, clearing my throat and sitting up straight, moving the hair out of my eyes. "I didn't come in because I was out all night celebrating with my girls after I made the team. I worked from home. You knew that. I know you're not trying to micromanage me, Eli. Don't start that shit, now."

"No, that's not what I'm doing. You're senior staff. I'm cool as long as our single keeps climbing the charts and you're in the important meetings, especially when Nigel and Mannie are in town. The rest is on you." He licked his lips and tilted his head to the side. "I saw his face, and super-baller wasn't happy to see me, with you all in your robe and shit looking hot."

"Why do all men go there? Believe it or not, women can have platonic relationships with men and have that be all it is," I said, trying to sound knowledgeable about the matter.

"Woman, please; you're way too smart for that shit. That ain't never the case, especially when the woman looks like you." He nodded his head as he sucked me in with his eyes.

"Thanks; I'm flattered. Now what do you want? I'm trying to get out of here early today."

"OK. We can play it that way." He cleared his throat. "I got your e-mail about Cobra traveling and taking on these additional responsibilities, and I wanted to let you know that I'm cool with it. But Hannah, hear what the fuck I'm saying to you. I swear if he fucks this shit up—even the smallest mistake—I'm gonna have your ass for it." He looked at me with that fatally powerful stare. "Rain is RockStar's Beyoncé; you wouldn't put an intern on Beyoncé, now would you?" he asked seriously.

"Cobra is not an intern, Eli."

"You know what the fuck I'm saying. Now I ain't mad at you giving the little man a shot. I remember how it was when I was a shorty and I was dying for somebody to put me on. Handle that, but don't forget what the fuck I said," he cautioned me before he stood up straight and walked out, checking his cell to see who'd just called.

Halfway down the hall he looked back over his shoulder and yelled, "I thought I told you to get a fuckin' intern."

"Working on it," I called out into the thick air.

"Cobra!" I yelled, again from my desk.

"Right away!"

AUGUST WAS ALWAYS A HOT, HUMID, STICKY MONTH IN CHICAGO, AVERAGING somewhere in the mid to high nineties, and this year it didn't deviate from that in the slightest. Skin was in, and skimpy fitted pastel tank tops and flip-flops ruled as the city went from enjoying July's highly anticipated Taste of Chicago to August's Freon Fetish.

It was common to walk out of my office onto Michigan Avenue and see businessmen in perspiration-stained shirts dashing for the nearest air-conditioned den. Even the occasional jaunt across the street to Oak Street Beach for an ice cream cone and the cool lake breeze didn't much help relieve this early August heat.

I needed to take the Rover in to have the air conditioning checked out, but the last four weeks had been filled with tying up loose ends and loosening tight ones. Between traveling with Rain to do publicity all over the place, being in the studio, and practicing with her choreographer for her performance at the VMAs, I was trying to fit everything I could into the four free weeks before I officially began my cheerleading season.

Sitting at a red light on Wabash Avenue on the way to my first official Diamond Dolls practice, I wiped the sweat from my forehead. I hung my head out the window like a hot dog gasping for air while I fiddled with the air jets for the ninth time. It should have been a quick ride from the office on North Michigan to the American Dance Center in the South Loop, but it seemed as if two lifetimes had passed and the sun just wouldn't stop laughing.

A metered spot opened on Wabash. I looped around and threw enough coins into the timer to cover me for the next four hours.

"Hannah! Hey, Hannah."

Now that was a familiar voice.

"Hey, Minn, how's it going? Oooh, did you get a tan?"

"Dunno. Maybe. I've been at the beach," she said, and inspected her arms as if she'd never really looked at them before. "I'm so excited. It's like I've been looking forward to this day for, like, forever."

We jaywalked, dodging the three cars in oncoming traffic.

"I know; I'm excited too. It'll be intense, but I guess that's part of what we signed up for."

As everyone filed into the dance center the energy was volcanic. I was swept away in the possibilities of the upcoming year and all that it had to offer. And what would a first day of school be without the big bad bullies?

"Look, the veterans all have those awesome duffel bags," Minnow said, nudging me when a group of them walked in together, wearing their warm-up suits and already in full hair and makeup.

"I know. I just hate drooling over them," I said, imagining the day I'd be officially outfitted.

We changed into our dance clothes and went into the studio to begin stretching.

"Ohmigod! You guys, I totally couldn't sleep," said Chloe as she and Brooklyn rushed out of the dressing room and joined us on the huge hardwood floor.

"I know. I've been talking about this nonstop," Brooklyn gushed. "My boyfriend—his name is Jack," she giggled, "he swore he'd kill me if I mentioned one more word about it."

"What about you, Hannah?" Brooklyn asked.

I thought about the intense heat, my broke-down air conditioner, and the sweat that was still drying in the crack of my ass. "My day was pretty cool."

"You look really good," Minnow said to Brooklyn. "I can totally tell you've lost already."

Truthfully, I couldn't. And I felt bad for her because I knew the weight on our thighs was always the last and the hardest to go, no matter how much white blood was circulating through.

Nikki and Shortstuff rushed in with a big boombox and a huge duffel bag. "Hello, ladies; so good to see all of you. Now gather around and let's get started. We've got tons to do tonight, but let's go ahead and get the housekeeping out of the way."

She had twenty-five black notebooks with our names and the Diamond Dolls logo on the outside, and everything, including our schedules and costume options, inside. I was thrilled at the thought of finally having something official—notebook first, maybe that damn duffel next.

"First of all, congratulations again. You should be so proud of yourselves. Welcome to your official practice space," she said, looking around the room, inspecting each of us. "Great, I see everyone remembered what to wear."

"Now, you don't have to wear *full* makeup for practices, but you should always be picture-ready. You never know when there will be photo ops, so make sure your hair is always camera-friendly." She flipped hers over her shoulder. "And remember: you are a Diamond Doll, and you rep everything that goes along with the Diamond Doll brand. Yes, you rep beautiful, talented, glamorous, fabulous . . ."

I got the damn point: don't forget to brush my horse.

Nikki droned on. "I have been the coach of this team for twelve years, and there is nothing I enjoy more than the time I spend with you all. I want you guys to bond and enjoy each other as much as I've enjoyed you over the years. So we're going to have a Diamond Dolls party next weekend to get that bonding started. You'll get more details about that later, but for now, keep your schedules clear for next Saturday. You can bring one person if you want—a friend, a boyfriend . . ." Nikki rattled on.

Minnow nudged me. "Are you gonna, like, bring him? You should like totally bring him," she whispered annoyingly.

I looked at her sideways. "Are you like, *crazy*?!"

"Now speaking of boyfriends, I know this should go without saying, but I realize that I have to say it each year, so no one can ever say that I never said it." Coach took a nice long deep breath and filled her lungs. "You are not allowed to date *any* of the players on the home team as long as you are a Diamond Doll. You can date anyone else in the entire world that you'd like, but not a Chicago Diamonds player. That is a league rule, not a franchise rule, and if you have a problem with that, call the commissioner, or date *him* if you'd like. I just hope I have made myself absolutely clear. That means you can't be spotted out at the club with them either. Nothing. Period. If you happen to be at the same club with one of them, be advised that it's going to get back to me, and what I'll hear is that you were having sex in the club on top of the bar. Doggie style!" She stopped when she heard giggling. "You'd really be surprised at what I hear. You'll be asked to turn in your uniform and resign from the team, no questions asked. Now are there any questions about *that*?"

I could feel eyes boring through me, but I didn't dare take my eyes off Coach.

"You'll be sized for one uniform, and once you get it, it's yours till the end of the season. If you put on weight, you will not be given a new one. It doesn't work that way. You will have free gym memberships at the Crunch gym on Grand and Wabash. Also, you'll have passes to Mario Tricoci's hair salon in the Bloomingdale's building, redeemable once a week. Some of you need to make that trip immediately. Diamond Dolls don't do brassy; we do blonde. Finally, rookies, you'll get an assigned big sister next week," she said, and smiled at the veterans, who were huddled together on the far side of the room. "Now let's stretch and learn this routine, which is mostly a combination of all three routines you learned over the course of your auditions last month. Then we'll teach a couple of sideline repeats, and then we'll wrap," she said, clapping her hands neurotically. She flung her jacket in the air.

Shit, I was already tired!

"Hey there, rookie," said my nemesis, Mona. "I was hoping you would've gotten too chicken or too busy or too whatever to like join us this year. I see I just wasn't so lucky." She flipped her very brassy hair over her shoulder.

"Hey, Mona—I've got a Snickers, a Baby Ruth, and a Mars bar for you in my bag. I'll let you scarf them down on our water break."

"Oh grow up; you're such a little bitch. You think you're so smart. You don't know anything. You're just a fucking rookie! I'm warning you," she hissed before huffing away to join Pepper and Hilton.

I was afraid. I was very afraid, but I didn't dare let the dirty dog smell fear. I had worked too hard to get here, and it was going to take more than a growl of intimidation to send me scurrying away. I tried hard to shake it off and concentrate on practice, but the bass in her very scary bark terrified me. I was long overdue for a rabies shot.

The practice was both exhilarating and exhausting. When we finally got our water break, two and a half hours later, I was dying to pee. I darted down the hall to the bathroom and into a stall before anyone else.

I had flushed the toilet and was ready to exit the stall when I heard the outer door open and shut.

"No, Mona, they really hurt."

On second thought, maybe I'd chill for another second. *Didn't people look under stall doors anymore to see if there was anyone already in the bathroom, or was that just in the movies?*

"I told you the other day that you shouldn't be jumping up and down like that so soon after," I heard Mona respond to someone.

"Yeah, but Dr. Pryor said I could get back to my normal activity after last week."

"I'm sure you didn't tell him that part of your normal activity involves toe touches and kick lines, Pepper. That's enough to spread the pocket. You could get that double bubble."

What!? I tried to hold in my laughter. I pushed my eyeball against the opening in the door and tried to focus.

"What the hell is double bubble?"

"You know, double bubble, when they slide down below your tit crease."

"Can you just feel them? See if they feel right. I think there's something wrong."

"No. I'm not going to, like, squeeze on your tits. I told you that you should've just told Coach so she wouldn't make you do everything full out."

"Yeah, right, and let one of those rookies take my spot. I so wanna be a captain this year," she whined. "Just feel them for me, pleeease."

"OK, stop whining; I'm only gonna squeeze them super fast. Don't move. Here, pull up your bra."

"OK," said Pepper, thrusting her overinflated breasts in Mona's face.

I burst out of the stall, snorting with laughter at the soft porn scene: Mona, with both her hands cupping Pepper's breasts, touching and squeezing them meticulously.

"Ohmigod!" Pepper screamed. "Ohmigod! It's so not what it looks like, Hannah. Hey, come back here," she called after me as I hurried into the hallway.

"Come back here, roookkkiiieee," Mona yelled.

PULLING THE CAR AROUND TO THE DRIVEWAY OF MY BUILDING, ALL I WANTED TO do was climb into the scorching bathtub, my body's new best friend, and listen to Goapele.

"Hey there, Dallas," I said, handing him the keys.

"Hi, Hannah. How was your day?"

"You wouldn't believe it if I told you. Make any house calls this evening?" I could feel my flushed face releasing a smile.

He broke a slight smile himself. "No ma'am," he answered. "And how's Brittany, anyway?"

"Good. Why do you ask? Been thinking about her?"

He shrugged and exhaled with satisfaction.

"Be careful, Dallas; she's lethal."

"That's one of the things I really like about her."

He tossed my keys into the air, and I walked into the lobby, contemplating whether to douse my bathwater with organic orange or lathering lavender bath gel. Just then the elevator doors opened. From the corner of my eye I spied Max strolling leisurely through the corridor with that same stunning exotic woman from the Signature Lounge. I ducked behind the mailboxes, watching him open the lobby door for her and lead her toward his car. I scooted to the concierge desk and stooped down behind it. Just as he had done with me, he handed her a rose. What was this? The goddamn Bachelor?! My little heart did a cartwheel. She looked up at him and smiled as he bent down to kiss her on the cheek. My heart finished off the combination with a back handspring. He closed her door and smiled. Bang! My heart landed painfully.

"Hannah, you OK?" Dallas asked, throwing me a concerned look.

I poked my head around the desk to make sure they'd pulled off. "Yeah, uh, sure, I'm fine," I stuttered, bolting from the floor and tugging at my white tennis mini. "What had happened was—I, uh, dropped a piece of mail behind your desk over here, right, and I was bending down, right, and then—"

"And then you saw your prince giving someone else a ride in his chariot?"

"Huh?"

"Hannah, everyone knows that the prince has only one princess, but sometimes she doth protest too much after listening too often to the jesters in her court."

"Huh?!"

43

I SLAMMED THE PHONE DOWN AND SAT BACK IN MY CHAIR AFTER UNSUCCESS-fully trying to explain to Spike the inflexibility of Rain's schedule. Letting my fingers run over the delicate tips of the lavender orchids that had been anonymously delivered this morning, I closed my eyes and exhaled.

"Cobra, come here please," I called out, exasperated. I don't know who said Fridays were fabulous; my Fridays were usually fucked.

"Yes, Bosslady?" Cobra appeared next to my desk with pen and pad in hand. "What's up?"

"What's up is that I have a very irate manager who doesn't wanna cut one of Rain's choreography days because she can't get the turn-pump-pump move down. And I need her back in New York on Monday afternoon, at the very latest, to do Conan and rested for Regis and Kelly and TRL on Tuesday. This is now officially *your* problem." I rested my head in my hands and closed my eyes for a second. "Hand me one of those Red Bulls out of the minifridge."

"No problem; I'm all over Spike—if you know what I mean. I'll see to it that he's cool with everything. She can practice at the hotel in one of the conference rooms. We can have them move the tables out of the way, or maybe I can even book her some space at Broadway Dance for later Monday afternoon."

"Ooh, I like the sound of that."

"No problem, Ms. Hannah. Anything for you."

"Hey, how'd you know about Broadway Dance, anyway?" I popped open the can and swigged down half the energy serum.

"Last month when you sent me to New York, I did some sightseeing and tried to familiarize myself with the area, since our artists will be spending most of their time in the Midtown vicinity anyway. I mean, between the hotels and the radio, cable, and network stations, I thought it would come in handy to know the nearest spots where they could pop in for a quick band or dance rehearsal." He stood in front of my desk with his hand on his hip and his chartreuse Sharpie to his lips. "I'll go ahead and get Spike on the phone and make sure he's all good."

"I just bet you will."

"Well, it's the least I can do for that cute little Spikey. Maybe he'll send me some flowers that beautiful." Cobra nodded at the arrangement. "Now you know he's a cutie, Hannah. Admit it."

"C'mon, the man is five foot four, and I really need *you* to focus," I suggested firmly, flipping over the card that had come with the bouquet of flowers.

YOU'RE THE ONE, it read.

"Confirm your rooms at the Dream Hotel and then reconfirm them. Eli will be with you guys this time, so book him a suite too. It's his favorite." I flipped the card over again. *YOU'RE THE ONE*.

"Consider it done." He stood in front of my desk, and I could feel him staring at me as I perused my e-mails.

"What?"

"Nothing. It's just that—well, thanks again. I mean, I really appreciate it—the opportunity. I know it's work and everything, but this is too fierce. I never would've imagined I'd be booking *my* second trip to the City."

"Well, if you keep taking initiative and putting out fires like you just did, there may be more where that came from. Now, why are you still standing there?"

"Right." He spun around and was back at his desk with his ear to the phone before I could finish my Red Bull.

"Got a sec? I need to talk to you."

I looked up and saw Eli walking into my office in a more than flattering navy-and-white pinstriped Paul Smith suit. I took another deep breath, this time silently putting out my own fire.

"What's up, Eli? What can I help you with? Your suite has already been reconfirmed at the hotel, and your first-class ticket will be waiting for you at O'Hare, and your car will be waiting for you at baggage claim. Now I still haven't figured out what exactly it is that Cameran does over there for you all day, but I am *not* asking Cobra to pack your bags. I have no doubt in my mind that she can handle that just fine."

"Damn, woman, do I detect a bit of a caffeine fit going on here?"

"Don't even ask." I looked back at the computer. "So . . . what's up?"

"Listen, I just wanted to say that I'm not totally cool with you not being there for Rain's release, but I heard that little man out there did his thing at the *King* shoot last month. That's hot. So I'm not gonna beef too much about it. But that shit I said the last time still stands. You know what's up, and he'd better not—"

I watched him rest his firm ass on the edge of my desk. Secretly, a part of me wanted to reach out and smack it.

"Now we just have to max all this momentum and show everyone her unique identity. Then they'll be comparing everyone else to *her,* especially after she does her thing at the VMAs."

"Is she set for the show?"

"Yeah, I'm trying to work it out for her to go with Common," I explained.

"As his date?"

"Yeah. That would be a good look for her."

"I agree, and I think it would be a good look for you to meet me at Ruth's Chris in a couple of hours." He stood next to my desk in his best bad-boy stance.

"I don't know, Eli. I really need to get home and—"

"Those are beautiful flowers."

"Thanks," I said, and picked up the card, flipping it between my fingers.

"Very beautiful—almost as much as you, Angel."

"Uh-huh," I said, suspiciously. "And you wouldn't happen to know anything about who sent me these beautiful flowers, would you?"

Eli rubbed his hand over his chin and grinned mischievously. "Well, let's just say that a beautiful Angel deserves that and then some. So, let me take you to dinner."

"Sneaky, sneaky. OK, I like a little mystery."

"No mystery here, ma. I'm an open book. It was the least I could do. Now, dinner? Tonight?"

"Well . . ."

"I'm not trying to hear that, woman. We need to go over some more shit for next week anyway. Your ass is goin' be here droppin' it like it's hot and not in NYC where we really need you. Let's just make sure all this shit is in order. I ain't mad at little man out there, but I need to go over a few more things with his mommy first. I'll have a car at your crib at eight." He stood up and turned around with his cell to his ear.

"But—" I yelled out after him.

"He's already gone," I heard Cobra whisper loudly from his desk. "But Case 135 of the Phantom Flowers has officially been solved," he said, and pounded his makeshift gavel, the Barbie snow globe paperweight, on his desk.

44

THE VALET OPENED MY CAR DOOR, EXTENDED HIS HAND, AND HELPED ME OUT onto the sidewalk. The August days were a scorching bitch on her period, but the nights were hot, heavy, and heated with passion. I thanked the valet and aligned the ruby-red ruffles on my Cynthia Rowley tiered minidress. I touched the Tiffany diamond necklace on my neck and made sure the clasp was tightly secured.

Nervously scanning the crowded restaurant, I immediately found Eli enjoying his usual vodka tonic. When the host guided me to his booth he came to his feet like royalty, looking distinguished in a Neiman Marcus exclusive black tuxedo suit. And for a moment, he took my breath away.

"Wow, you look great," I said, allowing the host to push my chair in beneath me.

"Damn, girl, so do you." He smiled and sat down. "I knew that necklace would frost perfectly against your collarbone."

I touched the diamonds again and smiled, feeling flushed. I wasn't sure if it was the summer sizzle or the U.S. prime beef, but I was unmistakably hot. He ordered for us both—usually a serious turnoff for me, but I let him. I couldn't care less; I hadn't planned on eating anyway.

"So, did the New York office take care of the release party for Tuesday night?" I asked, trying to get down to business right away.

"Yeah, it's going to be downtown at Capitale. All A-list, the usual hip-hop glitterati, the media, and select fans from a promotion America Online has been running."

"Sounds hot. Sorry I can't be there."

"Gimme a break. You hate that shit anyway. Don't think I don't know that you run from 'the scene' every chance you get. You ain't gotta play all professionally interested with me."

He was right, and I'd forgotten about all the conversations we'd had when I still lived in New York and we'd bump into each other at this spot for this person or at that spot for those people.

"You're right. I sometimes forget about the history we have."

"I don't."

The music was relaxing, and the wine was easing my heat a little. I drifted off momentarily and thought about the long week I'd had and the team party tomorrow. I turned the glass all the way up and let the Cabernet coat my throat.

"Damn, is it that bad?"

"No, it just hasn't stopped. I feel like I'm on this waterslide on this crazy hot day and it won't drop me into the pool. I just keep going around and around and—"

"What?"

"What I mean is—everything I'm doing right now is great. It's just that I can't seem to get to that point where I'm actually able to enjoy it. You know, get off the waterslide, slow it down, and just enjoy being in the pool."

"Uh-huh. Well, not to keep you on that motherfucker or anything, but what's the status of the Chicago release party?"

"You really need to start reading my e-mails."

"I read your e-mails."

"No, *Cameran* reads your e-mails."

"Same damn difference."

"No, it's not. If *you* read them you'd know that it's going to be at a hot spot, The Victor, downtown."

"Yeah, been there. So who's coming?"

"Anybody who's anybody that already lives here and the top shelf that are in town that night."

I eyed the bottle of wine on the table.

"My bad." He picked up the bottle and poured me another glass.

"It's scheduled for the night you get back from New York. I'm still trying to convince Nigel and Emmanuele to fly in for it. They're just not feeling me. I think it would be a good look if they flew into as many of the primary markets as possible to do local photo ops and give Rain their stamp of approval for the media," I explained, and took two big sips from my glass.

"Oh, you do? Well, I'll see if I can talk to them. I'll talk to Mannie and see what he says. I've got a little extra pull with him."

"Good. Rain's still new, and we really need the machine behind her from the gate." I took another big gulp and eyed the bottle again.

"Are you for real? I know your job is heavy, but I'm positive I ain't putting no shit on you that would drive you to drink—at least not like that."

I looked at his lips. Lord have fucking mercy!

"No, you're not. It's not the job. I have to go to this party tomorrow night for the team or with the team, or whatever," I said, feeling a welcome fuzziness in my head. "And I know that I'ma have to deal wit some bullshit. That's all; nothing I can't handle. Now pour."

I pointed at the bottle, and he looked at me with coyote eyes and did as he was told.

"What? What's that look all about?" I asked him guardedly.

"Nothing. It's just that your ass is funny. You think you bit off more than you can chew with that cheerleading shit?"

"Why does everybody keep fucking asping me that?" I said, slurring my words. "No, I don't. It's just that with any kind of team thang, there's gonna be some fucked-up da-namics."

"You're cute when you're tipsy." He reached across the table and touched my lips.

"Watch it, boy."

"Now if there's one thing I'm not—I'm definitely not a boy. I am *all* man; please believe it."

"So, am I really *THE ONE?*"

"The only one," he said, locking eyes with me.

"OK." I cleared my throat. "Pour or die."

He poured another glass just as the filet mignon came. By then I was hungry, and the smell of it all was inviting. But I couldn't take my mind away from the hell that was sure to be the team party. Besides, the heat had started to flare—between my legs this time—and I thought I'd better make a move for the ladies' room.

"Excuse me; I've got a meeting in the ladies' room, and I'll be back real soon," I said, and snapped my fingers to the imaginary beat of the eighties song. "Oh come on, you remember that song. I've got a meeting in the ladies' room/and I'll be back real soon/Ooh yeah/ooh yeah," I sang and threw my head back. "Who sang that? You know—"

"Klymaxx, woman. The name of the group was Klymaxx."

Right. And I hadn't done *that* in a while! I so desperately needed to get to the bathroom, but when I stood up Eli followed suit, grabbing my hand and helping me with my chair.

"Thank you."

He pulled me close to him. "Sure," he purred into my ear.

For what seemed like an eternity, I stood against him, so close that I could feel his heart beating through my dress. He'd entangled his fingers with mine, and every tiny hair stood at attention on my neck. He took in my breath and drew me closer. I cleared my throat and tried halfheartedly to step away from him. He held on tighter and squeezed my hands. I looked up into his eyes, pleading for mercy. But he denied me that and bent down to brush my lips gently, softly, precisely. Finally he pulled away, and I just stood there with my eyes closed, trapped in his web of crazy sexy twisted tipsy fucked-up—wait! He's *so* my boss!

"Uh, what was that?" I purposely pulled away and reshifted my ruffles. I touched my lips with my fingers.

"Sorry, I couldn't help—"

"Excuse me—I have to go pee." I stepped away from the table and snatched my Prada clutch and finally headed for the goddamn ladies' room.

Strangely enough, I wasn't upset at what had happened. The man was sex. And between the wine, the music, and the smell of his custom-aged U.S. prime beef—hell, I went for the beef.

I blew it off, deciding that I wouldn't have a hissy over the *exchange* (that's what I'd decided to call it), and continued on with the evening. Opening my purse, I slid the card from inside. *YOU'RE THE ONE.* I quickly stashed it again and accepted the towel being offered by the attendant before haphazardly dropping her a twenty.

"Listen, Hannah—"

"Ah ah ah, don't you worry about it," I said, pointing my finger at him as he pulled out my chair. "Just pour."

"You're just so damn—"

"Nope, that was my fault. You just finished explaining to me that you're all man. I have to keep that in the front of my mind when I'm around you. You see, Elijah, I'm all woman, and part of being a woman is being able to handle her surroundings. Because if I can't, then I'm no better than a woman-in-training. And that would make me a girl."

"Uh-huh," he said, arching one brow as he refilled my glass and cut into his cow.

After he'd finished his meal and I'd finished the bottle, I looked at my watch and realized I needed to head back to the house. I'd basically cleared my schedule for the next day and had planned on just hanging around and doing some laundry (ugh!) until it was time to go to the party.

"Listen, I've really gotta go. I'm nice and buzzly and I really need to get some rest. And I'm sure you have somewhere cozy and sexy to be yourself."

"I'm already here," he said, and touched my fingers with his from across the table. A jolt of electricity shot through me on contact. "But it's your call. As far as Rain goes, I'm satisfied with how everything should roll out next week, but I'd be lying if I said I wasn't going to miss you being there complaining about all the flossy flashy froufrou faces on the scene."

"Oh my God, you sound just like me." I threw my head back in laughter.

"I know. I've been listening to your shit long enough now. I know how you get down."

"Is that supposed to impress me?"

"Is that all it takes?"

"Well—"

"Cuz if that's the case, I've got more where that shit came from. But somehow I have a feeling that it's gonna take a tighter game than that." He reached across the table and ran his index finger across the diamonds on my necklace. "Get up; let's go." He pulled out my chair. "I paid before you got here."

"But how did you know what I—"

"It wouldn't have mattered."

I laughed and wiggled my index finger at him. "I'm not mad at that," I said, and swayed when I stood up. "Whoo!"

He put my arm through his and laughed at me as he walked me out.

"Goodnight, Mr. Strong, and thank you again," the server said. Eli raised his hand in return, never looking back at the man.

We got into his XJ8L Jaguar, and I felt my head tilting to the side without my permission. It felt good to release and just let my body go with the flow, though I wondered if an AA meeting wasn't in order. I was enjoying the wonderfully seductive fog—maybe a little too much.

"Hey, you gonna be OK?"

"Yeah, I'm just zoning out. And to be honest, it feels kinda good," I said, giggling.

"You are done, ma."

"Oh, shut up and just join in the giggles, Mr. Riley Coyote."

"Who?"

"You know the coyote, from the show, when we were kids? That's who you are. That's it—Riley Coyote!" I exclaimed and hit him on the shoulder, still giggling.

"Woman, that was Wile-E-Coyote. Wile-E."

"Whatever, don't try and get all proper and shit on me now."

We pulled into the driveway of my building, and I looked at him seriously. "We cool?"

"Yeah, of course. It doesn't change the shit I'm feelin' for you—but yeah, we're cool."

"Good," I said, and tried with difficulty to open my door.

He put the car in park and got out. "If you would give a nigga a second—I'm coming."

He pulled me out and closed my door. "I'm gonna help your twisted ass upstairs."

"No, you don't have to do that," I said, still giggling.

"Yes, I do. It would be some serious shit if you fell out in the elevator."

I obliged, and we walked through the lobby.

Dallas nodded. "I'll keep an eye on the car, sir," he said.

"Thanks, man. I'll be right down."

"He's my bwuther," I said to Dallas, giggling much harder. "My bwuther."

Eli pressed for the elevator and secured my arm in his. "Despite what you might think, I had a good time with your drunk ass tonight."

"I know. /Cuz the men all pause/when I walk into the room/the men all pause/ooh yeah/ooh yeah/," I sang and snapped my fingers. "Klymaxx again, Klymaxx, negro." I threw my head back in continual giggles, this time cracking my neck. "Ow!" I fished my hand behind my head and halfheartedly grabbed my neck. "Klymaxx—" I said, almost in a whisper, before drifting off into another thought.

"You don't have to tell me," he said, and ushered me onto the elevator. "I been in the music game since you were in diapers."

"Hey, hold that elevator please!" I heard a voice call out just as the doors were closing.

Max and his stunningly striking lady friend stepped onto the elevator, and I sobered up instantly. I'd never known myself to be claustrophobic, but tonight had been chock-full of surprises. The metal walls closed in on me, ready to crush my insides joint by joint, taking with it the bone marrow that was as transparent as the look on Max's face. I felt flushed and hot all over again, clearly for totally different reasons this time.

"Oh, hi Hannah," Max said, looking over at Eli.

"Hi." It was all I could get out with the guarantee of not vomiting on his black Tod's lace-ups.

The tension in that tiny box was as thick as my head had felt just ten seconds earlier. Eli looked at Max, and they exchanged some sort of testosterone-filled silent dialogue before Max finally extended his hand and said, "Hey man, I'm Max, Max Knight."

Eli looked at him and puffed his chest out as far as his Burberry striped satin shirt would allow. "What up? Eli, Eli Strong."

Great. I looked over at the incredibly stunning, exotic woman and realized she was even more beautiful than I'd remembered. She smiled and I smiled back. I didn't even want an introduction for fear that what I was sure would be a beautiful name would haunt my fucking dreams forever!

The elevator doors finally opened on Max's floor, and the woman got off. He held the door with his oversized hand and looked back at me and parted his lips through a very deliberate earnest smile. "It's really good to see you. You look great. And nice to meet you, Eli."

Then he moved his hand and released his grip on the doors of the elevator—and on my heart.

I didn't move for fear of doing just what Eli had predicted—falling out on the goddamn elevator floor.

"So, that was Max Knight. He ain't so big in person, when you're standing up on him and shit."

Eli walked me to my door and gave me a hug goodnight. Without even looking at him, I turned the key and slipped inside. I closed my eyes, and as the room started to spin I quickly realized that the nameless beautiful stunningly exotic woman was still going to haunt my fucking dreams!

45

I'D DEBATED ON TAKING KENNEDY TO THE PARTY WITH ME BUT CHANGED MY mind when she told me how excited she was about her new trampoline workout class, and I already knew that Britt had to show some pricey estates in Highland Park to a couple of A-list clients who'd flown in from L.A.

I pulled up to verify the address of the historic mansion on Astor Street where the party was being held in our honor. I was tired, sad, and still dragging from the night before. I checked my hair and makeup in the visor mirror and pulled at the top of my dress. I was happy that I'd decided on a Helen Wang white linen strapless belted outfit with black piping. It provided the "damn" accent that would, I hoped, distract people from the bags under my eyes, which had been filled with day-old tears.

"HEY ROOKIE, DON'T YOU JUST LOOK SO CUTE," MONA SAID AS SHE AND PEPPER excused themselves from an older gray-haired woman at one of the satellite bars just beyond the massive foyer. I looked over my shoulder to make sure Hilton wasn't going to pop up somewhere so they'd have me surrounded. Nope. Just huddles of anonymous linen from everyone except Mona and Pepper, who'd donned white denim Bebe jeans and wraparound ballerina-inspired satin cami tops.

Ignoring them, Skye approached and led me away by the elbow. "So how've you been, rookie?"

"Good," I said, looking around in awe. "Whose house is this anyway? It's huge." I tried to talk over the music, a mix between sleek hotel retro and elevator easy.

"It's a landmark, but I hear it's going on the market soon." Skye snapped her fingers to the music and bobbed her head. "So if you know any super–filthy rich guys that are interested in buying—"

"Well, we already know she's good friends with one $35 million man, right?" Katie said, appearing out of nowhere and walking up with two drinks in her hand. "Oh wait, he's just family; isn't that right?" She passed one of the cocktails to Skye.

"Whatever! Catch up with you later, Skye."

I tried to plot a course through the legions of linen that appeared to be on every level of this monstrosity. Guessing that the second floor might not be as packed as the first, I headed for the glass stairs across the room. I recognized a couple of the tall men from the minimal research I'd been doing on the Diamonds team—per Max's earlier advice. I didn't figure they'd be attending this event; I thought it was just a small party for us to "bond." But I was quickly beginning to see that there were double meanings for a lot of the things we'd been told when I pushed open the door of a darkened room and saw Hilton on a king-sized bed, straddling one of the players.

Holy Sluts, Batman!

"Sorry, I—"

The door closed in my face just as quickly as I'd opened it.

Feeling awkward and alone in the houseful of strangers, I started to jet just before I looked through the massive floor-to-ceiling glass wall framing the back lawn. There, most of the team was mingling and dancing under an ivory-white-and-metallic-gold tent.

"Minnow!" I shouted, walking on my toes through the dewy grass in the overpriced shoes. "What the hell *is* this place? I was just in a very bad episode of the *Twilight Zone* in there."

"You totally came through the front door, didn't you?"

"Yeah, just before I got run off the second floor."

"Glad you made it. We were all talking about Rain's CD dropping on Tuesday, and we were wondering whether or not you'd have to be at some hot shindig or whatever today," Elle said.

"No, I wouldn't miss being here with you guys for the world," I said, and looked around for the nearest bar. I could smell the Pinot on their breath and realized that Brooklyn and I were the only ones standing around without a drink. Brooklyn didn't indulge because of her religious restrictions, but since I sure did, I surveyed the manicured landscape.

Whatever your appetite, there was an edible delight. Ivory-and-gold tablecloths covered the food stations that bordered all four sides of the tent. A big stage for the live band and DJ fronted the huge dance floor that had been constructed in the middle of it all. It wasn't a total scorcher today, but it was still too damn hot to be cutting anybody's rug!

"Shiraz, please," I requested as I watched Mona pack several plates so full of food that a couple pieces of over-fried chicken fell off. Before they ever touched the ground a server appeared out of nowhere and caught them in midair.

"Hey Hannah, did you meet Brooklyn's boyfriend?" Minnow slid her arm through mine and walked me through more grass to catch up to Brooklyn and her super-cute guy.

"Nice to meet you," I greeted, and extended my hand.

"Jack has a modeling agency. He works with *real* models," Elle gushed, never taking her eyes off Brooklyn's beau.

Brazilian, sexy, and gorgeous, Elle had told us over and over how "everyone says *I* should be a model" and that she'd done a few things "oh here and there."

"Actually, it's a boutique modeling website. I'm working on the expansion now so clients in all the major cities can log on and choose which models they want for their promotional events and conferences," he rattled off, sounding more like an educated used-car salesman.

"Exciting," I lied, watching Elle and Six fawn over him. "So, Brooklyn, having a good time?" I asked, eyeing the thick black slimming jersey sundress and black peek-toe flats she was wearing.

"Yeah, I'm having fun—just a tad hot."

"Well, you look good," I said, noticing that she did look a smidge slimmer.

"I'm doing my best. I had some of that fruit salad and a couple chicken skewers—well, actually four, but I know it's *all* protein. OK, so maybe I had five."

Jack leaned over and kissed her on the cheek and said just loud enough so we could all hear, "Babe, you know I like you just the way you are."

"I know, honey; it's just that I've gotta lose thirteen more pounds for Coach Jenny Craig."

I looked around. "Where's Nikki, anyway?"

"Excuse me girls, I'll be back—little boys room." Jack kissed Brook on the cheek and disappeared inside.

"She's smashed between those two older guys on the dance floor— Stan and Bob."

"Uh-huh, I see. Excuse me, too. I'll be back." I'd decided to bravely venture back into the estate and look around. I secretly wondered if Max had planned on showing, since some of his teammates had dropped in.

There were people everywhere—smiling, talking loudly, and laughing on cue. In one of the kitchens adjacent to the stairwell, I saw Mona, Pepper, and Hilton clustered next to the subzero, stuffing their faces. A carb feast was stacked on the four plates that Mona had managed to bring back inside. She caught my eye and nudged Hilton toward me.

Whenever anyone needed a "hot" barometer for comparison purposes, Hilton was it. Initially, I'd been on her bandwagon until her personality forced me to gladly give up my seat. Grandpa Red always used to say, "You got to live with what's on the inside eternally; that pretty on the outside will surely fade. Now don't go wastin' the pretty, Doll-face, but don't damage the soul."

Taking her cue, Hilton rushed toward me, but I took the last sip of my wine and ditched her and the glass. I didn't want to be snuffed in that castle and left for dead behind some trick wall because I'd glimpsed her slut card.

Roaming somewhat aimlessly, I stumbled onto another set of stairs that led to a steel catwalk overlooking the party. From there, I zoned out, meticulously scanning the crowd.

"Enjoying the festivities?" a soft voice beside me asked.

I jumped out of my skin before taking a second to center myself. "It's definitely been interesting," I said, cautiously.

"I'm Aliyah," she said with a welcoming smile, and leaned comfortably against the rail with me.

Keeping mostly to herself, Aliyah often helped Nikki with coaching duties, so I hadn't been able to put my finger on where she fell in this hodgepodge of personalities. She was a thin black woman with long legs and curly eyelashes. Her dark hair was permed straight, and on the rare occasions that she took it out of its thick ponytail, it brushed against the bottom of her sports bra.

"Nice to officially meet you," I said, shaking her hand.

"You're really good," she said, smiling, causing her eyes to slant and her right cheek to dimple. "But a little advice."

I leaned away from the rail on the catwalk and turned to face her.

"Always remember why you joined this team—to dance, to be on the court in front of the fans. And if you're anything like me, you wanted to be an example for others." She stepped away from the rail and slid her slender fingers into her denim Betsey Johnson mini.

"I've wanted to do this since I was a little girl."

"Me too." She put her hand on my shoulder. "And that's exactly why I don't want you to let anyone ever get to you—not Mona, not Pepper, not Hilton or anyone else." She was counting the vixen veterans on one hand. "You have to remember that you're here because you're special."

"Thank you." I started to feel at ease and comfortable for the first time. "How long have you been on the team?"

"Four years. And it's been one of the most fulfilling things I've ever done."

"Was it tough when you were a rookie?"

"Sometimes. But you rookies have to stick together. That's part of what being a rookie is all about. And next year, the cycle will repeat itself."

"Does it get easier?"

"Of course," she said, and laughed. "Welcome to the other side. You're in the big leagues now. Just try and remember what I told you, and you'll do fine." She leaned closer to me. "And one more thing. Whatever you've got going on with Max Knight, keep it to yourself. That's your business and nobody needs to know. If I wasn't already seeing someone, I'd probably be checking for him too."

"Oh my God," I uttered, and covered my face with my hands.

"It's all good, girl. He's different from most of these other ballplayers. I don't know how he does it, but he's managed to keep the things that have always been important to him close, despite being one of the highest-paid players out there. That man loves his family, and he loves helping people. He's special, that's for sure, not like some of these other knuckleheads running around."

"I know what you mean," I said, and turned away from her and leaned against the rail again, looking out over the sea of plastic people. I drifted off, remembering the look on his face when he'd stood at my door with the bag of flower food. But being trapped on the elevator last night convinced me that we were in two totally different places right now. "If only things were that simple," I said, and looked over at Ali, who had disappeared into the abyss.

I walked back across the catwalk toward the hallway in search of the bathroom. I opened the first door I came to and saw Jack leaning against the sink with his pants around his ankles.

"Ohmigod!" I yelled.

"Uh, Hannah, right? This isn't what it looks like," he said, pushing the blonde head away from where his zipper should have been. It was all I could do to cover my mouth and run the other way, just the way I did when I was seven and saw Grandpa Red sleepwalking—NAKED!

46

PICTURE DAY AT SCHOOL HAD ALWAYS BEEN THE MOST EXCITING EVENT OF THE year for me. There's just something spectacular about capturing the robust flavor of an entire year in a single simple snapshot. I walked into practice and hoped that Dolls Day would prove to be just as fulfilling.

The dance studio had been converted into a three-station prep and photography suite. There was a station just for makeup, where Elle was happily being dabbed and blended; a station for hair, where Chloe was being spritzed and sprayed; and a station for fittings, where Brooklyn was being poked and pinned. Nikki had surprised the team with uniforms and had squeezed two of the most anticipated days into one.

"Isn't this so cool?" Minnow gushed, rushing me as soon as I walked through the door.

"I don't know what to say. I had no idea all of this would be going on," I said, standing in the middle of the room and watching the behind-the-scenes prep show.

Minnow held up a sheet that listed the big sis/little sis match-ups. "Ohmigod! Skye is your big sister! You're like, so lucky—you got Skye."

"Gimme that. Lemme see." I took it out of her hands and reviewed it carefully. Aliyah had been paired with Brooklyn. Now all was right with the world.

"Hey little sis; what's up?" Skye walked over to us.

"So glad I got you."

"Yeah, me too. But now we've gotta do something about those sad high kicks of yours. You can't be on my game squad with wimpy kicks."

"I'm on your squad too? You're my captain? That totally rocks! So who's my other captain?"

"Well, Nikki hasn't released the list yet, but I'll tell you now so you can prepare yourself." She squared both her hands on my shoulders, and an acid ball blistered through my gut as the name rolled off her lips. "Mooonnnaaa."

"You've got to be kidding!"

"Sorry; there was nothing I could do about it. Coach had her mind made up. Something to do with 'balancing the aesthetic variables.' "

I wanted to close my eyes, click my heels, and wake up in the land of fucking Oz. I groaned, "You mean I'm gonna have to spend all season on the court with that bitchy bulimic?"

"Well, listen, you'll only have to cheer with her half the season when you're cheering with the A squad. The other half of the season you'll be with me, on the C squad." She smiled encouragingly.

"What if she tries to kill me out there? What if she *really* tries to kill me out there?"

"In front of tens of thousands of people? She's crazy, but she's not mental—*is she?*"

"Hi there, little rookie," Mona said, drumming her nail into my shoulder. "So, I'm sure your wonderful big sister has informed you that I'm one of your loving captains. Understand, rookie—I run a tight fucking ship, so be prepared to work."

"Mona, give the girl a break. You've got plenty of time to terrorize her," Skye said, grabbing my hand.

I felt as if I were in the middle of a custody battle and the big bad *Flowers in the Attic* mommy was taking the lead.

"Hannah, could you come over here a second, hon?" Nikki yelled out over all the buzzing and snapping and spraying.

The moment I'd waited for! My turn to put on the uniform that I'd longed to wear for five million forevers. The celestial gates to heaven were opening! It was a very special moment, ranking up there with getting my first menses.

"You are now a woman. The strength and power of our species is being passed on to you. Use it wisely. Now get off my couch and go put on a pad," my Nana had said, and cried the rest of that night.

"Here, honey. We're running a bit behind schedule tonight." Nikki handed me the uniform hurriedly. "Great party Saturday, huh?"

"Yep," I fibbed.

I took the pristine two-piece white-and-gold miniskirt and white midriff top with gold sequined lettering. I held it in my arms, and angels began to sing.

"Now this is your signature two-piece white, and you'll need to wear this to all of your autograph signings and high-profile promotional events, OK? Sometimes you'll have other uniforms to wear, but this will be your primary piece." She reached behind her. "And this is what you should always carry your Diamond Dolls gear in from now on. You can do away with your Sienna Miller or whatever it is you girls carry around to look trendy. This is where it's at." She pulled out the oversized white-and-gold Diamond Dolls duffel, and the choir of angels sang the second verse.

Ali, standing nearby, now leaned over and whispered something in Nikki's ear.

"Sure, go ahead," Nikki agreed, and handed Ali a box.

"Turn around and pull your hair up, Hannah."

"Ohmigod, you guys! Is this what I think it is?"

Aliyah placed the 18k-gold Diamond Dolls necklace around my neck, and I knew that somewhere up there an angel was getting her wings.

"It's nice to have you on my team," Aliyah whispered sweetly. I turned around and gave her a warm hug. I never imagined it would feel this good.

FOR THE NEXT HOUR, I POSED AND VOGUED, THINKING HOW PLEASED GRANDPA Red would be with how I was using "the pretty."

47

BY THE TIME I'D GOTTEN MY SHOWER, SLIPPED INTO MY JAMMIES, AND MADE A quick sprint through my e-mails, it was almost midnight. I found an extra box of cheddar chips in one of the pantries and copped a squat on the sofa to flip through the channels. I'd checked my voice mail on the way home and was getting comfy before returning Cobra's call. The day in New York had been one of the biggest for the label, and I needed to get updated before I went in to work tomorrow. But the phone rang before I could even put the first chip to my lip.

"Hello, Eli." I smiled into the phone, not quite sure why.

"Hey, Angel. What's really good?"

"I'm cool, just a little tired."

"How was your photo shoot?"

"Heavenly."

"Good. Now, tell me what you're wearing." The man seriously sounded like ecstasy.

"What I will do is let you screw the dial tone if you're not careful."

"You know I just be saying that stuff to make you mad," he said and laughed.

"Mase, Harlem World, circa ninety-seven."

"Good girl. Now, really, what are you wearing?"

"Eli, come on. How'd everything go? Don't keep me waiting in suspense like this."

"OK. OK. She was hot! She was so fuckin' hot I almost had to pull out my Hermes hankie and wipe away the sweat."

"So what you're saying is that *Rain was on fire.*"

"These cats are still out here talking about how you came up with that hot tag line. That's what's up: *Rain on Fire!* Mannie wants to put it on all the T-shirts and baby Ts for giveaways. Yes, woman, our golden girl was on fire!"

"I told you twice already that Cobra helped me come up with that." I filled my mouth with chips. "So she did good, huh? That's the news I've been waiting for all day." I kicked my feet up on the ottoman and crunched into the phone.

"She did her thing last night on Conan, but she wasn't really feeling it too tough, so little man went ahead and booked space so she could rehearse with Darren for a couple hours right before TRL. You shoulda been in the studio! I'm telling you. She was sick wit' it. And that single, *Rain on Me,* was the most requested of the day on TRL *and* 106 & Park. Now, that's what's up, baby girl!"

"What kinds of numbers do you think she'll do in her first week?"

"I'm already hearin' three hundred thousand, but I'm predicting two-fifty."

"Nice," I said, and took a deep breath. We had a lot riding on that show, and deep down I was glad it was over.

"So where're y'all headed now?"

"We're over here at Cipriani's on 42nd, just showing her some love. Big brass is here with a helluva lot of industry types. She's having a crazy good time."

"I'm glad. How was Regis?"

"You know that cat is whack. He knows nada about the game. But in all honesty, he thought she was fine as hell. She even made Kelly look average today. And that's what's up; you know brothers be lovin' them some skinny-ass Kelly Ripa."

"That makes me proud. Now put Cobra on the phone."

"What! Call that little man on *his* phone. He got a phone. RockStar fitted him with a goddamn phone—I should know. I signed off on that shit."

"Put him on the damn phone, Eli," I yelled, getting a chip stuck in my throat.

"Here, your mommy wants to talk to you," I heard him say over the commotion at their table.

"Hey, Bosslady." Cobra was a little hoarse. I could only imagine all the yelling and screaming he'd been doing.

"Are you having a good time?"

"Oh man, she was so fierce. She got in that extra practice right before she did TRL, so she was super ready. And did I tell you that the child was fierce? All the kids loved her, and I'm not talking about the teenyboppers in the audience either." He was talking so fast he was running out of breath. "And this restaurant—I've never seen anything like this before."

"Cobra, honey, are *you* having a good time?"

"Yes, Hannah, the best time of my life."

"Gimme my goddamn phone! Call her on your own fuckin' phone. I'm paying for it."

"Gotta go; the coyote is growling, but I can call you back if you want."

Eli huffed at Cobra, "What did you just call me?"

"No, that's OK. Just enjoy it all, every minute of it," I told him.

I heard Cobra call for the waiter as he passed the phone.

"Does little man have a goddamn phone or not?"

I ignored his raging. "Eli, have a blast at the party, and don't forget to see what kinds of feelers you can put out for Rain to do a guest spot on a couple of shows, like *Veronica Mars* or *Girlfriends* or—"

"I know how to do my job. Take your ass to bed and get some rest. You did your thing and worked magic all the way from Chicago. Everything flowed like butta—like butta, baby! But I wouldn't expect anything less."

Grinning, I hung up the phone and slid deep into the sofa, thinking this was exactly what winning was supposed to feel like.

48

MY WHITE THIGH-HIGH FISHNETS WERE SLOWLY SLIDING DOWN MY LEGS. I fussed with the garter and adjusted my wings over my left shoulder for the third time.

"Kennedy, come here. I need you to fix my wings. They're gonna fall off, and I'll never be allowed back into heaven," I yelled over the staircase, and heard her heavy feet pounding the hardwood.

"I'm coming. I'm having the same problem."

I stood in the balcony doorway of my bedroom in the white sparkly angel costume and looked out at all the traffic on Lake Shore Drive. The air was crisp and the streets were festively lit. I scanned the crystal-clear October sky and was glad the gods had decided to be good to all the tiny toddler and teenybopper trick-or-treaters. Our Indian summer was already in full swing, and the autumn evening promised to be gentle to my scantily clad crew.

"Mine are hanging lower on the right side, Hannah-Bug." Kennedy stood in front of me, pointing to her back, and I adjusted her pink feathery wings and secured the snaps on her pink satin-and-lace bustier.

"Damn, those kids are little punks," Brittany bitched, walking into the room in her salacious red angel outfit. She sizzled in red stilettos, flesh-tone fishnet thigh-highs, a red lace off-the-shoulder micro-chemise, and big red feather wings that hung daintily from her back.

"You answered the door like that?" I looked over Kennedy's shoulder.

"What? The goddamn doorbell rang. What the hell was I supposed to do? I opened the door and gave the little fuckers some Snickers."

"Oh my God. That'll probably haunt them for the rest of their lives," Kennedy said.

"No, I did them a favor. I'm certain they'll only see *this* in their dreams." Cupping her abundant double-Ds, she ran her tongue across her lips and stuck her juicy round rump out from under the bottom of her wings.

"You're right, and I don't wanna think about what kinds of dreams those are gonna be." Kennedy giggled.

"Whatever, Annie."

"Don't call me that. There's nothing wrong with the way I eat. Some of us just like being fit," she retorted.

"Implication being? Never mind, Annie; I am fit: fit, thick, and fabulous. Don't hate. And trust, I get NO complaints."

"Like you'd ever know. They're always gone by the time you wake up out of your stupor," Kennedy taunted her under her breath.

Brittany dived for her sister, and before I could call ref, she'd yanked a handful of feathers from Kennedy's wings.

"Hey!" I screamed. "Not tonight. It's the devil's day. Let's play nice."

"OK, now I seriously need a drink." Britt threw the feathers in her sister's face. "Are we still going to Whiskey Sky or not?" she fumed as they stared at each other. "I'm not gonna tell you thrift shop angels one more time that I need a fucking drink!"

I grabbed both their hands. "Come on now, let's be ghosts and disappear from here and go play 'Haunt the Hotties' at the W."

THREE NAUGHTY ANGELS SASHAYED CELESTIALLY THROUGH THE LIVING ROOM OF the W Hotel before deciding to take the elevator up to the Whiskey Sky.

Countless costumed folks were in a frenzy to get to the top-floor sky bar and had formed a line that stretched out the door. As we made our way past them, several French maids, wicked witches, and variations of Village People applauded. Hector moved the red velvet rope and kissed us each on the cheek as we got on the elevator to the swanky 33rd-floor fantasy festival. The sky bar was decorated like something out of Hef's Playboy pad, and we fit right in with the rest of the could've-been bunnies.

"So, Hannah, how are things with the team?" Britt inquired, once we were situated at a table in the VIP section overlooking the city.

"Can I just tell you that I am so ready for the season to start? If we practice one more damn sideline repeat or one more signature routine, I swear—"

"When is your first game?" Kennedy picked up a pretzel from the dish on our table and put it back down. We all looked at her.

"Eat it, Annie. You need to feed yourself some carbs every once in a while," Britt said, obviously still pissed.

"Ew! It's not the calories." Kennedy rolled her eyes at Britt and looked directly at me. "I just remembered there are more germs in these communal snack dishes than on toilet handles."

"Now, that's just nasty." Britt turned her nose up and took a handful anyway.

"It's next Friday," I said, taking a sip of my specialty caramel martini.

"It's gonna be bananas when you and Mona are out there cheering for the multimillion-dollar man. She's gonna hate you through all four quarters. And heaven forbid the game goes into overtime," Britt warned, dipping her finger into her orangetini. "Now if you want, I'll find a way to get two courtside seats on *both* sides of the court, so when you change sides at halftime, this full-figured ass will change right along with you."

"That makes two of us, my ass included," Kennedy said.

"Thanks, guys. You definitely rock!"

"But since she's already been cheering with the other veterans for the past three weeks in preseason, she should be used to being out there with Max," Britt said. "So maybe she's over it already."

"Maybe not," I answered, still unconvinced.

"Have you seen him at all?" Kennedy put her glass down and leaned in.

"No, not since the elevator incident."

"Thirty flights you had to suffer through with him and his girl," Britt reminded me.

"Is he still seeing her?" Kennedy was treading lightly.

"I dunno. Minnow said there was a woman matching her description at the Cleveland game she went to. She said he kept looking back at her and smiling."

"See—so you shouldn't be worrying about Mona anyway. He's already on lock with some other bitch," Britt said.

"Brittany!" Kennedy slapped her hand down on the table.

"What? Spilled milk, bitches. She's got eleven other players running their rich asses up and down the court to choose from. Keep it moving. Grandpa Red told her ass, 'don't waste the goddamn pretty.' "

"That's so not what he said," Kennedy defended.

"Well, hell; that's what the fuck he meant." Britt put her empty glass down on the table and motioned vehemently for the server. "Now pass me your drink while that slow heifer goes to fetch mine." She reached across the table and took Kennedy's chocolate martini.

"Yeah, well, anyway I think Dr. Ivy was right when she said I need just stay focused on me right now. I just should've listened."

"Again, spilled milk," Britt said, rolling her eyes at the overwhelmed server.

"And what about Eli? Have there been any more accidental kisses?" Kennedy asked, rubbing her hands together.

"Yeah, what's up with that? Another fine-ass rich man who has his shit together." Britt was getting pushy.

"Now you know that man is a self-proclaimed player, and he just wants Hannah cuz she ain't giving him the poochie," Kennedy spelled out.

"Her loss. Maybe that would loosen her up some, or at the very least get her mind off something that's apparently off the $35 million market."

"He's my boss!"

"No, he's your fine *virile* boss!" Britt corrected.

The server put our second round of drinks on the table, informing us that they were courtesy of the gentlemen at the bar. I looked over and saw two white and one black man costumed like Donald Trump, Spiderman, and a very dark one-eyed pirate, all perched on the retro sixties bar stools.

"Now that's what I'm talking about." Britt raised her glass and smiled in their direction.

"How the hell can I take anybody dressed like Donald Trump seriously?" I asked while Kennedy sipped without acknowledging the suitors.

Britt crossed her netted legs and continued to smile at the costumed men. "Speak for yourself; I can take The Donald's money seriously any day." She winked.

I turned to Kennedy and attempted to poof up her featherless wing. "Lately Eli's been doing these really sweet things. When I come into work, different arrangements of flowers will be on my desk with a note that says simply, 'You're the one.' Some days I don't even see him, but there they are, already beautifully arranged on my desk."

"He must mean you're the one not giving his ass any, and probably the *only* one," Britt said.

Kennedy put her glass down, pulling at one of the few remaining feathers poking her in the shoulder. "What does he say when he sees you in the office?"

"Nothing really—just his normal flirtatious slush. Other than that, it's business as usual. We've gone to lunch a couple of times, but it's always the same thing: crazy attraction, some sparks, and lots of shop talk. Besides, Rain is about to go platinum, and there's buzz about her being nominated for a Grammy. Best new artist. We've been spending more time together since she rocked Miami at the VMAs."

"She was so hot in Miami, it was unbelievable," Kennedy said.

Britt crossed her arms across her chest. "She was all right." She finished her drink and was starting to tap her glass on the table and stare indignantly at the men at the bar. "Well, Hannah, that shit with Elijah sounds sexy to me. I don't know how you work so closely with him and manage to maintain your cool. New York reads promising. I'd explore that a little more if I were you. Sounds like he's trying to show you a softer side of Sears." She turned her body completely around to wave a finger at the masked men.

Kennedy laughed. "You're fucking pitiful."

"No, bitch; my drink is gone."

49

I PUT THE ROVER IN PARK AND STARED INTO THE DISTANCE. I RUBBED MY HANDS together, breathing into them as if the intense heat shooting from the dashboard weren't already making my MAC foundation clump. The layers of ribbed long-johns I'd thrown on in response to the weather channel's "First SEVERE Windy City cold front" advisory was the sole cause of the sweat trail that was making its way down my legs.

It was a little over two hours before game time. My very first call time. I'd made the cut for my game squad, but I couldn't help but be nervous about tonight's big performance. I centered myself and attempted to go over the steps to the show-stopping halftime routine in my head. I closed my eyes and was in the middle of the court, whizzing through the steps and shining like a beacon of hope to all who aspired to one day be a part of the larger-than-life well-oiled NBA machine when I suddenly froze in mid-pirouette! All I could think about was the moment my eyes would lock with Max's. Shit! I pounded on the steering wheel and screamed, "What Would Jesus Do?!"

I called on the gods, Grandpa Red, and my first dance teacher from the Pretty Princess Pageant before reaching into the glove compartment for my official Chicago Diamond Dolls "All Access" ID badge. Reverently, I placed the laminated picture around my neck, rubbed my hands together one last time, and took a deep breath before putting on my winter-white leather gloves.

Adjusting the duffel on my shoulder for the fourth time since entering Gate 4, I walked through the Hall of Fame, down the stairs, and through the concourse. The smell of hot dogs on poppy-seed buns and nachos with packaged processed cheese added to the stench of barreled beer and popcorn. My stomach turned. Arriving at the third room on the right, I read the engraved sign on the silver door: "CHICAGO DIAMOND DOLLS." My stomach turned again.

I did a quick once-over and manually volumized my hair with my fingers. A bolt of lightning raced through me when I gripped the shiny doorknob and entered the almighty cheerleading sanctuary: the Locker Room.

It was much larger than I'd imagined, even though my main reference had only been the ones built for the movies and TV studios that were always filled with über–fine men. Prince's "When Doves Cry" cranked from the CD player next to the water fountain. I inhaled the energy. All the veterans were huddled together, just like that cheerleading clique in junior high that all the girls loathed yet secretly imitated in the safe confines of their glossy-postered bedrooms. It was probably too much to hope that one of them would take pity on me and spill the deal about locker room etiquette. Like getting my cherry popped by Bobby Sachs in the eleventh grade, I smiled nervously at nothing in particular and tried to go with the flow, showing no signs of confusion or discomfort. I loosened my Ralph Lauren goosedown puffy jacket and looked around. Mona and Hilton were brushing their hair, and Katie stood against a locker in her white thong, pulling her nude sheer-to-the-waist pantyhose up her long, shaved legs.

I looked past the narrow row of lockers behind me. The far side of the room opened into a massive bathroom complete with showers, a sauna, and a svelte platinum-blonde masseuse, who now stood next to the massage table waiting patiently while a few of the girls discussed who was due the first pregame rubdown.

Several deli tables had been set up against the wall opposite the vanities with enough food to feed the girls, the players, and probably the mascot. I wanted to grab a few oatmeal cookies but realized I would have to disrupt the veteran inner circle in my maneuver to get to them.

"Hey rookie, just pick any locker that's not already taken on that wall," Skye advised, without looking at me.

I obliged and started opening random lockers.

"Just don't take locker 115."

"—or 112."

"—or 96."

Well damn, why didn't they just pick out a locker for me and shove me into it? I fumbled along the wall, being careful not to touch any they'd already claimed, when Minnow, Elle, and Chloe rushed in.

"I'm so nervous about tonight." Minnow's voice quivered when she whispered. She ditched her coat and opened the empty locker next to mine.

"That makes two of us," I agreed, taking my white two-piece signature uniform out of the garment bag and hanging it in my locker, careful not to snag it on anything.

Nikki's entrance cranked the night up to a maddening momentum. After a quick head count and welcome, she turned to address the rookies delicately and deliberately.

"Try not to be nervous, you guys, even though it's normal for you to feel first-day jitters. All these old gals in here have been in your shoes at one time or another. They'll help you through any uncertain moments you may have. But more than anything, just try and enjoy tonight. You'll never have a first night on the court again. There's only one first time."

Nikki's sentiment was sweet but unrealistic. I looked over my shoulder at the veterans, who smiled disingenuously and nodded unapologetically at all of us.

"These are your halftime outfits. You'll only have a couple minutes to change after second quarter, so put them away immediately where you can easily put your hands on them," she advised, as everyone fussed with the hairspray, falsies, and lipstick strewn across the well-lit wall-length vanity. "Then meet me on the court in five for a quick pregame run-through of the halftime routine."

Systematically, she distributed the Holy Grail: a sexy gold-sequined halter top with a diamond in the center, a black micromini skirt with gold rhinestones along the waistband, sequined scrunchies, and black briefs to go under the skirt.

Unable to control myself, I put the halter top and the skirt to my nose and inhaled slowly. It was the sweet smell of success. So worth it!

"Run-throughs right now, Dolls!" Coach yelled after looking at her watch.

Ready or not, here I come.

50

WALKING THROUGH THE TUNNEL AND ONTO THE COURT FOR RUN-THROUGHS HAD a ceremonial feel to it. Anyone with a pregame job was hastily moving about. The ushers were arranging the courtside seats, and the announcers were fidgeting with microphones and adjusting lights for *Showtime.* But there was no mistaking who the stars of the night were: the players. They were scattered about the court in their warm-ups, effortlessly shooting around or prepping for lay-ups and easy dunks.

"We don't have all night to get this done, ladies, so take your places and we'll walk through the routine a couple of times to my count," Nikki instructed, after signaling—a double handclap—to the players.

We ran to our spots and marked the choreography three times until all rookies were hitting their marks before and after transitions.

Wrapping run-throughs, most of the girls headed back to the locker room. Even though I was feeling pretty confident about my routine, I looked out at the court and went over it all in my head once more.

"Hey, you look like you know what you're doing out there."

Max had changed back into his warm-ups and was standing next to me, holding a ball under his arm. I managed to stand there, frozen, clenching my teeth and tightening my knees.

"Don't talk to me. You can't talk to me. You can't do this right now. Go away," I said through my teeth, motioning for him to shoo.

He laughed and took a step closer. "OK, OK, whatever you want. But you look good out there. I don't know how I'm gonna focus on my game tonight," he said, bouncing the ball that had been under his arm. "I need all my attention focused on L.A. I'd be lying if I said it wasn't gonna be hard."

In spite of myself, I smiled. I wanted to ask where his girlfriend would be during all this distraction, but discovered that I couldn't speak. I turned to walk away.

I was almost to the tunnel when Max called out after me. Was he deliberately trying to mind-fuck me? Maybe *he* could handle the distraction, but I sure as hell couldn't.

"Hey."

I turned around slowly.

"You look great."

The ball fell from under his arm, and a ballboy ran over to scoop it up and toss it to another player.

"Thanks."

I headed toward the hallway and jogged to the locker room, feeling his eyes through my silver Diamond Dolls sports bra. I imagined him taking his hand to his head and running it through the curls at the base of his neck, and suddenly I couldn't remember how the halftime routine was supposed to start.

51

"WE WILL/ WE WILL/ ROCK YOU!"

The fans were going bananas, and the show was finally about to begin. We scampered out and formed a tunnel with our pompoms for the players to run through. Nervously, I stood next to Aliyah and followed her lead. She shook her wrists spiritedly as each of the players ran out onto the court before the lights went down for their big intro. Max winked as he ran past me.

Along with the rest of the Dolls, I screamed, howling between high kicks, back flips, and toe touches as the announcer got the crowd even more hyped.

"Ladies and gentlemen, stand on your feet and prepare to meet the biggest baddest team in the NBA. They're precious and they're rare. They sparkle and they shine. They're your Chicagooo Diamonds!"

Instant insanity!

There wasn't a single soul seated anywhere in sight. The strobe light bounced around, and the arena had a pulse of its own. The stadium was alive, and I was a part of it all.

My heart beat speedily, in sync with the roar of the crowd. Shortly after tipoff I was beginning to relax and ride the frenzy, but it wasn't until after an entire first quarter that I finally managed to settle into the routine of the night. Toward the end of the second quarter I realized that I'd only forgotten a couple high Vs in two of the sideline cheers. What had I been so worried about, anyway? I looked over at Mona, who grimaced back. Now I remembered.

The game was tied, and the end of the first half was rapidly approaching. Anxiously, I scanned the stands searching for the Brats. I looked out onto the court and threw my arms in the air, shaking them wildly when Max stole the ball and charged down the court, pulling back while Shep hustled inside the paint and reached around the defender. Shep caught the pass in midbounce, laying the ball in the net effortlessly, finally putting the Diamonds in the lead. Jumping up immediately, my squad hit toe-touches and herkys, except for me. Distracted, I haphazardly kicked my leg into the air as my eyes darted in and out of the stands searching for the Brats. Movado check: LATE! Damn. I really didn't want them to miss the big halftime routine.

With five seconds left on the clock at the end of the second quarter, Max got fouled, and the Diamonds coach, Winston Rollie, called for a time-out. We scurried onto the court for a sixteen-count sequence we'd worked on for quick dead spurts like these. That's when I spotted them filing down the stands.

"Go Hannah! We see you, girl," Britt screamed as she led the way down the concrete steps into the first row, off center, next to the home team. Those weren't the tickets I'd given them.

Britt waved and Kennedy screamed out my name. "I see you, Hannah." Who knows what favors had been redeemed for those seats. I'd be all ears later. They looked fabulously hot. Relieved, without a second to spare, I waved back before flying off the court and into the Batcave to get changed for the big number.

I opened my locker and laid my costume neatly on the bench. My hands were wringing wet. I hung my uniform skirt on one of the metal hooks and quickly, carefully, pulled my white top over my head. And though annoyed, I ignored my sweaty palms and tried to go over the routine in my head one last time as my heart pumped premium un-leaded anxiety. I kicked off my shoes, socks, and white briefs and laid them on the bench on the opposite side of me.

The frenzied chaos in the room was ridiculous, and I understood why Coach had repeatedly stressed organization.

"Three minutes, ladies," Nikki yelled from the water fountain. Her headset was linked to her walkie-talkie. She was continuously confirming time with the game coordinator.

The locker room blurred as I moved in record speed to get dressed. I tied my black jazz shoes, stood up, and reached for the black briefs I'd placed on the bench. I looked under the bench. Nothing. I looked in the locker. Nothing. I looked under my skirt to make sure I hadn't already put them on. Nothing. Gone. They were nowhere to be found!

"One minute, ladies!" Nikki yelled out.

Holy bloomers, Batman!

"Minnow, I can't find my briefs."

"What? You just had them. I saw them," she said as she pulled her hair back into her scrunchie. "Are you sure you're not wearing them?"

"No! I'm not wearing them. I checked twice. I had them a few min-utes ago. I can't find them now."

Panicking, I looked through my locker, under the bench, and in my locker again.

"Thirty seconds to line up, ladies."

"Shit! What do I do?"

"Put your white uniform briefs back on. At least you'll have on something, and just pray Coach doesn't see."

I looked through the locker for my white briefs, but I couldn't find them now either. What the hell was going on? I glimpsed Mona in my periphery. I dared not make eye contact. She was leaning against her locker directly across from mine, tying her black jazz shoes and watch-ing while I searched relentlessly for either pair of uniform bottoms. My heart sank into my gut when Nikki yelled out "last call!" and I still hadn't found my fucking drawers.

"Minnow, let's go right now!" Coach yelled.

"You want my briefs?" Minnow asked just as Mona grabbed her by the elbow and pulled her out of the locker room, slamming her locker door shut.

I snatched the black sequined scrunchie, pulled my hair back, and ran to catch up to them in the tunnel.

"Go! Go! Go!" Nikki pushed Hilton, who led the team to the center of the court.

I took my position, ready to dance—with my uniform black micro-mini barely hanging over my neon-orange thong!

52

ALL 23,140 FANS WERE ACCOUNTED FOR AND ON THEIR FEET, BELLOWING AT THE first beat of the Grammy award–winning Outkast song. One single tear fell from my right eye as I stood motionless with my head down, waiting for the music to cue my first move. *Surely* I'd be inducted into the dishonorable cheerleading Hall of Shame. *Surely* they'd force me to relinquish my Diamond Dolls necklace. *Surely* they'd confiscate my official Chicago Diamonds ID badge—just before I'd *surely* have to burn this goddamn neon thong.

I'd made it through the first two transitions and was praying to everyone, including Outkast, that my luck would last. Just then I spied Max jog through the tunnel and stand on the sidelines, directly in front of me. Ohmigod!

He tossed a towel over his shoulder and crossed his arms over his chest. A red-haired freckle-faced boy kept trying to serve him Gatorade, but he didn't take his eyes off me. Ohmigod!

A commentator in the middle of a live halftime broadcast proffered a microphone, requesting an interview from Max, but he wouldn't take his eyes off me. Ohmigod!

I tried to force a charismatic smile with just the right amount of Diamond Dolls attitude. Oh. My. God.

The Brats were screaming my name, clapping their hands, and stomping their stilettos into the concrete floor just to the right of the bench. It was going by so fast, and though I couldn't see everyone around me on the court, it felt as if the routine had been flawless up to this point. I just prayed I could finish the last eight counts without any unexpected fireworks.

Counting down the final four counts, I was into the third formation change when Mona cut around my left side a millimeter too close and swiped the tip of my foot.

And—my—face—met—the—hardwood!

I knew this couldn't be a good thing when my left *and* right butt cheeks caught a cool breeze. I rescued my hands from underneath me. They'd broken my fall, and now I needed them to cover my ass. When I looked up from the corner of my eye and saw two cameramen in my face, I wondered if everyone with an NBA league pass was watching the most embarrassing moment of my life!

What seemed like a lifetime couldn't have been more than a few seconds before I jumped up, pulled my skirt down, and ended the routine on cue in my final pose. I looked over at the Brats as my eyes welled with tears. One by one, they took their seats, eyes wide with shock, mouths covered with both hands. I just couldn't bear to make eye contact with Max, who I was sure was no longer my biggest fan, but as soon as Kennedy's butt hit her chair, my eyes locked with Max's stunningly beautiful companion, who'd been standing behind her. Could this night get any worse?

"Now, how does it feel to be the center of it all?" Mona cooed into my ear. "I think I even saw Maximillien laugh when your shiny neon-orange G-string greeted everyone. Welcome to the big leagues, rookie! Now smile—you're on *Candid Camera*."

I forced a pathetic grin. It wasn't bad advice. As Mona strode off the court she turned back and yelled with deep satisfaction, "And keep on smiling, rookie; your ass is plastered all over the Jumbotron!"

THIRD QUARTER

53

AFTER I'D LEFT DR. IVY'S OFFICE FOR AN EMERGENCY SESSION, THE RIDICULOUSLY rapid rate of my thoughts kept up with my speedometer all the way down Lake Shore Drive. No yachts to count; the harbor was empty. "You're not a quitter," Dr. Ivy had responded after I'd admitted being afraid to go back to practice after being sidelined until the Christmas game. *What did she know? She said I needed to get to know who Hannah was; well, maybe that's exactly who she was—quitter No. 108.*

I passed the Field Museum and turned off into the museum complex adjacent to Soldier's Field. I was on automatic pilot and found myself shifting into park beside the Shedd Aquarium. I beat my head against the steering wheel. *What have I done?*

I shut the door and tightened the mint-green Ralph Lauren scarf around my neck before zipping the creamy white RL jacket. I could see my breath trail into the frosty air. The vibrant leaves hummed in the wind, and the seasonal hymn almost went unnoticed as I hoisted myself onto a boulder next to the spot where Max had reintroduced me to life.

How was I ever going to face him again?

Pulling my knees into my chest, I looked out at the still water. It lacked the infinite possibility that the summer had held. Still. Lifeless. Shades of gray. The wind blew, and the few tears that had been on reserve fell. I wiped them away with my leather glove.

I thought about Max's legs wrapped around me and snuggled the insulated legwarmers clinging to my calves. Already, I missed the hope in that intimacy. He would never look at me the same way again. Not like he did that night. A cluster of leaves had been riding the current from a gust of wind and settled softly in front of me. I stared at their textured November hues.

Eli would never understand, either. Inevitably, Cameran's shift at the rumor mill would ensure his awareness. He'd never look at me the same way again. I'd lose serious 'cool points' with him. Being vulnerable, or not measuring up, wasn't something he subscribed to, and the possibility of defeat never registered with him. Eli understood making moves—power moves. Max embraced hard work and dedication, pushing yourself until you got it right. Max had supported his family and kept them grounded in hope. He'd believed in me. Grandpa Red had believed in me.

How was I going to explain to Max that I wasn't directly responsible for the embarrassment I'd brought to his team? She stole my goddamn briefs!

At least, I knew I could still count on him to be honest and straightforward about my ineptitude. Eli, on the other hand, had been trained to manipulate situations to satisfy his end goals. It was what he did and who he was. Money! Power! Respect! They coincided with his *Make It Happen* mantra. He'd never understand how I just didn't *Make It Happen*. And what I had made happen would be totally sub-par and absolutely unacceptable to him. I was an embarrassment.

I buried my head between my knees and shuddered. The cluster of leaves that had peacefully settled in front of me was whisked away. Where had the blades of grass gone that Max had plucked from between the sandy grains? Holding my head up, I breathed in and murmured aloud, "I miss you."

54

ON THE WAY HOME, I STOPPED OFF AT ONE OF MY FAVORITE TAKE-OUT SPOTS, JU-bilee Juice, just down the street from Harpo. Their grilled chicken Cae-sar salads and pineapple smoothies had a simple way of soothing me. But even though it smelled inviting, I set the brown paper bag on the is-land and trudged into the living room, tracking slushy water from my sand suede Donald Pliner Gracie snow boots and pink lemonade leg warmers.

The sun was already calling it quits, and all I wanted to do was cud-dle deep into the couch, curl up under the cozy chenille throw blanket Nana had bought for my very first apartment, and watch the noon *Law & Order* episode that I'd Tivo'd. I pulled the rubber band from my hair, loosened my ponytail, and slid my hands deep between the sofa cush-ions in search of the tube of Carmex I remembered seeing slip between them yesterday.

There was a knock on the door. Whoever it was would just have to go away. I wanted to fire up a good joint, but I didn't smoke pot. A good Chardonnay would have to suffice, regardless of all the wine bottles I'd already tricked out over the weekend. I made a quick call for three bot-tles of J. Lohr, trying to ignore the insistent knocking at the door, before turning up the volume on the flat screen. Sweet. It was an old episode with Jerry Orbach.

"Hannah, it's not like I can't hear you. Open the door please."

Shit! What was Max doing here?!

"Hannah, open the door! I'm not going away. Trust me; I'll go to great lengths to get you to open this door, just short of breaking it down or—"

"Please go away!" I slid deeper into the couch.

"—calling Dallas to come up here and open—"

I swung the door open. "What're you doing here?" I fussed with my tousled hair.

He stood in the doorway, holding what looked like a videotape and rubbing his perfectly lined five o'clock shadow. "I need to talk to you. You probably don't want to talk to me or anyone else right now, but I really do need to talk to you." He stepped closer, looking down at me, then touched my chin with the same hand he'd just rubbed against his chisel.

I thought about how I must look, completely washed out and in disarray, just like my pad—and he wanted to come in?

"Listen, I'm not feeling so good and—"

He put his index finger to my lips and shook his head. "I'm not taking no for an answer. I need to talk to you. That's all there is to it. At the very least you're gonna listen to what I have to say, even if we have to stand here in your doorway."

His eyes were intense and had that exact look I'd seen when he owned the court, driving to the basket for a dunk over his defenders. And what was my defense? Oh yeah—I'd just been facedown on his turf with my ass in the air for *all* to see.

"I'm sorry, Max; this really isn't a good time," I was saying when the phone rang. Saved by the wine. "Hey, I've gotta get that; I'm expecting a very important call from New York, and I really need to concentrate."

He didn't move. Instead, he shifted his weight and leaned against the door, running his hand through his hair. "Get the phone. I'm not moving. You're gonna listen to me, even if I have to sit in your living room and wait for you to finish all your work tonight."

The phone was on its fourth ring when I turned to snatch it from its base. "Yes, thank you. You can send it up," I whispered into the receiver. I felt dizzy. Maybe I needed to eat that salad after all.

When I turned back toward the door, Max had already closed it and was standing only a few feet away from me.

"I take it that wasn't your business call." He smiled for the first time and took a step closer in his white-and-blue UNC Carmelo Jordans. I'd heard that Nike was in talks with his management to develop a Max Knight shoe (I really needed to get that stock).

"No, but they should be calling any second now." I walked over to the door and opened it as the delivery guy was coming down the hall.

Max came over and took the big bag of bottles from my arms. He grabbed my hand and walked me to the couch, placing the bag on the island on the way. "Sit. Sit right here next to me."

He sat in the middle of the sofa, grabbed the remote, and paused the *Law & Order* episode as if he'd been handling my remote longer than me. He grabbed my hand, and I realized I still had on those damn leg warmers. I fidgeted with my feet, trying to maneuver the warmers down and off my legs. Max let go of one of my hands and held my knee. I was trapped, and he had my undivided attention.

"In life, Hannah, there are winners and there are losers. Winners face defeat all the time. I understand that what you just went through must've made you feel awful."

I looked away as tears began to collect.

"Please, look at me. I need you to hear this." He turned my face back around to his and stared into my eyes until the first tear fell. "I'd like to be here for you right now. Let me be your friend. I wanna put my arms around you so you can feel safe—even if it's just for a little while."

When I didn't object, Max moved as close to me as possible, put his arm around my shoulders, and sat silently still. I fought back the tears with all my might but quickly lost that fight. Two tears turned into five, which turned into a whimpering waterfall. He rocked me back and forth, getting comfortable in the cushions, and I buried my head deep into his chest. He stroked my hair with his left hand and wiped away the tears with his right, kissing the top of my head repeatedly. We stayed that way for what seemed like hours, in the quiet of the room.

When there were no more tears left, I opened my eyes and looked up at him. "I didn't mean to cry all over you like that. It's just that I know you must've been so embarrassed the other night. I mean, you had faith in me, and I let you down, and—"

"Don't tell me how I must feel. That's what I need to talk to you about—exactly how I *do* feel."

"Well, I mean, I completely—"

"Fumbled. You fumbled. It happens to athletes all the time. It happens to presidents, it happens to teachers, and it happens to professional cheerleaders. You fumbled. At some point you have to look at it for what it is, darlin'. I know it's almost easier to sulk and hole yourself up with a bottle of wine, but it's healthier to look at it for what it is—nothing more, nothing less. Everyone who puts themselves out there will, at some point, fumble. It's part of playing the game. You just did it on your first time out, and that can feel far worse than doing it after you've gotten some experience under your belt. After a couple times on the ropes it's easier to see things for what they are. Trust me on that one." He rubbed my arms and rocked me against him.

I could feel myself begin to relax again. "Have you ever fumbled?"

He laughed to himself. "Darlin', I'm one of the best guards in the league. You don't get to be one of the best without fumbling—and on more than one occasion."

He disentangled himself from me and reached for the videotape that he'd set on the coffee table. And after studying the remote for a sec and jabbing a few buttons, Max appeared on the oversized plasma screen, already in the middle of a game, running up and down the court. I glanced at the now empty box; it was marked Diamonds/ Knicks playoff finals. Right away I knew it was an old game; his hair was wavy and cut close, and there was an imprecision in his eyes.

"OK, this is an old tape. Check out that hair." He looked over at me and laughed. "I wanted you to see for yourself."

He sat back down in the middle of the couch and pulled me even closer to him this time. My blood bubbled, and I ditched the leg warmers.

"You ask if I've ever fumbled?"

I watched him charge for the basket and go up for an easy dunk with absolutely no one around him. He tried to execute a funky between-the-legs showoff move and completely missed the basket, landing clumsily on his leg and twisting his ankle in two directions.

I winced and forced my eyes shut as he lay there on the court in what appeared to be excruciating pain.

"Ouch."

"Exactly. Not only did I injure myself, but I also got reamed for even thinking about showboating on a play that should've been an easy lay- up or a simple dunk at best. Because of my ego, time ran out and I lost the game for us. A win would have put us in the championships, which we were favored to win that year. Instead, I handed the ring to the Knicks on a silver platter." He shook his head and stopped the tape. "I had to come out the following year and really prove myself all over again: to my team, to my critics, and most importantly, to myself. It's about what you do on the next drive to the hoop or the next drive down the lane—or the next halftime show." He moved my bangs and kissed my forehead once, then again. "Besides, I'm looking forward to you getting back out there and showing me what you've got. I was impressed the other night. You looked good. I couldn't take my eyes off you—and believe me, I wasn't the only one." He licked his lips and cocked his head to the side. "You didn't give Mona much of a choice *but* to trip you up."

My body temperature shot up a zillion degrees.

"Are you kidding? You mean you saw her trip me too?" I leaned as far back from him as I could.

"Of course. I said I couldn't take my eyes off you. I saw every single move you made. So how could I miss it when she stuck her foot out just about when you were making that move around the little Brazilian girl?"

I leaned back into his chest and smelled his delicious cologne. Tonight he was wearing just a touch of Angel for Men.

"But hey, listen. Never mind that she tripped you. That's not what matters. What's important is getting back up after you've fumbled, and making the most out of the next play. You hear what I'm saying, darlin'?"

"Yes," I said softly.

"Good." He kissed the top of my head again. "Now, what the hell happened to your panties out there?" he asked, and laughed slyly.

I leaned back and jabbed into his rock-hard arm, but my fist bounced right back.

He grabbed my wrist with his right hand. "You pack a pretty strong punch." He started to laugh even harder. "Sorry, Love, but you know I had to ask. Everyone wants to know. I promise I won't tell all the guys, but they were lovin' you already—that cute lil booty just put the icing on the cake."

"I can't believe you. What was all that sensitive comforting talk? You were just reeling me in so you could make fun of me," I fussed as I got up from the couch and stalked away.

Max grabbed me and pulled me over the back of the sofa and into his lap. "I like your sexy little ass. Actually I was wondering if I could keep those orange thongs you were wearing." he whispered, no longer smiling.

I sat motionless in his lap and looked into his intense dark eyes. Even though I wanted/*needed* to inquire about his dating situation, now just wasn't a good time. Nothing was going to make me feel better than being this close to him, even if it was only for a little while. I felt alive again. Finally. I stared at his lips, which were just inches from mine. He had both his arms wrapped around my body and was supporting all my weight on his thighs.

"I need to tell you something. Now listen very carefully, Hannah Marie Love." His lips parted. "I need you, darlin', and you need me too. But you keep running from me." He brushed the hair out of my face with the tip of one finger and leaned down into me, now just millimeters from my mouth. I could smell the fruity Gatorade on his breath. "Tell me you need me too."

Everything I'd been trying so hard to protect, from my spot on the team to my harried heart, now more fragile than ever, all mixed together in a jumble of fearful emotion. I felt a new tear fall from my eye, but before it could drop from the side of my face, Max wiped it away.

"Put your arms around my neck," he said.

"I . . . I . . . I can't do—"

"I'm not asking you. Put your arms around my neck."

"Max, listen—" I whispered. I could feel his heart through his shirt. The pounding was already in sync with mine.

"I'm going to count to three and you're going to put your arms around my neck. Then you're going to close your eyes because I'm going to kiss you. And maybe this will help you understand just how deeply I need you."

My body was already twitching, and I felt no need to try and hide it from him. Undoubtedly he could feel it. Hell, he'd caused it.

His neck was damp and his eyes were fixed on my brows, my eyes, my lips—

". . . two, three." He bent down to my ear. "Close your eyes, darlin'," he whispered. "Let me explain this to you with my tongue."

I did as I was told and braced myself. Just as he'd promised that night on the beach under the stars, he *really* kissed me. He gently brushed his lips against mine before inching away and pulling back. Even with my eyes closed, I knew he was studying me. Softly, he kissed me, this time lingering a while longer. He pulled away, just for a second, and kissed me again with familiarity. His tongue slid across my upper lip, tasting it before sucking it gently. Engaging my lips before parting them, Max took his time and introduced the inside of my mouth to his tongue. My nipples hardened and my heart pounded as he turned his head away slightly and held me tighter in his grip. I stared at him and waited impatiently, powerlessly, for his next move. Finally, he pulled me so close that I could feel him flex every major muscle in his body. His kisses now were deliberate and purposeful. His hands pressed into my sides, and I ran one hand through his hair, gripping the back of his neck with the other. I settled into my vulnerability, surrendering a soft moan while he kissed me with emphasis. His tongue felt good in my mouth. He tried to draw back again, and I released him into a deep sigh before grabbing his neck again to pull him closer so I could bite his bottom lip. He bent down for more, massaging his hands into my sides and moaning louder. My body twisted and turned on his lap. I was hot all over, wanting his hands to meet the rest of me. But I felt his momentum slow to long lingering kisses focused only on my lips. I opened my eyes and watched him brush them one last time before he leaned back and pulled my body into his embrace. His arms were strong, and I felt safe.

Max licked his lips and bit down on his bottom one. Taking my right hand from behind his neck, I traced his bottom lip with my index finger. He snatched it into his mouth, letting it slide out before kissing my fingertip. Then he sat with me in silence.

He opened his eyes and gazed at me. "Do you understand now?"

I could barely find my air.

There was so much I'd wanted to ask him and so much I still wasn't sure could ever be resolved.

"Talk to me, darlin'," he whispered.

I only knew that I didn't want this to end, but I was fully aware that the real world wasn't interested in what I wanted. There was too much to consider: my spot on the team, Mona, his breathtaking girl—consequences.

"It's complicated," I heard myself finally utter.

He took my face in his hands and made me stare directly into his sincerity.

"Things just aren't that simple," I said, looking away. "Believe me, I wish they were. Everything is just so—so—complicated right now."

"Darlin', nothing about that kiss was complicated."

My head was spinning. I wanted to ask him about breaking franchise rules and about the stunning striking woman I'd seen him with—and about Mona! But the words were stuck, and I couldn't get them out.

"Well, I don't know what else to do. I send flowers to your job every week. And I try and talk to you every chance I get." He ran the backs of his fingers down the side of my face. "We can work to make this less complicated."

"What did you just say?" I sat up straight, confused and shocked.

"I know we can make it less complicated."

"No, before that."

"The flowers? Well, I know you like beautiful flowers, so I wanted you to have a fresh bouquet each week when you got to work." He loosened his hold on me.

"You've been sending me flowers every week? To my job?"

"Yeah."

"With a note?"

"Yeah." He lowered his eyebrows. "What? You wouldn't talk to me. I was trying to respect your decision about the rules and the consequences without—"

"With a note that says *YOU'RE THE ONE?*" I pressed.

"Darlin'—you are. I knew that the first time I heard you at your audition." He reached for my hand. "You made every moment stand still. I've never felt that way before. Then when I spent time with you that night on the beach, well, I just knew."

He pulled me back into his arms and held me. But now I couldn't settle into him. My mind raced with thoughts of Eli taking credit for Max's gestures of affection. I felt enraged and violated and terribly confused. How could I have been so stupid, so naïve? All this time I'd thought Eli was vying for my affections and—

"What's wrong?" Max recalled my attention just as the phone rang. "Please, don't answer that."

"I need to get it."

He let me go with ease, and I went for the phone. Caller ID: Eli Strong. He'd always managed to be in the right place at exactly the right time. But tonight he was a few minutes too late.

"I really need to take this call. I'm sorry, Max. Can we talk more later?" When he didn't answer I turned around, but he was already on his way toward the front door. "I do wanna talk about this. Like I said, things are just a little complicated right now—for both of us. There are rules, and I've already screwed up royally, and then there are other things that need to be sorted out and—"

The phone was on its fifth ring when it finally stopped.

When he reached the door, he turned to look at me. "You mean there's someone else."

"That's not fair—in your life too!" I raised my voice at him, and he turned away from me to open the door.

The phone started to ring again. Glancing out the corner of my eye, I could see that it was Eli—again. He was managing to come between Max and me, even if I didn't want to see it for what it was. Why couldn't I just pick up the phone and tell him to go to hell, to kiss my ass after lying all that time to me? It shouldn't matter that he was my boss; this was personal. Max was getting ready to walk out the door and feel something that he should never feel, all because I'd let things get a little *complicated.*

"Hannah, I put everything on the line tonight. I'm done. Answer the phone and deal with him. Handle your business, darlin'. I won't wait. And I can't make you love me."

He opened the door and was gone before I could answer back, "But I think I already do."

I grabbed a couple paper towels from the countertop and wet them, bending down to wipe the floors where the slushy dirty water had dried. After I realized I'd been wiping the same spot for five minutes, I gave up and left the towel on the floor, having decided to call the housekeeper first thing in the morning. The bag with the wine was still on the counter, and instead of opening one of them, I put the bottles in the fridge for another fall-on-my-face-and-show-my-ass kind of day.

If there was ever a time when I needed to soak and think, this was it. I slogged into the master bathroom and turned on the faucet, letting the tub fill with hot water. Max had turned my world upside down, and now with the realization of Eli's deceit, I doubted myself more than ever. I'd neglected to ask Max about the striking, stunning woman who looked adoringly at him whenever I saw the two of them together. Fearful of being duped a second time with lies and half truths, I decided I just needed to back away altogether and think for a while. My track record with honest men had been perpetually disappointing and was getting more pathetic by the man.

I stuck my foot in the searing water and got burned. That made it twice in one day.

55

I STRUTTED INTO THE OFFICE IN MY FABBEST BLACK WOOL-AND-ANGORA-BLEND Prada skirt suit with faux fur trim and black leather knee-length stirrup stiletto boots. I was prepared to take on my world: Eli, Rain, her promo tour, and her Grammy performance. I was disappointed that there were no flowers waiting for me on my desk. I slammed the door and sat back in my chair. What did I expect?

With a timid knock, Cobra pushed the door open slightly. "Can I come in, Bosslady? You said you wanted to see me?"

"Of course. Have a seat and catch me up."

Cobra eased into the leather chair across from my desk and crossed his legs, flicking his pencil with the poofy tip.

I gave him a look that said "GO!" He situated his notebook on his knee and dove right in. "The *Seventeen* shoot is scheduled, and I'm working closely with the stylist to put all the looks together that you suggested. The accessories editor is faxing over pictures of more pieces to finish the ensemble. That will be in your box by noon."

"Great."

"Also, you have a conference call with the big brass at two. That was scheduled this morning just before you got here."

I looked up from my day planner and maximized my computer screen. "Really? Do you know what it's regarding?"

Cobra pushed the door closed with the furry tip of his pencil. "Couldn't get any info from the New York temp."

"Is Eli here yet?" I asked, without looking away from my screen.

"Yes, he got here at eight this morning. When I went to the kitchen to make my morning oatmeal, I tried to listen in on Cameran's call with him to find out why he was in the office so early, but homechick wasn't giving up any juice when she peeked around her cubicle and saw me standing there."

"No worries. Thanks for holding everything down for me. Things've been kind of crazy, to say the least."

"Well, you look hotter than your piping nonfat caramel macchiato this morning."

"I'm actually feeling a bit better."

"What, no flowers this morning?"

"Long story. Let's just say that if you want flowers from now on, order them and expense it to the label. My treat. Today I'm really gonna need you to handle *Seventeen* so we can finalize the outfit and layout for our rock star."

"No problem," he said, heading back to his desk.

He wasn't the only one who missed the flowers, but I was missing the uncomplicated note more than anything. I grabbed the mirror in my desk and checked to make sure my lipstick hadn't skidded across my teeth before I grabbed a spiral notebook to head to Eli's office for a debriefing. Keeping my cool was going to be the priority task of the day—the entire effin' day. The office wasn't gonna be that place where I aired my dirty thongs.

I walked past Cobra's desk and heard him talking to his new intern. "Now when you talk to Spike, be prepared for him to ask a ton of questions. He's rough on the outside, but he's really a big softie. Hands off, though, he's spoken for."

I trudged down the hall and around the corner, listening as assistants handled buzzing phones and meticulously went over itineraries with agents.

Cameran was at her usual spot behind her desk, headset on, yapping away to her counterparts in the New York office. She always managed to have her chair pushed back just enough so everyone could get a glimpse of her thighs under her miniskirt. Today she wore fishnets. Instead of the usual forced smile I'd come to rely on when she greeted me, today she was pouting. She even looked indiscreetly upset—borderline annoyed.

"Good morning, Cameran. Is Eli available?" I couldn't figure out for the life of me why Eli continued to allow her wardrobe to shrink by the week.

She looked at me and winced before forcing the recognizable smile I'd come to expect from her. "Uh-huh, he's in there," she said dryly, and continued with her long-distance convo. I'd never been able to make out what she was saying into that headset. She'd perfected the exact tone and pitch necessary to let you know that she was on the phone, but in no way allow you to decipher a word of what she was saying.

I knocked lightly on Eli's door. Not hearing anything, I turned the knob and pushed it open. I should have knocked louder, because my thumbs went numb when I saw Eli standing behind a woman, so close to her right ear that it looked as if he would take a Tyson bite out of it. She put something into her purse that looked like a small blue box WITH TRANSLUCENT RIBBON. I cleared my throat, kicking myself for not answering the phone and giving his ass a piece of my mind last night when I'd had the chance. I coughed louder and heard Cameran laugh from her desk.

"Oh, uh, hi, Hannah."

"Morning, Eli."

He took a few steps away from the woman and slid his hand down the back of his freshly faded head. "You know Morgan, don't you? Rain's publicist?"

"Yes, of course," I said through tight teeth and locked jaws. "How are you? Good to see you." I walked up to her and gave a perfunctory kiss on both cheeks.

She returned the obligatory gesture, simultaneously smoothing out her frayed Fetish denim asymmetrical skirt, which made her look a bit hippy. I stood, letting them squirm for a moment, dragging it out as long as I possibly could.

Morgan looked like one of those women who'd been a pudgy tomboy most of her teen life and had recently discovered that she had curves but couldn't quite decode the world of fashion enough to understand how to flatter her size 8 figure. Her long straight weave had grown out enough to make it evident—at least to everyone else—that it was time to touch up her raggedy roots and invest in several new tracks. But then maybe I was being a bit too judgmental. I thought about the tiny boxes that Eli had given me and about the annoyed look on Cameran's face and decided that whatever was going on, I needn't pick at it. This scab would eventually fall off on its own.

"Uh, Morgan just stopped by because she was in town to pre-interview with some of the local press on Rain's behalf for the big Grammy campaign. Isn't that right, Morgan?"

"Yep, just trying to make sure we keep everything on lock over here. Rain may be in town toward the end of the week, so I wanted to set the stage."

"OK. Right. Well, I was just coming in to find out more about this two o'clock conference call and what you may or may not know about it, Eli." I shifted in my stiletto stirrups and fidgeted with the spiral notebook. "Just give me a ring when you're all done in here."

"No problem. I'll be over in a second."

"Good seeing you, Morgan. As always, let me know if there's anything I can do for you," I said, deliberately forgetting to close the door behind me. I glanced at Cameran from the corner of my eye. Her pout was even more pronounced, and her arms were now folded across her chest.

I couldn't get back to my desk fast enough, and within minutes Eli was in my doorway. He slid his hands into his pockets and gave me the most pitiful puppy-dog face I'd ever seen, surely aware that I hadn't had ample time to process any of what had just happened.

I looked at my blank computer screen and pretended not to notice him, angry with myself for hating confrontation so goddamn much.

He stepped into my office and rocked back and forth on his square-toed lace-up black Ferragamos. I wanted to beg him to stop for fear he'd crease the smooth Italian calfskin.

"Can we talk? Stop looking at that screen. You and I both know it's blank."

I looked away from the computer and flipped my freshly washed and curled hair over my shoulder, enjoying the extra wisp in my bangs.

"Hannah, what's going on? Why didn't you answer any of my calls last night? I was trying to get at you, Angel." He slithered closer to my desk.

"Huh? You called me last night? I got sleepy and called it an early night."

"Or were you too busy with your baller boyfriend to take my calls? I called you at least three times."

I idly flipped the pages of my day planner and motioned for him to close the door. "Whatever, Eli. You've got your hands full, or at least it seems that way to me. What did you want, and why do you care who I'm spending my personal time with anyway?"

"What do you mean, ma? You know you're my Angel, and since you didn't come into the office yesterday I just wanted to make sure no one was try'na clip those wings." He smiled proudly at his latest delivery of bullshit.

I sat back in my chair and crossed my hands in my lap. This man was good. I watched him go through all the motions. He looked especially tasty this morning, and I could smell the Gucci cologne on his crisp white shirt and perfectly knotted Burberry woven patchwork tie. I decided to avoid the outright confrontation and take a different approach.

"So what's the two o'clock call about today? And cut the shit; I've got a lot to get done before then."

He stepped back and cleared his throat, obviously caught off guard—not something I'd been very good at effecting with him in the past.

"I'm not sure. Nigel and Mannie said they needed to holla at all of us and to make sure you were on the call. So I two-wayed Cobra and told him to put it on his mommy's calendar."

"Is that all you know? Is there any reason I should be worried? I mean, really, I'm aware of the meetings that have been going on with

Universal, and I just want to know if there's any need for me to be concerned."

"Hannah, Angel, I told you before that I'd watch your back before I watched my own. You've been real sweet to me, and that deserves nothing but sweetness in return. I'll tell you what—let's get together tonight and go over everything that happens on the call. I'll even put out some extra feelers and see what else these jacks have up their sleeves."

"I can't. I have practice."

"What about after practice?"

"That's not gonna work for me, Eli. I'll be exhausted and barely able to think straight."

"Ooh, holla at your boy. You, not on your toes and thinking straight? Now a man like me needs to take complete advantage of some shit like that."

"Down, boy."

"Aight, suit yourself. Let a nigga know if you change your mind." He stood up straight and scaled around to my chair, leaning in to kiss me on the forehead like an unholy reverend.

I held my breath until he turned away, determined not to let him gauge my racing pulse. Reluctantly, I was turned on just as much by his cologne as I still was by his access and his ability to "put out feelers." The Ferragamos didn't hurt either. But now I was clearly hearing Grandpa Red in my ear: "Baby girl, if it was a snake it would have bit you." And since I didn't want to get bit, I knew better than to play with this snake's rattle.

"Hey Eli; I didn't get any flowers this morning. What happened?" I asked as he opened the door and froze just before stepping into the hallway.

"Oh, uh, I'm gonna have to talk to Cameran about that. I don't know what happened. Either she's slippin' or something went wrong at the flower joint."

"Oh? Well, don't worry her about it, I can ask her myself."

"No. No, don't do that. I wouldn't wanna put her on the spot; know what I mean? I'll handle it. My bad, baby. You know you're my Angel."

SSSsssssnake!

56

THE HOLIDAYS WERE RIGHT AROUND THE CORNER, AND THE CITY HAD A HIGH winter wonderland fever, evident by the red, white, and green lights on the trees that lined each and every downtown street. The holidays in Chicago were the only thing that made the frigid weather bearable for most of its warm-blooded dwellers, and driving down North Michigan Avenue was always a seasonal treat. Mums in extravagant kitschy furs with their nannys carrying their starched shopping bags were easy to spot exiting Saks, American Girls Place, or Neiman's. And you didn't have to look hard to find little girls dressed in furry hats, knitted scarves, and colorful mittens, holding their fathers' leather-clad hands, or couples sipping hot cocoa, strolling leisurely to the tune of their own romantic beat.

I sat at the red light on Michigan and Ohio and watched as the oversized corner Santa rang his bell and handed out candy canes to anyone who would cast the requisite caricature smile his way. White billowy gusts of air rushed from his mouth each time he exhaled. I glanced at the dash: twelve degrees (just wrong on so many levels)! Santa reached for his hat a millisecond too late when the Chicago hawk charged around the corner and snatched it in its frosty beak. St. Nick's cap went flying through the street, right past my windshield, and the expletives that suddenly barged from his mouth threw the earlier "ho-ho-hos" into question.

I pulled into the lot for practice and shook my head in disbelief that I'd been suspended until the bloody Christmas show. What had my life turned into? I was sacrificing everything and was being denied just as much: no team, no court time, no love life, no dignity!

Walking the hall to the practice room was humiliating. Some of the veterans ran past me and giggled. I even heard one of them spout out "Cheeks" as she passed. At least they were cute cheeks, I thought to myself. There was also the fact that the most eligible bachelor in Chicago had taken a liking to them. And I held on to that thought tightly during practice each time one of my teammates eagerly employed my new nickname.

For the most part, my fellow lowly rookies had my back. They patted my shoulder in support when we all lined up along the wall for weekly weigh-ins. Even Brooklyn, who still hadn't seen the court, whispered words of encouragement in my ear: "It could have happened to any one of us."

Brooklyn prepared to get weighed in with tears in her eyes and, having picked up Minnow's nasty habit, was chewing on nails that already were nearly nubs. She looked good to me, and I could really tell that she'd been working out. The definition in her arms and her back was flattering.

"I don't know if Coach is *ever* gonna let me get my shot." Brooklyn sighed. "It's different for you. Everyone knows you were set up."

"What're you talking about?" I forced under my breath. My eyes bulged like saucers, and my fingers were beginning to numb. Brooklyn hadn't even been at that game.

"Your briefs; everyone knows Mona and Hilton were behind that. But you're on your own with your personal choice in neon undergarments," she whispered, shaking her head before turning around to step on the scale.

"Come on, Brooklyn; let's see where the numbers fall for you," Coach said.

Brooklyn sucked up to the scale, and I thought I actually heard her knees knock.

"Well, Coach? Can I audition for my spot tonight?"

Coach looked at her clipboard and took the pen from her mouth. "Sorry, honey; maybe next week. I can totally tell that you're making great progress. But overall, you're not quite ready to represent us on the court. I'll line up some promotional work for you to do with some of the veterans, though. Hang in there. Maybe next time."

Brooklyn looked at Coach with despair and stepped down. My heart went out to her.

Coach looked at me and nodded at the scale before I manned up. But it wasn't my weight I was worried about.

"Hi, Coach," I greeted her, against my better judgment. She just looked down at her clipboard. I should've kept my mouth shut.

"Do you know how many phone calls and e-mails I've gotten from people about you? Do you know how many people would like to know if you've been relieved of your Diamond Dolls duties? Did you know the franchise owner called a meeting with me earlier today? Do you know what the topic of conversation was?" Nikki said all of this without taking a breath or looking up at me once.

"I apologize, Coach," I managed to get out. "Nothing like that will ever happen again." I watched her scribble a number next to my name and shoo me away with a nod, refusing me eye contact.

Dejected, I sat on the floor and watched as teams were selected for the game the following night. Sigh. Mona interrupted her conversation with Hilton to end my night on an even sourer note.

"Hey Cheeks, I thought you'd like to know that you have single-handedly destroyed in your two-second flash dance what we have worked years to build. This isn't a strip show; it's a professional cheerleading team."

The room had gone silent, and most of the team was listening to this abuse while Coach yapped away on her cell.

Mona tossed her platinum-blonde hair over her shoulder, and her ice-blue eyes rolled into the back of her head. I sat on the floor and outlined the scuffs in the hardwood and patiently waited for her head to spin around her neck.

"Mona, give it a rest. She gets the picture."

Was that a voice of reason I was hearing? I looked up from the floor, and saw Skye standing with her hands on her hips next to Aliyah.

"Whatever. I'm watching you, Cheeks." Then she bent down and whispered, "It's not like you weren't warned. Stay away from what doesn't belong to you." She turned around to strut back over to her squad.

When I got up to stretch for warm-downs, my notorious cheeks were aching from sitting so long. Aliyah stood next to me in the back of the room and winked. I wondered if she was also aware of Mona's secret sabotage. I stretched out my hamstrings and grabbed the back of my ankles, jutting my head through my legs. The blood rushed to my brain, and I thought I must have been short on oxygen when I saw Ali wink at me again. We rolled back up to a standing position and clapped to signal the end of practice. I eyed the door and prepared to make a run for it.

"Got a sec?" Aliyah asked as she sneaked up on me from behind, halting my escape attempt. "Listen, don't let her get to you. You've got to stay strong if you're gonna come out of this on top. Remember what I told you."

"I know, but it's hard. She's just so cruel."

"Sounds like you need a fun night out. What're you doing this weekend?" Ali was talking so low I could barely hear her.

"It's my girls' birthday, so we're going out. Other than that, I might have to work." I lowered my voice to match hers.

"Where are you going to take them?"

"I dunno. We haven't decided yet," I said, looking around the room discreetly.

"Let me recommend a place I know you guys'll love. I'll give you the address. Trust me; you'll have the time of your life." She jotted down some info and folded the tiny piece of Diamond Dolls stationery before taking my hand and wrapping it tightly around her note. I bent over to put the tiny paper in my bag, and when I looked up to thank her, she was gone.

57

"HERE'S TO HANNAH'S CUTE LITTLE ASS," BRITT SAID, AND RAISED HER CHAMpagne glass for a toast. "We've all seen it before, but there's something to be said about seeing it under LIGHTS, CAMERAS, and in the middle of all that ACTION!"

We sipped our floating orchid cocktails on one of the draped daybeds on the enclosed riverfront terrace at Japonais, the ultra-chic Eurasian Japanese restaurant. It felt like forever since the orange thong debacle had gone down, but we hadn't had the opportunity to all get together to veg out and vibe. The twins' birthday celebration had had to be pushed back when I got called out of town to New York for a mandatory executive meeting on their b-day weekend. But tonight we'd managed to sync our calendars and have our Brats' night out in belated honor of Brittany and Kennedy.

I picked up a lobster spring roll from the myriad of delicacies on the oversized wooden candlelit table. "It's been over a month; I guess I should be able to laugh about it," I said through a mouthful of buttery lobster. "But I'd rather toast the birthday girls, even if we are a little late."

Britt smiled and took another sip of her Stolichnaya vodka cocktail. "Hey, it's cool with me; it's not like I'm aging. That'll never happen." She flipped her bone-straight weave over her shoulder. She'd been trying out new looks that Poppie, her new mystery "plumber," had hinted he might like. Her new coif was straight to the bone and sweeping her ass. She said he liked the Pocahontas meets Cleopatra ride and that she'd taken to giving it to him whenever he requested.

"Well, they say some things get better with time," Kennedy said, looking even thinner than I'd remembered just a month ago. She was in a very sexy black A.B.S. sheer-chiffon-over satin minidress with a seriously plunging V-neck. I couldn't help but notice how her collarbone jutted out from her chest and how the definition in her ribs made her look emaciated. "Isn't that right, Hannah-Bug?"

"Yep, that's what I'm counting on at Monday's big Christmas game. You guys still coming?" I took another spring roll and shoved half of it into my mouth.

"I'll be there. We won't start filming again till after the Christmas holiday," Kennedy said, swigging back her drink and batting her naturally long eyelashes.

"Sweetie, how the hell is that a reality show if they're not taping you doing *real* shit *all* the time? Like they should be here right now watching Hannah snort up all her food," Britt said as I reached for a Tokyo drum. "That shit ain't reality TV; it's an oxymoron of a sham, just like that jumbo shrimp she's about to stuff into her mouth. What's jumbo about a goddamn shrimp?"

I bit down on the Yaki Yaki and sucked up the sake-garlic soy sauce.

I'd been ignoring the hunger pangs I'd felt all day just so I could reserve my appetite for their delish Japanese cuisine.

"Happy birthday, guys." I toasted them and raised one of the Japonais Startinis the waitress had brought over. The terrace was packed with beautiful people, and most of the men had attempted to patronize our private soiree at one point or another. The twins picked up their fresh drinks and yelled out in response to my call.

"Happy birthday, us!"

All the men and several of the women on the terrace followed suit. Britt stood up from the bed and moved one of the sheer drapes aside to take a bow before raising her glass and mouthing "thank you" to her admirers. She was looking oh-so-fab in all her thickness, rocking a black Stella McCartney open-bra-back dress with a deep sweetheart neckline. We giggled to see her tug at the bottom of it whenever she stood to prevent it from rising to greet her bikini wax. She liked it that way, and apparently so did the rainbow coalition of slick Gucci- and Armani-clad men.

We finished our food, politely declining several offers for seconds or thirds from various partygoers seated on the daybeds and cushy lounge chairs nearby. Kennedy looked at me with a twisted expression and threw her arms into the air. "Where to now, chickies? I'm feeling realll good."

I opened my Neiman's Giselle bag and rifled through its compartments in search of that tiny piece of paper Ali had entrusted to me. "I'll handle that; let's just get the bill and get out of here," I said, motioning for the waitress, who informed us that our exorbitant tab had been covered by one of the owners (a close *personal* friend of Brittany's) before handing us our coats.

We headed out into the December frost to hop into the limo, and I promptly gave the chauffeur the folded Dolls stationery with the scribbled address. I was confused when he turned down an industrial street just off North Avenue and pulled up to the valet who was standing beneath big neon letters atop the building: VIPs. Chauffeur lowered the dividing window and assured me of the address. Britt grinned at Kennedy and me as if she'd just been handed disease-free hot sex on a platter with no strings attached!

"Ooh, Hannah, why didn't you tell us this is what you had up your sleeve?" Britt ran her fingers through the ends of her hair and grabbed her black Tod's snakeskin clutch. "What the hell are we waiting for? This shit is gonna be hot. Happy birthday to me!"

The music blared from several speakers except when the invisible emcee introduced the next dancer over the microphone as we were led to the general seating area in the middle of the adjacent carpeted room.

Brittany was already talking to a server in a black-and-white polyester micro cocktail waitress uniform, custom fitted for her 36DDDs, when I got over to our table, left of the main stage. The two big shiny poles made me think of Chris Rock's comment about fathers being solely responsible for keeping their daughters off the pole. That would have been quite a challenge in here tonight, I thought, as a long-legged blonde with very augmented rippling breasts attacked it awkwardly. Her schoolgirl costume remained on the floor when she was done with the shiny silver prop. She pranced around, collecting bills in her feathery green garter from middle-aged googly-eyed men with wedding rings.

Numerous couples, a few women, and a large throng of enthused men were partying, drinking, gawking, or fumbling through their wallets. With the exception of the waitresses who prowled from table to table, the aisles remained clear and free of traffic so the dancers could give twenty-dollar lap dances, or aggressively solicit them.

"Ooh yeah, you guys pick out a good one. You know I like my girls on the thicker, more natural side," Britt said, looking around the club at all the prospects. "And don't bring no skanks over here. I see some skanks up in this place," she yelled, and turned her nose up in the direction of a very buxom stripper with hairy legs and ashy elbows, mocking her apparent shortcomings. I wondered how the hell she was able to be so discriminating under the dim fluorescent lights. This was definitely not my usual scene, and I couldn't imagine why Aliyah had suggested it—even if it did suit Brittany purr-fectly.

Fascinated, I looked around and noticed an older gentleman in a crisp tuxedo concealing a hidden headset. He was standing at the entry to a private room and channeled a secret service agent or a very cute Bond Boy. I wondered if a senator or a congressman was behind the tinted wraparound windows with an Anna Nicole look-alike. The big steel door behind him opened, and Maverick Mason and Derrick Styles strolled out together, talking on their cells. Both the Chicago Diamonds guards were notorious derelicts, but Mav definitely had more miles under his belt. When they looked over in my general direction, I slowly slid halfway under the tiny round wooden table, putting my hand up to shield my face, unsure why I even cared if I was seen in this particular establishment. Somehow it just seemed wrong.

"Kennedy," I whispered loudly, trying to snag her attention as she unscrupulously watched the new girl on the stage perform intricate pole and Marlboro tricks. Snoop Dogg's "Drop It Like It's Hot" blared from the speakers in the ceiling, completely drowning me out.

"What're you doing down there?" she asked after I poked her with my French manicured tip.

"Look behind you and see if Maverick and Styles have left already."

"What?"

"Just turn around and look for me." I tried to scoot back into my seat but was somehow stuck between the chair and the table.

"Maverick Mason and Derrick Styles? In here? They're in here?" Her voice climbed an octave with each inquiry.

"Yes! In here! At least they were. Now I need you to sneak a peek and tell me if they're *still* in here." I pushed at the damn chair with my back and fell completely under the table onto the carpeted floor. As I stared at the globs of gum that had been squashed and stuck beneath the table, the song came to an end, and I heard the emcee tap on the mike, preparing to announce the next girl. I hauled myself off the floor and back into my chair, ready to give my complete attention to the amnesia-in-a-shot-glass I'd ordered.

"I hope you enjoyed the talented Susannah coming down from the main stage. But trust me, boys; you're gonna want to cash your checks for this next duo and maybe reconsider paying that mortgage this month. Coming to the stage next are two of the sexiest dancers this side of the Mississippi. Brace yourselves, sailors, for Sugar and Spice."

As Sugar and Spice sashayed from behind the curtain in teeny tiny purple-and-white cheerleader costumes and five-inch thigh-high white lace-up stripper boots, I spit out my tequila shot and the Mexican drink went everywhere.

Kennedy shook me and yelled over the music. "What's wrong?"

"Ohmigod! Sugar and Spice—" I blinked hard and looked back at the stage. "Also known as Mona and Hilton!"

58

THE STALL DOOR IN THE LOCKER ROOM BATHROOM CLOSED BEHIND ME. I pulled up my uniform skirt and double-checked that my briefs were securely in place—both pair! We'd been given red briefs to go with our red-and-white sexy Santa halftime costumes, and mine were neatly tucked away under the white briefs I had to wear for the first half of the game.

I still hadn't said a word to Mona or to Hilton about their part-time side hustle, and for the moment I'd decided that the very fact that they knew that I knew that they knew that I knew was adequate ammo to get me through the night. Mona had been keeping her distance since I'd walked into the locker room, and Hilton had switched lockers so she wouldn't have to make eye contact with me. They'd gotten the surprise of their lives when they looked down at the idiot who'd spit tequila all over the bottom of their stage only to find that the idiot was their arch-nemesis, Cheeks.

Tonight, the locker room rocked with heightened energy. Traditionally, every Diamond Doll on the team participated in the Christmas game halftime show. It was the biggest, most hyped-out show of the basketball season, and the only way anyone was excluded from the festivities was if she didn't make weigh-ins. There were twenty-three Dolls scheduled to perform together at halftime. And Brooklyn wasn't one of them. The sinister scale had denied her by a measly half point.

Needless to say, with the intense energy and chaos, the mishap potential was exponentially greater than on any other night. I'd arrived a half hour early to secure my locker, touch up my makeup, and get dressed before the blow dryers, hairspray, and estrogen seized the room. We had a makeup artist on hand for the game, and I made sure I was the first in her chair. My lashes were secured and my red pout perfected before anyone else could dull her liner pencils. I couldn't wait for Minnow to arrive so I could share the highlights of the previous weekend with her. But there was one other person I needed to have a word with first.

"Hey Ali; how's it going?" I touched her on the shoulder and settled into a most victorious smile.

"I have a feeling I know what that look of sheer satisfaction is all about. I was wondering how long it was gonna take before you took that little trip to the Promised Land."

"Oh-my-God!" I said. "I don't know how to thank you. I just—"

"No need; just leveling out the playing field. Now you can concentrate on your game." She pulled at her white skirt and turned around so I could help her with her zipper. She'd put on a couple pounds, and it actually looked good on her.

"Thanks," she said, and aligned the skirt's zipper with the small of her back. "I know it's a bit tight, but there's nothing I can really do about it now." She turned back around to face me and whispered into my ear, "I'm pregnant." She smiled and threw her arms around me. *OK.* I hugged her back. She pulled out of the embrace and looked down at her watch before grabbing my arm and rushing me outside into the hallway.

"You can't say anything to anyone about this. You and Skye are the only two people on the team who know." She looked up and down the hallway.

I didn't know what was up, but I waited patiently in the hallway for her to elaborate. In a matter of seconds I heard a whistle sound from the opposite direction. She grabbed my hand and pulled me with her as she ran down the hall and ducked into one of the smaller rooms off the concourse that was occasionally used for interviews.

"Shh; don't say a word."

She opened the door, and I closed it nervously behind me. Before I could turn around she'd jumped right into the arms of Shepherd Hunt. I watched uncomfortably as he kissed her deeply. Lately, he'd been playing exceptionally well, and all the sportscasters were commenting on how he'd "really found his rhythm" and was in this "great zone." A six-foot-six guard forward, he'd taken his average points per game from 13.5 to 22.7 in a matter of a month. If they only knew.

Shepherd put Ali down and bent over to her tummy and rubbed it, cooing softly. He'd turned to mush in front of my very eyes.

"How you feeling, babe?" he asked, straightening. He smoothed her hair. "Feeling sick at all?"

"I'm OK. A little yucky earlier, but I'm better now. Look—my skirt is getting tighter already. Hannah even had a rough time zipping it for me."

I looked at the two of them gushing in their own private world and couldn't help but be a little envious.

"It really wasn't that rough," I mumbled.

I had no idea why my presence had been requested, so to speak; this was clearly a family moment. I leaned back and felt the doorknob press into my spine. Shepherd watched me as if he were sizing me up and making decisions. Finally he smiled. I returned his gaze, concluding that he was handsome in a slightly nerdy kind of way. He had a goatee and smooth dark skin, and his wavy hair was faded low. I'd noticed that his exceptionally long lanky arms must've made it easy for him to carry the ball, and I figured his deep brown eyes and striking features would probably mix well with Ali's soft dark hair and—

"You know you look like a pretty smart girl, Hannah. But I can't figure out for the life of me why you passed on the best thing out there—second to me, of course," he said, ending my game of "What's Your Baby Gonna Look Like." "But since I'm taken, that would make my man, Max, the absolute best catch on the free market." He furrowed his eyebrows. "Now, Ali thinks you're pretty adorable, and Max had nothing but good things to say about you too—except, of course, that you wouldn't give him the time of day." He'd let Ali's hand go and was now standing directly in front of me with his arms crossed over his chest. "Don't get me wrong; I'm all for making a man chase you for a minute—you know, let him figure out that you're worth it. But there comes a point when he doesn't wanna play that game any-more. And when that happens, he's gonna move on to someone else. And believe me, there will be someone else. There's *always* someone else."

"Honey, that's enough. She's still figuring it out. I know you want what's best for your boy, but it'll work itself out." She glanced at her watch. "We've gotta go."

"OK. I just hope she knows she lost a good one, and I'm not just saying that cuz he's my boy." He ended and turned back around to face Ali. "Now, give me one more of those kisses." He grabbed her by the hand, wrapped his arms around her, and lifted her in the air. "Take care of my baby in there," he whispered sweetly into her ear. "Love you both." He blew her another kiss as we slid out the door and back down the hall in the opposite direction.

I followed Ali all the way to the locker room in disbelief. What had I just seen? My fingers were throbbing.

"What about the rules, Ali? Couldn't you get in a world of trouble for that? I mean, you guys are sooo cute, but what about—"

"Listen, I can't really go into it, but we've been together for over a year. The baby wasn't planned, but as you can see, we're excited. This is gonna be my last season cheering, and after this, I'll only be cheering for Shep and signing autographs as his baby's mama," she said proudly.

"But what if someone finds out?" I asked naively, still without a clue.

"Like who?" She pulled me away from the locker room door.

"Like Coach, that's who."

"You mean Nikki? Who do you think set me up with him in the first place?"

With only two minutes left on the clock in the second quarter, we filed into the locker room to get ready for the big number. No one had called me "Cheeks" all night, and I knew Sugar and Spice had put the word out: "Ix-nay on the Eeks-chay!"

The hair and makeup crew touched everyone up while we nipped and tucked tags, hems, and anything else that needed attention on each other's sexy Santa suits. Coach counted down the minutes till liftoff, and I pulled up my red velvet miniskirt and happily saw my red briefs right where they belonged. Coach winked, never uttering a word.

We were halfway through the "Jingle Bells Rock" medley and were coming to the part of the routine where we pair off and face each other in our kick lines. The set choreography was to toss the basketballs to our partner as the song hit **"Jingle bell, jingle bell, jingle bell rock/ Jingle bells chime in jingle bell time/Dancing and prancing in Jingle Bell Square/ In the frosty air."** And on cue, the Diamonds mascot initiated the big basketball toss and threw the first one to Elle, the second to Six, and the third one straight to Mona, who appeared to be a half count behind the music. I looked over my shoulder when I heard an ear-splitting shriek so piercing that Elle immediately dropped her ball to the floor instead of tossing it to me. Everyone looked down the line at Mona, who was doubled over in apparent pain. In slow motion, she fell forward straight to the floor as her screams reverberated through the stands. At first I thought she'd been pummeled in the stomach with the ball, but when she stood up I quickly realized that she'd been hit directly between the eyes in her recently resculpted nose. That had to hurt! Blood was quickly filling her cupped hands as she hobbled off the court, never looking back.

Chloe quickly shifted her position in the kick line, and Hilton happily picked up where Mona had left off. She tossed the last ball back to the mascot and began the kick-split ripple as if nothing had ever gone awry. Jumping in the air and landing on cue in my infamous Chinese split in front of my squad kick line was pure perfection. I lifted my head on the final count, looked into the camera that was bobbing in my face, and winked my super MAC-lashy eye.

FOURTH QUARTER

60

THE MACARONI AND CHEESE AND THE CORN BREAD WERE BAKING IN THE OVEN while Nana was on the phone explaining to me, from the Sunshine State and for the third time, how to finish the sweet potatoes. Roman had recently grown bitterly tired of the Chicago arctic and, after a three-minute discussion with Nana, had decided to set up shop in West Palm Beach. Nana couldn't stop gushing to anyone who'd listen about her very big house on the golf course "with a real live palm tree smack-dab in the front yard." But tonight, between culinary lessons, I was growing impatient still trying to finish the potatoes while being forced to hear about the hairless cat who'd jumped into her new pool. Brittany was no help, either. She was far too busy taste-testing absolutely everything, regardless of whether or not it was done, so Kennedy graciously grabbed the phone from my ear after I'd nearly dropped it into the boiling pot of waiting water.

"Gimme the phone. I'll finish them. Go check on the corn bread," she directed, and started talking into the receiver. "Hey Nana, it's Sweets. So how's Florida?"

The kitchen smelled delish, and the dinner that I was secretly preparing for Max was coming along nicely. Britt sucked her fingers between finishing the bottle of Cab that had been opened a few minutes earlier.

It was the biggest holiday of the year, New Year's Eve. The team had been on the road since the Christmas game, which had given me plenty of time to think about Max and make some serious decisions. After Aliyah's revelation about her relationship with Shepherd, I'd decided shortly thereafter to take matters into my own hands with my own nonexistent love affair.

Because of the holidays, work had slowed considerably, and the time away from Eli had been just enough to allow me to formulate a plan. He'd informed me that he'd be going back to New York to be with his family until the new year. Coincidentally, Cobra had called last night to talk about Rain, and after beating around the bush for thirty minutes and assuring me yet again that he wasn't one to gossip, so I didn't hear it from him, but he'd overheard Cameran booking a flight to accompany Eli. Same flight! Same hotel! Same room!

Oh, well. It was what it was. Even though she wasn't my top choice for Assistant of the Year, I still hoped she was capable of handling that ride.

The Brats had come over earlier that morning, and we'd planned the entire evening. I made a big soul food dinner complete with collard greens, corn bread, sweet potatoes, mac and cheese, corn on the cob, and fried chicken. I also put together a gift basket with candles and chocolate-covered strawberries for the first half of his dessert, and for the second half—well . . . me! I envisioned him opening the door to find me holding the basket of goodies wearing my new red silk Frederick's long slit silk dress with a rhinestone side, spaghetti straps, and mega-low cleavage.

I balanced against Kennedy's shoulders and slid my feet into the clear two-band stripper shoes that had been gifted by Britt. Ahhh—the pièce de résistance!

"Now, you don't think this is too over the top?" I turned to the side and sucked in my stomach. "Look at all this skin."

"That's the damn point," Britt said. "It's a gorgeous dress. I know it's a lot of skin, split straight up to your crotch. Scrumptious. And it's not like it's gonna be on for long anyway," she reminded me.

Kennedy walked up the stairs and down the hall into the room. "OK, the food is all packed up on the cart I borrowed from Dallas and ready to go downstairs to Max's place."

"Now remember, five minutes after I leave, that's when you come down and knock on his door to deliver the food."

"No worries," Kennedy assured me, turning me back around to look in the mirror with her. "Damn, you look good. He's not gonna know what hit him."

"Yeah, a real come-fuck-me dress." Britt licked her teeth. "Arrrggghh," she growled.

"Too over the top?" I turned to look at Kennedy for approval. I was growing more nervous by the second.

"Not for what you're after tonight, Hannah-Bug. This will definitely be something he won't forget. And that's the whole point, right?"

"You're pulling out all the stops tonight. Shep must have really gotten to your ass," Britt teased.

"You think?"

Movado check: eight forty-five. It was time to get moving. Britt had called downstairs much earlier to ask Dallas whether Max would be spending the evening in or out celebrating. He informed her that Max had come in around five and had asked Dallas to put his car up for the night. He'd told him something about spending New Year's Eve relaxing at home so he could be ready for the big game the next afternoon. They'd be playing Orlando, and I knew he was going up against his rival from college, Zach Palmer. Their rivalry was the biggest deal and had been written up in all of the local papers. So it looked like all systems were go and operation "Go Get Your Man" was on course for phase three.

My glam-squad was on the clock. They fussed for a few more minutes with my hair, which I had to admit was now perfect, and Britt did her due diligence and dabbed a touch of Dior behind my ears, "specifically for when he hugs you." A divine visual. I exhaled and knew it was game time when Kennedy grabbed my wrist to sync watches.

61

THE BRATS WERE BOTH STANDING IN THE CORRIDOR MAKING LEWD REMARKS AS the doors to the elevator closed. I was trembling as I rifled through the love basket. There was a sheer mesh-and-satin chemise embroidered with hearts that I'd hidden beneath the candles and Shiraz in the goodie basket—just in case. I crossed my fingers and closed my eyes, and as soon as the elevator began dropping floors, I lost my balance and swayed a little too far to the left in my five-inchers, almost toppling over onto the wicker basket. In the name of the Father and of the Son and of the Holy—

The doors opened, and I peeked out to see if Max was anywhere around. Timidly, I inched off the elevator before turning around and jumping back on. My fingers were starting to go numb, having nothing to do with it registering a frigid twenty-one degrees outside. The elevator doors started to shut—with me behind them. *In Nomine Patri, et Filii, et Spiritus Sancti. Amen.* (Two languages were better than one, even if one of them was already dead.) I sucked in a gust of air and threw my hand against the door. I peeked out again, and stepped off—this time for good.

Walking the length of the first long hallway, I fidgeted before turning down the second shorter hallway. Once in front of his door, I knocked.

Nothing.

My stomach was churning, but I forced myself to knock again, this time even louder. I inspected my breasts, which had been plumped and tweaked and were situated quite openly in the barely-there bra inset of my dress. I wanted very badly to wipe away the perspiration that was prepping to drip down onto the satiny silk bodice. While still contemplating my next move I pushed my ear against the door to see if I could hear inside.

"Maxie, there's someone at the door. Can you get it, sweetie? I'm still in the shower."

Ahhh!

I pulled my ear away from the door and pressed it right back against it. After a few seconds I heard the water shut off.

"Never mind, Maxie; I'll get it."

On automatic pilot, I bolted down the first hallway, running all the way on the balls of my feet in the friggin' five-inchers. Just as I heard the locks turn, I ducked around the corner and dropped to my knees. The door swung open, and I heard the woman's voice again.

"Hello? Is there anyone out here?"

I bit my lip.

I could feel her presence and was desperate for a peek. I crouched as close to the nubby carpet as possible and cautiously eased my head around the corner.

I could see the bottom of her robe swinging around and brushing the carpeted floor. I slowly raised my eyes to her face. It was that same striking, exotic, beautiful, no-named chick! She stood in the hallway, tightening her robe, while water dripped from her long curly hair onto its white satiny hood. Daintily, she dabbed her face with a towel.

I held my breath, hoping it would somehow prevent her from smelling the perfume that now overpowered the hallway.

As she was closing the door I heard Max's voice. Surely if he came into the hallway he wouldn't give up the search as easily.

"Who was it?"

"No one; I must be hearing—"

The door closed, locks turned, and I sat crouched in a leapfrog position for what felt like ten minutes, partly overcome with disappointment and just too damn weak to move. The elevator doors opened, and I glanced at my watch. Hell, if it was anyone other than Kennedy, I'd just stretch out and play dead!

"What are you doing out here on the floor?" She ran over to me, leaving the cart filled with food next to the elevator.

"Shhh" was all I could manage.

"Are you OK?" she whispered in a panic.

I pointed feverishly at the elevator, grabbed her hands, and pulled myself up from the floor. Holding on to her arm for dear life, I scurried down the longer hallway, looking back over my shoulder furtively. The elevator doors rebounded, and I stepped on, catching one of my heels in the tiny space between the shaft and the floor from hell. I yanked and yanked at it. And the spiky shitty fucking five-inch stripper heel snapped right off! Perfect.

Happy fucking New Year!

And then I just went numb for a while.

Getting through the January game/practice schedule was simply a grinding exercise in self-discipline. I dragged myself listlessly through the days when I had to be bothered with anything Diamond Dolls. I couldn't manage to extinguish the burning blahs no matter how hard I practiced or how hard I performed. Blah blah blah blah blah blah. It stayed with me for the first three weeks of January practices and all four of my mandatory squad games.

The first couple of games I'd cheered that month were like a smoky blur. From the moment I stepped foot into the stadium, everything sounded like drowned-out noise, especially the locker-room babble that was barely audible because of the incessant buzzing in my head— a sort of humming pitch that resounded loudly and continuously between my goddamn ears!

Eventually all the games became routine, and I just went through the motions, comfortably numb. What I'd been so connected to, so passionate and so fanatical about just a few weeks prior was now just another series of steps I had to go through to get to the end of my day.

Coach even commented on my lackluster sideline cheering and strongly suggested that I turn it up a notch. "Whatever is going on in your personal life, I'm here for you as a coach, but you just can't let it affect your performance on my court. This just isn't like you, Hannah." My attitude wasn't exactly dismissive, but it definitely bordered on complacent.

Kennedy suggested that I put all of my negative energy into my routines. "No really, Bug; it might help. It's just one example of method acting, you know, like channeling." Great suggestion, I'd thought, and hoped it would help me snap out of this slump. Something was gonna have to help me get my head back in the game, especially after Coach told me that I'd be one of the Diamond Dolls appearing on the Fox morning show at the beginning of February. She'd said she wanted to show diversity, and a rookie, especially one with my level of media experience, would add flavor to the mix. Ironically, I'd be taking Mona's place, since she'd still be recovering from a series of necessary surgeries (something about missing bone cartilage) when it was time to tape the show. But even that amazing news didn't do much to relieve my heavy case of the blues. I just blamed it on the latest trendy diagnosable disorder: <u>S</u>easonal <u>A</u>ffective <u>D</u>isorder. SAD! I was just plain <u>S</u>-<u>A</u>-<u>D</u>!

63

FEBRUARY BLEW IN LIKE AN UNHAPPY BLIZZARD AND TURNED MY ALREADY SOUR mood to shit. Work was the only thing not negatively affected by the four-inch slushy snowstorms or the below-zero Windy City wintry days. Nigel and Mannie could have given less than two craps about cars not starting because the damn engines were fucking frozen or about tires rotating in place and refusing to budge, stuck deep in the Chicago snowbanks.

These days, all that mattered to the big bosses was Rain's performance at the Grammys and the aggressively pushy campaign to nab her an award or two and inevitably up the equity at RockStar. Everything in my world was now black and white, and it was becoming more apparent that I was gonna have to request some time off from the Dolls so I could be in Manhattan for the overhyped awards show.

Great. More time with Eli the s-s-snake. I now dreaded being around him longer than a New York minute, and lately that was still too long. I couldn't figure out for the life of me what had made him so attractive in the first place. His cologne now smelled slimy; his square-toed shoes, slimy; his designer suits, slimy; and his creepy thousand-dollar gifts in the creepier little boxes that he gave out whimsically to anyone old enough to have pubic hair—slimy! Cobra had been right about him and Cameran—not that I'd ever doubted him, cuz if he says so himself, he's just not one to gossip.

After the holidays, Eli went back to being the senior vice president, and for a short time Cameran tried to become the SVP's hottest honey. He allowed that to go on for a little less than a week before calling her into his office for a "chat." For a while she'd been sad and had moped around. Then she got mad and slammed doors and desk drawers, before finally deciding to get even. She took a week to carefully survey the office landscape before deciding to make Cobra her accomplice. She befriended him with lunch dates and homemade cookies just prior to divulging confidential information about the fate of the company: a probable merger and acquisition of RockStar by Universal, and Eli's first-hand knowledge and assistance with it all.

Cobra made a beeline straight for me, especially after Cameran bent over his desk and leaned in closely to say, "Oh yeah, I almost forgot—Eli isn't planning on taking anyone from RockStar Chicago with him to the other side!"

I sat back in the chair while Cobra dished the news, and though I wasn't surprised, I didn't want to let on that I'd been remotely aware of the situation. All along it had been my plan to take Cobra with me, no matter what was going to happen around here. But because I hadn't made any definite future decisions, I'd put off telling him and thought it unfortunate that he'd found out this way.

"Cobra, I know things seem bleak right now, but you'll have my total and complete loyalty no matter what." I fiddled with the texture of the double-belted lime-green Valentino suede pants Kennedy had given me when she'd hit size 0 last month.

He looked around the room in a disgusted daze and took one deep breath after another. "I know you've always had my back, Hannah, but did you know about this?"

The expression on his face resembled that of a little boy who'd just been told there was no such thing as Santa.

"No, but it doesn't surprise me."

I leaned back again in the chair and intertwined my fingers like a steeple, feeling slightly sinful to be telling a partial white lie so close to a church.

"This is a shady, cutthroat business, and you only have a couple of choices when you're dealing with those who would rather slice your throat. You can run until you find a company that embraces a different set of morals and values, or you can fight back. And frankly, morals and the music industry rarely go hand in hand."

He leaned in and for the first time completely focused on what I was saying. "But how do I fight back?"

"You have to play their game. You've got an ally now, even if it's for the wrong reasons. Use Cameran to your advantage."

"I'm listening."

"Well, Eli fucked with her head, among other things, and she'd love to get him back even more than she thinks she already has. She reads everything, e-mails and letters, and takes every single call, even listening in on most of them. She knows a lot more than she thinks she knows."

"So what you're saying is that I need to pull it out of her."

"Help her navigate her way through her own head."

"I think I see where you're going with this."

"Then, if we can manage to get something heavy on Eli, maybe we can expose his hand. That's all I'm really saying."

Clearly, I wasn't happy with Eli undermining me, and it was apparent that all his sweet slick talk about watching out for me before he watched out for himself was B.S. And now that I'd lost the best thing to come my way, I saw Elijah Strong for what he was—a total wackass!

I pushed back my chair and tightened the straps on my green snakeskin Jimmy Choo cutout pumps. "OK, you go work on your assignment and let me take care of the rest," I said, and nodded toward the door. "And make sure I'm booked to get out of here for New York first thing Friday. And don't forget to double-check everyone's seats for the awards show on Sunday. I need to make sure everything is in place for Rain. She's worked too damn hard for anything to go wrong now." I crossed my legs and put the pen in my mouth. "And get Kimber on the line. Tell her it's urgent."

64

THE WAITING AREA OUTSIDE OF TRU RECORDS HAD ALWAYS BEEN ULTRA-SLEEK and mod—a distinctive European vibe mixed with urban flavor. The last time I waited for anything in this office was when I'd had my very first interview with Kimber's assistant five years ago. It felt as if several lifetimes had passed since that fateful day when I exited the elevator banks in a Banana Republic navy blue wool suit that was an entire size too big, on loan from my college roommate, who'd convinced me that I'd needed to be trendy yet chic. Needless to say, when I got to the office wearing my borrowed duds and carrying my college backpack, everyone in the super-fab organization was decked out in Baby Phat, Ecko, and Tommy—complete with matching Timbs and Manolos. But even though I'd stuck out like a very sore thumb, I'd managed to win over Kimber's assistant, who said she'd made the exact same mistake her first time on the block and if it hadn't been fatal for her, it needn't be for me either.

The new receptionist seated behind the big glass-and-steel desk asked that I take a seat while she called for Kimber. I took off my fitted black Italian wool-and-cashmere Oscar de la Renta coat and sat in the burnt-orange leather-and-chrome chair. I flipped through the *Seventeen* magazine I'd picked up at the newsstand at LaGuardia earlier that morning and scanned every page. Rain was one of the features in the celebrity section, and though I'd given final approval on the photos selected, it was still exciting to see the layout in the actual publication. There she was, more chic and beautiful than ever. She looked hot: youthful, and approachable, yet definitely admirable—not always the easiest image to convey in pictures. Her quotes were funny and grounded, just as we'd practiced. And again, my team had done A+ work. I took out my cell to gush to Cobra for a job well done, just when Kimber appeared from around the corner.

"Well, hello, Ms. Love, so glad to see you." She held out her arms and hugged me tightly.

"Ms. Love? You know better than that."

"Why don't you follow me back?" she said, and nodded to the receptionist.

I followed Kimber down the long hallway and into a huge corner office. Framed gold and platinum albums hung on all four walls, representing the artists she'd worked with since she began her reign at Tru Records more than fifteen years ago. I especially liked the platinum album behind her espresso-tinged leather chair with Mink's name on it. She was the last artist I'd worked with before leaving Tru for Rock-Star and also the first to give me a taste of what it was like to break a baby act and take the artist to the next level.

Kimber sat down and thanked her assistant, who'd put two steaming cups of coffee on the sleek steel-and-glass desk between us. "Caramel macchiato with soy, right?" she asked, smiling at me as her assistant nodded and asked if that would be all. "For now, Farrah, thank you. Please close the door behind you."

I sat down in the seat across from Kimber and crossed my legs. "You remembered?" I fondled the cup. "You have no idea how much I need this right now. I haven't had a second to stop and do anything since I stepped off the plane this morning. And I really hope you know how much I appreciate your seeing me on such short notice like this."

"Of course, Love; why wouldn't I? You're one of the only level-headed execs still in this crazy business. I have to keep you on my good side. I've been watching you, and you're really making some serious moves with Rain over at RockStar. The buzz around her Grammy odds has been really strong. You must be thrilled."

"That's what I wanted to talk to you about."

"By all means. I'm all ears when it comes to the hottest new female artist to hit the airwaves in five years."

I rummaged through my black LV skinny briefcase and pulled out an envelope marked "confidential" that Cobra had prepared for me. "Like I told you on the phone, this can't go any further than this office. It hasn't been leaked to the trades yet, and I'd hate for that to happen before it's time."

Kimber picked up the phone and told Farrah to hold all calls until further instructed. "Of course, but is this about what I think it's about?" she asked as she pulled out her black rectangular eyeglasses, which were a bit thicker than I'd remembered.

She opened the envelope and read through the package of documents that had been discreetly organized at my office back in Chicago. She shook her head and furrowed the arched brows on her perfectly made-up face.

Kimber was a tall, very thin woman who always looked as if she was in the middle of taking care of extremely serious business, even when she was lunching with her mother, which she'd done every Wednesday at noon since the day I'd met her and begun confirming the hour-long dates with the elder Mrs. Dawson. She was extremely astute and had earned her MBA from Harvard two years after she'd finished her undergrad work in music management. Though most people would agree that she was an attractive woman, she never let her sex appeal overshadow her intellect and business savvy in the workplace. She'd lived on the Upper East Side as long as I could remember and had never married or had any children.

I watched her thumb through the pages again, carefully and with precision. Her fingernails were flawlessly manicured, and I knew Farrah had already confirmed her standing 7 p.m. Friday mani/pedi appointment. I'd always respected her sense of style, which was impeccable, and had started emulating her sophisticated business semicasual dress the first day I'd gotten hired to be her second assistant. She didn't believe in wearing sneakers or mules to work, but she never berated anyone else who did. Her belief was that they'll see you before they hear you, and she always wanted "them" to know that she meant business. I'd spent many weekends at Lerner, TJ Maxx, consignment stores, and occasionally Strawberry looking for the appropriate separates to piece together to show that I, too, meant business—though on a much smaller budget.

The enviable thing about Kimber was the way she always made everyone feel that she could relate to them, regardless of their rung on the ladder. And her presence was powerful, which made it nearly impossible to ignore just how fierce she looked whenever she walked down the hip-hop halls of one of the youngest record labels to successfully compete in the game.

Kimber always called everything she did strategy, and I'd sit and listen for hours about the mechanics and relevance of "the most power-ful tool in business." It was when I became her first assistant and a ju-nior product manager that I'd decided to go to business school at night. She'd said that if I came to the table fully equipped, I'd already be two steps ahead of the game, but she warned that being a woman would automatically put me one step behind. At her own insistence, she made a few calls and wrote a dynamic reference letter on my behalf. Though never one to accept excuses, she'd surprised me when she cut me some slack when I'd needed to study during finals weeks and dele-gated my secondary responsibilities to other department assistants. I worked my ass off and finished with honors in under a year and a half, with Kimber by my side to share in the success. And she promptly re-warded me with a promotion to senior product manager.

She was deep in thought as she studied the last page of the docu-ment. "This is some pretty heavy shit," she said, and looked up from the papers.

"I know. Universal already has the most market share; this will def-initely put a monkey wrench in every other label's fiscal program." I took a sip of my coffee and relished the sweet caffeine I'd grown to love.

She blew at the top of her cup and took two big gulps. "So, what are your plans, Love? Doesn't look like they're preparing to bring anyone from RockStar Chicago into the restructuring."

"No, they're not, except the SVP. Truth be told, that's why I'm here. I'm so over them." I took a deep breath and lowered my voice. "I want to impair the strength of their brand by realigning one of their strongest assets."

"Well, that would be Rain." Kimber looked at me over her specs be-fore removing them altogether. "You mean Rain? Oh my God! Of course! Now *that's* strategy, Love." She looked at me with discernible pride. "And exactly with whom did you want to realign said asset?"

"Tru Records, of course. Who else?"

Kimber swallowed more of her coffee and stood up from her chair to face the enormous window. It overlooked Madison Avenue from her 35th-story office and engulfed her as she positioned her glasses on top of her head. I could tell she was deep in thought and working through a number of scenarios that could potentially leverage both her and the label's standing. "So now we're talking about a buyout? Hmmm. Do you have Rain's contract?" She turned around and held out her hand, knowing damn well that I'd come prepared with everything necessary to get this ball rolling. After all, I'd been her grasshopper.

I took a manila envelope out of my briefcase and handed it to her. She sat down and began carefully reading over the terms of the agreement. She picked up the phone and told Farrah to get Dean, the label's head legal counsel, on the phone. Within seconds, he was holding on her private line.

"Listen, Dean, stop whatever it is you're doing and get up here. I need you to look into a private matter for me and give me the long and short of it ASAP," she said into the speaker. "This doesn't go beyond the two of us or that'll be your ass," she threatened, and disconnected the call while scribbling some notes on a few stickies and attaching them to specific pages in the contract.

With a quick prompt, Farrah walked silently into the office and took the sealed envelope from Kimber.

"Dean," Kimber instructed sternly, locking eyes with the distinguished, though very young-looking first assistant. Farrah nodded, pivoted, and walked out, silently closing the door behind her.

"Now, let's talk *great* strategy. What on God's green earth makes you think they're gonna let her out of that contract and even talk numbers with us? She is their brand. She's their Alicia Keys, their Beyoncé, their—"

"I've got that covered. It's nothing I can fully disclose yet, but you'll just have to trust me. Before I leave New York on Sunday, I'll have the necessary leverage, and they'll consent to whatever it is you're asking. That would leave them with only Treasure, their next R&B crooner, whom they're positioning to compete directly with Usher. So they'll just be crippled, not dead."

Truthfully, I'd been toying with a couple of different tactics since I'd had the conversation with Cobra earlier in the week. But I'd yet to decide on any particular course of action. Still, nothing was going to stop me from salvaging at least one thing in my life that I'd put my heart and soul into—my career, and the people who had worked diligently on my team to advance it. My hatred of confrontation was now null and void. I was ready to go to war.

"OK, Love, dear, here's the long and short of it." Kimber spoke in a barely audible whisper. "I've been promoted to President of Tru Records. No one knows except the CEO, his assistants, and Farrah, of course. That information won't be made public until the end of the fiscal quarter, and I'd love nothing more than for you to rejoin me at Tru and take over my position as vice president of the label—not a department, but the entire label." She walked around her desk and leaned on its edge next to the lamp she'd picked up in India, and stood directly in front of my chair.

I was speechless, and suddenly thoughts of my life in Chicago sprinted back and forth through my mind. It wasn't that my life was so fabulous back in the Windy City. I'd decided not to cheer next season— my heart just wasn't in it now. I wasn't involved with anyone, and I clearly wouldn't be working for RockStar anymore.

"Kimber, I don't know what to say. You mean move back to New York? This is so sudden. I didn't come here looking for a proposition. I just want my artist, whom I've worked hard to develop and nurture, to have a home where I know she'll be taken very good care of. There's no denying that this is the best place for her. She'll have longevity here, and I know you'll diversify her career. I wasn't prepared to—"

"Listen, Love, you'd be my first choice anyway, no matter what. I trained you, so I already know you're the perfect candidate for the job. You'd be third in command around here, and you'd be able to look after your investment yourself. I wouldn't have to think twice about spending the millions to buy out her contract if I knew you'd be here running the label with her as your personal priority. See, I have a lot to gain as well—if I can persuade you to come over to this side."

"And I could bring whoever I wanted with me?"

"Your choice. I'm sure we could work something out."

"I have the perfect product manager for Rain."

I stood up from the chair, pulled at my low-rise custom black leather pants, adjusted the matching tight long-sleeved leather jacket, pacing into the conference area adjacent to her desk. The spiky heels on my black midcalf leather Versace boots sank into the quicksand carpet. Was I actually thinking about this? My mind raced and raced and raced before she finally grabbed the baton.

"You don't have to make a decision right now. Of course, the sooner the better, but you've got some time. I don't officially take over the company until April. Now, there are some other people I'm considering, but no one I'd rather have than you, especially with this new set of circumstances. Take some time and think about it. Why don't you take a month or so and let me know by the middle of March, say around the fifteenth? In the meantime, I'll draw up an official offer letter. And of course, Love, money won't be an issue. We're prepared to put you in a brand-new tax bracket. How about I just have Farrah messenger that over to your hotel later this evening?"

"It's an opportunity of a lifetime" was the last thing I remember her saying when I walked out of the main lobby onto Madison Avenue, becoming one with the organic bustle that is New York City.

65

RUNNING ERRANDS IN THE CITY THAT DAY WAS LIKE NO OTHER DAY I'D EVER SPENT in the Big Apple, amid the movers and shakers at the center of the universe. New life had been breathed into me, and I was barely prepared for the sudden rejuvenation. I stopped off at the rehearsal space on 57th Street and stood in the doorway next to the ballet barre, watching Rain prepare with her choreographer for her performance on Sunday. She looked absolutely amazing. I knew I was doing the right thing for her and her career. And it felt natural, for the first time since I could remember, to fight back.

"Hey, Hannah; what's up? Where you goin'?" Rain asked, breathless, as I was trying to ease out the door just as quietly as I'd come in.

The music stopped, and everyone turned around when she ran over to me and threw her sweaty arms around my shoulders.

"You leaving? No, don't go. Stick around. Watch and tell me what you think." She ran back over to the middle of the dance floor and cued the music before I could protest.

In Miami at the VMAs she'd been breathtaking, but she'd improved tremendously since then. The way she moved was sensual and captivating. She was performing one of two songs for the show: either "Rain on Me" or her latest single to drop, "Can't Stop the Rain," which was a more up-tempo track that showcased her personal style and dance ability. For the first time I had no critique to give, except to not change a thing. It was perfect. She was perfect. She'd lost a couple of pounds from all the intense rehearsals, and her hair stylist, Nia, had lightened her locks with golden streaks.

I marveled at the great job we'd done assembling her glam squad; she was now ready for the big leagues. I'd already lined up a commercial shoot with Coca-Cola and had finally closed the deal for her to do a cross-promotion with Nelly and Apple Bottoms. Down the road we'd be launching her own line, of course: apparel and quite possibly a line of tricked-out shades.

"So, what do you think?" she gasped after finishing the second number.

"I love it."

"No, seriously, are you just saying that?"

"No, really, I love it! Don't change a thing."

"Yeah? Thanks. That means a lot coming from you. We've been going at it since yesterday—nonstop."

"Cobra told me," I admitted, reaching into the LV briefcase. Did you see your spread in *Seventeen*?"

"Yeah, super cool—but truthfully, I liked the one in *King* better. I got to show off my sexier side," she said, giggling.

"Well, just remember we're appealing to everyone with your imaging, not just the horny boys and dirty old men."

"I know—you're right. You're always right." She caught the towel that her assistant threw at her. "So, is Cobra really gonna miss the show Sunday?" she asked, looking disappointed as she blotted her face.

"Unfortunately, he's gonna miss this one. But, trust me, this is only the beginning. It's just that I needed him to keep an eye on some very important things for me back at the office."

"Oh, well, when you talk to him, tell him I'll call him later. He takes such good care of me."

"I know. Now finish up your practice. I'll see you tomorrow at Radio City for your run-through. Try and get some rest."

She threw her arms around me again and squared my shoulders.

"Thanks for everything. I know I wouldn't be here if it weren't for you." As she walked back over to the choreographer she dabbed the back of her neck with her towel, insisting that they do it again until she thought it was perfect. But it already was.

66

BY THE TIME I GOT BACK TO THE HILTON I WAS POOPED. BETWEEN MEETING with Piper, Rain's stylist, to go over her costumes, with Spike to discuss the itinerary for the next couple of days, and with Morgan to ensure that she'd set up all the interviews and photo ops for the entire weekend, I hadn't been able to give much thought to Kimber's proposal. I'd even managed to suck it up and poke my head in Mannie's and Nigel's offices to reassure them that everything was on schedule and running smoothly.

I'd barely had time to grab a bite and resurge when Eli texted me about meeting him in the bar of the hotel for a briefing. I reread the message and realized that he hadn't specified in which of the two hotel bars he'd wanted to meet, so I decided to slip around to the back bar. I figured I could hide out in the dimly lit lounge if he hadn't already arrived. A drink or two and a little alone time would do me some good.

"A lemondrop and a vodka tonic, please," I told the bartender when he finally made his way over to my stool at the end of the crammed bar. To cover my game, for now, I was prepared to do whatever it took to avoid arousing any suspicion from Eli, even to having his drink ready when he arrived.

Cobra answered his cell on the first ring while I was still trying to become one with the relatively mellow energy of the room.

"Hey, Bosslady. How'd the meeting go with Kimber?"

"In the words of our resident anaconda, who I'm waiting on as we speak, 'like butta, baby!' "

"That good, huh?" Cobra sounded shocked and excited. There was nothing like watching a good plan unfurl.

"She bit, and she bit hard. Two points for the good guys."

The bartender brought the drinks, and before I knew it I'd sucked down the sweet and sour vodka cocktail and was motioning for another.

"Awesome! So . . . phase three?"

"Not quite. Now, we've gotta sit still and pray that it plays itself out." I took a deep breath, hating on all the industry parties I was supposed to attend later that evening. "I really wish you were here to handle the late-night show-and-tell and meet and greet the posers and pretenders."

"Dish. Who's hot tonight?"

"Let's see," I griped, dejected, watching the bartender deliver my second lemondrop, which I knocked back faster than the first. "Jessica Simpson and all of Sony will be at Marquee, Diddy and his entourage will be at Show, and everyone who's anyone will be doing last call at Cain with Dame Dash," I said and shook my head in despair.

"Sweet. All the fierce stars'll be aligned. I wish I could be there too," he said wistfully, sounding more dejected than I was.

"You really like New York, huh?"

"Do I *have* a pulse?"

"Would you ever consider moving here?"

"I don't wanna leave you. This is a rockin' gig," he affirmed without hesitation.

"Uh-huh." I looked around for the little girls' room. "Gotta go. Great work," I said, cutting our chat short. "Oh, and your girlfriend says hi," I remembered.

"Who? Spike?"

"Even better. *His* boss," I clarified, and snapped the cell shut.

Before heading for the ladies' room, leaving Eli's vodka tonic to fend for itself, I stared at the bottom of the empty martini glass. Things were moving really fast, and the lemondrops had been extra strong.

My hands were gritty and sticky, so I scrubbed them in the sink before sweetening up with a dab of the Dior that I'd grabbed from my samples collection and tucked into my briefcase. Finally starting to calm down and welcome the warm buzz, I got ready to head back to the bar to order yet another lemondrop and wait patiently for the label traitor. Haphazardly, I reached for the handle as a striking, stunning woman pushed the door open from the other side, almost knocking me into the tiled wall.

"Oops. So sorry. Please excuse me," she said ever so sweetly, exposing her brilliant smile and deep dimples in her seemingly sincere request.

"It's OK," I said, and tried to hightail it out of there before she recognized me.

"Wait—don't I know you? Don't you live in Maxie's building?"

I squirmed as she stepped back and put one hand on her hip and the other up to her ruby-red lips.

Maxie? Balancing myself on the stiletto heels, I cringed when I remembered freezing on all fours in that embarrassing frogger moment in Max's hallway. I could still hear her voice echoing in my head when she called out to him on that dreadful night. *Maaaxxxiiieee.* Ew!

"That's where I know you from, right? You're a Diamond Doll too, right? I've seen you at some of the games."

Busted!

"You're really good."

"Uh, well, uh thanks." Great job, Velveeta!

It was all I could get out. And I just stood there in the now-sweaty clingy heavy leather, feeling the vodka rush to my head while she leaned in the doorway, looking fresh and fab, in a Calvin Klein black satin minidress glammed out with amber crystals.

"I thought so. You know I'd never forget a face, especially yours." She walked over to the sink and played with her long, lush, naturally curly auburn tresses, delicately blinking her feathery lashes. "So, what're you doing here?"

Was she fucking kidding? I refused to stand there and talk to the "other woman," no matter *how* nice she seemed. And what was that supposed to mean: "I'd never forget a face, especially yours?" Why, I oughta—

"Are you in town for business or pleasure?"

"Oh, uh, business," I chickened, promptly realizing that my voice had hit quiver mode and that I was in desperate need of a get-out-of-jail-free card.

"I've gotta go. Nice talking to you, but I've gotta meet someone. I mean, I was supposed to meet someone and well—I just gotta go."

"Oh, OK, sure. Hopefully I'll see you around," she said, killing me with her crater dimples. "Oh, and great perfume," she said, settling comfortably into a megawatt smile.

I dashed out of the bathroom and past the bar, looking around to see if Eli had arrived, wondering if I'd just been outed by her perfume comment.

"What?!" I fumed, flustered and irritable, to the bartender, who was motioning to me.

"The vodka tonic came by looking for you while you were in the restroom. He asked me to give you this."

He reached into his vest pocket and handed me a room key and a napkin with a room number on it.

"Your friend said he needed to go upstairs and make some calls and for you to meet him up there," he delivered, smiling devilishly as if he knew the inside scoop on some secret seductive scheme. It made me wonder what Eli had implied or just out-and-out stated to the liquor-serving stranger.

Whatever, I thought, and slid the key and napkin into my briefcase. I got all the way to the elevator bank before realizing that I'd forgotten my coat on the barstool. Great. Another chance to run into the Queen of the thirtieth floor. Very Pink Panther–like, I peered around the corner. Keeping my eyes on the ladies' room, I inched over to the stool. I bumped right into a hard body. Max!

"You should really watch where you're going."

"Yeah, yeah, I know—I just might miss something," I snapped, immediately overcome with irritation.

"I think this belongs to you." He handed me the coat. "I watched you storm out of the bathroom and take the room key. You left your coat when you ran for the elevators."

He stated the facts without emotion, shifting his weight and putting his free hand into his faded Dolce & Gabbana jeans.

"Thanks," I muttered, and slung the coat over my arm. "I'm kind of in a rush." I turned to walk away from him before any residual pain could boil over in my stomach. I'd completely forgotten that the Diamonds were playing New York at the Garden tomorrow. Of all the bars in all the hotels!

"I see you're in a hurry; don't let me keep you. You wouldn't wanna keep him waiting, I'm sure."

I winced, stopping dead in my tracks. Had he really had the gall to say that to me when I'd just dodged a "let's be girlfriends" chat with his amazingly beautiful away-game companion?

"What did you just say to me?" I threw the coat across a booth and thrust my hands onto my hips. For the first time, I was actually angry, and my anger was directed at the man I'd wanted to spend the rest of my life with just one month two weeks and three days before.

"You heard me. I said you don't wanna keep the vodka tonic waiting—in his room."

Max didn't budge, smile, laugh, or hint at easing up in the slightest. In fact, he seemed angry—at me! He zipped his rust-colored leather jacket and looked right past me as if I'd just been dismissed.

For the next few minutes I forgot that we were in the lobby bar of the upscale New York Hilton with high-profile professionals, theatergoers, and tourists from all over the fucking world. I felt the power of the lemondrop push me right over the edge. And I completely lost it.

"Where the fuck do you get off insinuating that *I* am doing something that I should feel remotely bad about? Who the hell are you to throw anything in my face? Not that it's any of your goddamn business, but that prick who left his room key for me is my boss, and we have business to take care of. It's not like any of that matters in your fucking world, anyway."

"Right—your boss. And I'm sure you have serious business to take care of. That's really funny, Hannah. If he's your prick boss, then he's the same prick boss I saw in your apartment a couple of months ago when you opened the door in your robe with a glass of wine in your hand. Or were you two in the middle of taking care of business that night too? And in the elevator—"

"Are you fucking kidding me?!" Apparently, my tone had reached a rather undesirable pitch, since the bartender was now pleading for me to keep it down. "Are you really gonna go there? He'd just stopped by—not even ten minutes before you did. What you saw was me escorting him to the door. I didn't know he was stopping by, and he didn't stay long. And yes, for the second time, that prick happens to be my boss."

I turned around and saw his girlfriend leaning against the booth behind me with crossed arms, watching us fight. Before I could catch myself I lashed out one last time.

"Besides, you've been with *her* all this time anyway. Probably even *before* that night you saw me in the elevator with my boss, the goddamn prick!"

I turned toward her. "Yeah, all this time he's been trying to get with me while he's been with you, probably talking that same smooth game that made me fall in love with him."

I went from being pissed to being choked up and felt the tears race to my eyes.

"Hannah—what the hell are you talking about?"

"Just let it go. And leave me the hell alone."

I grabbed my coat and squeezed it tightly as I walked away before turning around one last time. "I thought you were the one." My voice was softer and now trembling. "I tried. I tried hard. I cooked you that big meal and planned out that great night—but I saw her. I saw her!"—I pointed in the woman's direction but couldn't bring myself to look at her—"in the hall, dripping wet from the shower." I was crying now and was totally aware that I'd passed GO on the make-a-goddamn-fool-of-yourself meter. But somehow it didn't matter. "Fuck you, Max. Just-Fuck-You!"

I ran for the elevator and jabbed the call button mercilessly. I could hear her muttering to him while I waited impatiently, growing more and more neurotic with the damn button.

"I told you, Maxie. I told you it was her. I recognized the perfume."

When the elevator finally opened, I got on and pressed repeatedly for the doors to close, sobbing uncontrollably into the $872.36 coat. Before the doors could oblige, Max got on and pushed for the Penthouse. I could feel him staring down at me as we ascended in silence. He was breathing hard and fast, but I wouldn't look up at him until he reached for my face and held it in his hands, forcing me to surrender.

"I would never do anything to deliberately hurt you. You have to believe that, darlin'."

I was exhausted from mulling over the Tru Records offer, the extra-strong vodka lemondrops, and the painful rehashing of this complicated and volatile situation with him. I had nothing left to give nor anything else to say.

The elevator opened, and he led me into the still hallway, where the echoes of my whimpers could be heard even after he closed the penthouse door behind us. He sat me down on the king-sized bed where his suitcase lay open. The water running in the bathroom pressured my bladder until he reappeared and knelt down next to the bed in front of me. Holding a damp cloth, he took my face in his hands again, this time wiping away all the tears and the goo from my runny nose. I didn't object. I sat still on the bed—empty.

He handed me the washcloth and let his jacket fall to the floor before he dug around in his bag and, relieved, pulled out a silver rectangular picture frame. It was him, the striking, stunning woman, and a beautiful baby.

"Hannah, darlin', that's my sister. Cree." He pointed to the woman who had haunted the secret hiding places in my soul. "And that's a picture of Zoey, my niece, her baby girl."

He took the tear-soaked coat from my arms and threw it on a chair, eased onto the bed next to me, and leaned back against the headboard, putting his arms around me while I cried even harder.

67

"DID YOU REALLY MAKE A SPECIAL DINNER FOR ME AND BRING IT DOWN TO MY floor?"

I nodded.

"Were you really wearing sweet-smelling perfume?"

I nodded again.

"Hmmm—what else were you wearing?" Max asked as he kissed me on the forehead for the first time since that night he'd been in my apartment on the sofa with his arms wrapped tightly around my body. "Did you dress up for me?"

I'd finally stopped crying and was completely congested. "Yes," I whispered.

"Now, that's real sweet. Cree told me she could smell your perfume in the hallway, but she didn't see you and figured you'd left—or something."

"Or something," I said and chuckled to myself at the thought of my crouching-tiger-hidden-leapfrog imitation.

"She said she remembered you had on that same perfume when we were all trapped in the elevator that night. She never forgets a face or a smell, especially when she likes it."

"What, the perfume?"

"And the pretty face." He lifted my chin and kissed the tip of my warm nose. "I just can't believe that you've been dealing with this all this time. I had every intention of introducing you to her, but when we were on the elevator with your boss, the prick, somehow it just didn't seem appropriate or even necessary."

"Listen, I'm really sorry about that," I said, trying not to sound too nasally. "But he really is a prick. Things just got so complicated. That night, he was honestly just walking me up to my door because I hadn't eaten and I'd had too much to drink. Strangely enough, he didn't even try anything—probably not enough of a challenge for him."

He squeezed me tighter. "You don't have to explain anymore. I believe you. I'm sorry I ever doubted you."

"Can I ask you one other thing?" I cleared my throat.

"You can ask me anything and I'll tell you the absolute truth."

"Even if it hurts me?"

"I'll do everything I can to always protect you, but you should never be afraid to ask me. What's on your mind, darlin'?"

I pulled at the tiny hairs on his index finger.

"Mona. What's up with you two?" I looked him square in the eye. "She made it clear from the very beginning that you belonged to her."

Max started to laugh heartily and had to force himself to breathe as he wiped away the wetness under his eyelids.

"Oh, baby, I'm so sorry you had to deal with that too," he said, still chuckling. "She's what we call an inside groupie. She's got the access, but she's also been threatened with restraining orders from some of the guys—including me. She even showed up at Mav's daughter's second birthday party at his baby's mama's condo, uninvited, and his ex-girl had to call the cops."

"What!"

"Uh-huh." He wiped his eyes with the back of his hand as he laughed harder. "Whew."

I pounded my fist against his thigh. "Why didn't anyone tell me?"

"Probably cuz you're a rookie. You're not supposed to know anything. You have to *earn* access to information."

"Right."

"It's part of the game. The way they see it, information is power. And rookies aren't supposed to have any power."

"So, nothing ever—"

"Besides me having to change my numbers *seven* times over the last two years? No, darlin', nothing."

He pulled me into his arms and kissed the top of my head and indulged himself in another hearty laugh.

The phone next to the bed rang, and he caught his breath long enough to briefly talk to the person on the other end before hanging up. "That was Cree. She's in her room upstairs and wants to know if it's safe to come down."

He sat me up and pushed my curls behind my ear, wiping my face one last time before Cree came barreling down the spiral staircase in the middle of the duplex penthouse.

"Come in," Max said, responding to her knocks on the already open door.

She sat on the edge of the bed and held out her hand. "Hi, I'm Cree, Maxie's baby sister." She exhaled and smiled. The expression on her face was no longer threatening; it was really rather adorable. And shaking her hand felt like the beginning of a long friendship.

"He's told me so much about you," she said. "It's a pleasure to finally meet you."

"Same here," I said between sniffles.

"Are you OK? I know how affairs of the heart can be. I didn't mean to cause any kind of drama between you two." She shoved Max's leg that was dangling over mine.

"Yeah, she's fine—now," he answered for me.

"Good. Can I ask you one question?" she asked, with a suspicious smile on her face.

"Uh-huh."

"Weren't you at the door that night? On New Year's Eve?"

"Uh-huh," I said slowly, holding back signs of embarrassment.

"OK, so I wasn't going crazy," she said, and looked over at Max. "Well, what happened? Cuz when I opened the door there was no one there—or anywhere in the hall for that matter."

"Yeah, funny thing about that night—"

"Girl, never mind. You don't have to answer that if you don't want. Feel free to plead the fifth—I can hear it in your voice. I've been there with these men, and I tell you they will put you in some crazy positions."

If she only knew.

"Maxie, I'm gonna assume that you'll be staying in tonight, so I was wondering if I could have the tickets and maybe if I could go to the play with Miles. I just saw him downstairs, and he's not really trying to go hang out with Styles and Mav tonight. They said something about a strip club." She looked at him with big doe eyes and fluttered her lashes.

He didn't move for a second, and when I looked up at him he was making questionable faces at her. "With Miles, huh?"

"Yeah, with Miles."

"This is the third time I've heard you mention his name. What's up with that?"

She shifted her body on the bed and thought about her answer. "Well, if I'm not mistaken, you said I'd better not ever mention Styles, Mav, or Pierce to you. I'd ask Shep to take me, but I know he'd rather be on the phone with Ali all night. So, really, the only cool nice guy left is Miles." She shrugged innocently.

He picked up his cell from the end table and went into the bathroom, pressing numbers. Cree eased from the bed and tried her best to eavesdrop on him. I could hear "I dare you" and "you better not" and "don't let me find out" between muffled sentences. He came out, handed her the tickets, and kissed her on the cheek, giving his approval.

From the time she started rifling through his jacket to hand him his wallet, to waving goodbye to the both of us, she never stopped grinning.

"Be back by midnight. You both have a curfew. And keep your phone on. And no holding hands!" He screamed into the suite's living room, but she was already out the door mumbling something about 1 a.m.

He slid back into the big bed with me and pressed my head against his hard chest. "Now, what about your boss, the prick?" He cleared his throat and nudged my arm. "Weren't you supposed to go and meet with him in his room?"

"Uh-huh, I was. For real. I'm supposed to brief him on everything for the weekend. I'm out here working, Max. You know"—I counted on my fingers—"the Grammys, and Rain, and everything I've worked on these past eleven months that wasn't Diamond Dolls–related."

"I know what you're doing here, and I don't want to keep you from your work, but I'd really rather you talked to him somewhere other than in his room." He sounded serious, but not cold this time. I recognized the warmth in his voice.

"OK."

"I'm serious, darlin'."

"I know."

I got up from the bed for the first time since he'd sat me down and rifled through my briefcase until I found my cell. Eli had texted me three times already, and instead of returning any of his messages I decided to call him, partly so Max could hear me accommodate his wishes.

"Hey Eli, it's me. I know, I know. But we can meet downstairs. You're where? Oh. OK, sure."

I hung up and looked at Max, who pretended to be flipping through the *Seventeen* magazine I'd laid on the bed. He looked so good that I flipped the phone open again and snapped his picture.

"You're really, really cute," I said, looking at the picture on the screen.

"I'm glad you think so," he said. I leaned over and reached up to his face and slid my fingers through his silky curls. He sighed deeply and closed his eyes. "So, are you leaving me to go downstairs now?"

"No, it looks like the prick already left. He said for me to meet him out later tonight at one of the events and we can talk then."

I walked across the room to the window and looked out over the neon city. Suddenly, the excitement of the day caught up with me again, leaving me sober. I thought about this becoming my home again. It would be a far cry from my one bedroom in Fort Greene.

"OK, well, I understand if you have to go. I'll hang out till Cree gets back and catch a game on ESPN. We've got nothing but time, right?"

God, how was I going to tell him that I was seriously considering taking Kimber's offer and leaving Chicago? Why did everything keep getting so goddamn complicated? Now that it looked like I might finally have a chance at seeing where this could go with him, I get presented with the biggest offer of my career. I stood in front of the window of the penthouse suite and watched him watch me.

"Right, baby; nothing but time."

MY SUITE WAS DARK AND STILL WHEN I ENTERED. IT REMINDED ME OF HOW THE past month of my life had been before today. I flipped the light switch. The blinking red light on the phone alerted me to a message from the front desk. Before I even checked it, I knew Kimber had messengered over the offer letter. I needed to give that some serious thought. How easy would it be for Britt to sell my place, I wondered, and what would I do without my beloved pseudoroomie and best friend, Sweets?

"Well, you just *have* to move," Kennedy was saying from her bedroom when I finally sucked it up and conferenced the Brats to rehash the events of this mind-blowing day. "Max'll understand. Plenty of people make long distance work."

"Girl, fuck that job. That man is R-I-C-H! Who the hell would have to work if they hooked up with him?" Britt argued, listening in on the other phone in her kitchen.

"She hasn't even told him about it yet. Keep up."

"Semantics," Britt clarified, munching down on a cookie. "Put it on him so Jenna Jamison that he'll agree with whatever arrangement works best for *you*."

"Be happy, Bug," Kennedy begged. "He's 'The One.' "

"But what about us?" I'd been trying to keep my cool and not think about how my girls fit into this advanced placement equation. "It's all happening so fast. I'm not even sure that moving out here is best for me right now."

"Sweet's right. Be happy, bitch. Ain't shit here for you. If you want that job, take it. You've worked your ass off priming Rain for the majors. I'm sure loverboy'll respect the fact that you wanna keep your identity. And not to get all Matrix-y, but he is 'The One.' "

"What would you do if you stayed here?" Kennedy questioned, treading lightly.

"Be here all up under him, like Aliyah?" Britt challenged. "Not that I'm knocking *that* hustle, cuz please, don't get it twisted; I ain't mad at her."

"That's just not you, Bug," Kennedy avowed solemnly. "I'll miss you. But go, be happy. It's been too long."

"Oh, please," Britt interjected. "Kill the drama. Planes, bitches. Distance never slowed us down before." She slurped into the phone. "Where's he now?"

"Upstairs in his penthouse."

"And where are you?" Britt continued, biting into something crunchy.

"In my suite."

As soon as I said it, I prepped myself for the tongue-lashing as they both gasped and attacked simultaneously.

"What the fuck!" Brittany surged.

"Get your long-overdue-for-some-bomb-ass-sex *ass* off the phone with us and handle that!" Kennedy fired.

"Shit, I got mine this afternoon; what're you waiting for? The shit ain't goin' handle itself. You need to be a participant in the fornicating," Britt explained.

"But I have to be at—"

"There's only one place you need to be right now."

And that was the last thing I heard them say before they collectively disconnected me from all dialogue.

With renewed life, I stepped out of the two-person marble shower, wrapped myself in the oversized cotton bath towel, and searched through my suitcase to pull out the only sexy thing I'd brought with me—a bronzy cinnamon stretch lace halter babydoll with a matching cinnamon thong. Earlier this morning on my way out the front door, Dallas had handed me a Fed Ex package. "Hmm, La Perla?" he'd prodded when I took the package from him and jumped into the limo headed for Midway airport.

I applied a tad bit of Lancôme's iced cranberry Juicy Tubes to my lips, and three strokes of long-lash mascara. Since I wouldn't be joining Eli for any of the industry festivities tonight, I pulled out my laptop and updated the weekend catalogue of events Cobra had sent him this morning via e-mail. Impatiently, I logged on to the RockStar intranet and downloaded the original catalogue, printed it, and attached it to the updated one I'd just typed and proofed. Halfway there!

My old faithful MJ trench was knotted around my waist, and all that was left was to tie up my gold metallic strappy Christian Louboutin stilettos. I reached into my briefcase and double-dabbed the Dior behind each ear and in my knee pits (a seduction secret Britt had shown me ages ago). I'd Naired in all the right places (no time for that bitchy Brazilian) and was ready to do the damn thing. Speedily, I stuffed the matching gold Louboutin clutch with a toothbrush, floss, my cell, and the room key. I held on tightly to Eli's keycard and was halfway out the door before I turned back around to grab the updated detailed documents from the desk. Done!

69

On the first try, Eli's keycard worked and the green light on the doorknob permitted me to enter. The layout of his two-bedroom suite was exactly like mine and I wouldn't have known which room he was using if it hadn't been for the television left on in the west wing. The plan was to put the updates on his pillow so he'd be sure to see them when he came in from his night of schmoozing.

Jesus Fucking Christ!

I pushed the door wide open and stood in horror when I saw Eli stretched out in the middle of the bed, naked and spread-eagled! The back of a head with a low-cut fade was positioned between his legs giving Eli—well, *head*! When I realized that the volume and frequency of Eli's moans were steadily increasing, I flicked on the lights—just before he could really get *ahead*. Eli froze, his companion turned around aghast, and I snapped away with my little camera phone.

I gasped when I realized that not only was I immortalizing my boss, the senior vice president of RockStar Records, but also his boss, Emmanuele/Mannie, CEO of RockStar Records—in bed together—doing the goddamn thing!

70

Max was stunned to see me when he opened the door to the penthouse, but even more surprised to see me wrapped in the trench coat with all its lewd and fantastic implications. I could tell his eyes had already switched over to their x-ray-vision capabilities that every man universally possesses. He was clearly sizing up every inch of my body.

"Surprise!" I yelled, out of breath from running down both hallways.

"What's going on? I thought you had work to do and hot parties to attend and men to meet and greet." He reached down and grabbed me in his arms, swinging me around in the middle of the two-thousand-square-foot room.

"In one sec, baby; I've got a real emergency."

I freed myself from his grip and ran as fast as I could to the phone and dialed the concierge. "Yes, hello. Please listen carefully. I need someone to go to my suite ASAP and collect all my belongings and bring them to the east Penthouse. Please, it's an emergency. I need it done right away. Yes—Love, Hannah Love. Yes, that's correct. Please, right away." I hung up the phone and stared at the pictures on the phone screen as I scrolled down and saved every single one of them, still in severe shock at what I'd managed to accidentally digitally capture.

"You OK? What's wrong? Is there someone in your room? What happened?"

"Yeah, I'm OK for now. No one's in my room—yet! In about five minutes, my boss and my boss's boss will be at the front desk trying to get a key to get in there, if they haven't already broken the damn door down." I was trying to catch my breath. "That, I'm sure of."

"What're you talking about?"

I recapped the entire unbelievable story to Max, starting from the very *very* beginning. I explained about all the underground meetings Eli had been having with the CEO and the president of RockStar and the even more clandestine meetings that had been going on with the big brass at Universal. I told him about Eli's reassurances that he'd have my back and that I didn't have anything to worry about. Coming completely clean, I told him about the business dates we'd had to discuss him looking out for me, "no matter what happens" and also about Eli alluding to a possible promotion being in it for me if something was to unexpectedly occur between the two companies. Finally, I got to the part about Cameran and their fling and the vengeance of a woman scorned. And all that led me to my morning meeting with Kimber, the big job offer, and the leverage I now had over not only Eli, but also the CEO of the company.

"So needless to say, I might be in a bit of danger right now," I admitted, looking at him and realizing the full scope of what I had in my hands, buried in the memory of a single cellular chip.

Once my limbs began to shake, Max turned into Jason Bourne and took the phone from me, sending the pictures to his inbox "just in case something should happen to your phone."

He looked as shocked at what the pictures revealed as I was.

"Listen." He took a deep breath. "If you want Rain at Tru Records, then I want Rain at Tru. And I'm not gonna let anything happen to you, believe that. I'll get you around-the-clock security if that's what it takes to keep you safe when I can't be with you."

And with the touch of a button, he saved everything to the hard drive on his laptop that he'd had set up on one of the desks in the room. I stood over his shoulder and nervously watched him. When he was done he pulled me closer to him. We both looked at the pictures that were maximized on the screen.

I covered my mouth. "Ew!"

He slammed the laptop shut and turned to face me. "Are you OK?" He pushed his chair back.

"Yeah."

I exhaled and looked at him and knew I was going to be just fine.

"Good," he said, and gently tugged at the belt on my trench. He bit down on his bottom lip, then licked his lips while looking into my eyes. "Now, what's this about you being offered a position here in New York as the vice president of the label? I need you to talk to me, darlin', and be open and honest. Let's see how that works for us for a change."

I'd momentarily forgotten that I'd just told him absolutely *everything* that had landed me in this crazy predicament.

"Yes, it's true that the offer is on the table, but I've got a month to let her know if I'm going to accept or not. It was all so sudden, and even though I haven't given her an answer either way, when she made the offer I was still under the impression that there was nothing really keeping me in Chicago."

He stood up from the chair and picked me up, carried me over to the bed, and laid me down on my back. "I see. So now what are your thoughts about having something keeping you in Chicago?" he asked, and bent down to untie my coat with his teeth.

I ran my fingers through his curls and closed my eyes, remembering all the times I'd watched him do that and had wanted a chance to feel for myself. I shuddered at how good it actually felt, far better than I'd ever imagined.

"I'd definitely say that things are different now, very different, and I have something seriously keeping me in Chicago."

"Exactly, how *serious* is it?" He stood over me, gazing down at me as I lay on the bed with my trench wide open in the bronze lingerie and spiked heels. I was emotionally and physically exposed.

My heart skipped all kinds of beats looking at him look at me. His stare was like nothing I'd ever seen before, and he took his time taking in every part of me. "Very serious." I gasped for air.

"Uh-huh. Do you really want this job?" He kneeled down and placed both my feet on his shoulders. I was dying to kiss him. I hadn't had a single kiss since we'd reconnected. Instead, he untied the straps on my shoes, letting them fall to the floor, and began to caress my legs, starting with my ankles.

I was already starting to shiver just from the soft deliberate feel of his fingers and palms against my skin. He moved up to my thighs, and my thong panty caught all the juices that were beginning to flow freely. I tensed.

"I think it would be a great opportunity for me," I said, between short quick breaths.

"Uh-huh. Do you think that if you took this job and moved away from me you'd be willing to do whatever it took on your part to keep us together?"

The thumb of his right hand was now gently caressing me over the panty as his left hand explored my belly button and the skin around it. My eyes had been closed and I was forced to open them when he held my breasts in his hands and squeezed my nipples delicately, stopping only after I tensed again and let out a quiet moan.

"I think that no matter what it took to be with you, I'd do it—no matter what it was!"

His fingers had moved up to my mouth and were now going over my lips, and as he smeared my lip gloss off onto his fingers, he took turns putting them in his mouth or in mine to suck off the gooey gel. "And why would you do that? Tell me why you would be willing to do whatever it took?"

I watched him bite down on his bottom lip, lower his eyebrows, and stare at my mouth. His lips were inches away from me. I inhaled his breath, and a single tear fell from my eye.

"Because I love you."

His lips were barely touching mine when he whispered back softly, "I love you too, darlin'."

71

THE KISS THAT FOLLOWED WAS INDESCRIBABLE AND LASTED WELL OVER AN HOUR. Max had gotten on the bed and caressed every inch of me with his mouth, leaving no part of my body in need. And the passionate obsessive lovemaking that followed brought me to tears on more than one occasion. What started in the bed moved to the floor and finally ended in the shower. And though I'd only barely resisted getting my hair wet, he'd mumbled something at me about having the stylist of my choice in the penthouse first thing in the morning to take care of my "damn hair" right before he grabbed it and yanked it back, exposing my neck for his tongue.

When the concierge opened the door and put my bags in the foyer, I'd motioned for Max to be quiet and slow down, but that just seemed to intensify his passion. I was on top of him, and he grabbed my ass, thrusting harder, pulling my wet hair, and turning my loud moans into even louder screams. God only knows what the poor guy thought as he rushed out the front door. I found a "Do Not Disturb" sign hanging from the outside knob the next morning when I opened the door for room service.

We sat in the bed and fed each other pancakes, waffles, eggs, toast, chicken-apple sausages, and fresh fruit, and we drank apple, orange, *and* pineapple juice while college basketball played on the television in the background. It was pitiful how we couldn't get enough of each other. We were ravenous for food early that morning and even more for each other after we ate. It seemed that every possible Kama Sutra position had been tried, perfected, and thoroughly enjoyed. Never before had I known I was multiorgasmic—but this was ridiculous! Sometimes he would just kiss my neck, letting his tongue linger in certain spots longer than others, and my body would shake while he entertained my newly discovered G-spot. I moaned, twisted, and turned for several minutes, all the while grabbing his soft curls and rocking back and forth. It took me several orgasms to figure out that the only way he'd stop massaging, or pushing, or sucking, or licking during my climaxes was if I asked him to. And if I never asked, I'd keep on quaking—right off the Richter scale.

I closed my eyes, never wanting this to end. But my thoughts were drifting back to the things that could potentially keep us apart. "What about this job?" I rested on top of him, holding him tighter, fearful of the reality that we'd have to do the long-distance thing.

"Take the job. It's a great opportunity. I'm really very proud of you. You're kind of amazing, you know?"

"What?" I whispered in his ear. "You're the amazing one."

He closed his eyes and stroked my back. "I want you to take the job." He kissed my forehead again. "And there's something I should tell you, even though it's still pretty early." He opened his eyes.

I moved my head away from his and braced myself for whatever it was that he'd felt he couldn't tell me before now.

He grabbed me and pulled me back into him. "Don't pull away from me," he whispered. "Don't ever pull away from me again. I told you I'd never hurt you, darlin'." He nuzzled my ear. "The only pain you'll feel is the kind of pain you felt last night. And that's good pain, right?"

I pinched his ear. "You better tell me what it is."

"Ow! OK, OK." He sat up slightly, leaning on his forearm. "I'm not sure if you're aware of this or not, but my contract with the Diamonds is up after this season. I'll be a free agent and, well, the Knicks really want me to join their franchise."

I sat up and straddled him. "What! Are you serious? You're gonna play for New York?" I jumped up and down on his rib cage.

"You're killing me." He grabbed me by the arms and held me in midair, flexing his tattooed arms. "No, I didn't say that. Listen to me carefully. It's way too early to be able to say anything definitively. They really want me. I had a meeting with them yesterday and—"

"And what?"

"Well, I told them I'd think about it. But now that I know you'll be here, I'm gonna do everything in my power to make that happen. Do you think I want to be away from you one minute longer than I have to?"

I collapsed into his chest and held on for dear life.

He wrapped his arms around me and kissed the top of my head again. "I don't want to be away from you—I just found you."

"I know, baby. Me too."

72

IT WAS HARD FOR ME TO PULL MYSELF AWAY FROM HIM THAT SATURDAY MORNING, but I was quickly thrown back into the jaws of reality. Max had erased most of the illicit porn shots from my phone after double-checking that they'd been securely encrypted onto his hard drive. And just as I'd suspected, Eli didn't show up at all that day for run-throughs. Instead, he called Rain's manager directly for a midday update.

Rehearsals went smoothly at the venue. Rain's energy was electric, and her dancers were extraordinary, complementing her perfectly. She was already interviewing like a pro, and it was evident that the media coaching Cobra had arranged had paid off. The show was gonna be hot. We'd gotten so obsessively consumed by triple-checking the lights, music, and pyrotechnic cues that we almost ran overtime into Cold-play's slot.

Even though Eli hadn't shown his face at the venue, Max didn't take any chances and had prepared for the worst. He'd gotten one of his old friends, Tiny, from his "past" to pose as my cousin, guarding me while he went to his game that afternoon. When Tiny came up to Max's room earlier that morning, I was dumbfounded. The man weighed about three hundred and fifty pounds. He was huge! Max said he needed to know I'd be safe. He and I were both aware of how "accidents" just seemed to happen to certain people in the music game.

"Take care of my baby," Max had told Tiny and handed him an envelope with several hundred-dollar bills in it. "I love this one."

"Will do, Boss." Tiny winked at me and smiled, revealing one gold, diamond-encrusted front tooth.

Max stood at the door in his knee-length Chicago Diamonds shorts and nothing else, hugged me tightly, and kissed me on my neck. "Thank you," he whispered into my ear.

"You're welcome," I whispered back.

73

BY SUNDAY MORNING I KNEW THAT WAKING UP NEXT TO MAX WAS SOME-thing I could really get used to. Whenever I moved around in the bed he would reach over and pull me into him and kiss me on the closest body part he could find. He seemed to always have sweet dreams, I deduced, by all the smiling and talking he did in his sleep. His sentences were usually jumbled except when I'd lean over and kiss him on his cheek and he'd mumble back, "Ummm, good kisses."

I was trying to take full advantage of his being in the bed next to me while I had the chance. Originally, he was supposed to return to Chicago with the rest of the team that morning, but because they didn't have any games for the next four days, he said that he'd decided to stay and escort me to the awards show.

"Let me take you on our first date," he'd said.

MAX CAME OUT OF THE BATHROOM WITH JUST A TOWEL WRAPPED AROUND HIS waist. I had to pinch myself to make sure that this was really my life. His shoulders, biceps, six-pack, and calves were all rock hard and screaming for immortalization, but the chef d'oeuvre was his deep sweet dimples and even tastier smile.

I'd just finished applying the last of my makeup when he approached the mirror to help me step into the ivory silk Roberto Cavalli Harlequin gown, balancing me so I didn't snag the floor-length hem. The dress was exquisite, I thought, looking at the princess staring back at me in the mirror. I ran my fingers over the intricate beading that outlined the deep V neckline which stopped just above my belly button.

While I'd been busy shopping yesterday with Rain and Piper, Max had called Bergdorf and had them send over several dresses in my size. When he got back from his afternoon game at the Garden, Cree helped him go through them all and narrow it down to this ivory masterpiece. Later that evening when Tiny and I returned, exhausted from being on the set with Rain for her Coca-Cola shoot and from carting her into every Soho boutique imaginable, all I'd wanted to do was soak my aching feet in the Jacuzzi. Instead, there had been a seamstress waiting to snip the waist a tinge on my hand-beaded surprise. I'd been completely undone even before the Cinderella deal was sealed when Cree came running down the stairs to hand me the perfect pair of Manolo caged stilettos.

Max put on the black pinstriped wool-and-cashmere double-breasted Gucci suit that he'd picked up earlier when I was still making calls and going back and forth with Harley, my attorney, about the Tru offer. Max adjusted the lapel on his suit jacket and posed next to me in the mirror. He absolutely took my breath away. Caught in the moment, we just stood there, gazing at each other.

Max towered behind me, holding me in his arms. "I can only think of one other time when you'll look more beautiful than you do right now."

74

THE STRETCH HUMMER WAS OUTSIDE THE HILTON WAITING TO TAKE US THE EN-
tire two-block ride over to Radio City Music Hall. Image is everything in
this industry, and walking to the venue would have been just as wrong
as catching the bus!

Max squeezed and kissed my hand before the chauffeur opened my
door. He was far more aware of what we were walking into than I ever
could've been. I stepped one foot down onto the sidewalk and was
greeted by screaming fans, flashing bulbs, and tape recorders shoved
into my face—all before I could pull the other foot from the car. Bright
white camera lights glared from every direction, and my first instinct
was to cover my eyes when I thought I'd surely be blinded by the snaparazzi. But I knew better. Red-carpet etiquette; I'd taught this course
myself.

The media hounds yelled Max's name and shouted at him as if
they'd known him for years.

"Max, Max, over here!"

"Mr. Knight, can I get you to pose?"

"Max, who's your date?"

"Max, who are you wearing?"

And just as if we'd been doing it forever, we posed together, holding
hands for some and embracing for others. It was clear that our relationship wasn't going to be low profile, and by dawn, when the early
edition of the papers hit the stands, everyone on both of our teams
would be in the know.

We were making our way down the red carpet when an *E!* reporter
called Max over for an interview. She congratulated him on scoring a
career high of forty-six points in yesterday's game and asked what had
motivated him to dominate the way he did. Before I could inch away,
Max pulled me to his side.

"Love will do crazy things to you," he said.

"And who is she, Maximillien? You've been one of America's most eligible bachelors since your rookie year with the Diamonds. Is she just a friend? Or possibly a girlfriend?"

"Inspiration," he answered, and squeezed my hand. "And that's all I'm gonna give you guys right now."

He put his hand on the small of my back, flashed them a high-voltage smile complete with the down-home dimples, and escorted me the rest of the way to the end of the red carpet.

As we stood in the atrium waiting for an usher, I looked up at him and for the first time I saw a different person than the man I'd been with all weekend. The truth was that when we were together I forgot that he was a megastar in his own right. Rain was the only person I thought of as actually being on that dysfunctional idolized spectrum of celebrity. Part of that was because I'd worked so hard to get her there, and the other part was that I'd worked so hard to *keep* her there. It never even resonated that I'd been showering with a man who had celebrity and stardom stitched into his boxer briefs. He'd been such a pro at handling the attention, the media, the fans—and now me! He squeezed my side and pulled me closer to him, and I was as acquiescent as the masses.

"You're lucky—I started to tell them that you're my professional *and* personal cheerleader," he whispered into my ear.

He let go of my waist and reached for my hand. His fingers felt good intertwined in mine, and I remembered the first time that he'd grabbed my hand outside the Chicken Shack. That seemed like ages ago, I thought, smiling to myself at the innocence of the memory.

The ushers escorted us to our seats in the third row—three seats over from Lil' John and adjacent to Gwen Stefani. But I couldn't seem to get comfortable, worrying that Rain was having last-minute jitters like she'd had at the VMAs.

"Go check on her. Make sure she's OK." Max must've sensed my anxiety. "I'll be right here."

I made my way backstage and found RockStar's pride prepping with her glam squad in one of the dressing rooms allotted to the big acts performing in the first half of the show. One peek at her settled my crazed nerves. She looked up at me from the makeup chair in front of the vanity and smiled. No fear. I knew she was ready to show the world that she was taking what was hers. And I was proud. We'd come a long way in a very short amount of time, and she'd worked harder than any other artist I'd ever known. That first radio interview in Chicago was in no way a reflection of the superstar sitting in front of me now. It was her time. It was our time!

Just as the show was about to start, I gathered everyone round to rally and pray before hugging the RockStar and disappearing back into the celebrity-packed audience. Max watched me walk down the aisle as I tried unsuccessfully to pretend I didn't see him. He dismissed all the women who'd been standing around him, gawking, teasing, and flirting. As they followed his eyes up the aisle toward me, I'd never seen scowls turn to fake smiles so quickly. Max stood up and waited for me to slide into my seat, helping me with my enviable dress, before sitting back down and wrapping his strong arm around me. Without acknowledging his departed posse of potential pussy, he leaned over and kissed me on the cheek.

"Everything OK back there?"

"Yeah, she's perfect."

"So are you."

My phone beeped. I nudged Max and showed him Eli's name on the screen. My eyes bugged, and my hands were getting too slippery to hold the cell.

"Answer it. You're with me now." He put his hand on my knee and turned back to Ashton, who'd made a special trip across the auditorium to speak to him.

I wiped my hands on the seat. "Hello?" I didn't hear anything. "Hello!"

"Listen, I'm on my way over there now. I really hope you know what you're doing. That's all I have to say."

"I don't know what you're talking about. I really don't."

"For your sake, I really hope you know what the fuck you're doing!" he screamed into the phone, and the line went dead just as the lights in the theater dimmed.

I snapped the phone shut and whispered to Max what Eli had said. He shrugged it off and put his arm around me again and settled in for the first half of the show.

After two acts had performed and six awards had been presented, it was time for Rain to perform her hit, "Rain on Fire." All around me I could hear the whispers. Everyone had been looking forward to seeing her; this performance was slated to be hot.

I think I held my breath the entire six minutes she was onstage. I watched her bring everyone into her zone and have her way with them. When she wanted them to scream, they screamed. When she wanted them to gasp, they gasped, and when she wanted them to stand up and show her some respect, they jumped out of their seats and put their hands around their mouths and chanted her name until she was bored with it all.

Max stood up and yelled with the rest of the crowd when eight fire-eaters were left onstage tossing blazing batons over a now-empty cage after Rain elusively disappeared into thin air, still angelically, fiercely, unapologetically holding her last note.

Everyone seated around me jarred into my shoulders or threw me high fives. They all knew it was an enormously big night for Rain, for RockStar, and definitely for me! And only two minutes later, with no time for Rain to change out of her barely there fireproof costume, Sting announced that she was the year's Best New Artist.

The place was electric. Rain stood at the podium for what seemed like an eternity before the crowd settled down and let her begin her speech. I didn't hear a word she said after she thanked God, then her "mentor and biggest supporter, Hannah Love, who has taught me everything I've needed to know to ascend and succeed—even how to stand up here right now without falling apart like I really want to."

That wasn't part of the speech that we'd practiced over shrimp tempura the day before at Sushi Samba. She'd pulled that out of her trick bag and now had me emotional. One of the fans in the balcony screamed neurotically for her. I turned around to glance at her avid supporter and got choked up again when I saw endless rows of teenage boys and girls wearing shirts that read "Rain on Fire." And yes she was.

"I love you too!" she screamed back.

Toward the end of the night she graciously took the stage to receive her second Grammy. A cappella, she sang her thank-yous to a harmony she and her producers had come up with, showing the world once again that she was the real deal. Her voice was angelic and powerful, and even I, awestricken, clasped my mouth with both hands. When I looked around the huge theater I realized everyone was standing up. It was clear that this was her night. Single-handedly, she'd brought the house down.

"Damn! So this is what you do for a living," Max said as the lights came up.

"Welcome to my world."

"I hope you know you just changed the game." He looked at me adoringly.

"That's what I was hoping for."

We made our way out of the crowded theater, stopping to talk to some and speak briefly to others.

"Let's do lunch!"

"Let's do drinks next week."

"You know, we really need to talk."

And my favorite of the night: "Hey, let's get together in the next few days. I've got a way for both of us to make some *real* money."

I was standing under the marquee wearing Max's suit jacket, telling Spike which parties Rain needed to hit, when our stretch promptly pulled around. Max stopped signing autographs and insisted that the driver let him open the door for me just as Eli ran over to the car and shut the door before I could step in.

"Listen, we need to talk," Eli said to me, nodding at Max, who took two steps toward him before I could intervene and grab his thigh. I squeezed his quad muscles tightly (rock solid! But I digress).

"We don't have anything to talk about," I said.

"What's your deal? What the fuck have I ever done to you, except try to love you?" Eli boldly questioned.

Max's thigh tensed, and only in that millisecond of a moment when he saw me mouth "no" did he reluctantly move back. I knew it was killing him to stand there and let me handle this, but it was what I needed to do even though he could've easily grabbed Eli by the neck and bashed his head into the roof of the car.

"Listen, this isn't the time or the place. We can talk about this back at the office," I suggested to Eli, trying to avoid an even bigger scene.

"Oh, so you think after that shit you pulled in my room and then the disappearing act from the hotel that you still have an office to come back to?"

"What? Are you threatening me—no, better yet, are you firing me?"

"I don't need you no more, ma. I got Rain. That's all I need. She's hot, baby; she's hot. Did you see that shit she just made happen? History!"

Several people, including Spike, were still hanging around outside the theater, talking, star-gazing, or waiting for nothing in particular. And as Eli's voice grew louder, their attention was slowly diverted our way.

I looked up at Max, who hadn't moved at all. He was still standing next to me, waiting for Eli to step further out of line. His eyes glanced in the direction of the Escalade waiting behind us and I followed his gaze to find Tiny standing against the truck and two other gargantuan men, even bigger than him, toppling out of the backseat.

"I really don't think you're in a position to threaten my job."

"I've got Rain, and that's all that matters. They're gonna buy *her*, not some label cats. The fans could care less about us and how we get down. We're just some hype kings behind the scenes. It's all about Rain." He narrowed his eyes. "Didn't I teach you anything?"

I'd put my phone in the pocket of Max's jacket after he put it around my shoulders earlier. When I felt it vibrating I checked the screen and saw Kimber's name.

"You've got good timing. What's the deal?" I held the phone to my ear and looked back and forth between Max and Eli.

"I can't believe what I just witnessed. Unbelievable! We don't need any more time. We're ready to buy them out and sign her right now. She has a home over here, and so do you." Kimber was talking fast and sounded as if she was caught in the crowd, trying to maneuver her way out of the theater.

I looked at Eli, who was still blocking the car door. His arms were folded as he arrogantly sized me up. "Are you sure about that?" I asked Kimber.

"Whatever it takes—that is, if the offer is still on the table?"

"It is, but I don't think it's going to cost you as much as I'd originally thought. Let's talk first thing in the morning." I snapped the phone shut and looked at Max.

Tiny waddled over to the car, palming a BlackBerry, and handed it to me. There was the clearest, most lurid picture of Eli and Mannie on the screen. Out of all the shots I'd managed to snap that night, relying on the pinhole lens in the tiny cell phone, this particular picture was the most repulsive and, coincidentally, the clearest. I nodded to Tiny, who moved back a few paces and stood next to Max.

I took a deep breath and stood up straight. "Rain isn't going over to Universal with you," I declared, showing no signs of my previous affliction with confrontation. With this kind of ammunition, I knew I could be just as arrogant as him, even though my fingers were numb and so sweaty that the BlackBerry almost slipped from my grip. "As a matter of fact, she'll be going with me."

Eli laughed nervously, "What the fuck are you talking about?"

I looked past a couple of people and signaled to Spike, who I'd briefed on the situation earlier that day during one of my many calls. He motioned for his entourage to wait as he moved past the cluster that had formed in the street around us.

"I know all about the deal you all are making with Universal." I watched his eyes saucer and his left eyebrow twitch. "I also know that you restructured the deal in a way that doesn't include me or anyone else from RockStar Chicago."

Eli cleared his throat and ran his hand across the back of his neck. "I, uh, uh, see—where'd you hear that? Who told you that because—"

"Irrelevant! Rain is coming with me, and you're going to let her."

"Let that bitch out of her contract? You must be crazy!" He shook his head from side to side in adamant disagreement.

"Well, I think you will," I said, and held the screen up for him to see the disturbing down-low image of himself and his boss.

"I know it sucks that you'll have to go out and find another R&B princess to sign and cultivate," I whispered in his ear, "but it would be a very bad situation if Mannie's wife and three children were ever to open *Us Weekly* and find him in such a compromising position. I do believe that's your dick." I pointed to Eli on the small screen and turned back to his ear. "And can you imagine the divorce? You see, Eli, this has nothing to do with the fans. This is about one thing—the money. And maybe it's about a bit of dignity as well, of which you'll have none when they're done with you." I looked over at the snaparazzi, who were busy buzzing around the celebs they'd missed on the way in.

I heard Max chuckling and finally felt the muscles in his thigh begin to relax.

"I know the Universal deal is being leveraged on Rain's success. And that you all haven't even signed yet. You were waiting until tonight to see if she'd pick up any awards. So this is probably going to sting even more, now that she'll go triple-platinum after delivering the goods to the whole world the way she just did in there. But, as Mannie's lackey, and apparent boy-toy, it's in your best interest to tell him that you've extinguished this little fire, and he never has to worry about turning on *Access Hollywood* and seeing any one of the eleven pictures of him—naked and between your legs with his nose at your balls— that are still in my possession." I pointed to the *Access Hollywood* camera crew and waved at the reporter, whom I'd promised an immediate exclusive if Rain won a Grammy. She waved back excitedly, and I cut my eyes at Eli. "Yes, I think I have you both by the balls."

"Hannah, I can't believe you're doing this to me after everything I've done for you. You know you mean the world to me, Angel." Eli looked around and lowered his voice. He reached for my hands but Max stepped in front of me.

"I think you've heard everything she has to say to you. My boys will be over to clean out her office tomorrow. There's no need for you to contact her again—ever! Someone will always be watching her back." Max nodded to the two men who were still standing beside the SUV behind us.

Tiny pushed Eli aside, and Max opened the door for me and took my hand to help me in. I rolled down the window and handed Tiny the BlackBerry.

"Oh, and Eli, as you can see, the pictures have already been downloaded and encrypted into various files. So even if I did disappear into thin air one day, several outlets have instructions as to how they should proceed. All I want is Rain, that's it, and I'm willing to be fair and pay you what she's worth—well, close to it. So, first thing tomorrow, I'll have my attorney get in touch with RockStars' counsel, and we can get this ball rolling and put the sordid back-door mess behind us."

Max walked around to the other side of the car and got in, leaving Tiny towering over Eli in the street next to the curb.

"Hannah, please; can't we talk about this? I was gonna take you to Universal, Angel, really I was."

The chauffeur shifted gears.

"Who is she signing with?" he screamed as the car started to pull away.

I stuck my head out the window and smiled as the wind blew through my hair. "Tru, baby, Truuu."

75

I INDULGED IN A FIT OF SCREAMS AND STOMPS ON THE FLOORBOARDS. IN RE-sponse, the driver raised the dividing window, probably in self-defense. I couldn't believe what I'd just pulled. That was me back there, wheelin' and dealin', and I must say that I was a very, *very* bad bitch.

"Did you see that, baby? I was a very, very bad bitch."

"Yes, darlin', you were very very bad. I hadn't seen that side of you before—it was incredibly sexy."

I reached over and grabbed Max's shoulders and shook him. "Thank you so much, baby. I don't know if I can ever thank you enough. There's no way I could have done any of that without you."

"I told you not to worry about him, didn't I? Don't ever doubt me. I'll always have your back. No one will ever hurt you again—not if I can help it."

"I think we make a pretty good team." I snuggled up close to him.

"That's what I've been trying to tell your hot ass all this time—but no, you were on some other shit." He pulled me onto his lap, grabbed my hair, and nibbled at my neck until I closed my eyes and moaned.

"I'm sorry, baby; I'm so sorry," I whispered into his ear, and decided to leave my tongue there to explore for a while. I put my arms around him and bent down a few inches to return the above-the-collarbone affections. I could feel him through the delicate dress and knew he was already hard. Each time he pulled my hair and sucked my neck I worried about staining the silk gown, which was probable because tonight I wasn't wearing panties of any kind.

"Baby, stop; I really don't want to mess up my beautiful dress," I purred.

"Are you kidding? Did you just tell me to stop—and because of a goddamn dress?"

"But it's the most beautiful dress I have. And you bought it for me, and God knows how much it must've cost."

He pulled at the dress from the bottom, raising it over my hips, and maneuvered my leg over his lap to straddle him. "Is that better?"

I nodded, unable to speak because my lips were obsessively engaged, kissing him all over his perfectly lined five o'clock shadow.

"I'm glad you like your gift, but what do I care about a dress, no matter how much it cost, if it means I can enjoy kissing and grinding and fucking you—right here in the back of this ride? I'll buy you another one. Priorities, darlin'. You see, I have mine in order."

I pulled at his Gucci belt buckle and loosened his pants without saying another word. They hadn't hit the floor before he had on a condom and I was pleasurably, painfully, taking in all of him. He whispered things in my ear that I'd never heard spoken out loud before, and with each prompt to move faster or slower, I cycled into variations of euphoria. The space in my head was black, then fuchsia, then cherry-apple red—no, Corvette red—then deep-sea blue. I opened my eyes and watched his face—his eyebrows, his eyes, his cheeks, his lips—meet pleasure and spend a little time with ecstasy. He gripped my back with his hands, pulling me in to him.

"Can you feel me?" He'd repeated it twice before I could find the air to answer him.

"Yes, baby, I can feel all of you."

I grabbed the back of his hair and turned my head toward the window. The city was passing us passionately in the night as we turned corners, sped across streets, and weaved up avenues.

The window was getting too foggy for me to see anything, so I reached over and swiped at it with my hand. We'd headed uptown and were flying through Central Park. I leaned back and closed my eyes. The space in my head was now a fertile forest green. Max grabbed my ass with one hand and held one of my breasts with the other, tweaking my nipple, making me moan loudly. I pulled his hair harder and took in a deep breath, preparing to let out a scream. But he raised his head from my neck and whispered in my ear. "What time is it?"

I opened my eyes and saw him smiling and biting down on his lip.

"What time is it?" he asked again, and slowed my ride.

I looked at my watch and back at him. "11:59," I said, and held him tightly as he gripped my ass and resumed the fast crazy passionate pace, leading me straight into my orgasm in the Park.

"Happy Valentine's Day, darlin'," he said as I leaned all the way back and screamed, holding on to him for dear life.

76

"CLOSE YOUR EYES."

Max stood in front of the hotel penthouse door and fidgeted with the hotel keycard. "Are they closed?" He checked my eyes and pushed the door open.

"Yes."

He led me into the foyer and slowly shut the door. I could hear him moving around behind me but couldn't quite make out what he was doing.

"Can I open them?"

"Go ahead. Open them." He stood behind me and took my hands from my eyes. "It's our first Valentine's Day together. Enjoy it, darlin'," he whispered sweetly into my ear.

All the rooms on the bottom floor of the duplex were covered with red roses—even the rooms we weren't using. Fresh flowers packed the kitchen sink, the windowsills, the bathtub, and all the drawers. White candles in various shapes and sizes were lit everywhere, and vintage Brian McKnight was playing on the stereo—the same song that had played the night we cruised the lakefront and became believers. I closed my eyes again and opened them, unable to believe what I was seeing.

"Follow the white rose petals."

I looked down at the floor, which was also completely covered in roses, and saw soft white petals leading into the bedroom. Max leaned against the wall into the flickering candlelight and watched me tiptoe over the freshly cut flowers into the bedroom and over to a Louis Vuitton suitcase in the middle of the bed. I didn't recognize the luggage, but the last white rose petal stopped right at the handle of the bag. I turned around and looked at him as he walked toward the doorway, watching me intensely and rubbing his stubble.

"What's this?"

"I think you're supposed to open it. I said follow the petals, right?"

I knew I wouldn't be able to hold back the determined tears. "Uh-huh."

"Don't cry yet, darlin'. Open your bag and see what's inside."

I unzipped the suitcase and slowly pulled out the contents: a blue-and-white string bikini, a red halter one-piece, a yellow ribbed thong bikini, and one white strapless tankini. At the bottom of the suitcase was an overstuffed envelope. Max had both hands shoved into his suit pants pockets and was biting down on his bottom lip, trying desperately to suppress a smile. I opened it and pulled out two private charter tickets to Kauai, Hawaii. The departure date was Monday, February 14th. I screamed and waved the tickets around in the air and then ran to this thoughtful, considerate, generous man and jumped into his arms, trampling all the roses on the floor in my way.

"Ohmigod! Are you serious?" I hugged him and kissed him and hugged him some more.

"What do you think?" He let out the smile he'd been holding hostage and squeezed me tightly. "Are you happy, darlin'?"

"Yes, yes, yes, I am so happy. I've never been to Hawaii before."

He carried me over to the bed layered in rose petals and set me down before putting the suitcase filled with nothing but bathing suits on the floor. "I have a beach house there, and they have beautiful flowers."

He opened the top drawer and took out a piece of paper and handed it to me. Several sentences and words had been scribbled down and scratched out. After taking a closer look, I realized that it was the rough draft of the card he'd given me with the tropical bouquet months ago. After all the scratch-outs, he'd written out the final draft of the card:

> Hannah, please accept these beautiful tropical flowers and know that I'm sorry for upsetting you. Maybe one day you'll let me take you to the native island of each one so you can be surrounded by something as beautiful as you are to me.
>
> I miss you, darlin'.
>
> Enjoy.
> Max

He wiped one tear from my eye, and I caught another. What was I going to do with this man?

He sat on the bed next to me.

"I can't believe you kept this," I said, shocked. "You were so pissed at me that night."

I thought about how much I'd put him through.

"No, I wasn't pissed—just disappointed. You didn't owe me anything, and I understood that." He moved closer to me and stroked my hair. "I kept it because I still had hope. I only hoped that one day you would be right here with me, sharing the excitement of my life and allowing me to share in yours. Tonight was great. There isn't anywhere else in the world I would've wanted to be except right there next to you."

"Please—I was on *your* arm tonight."

"No, darlin', it was the biggest night of your career, and you let me share it with you. Those are the things I've been holding on and hoping for. Remember when I told you that hope is a very powerful, beautiful thing? I never gave up on you."

"How can I ever thank you, baby?"

"I'm sure we'll think of something."

• • •

AND ON THAT BED THAT WAS JAM-PACKED WITH ROSES, IN A MASSIVE HOTEL room that was dimly lit only by white candles, in a city grounded in eternal hope, Max found several ways for me to thank him.

With rose petals in my hair and stuck to my wet back, I rolled over. "Baby, are we really going to Hawaii in six hours?"

He held me in his safe, strong arms, panting and still out of breath. "And that's just the beginning."

FIRST OVERTIME

KENNEDY TOSSED ME THE DANCE SHOES THAT HAD BEEN ON THE FLOOR NEXT TO my closet.

"Did you hear back from Roxy yet? I thought you said she was gonna call by four." I stuffed an extra towel and a scrunchie into the Diamonds duffel.

"Not yet, but I know she never calls when she says she will." Kennedy paced the floor around my bed. "I don't wanna stay here anymore. What am I gonna do when you leave?"

"You've gotta think positive. No worries, remember? I know you'll get the part, and then you can move to New York with me."

"But what if my audition tape sucked?" She stopped in the middle of the floor and put her hands on her hips. "It's just that I've never done a soap opera before."

"There's a first time for everything, Sweets. The producer and the casting director said they thought you'd be perfect, right? Well, it's their job to recognize talent." I stopped packing my game bag and turned around to face her. "Look, you can't do reality TV forever. It's only supposed to be a stepping-stone. I know you're always the cast and crew's favorite, but that's two so far: *The Intern* and *The Second Assistant*. The producer loved you on both shows, but he also said that he thought you'd be perfect for *All My Children*. And I happen to agree with him." I tugged at my warm-up pants. "Now, Roxy's gonna call, and she's gonna call with good news. That's all there is to it." I zipped my bag and sat on the bed to tie my sneaks.

I'd been rushing because I didn't want to make Max wait for me for the very last game of the season. Despite his heroic efforts, the Diamonds hadn't made the playoffs, and tonight's home game had been hyped as the biggest of the year. We were playing the Knicks, and it was no secret that Max was planning on signing with them next season. Everyone was going bananas about the final game, and I absolutely couldn't be late for the last locker room romps. Besides, ever since I'd been promoted to squad captain, Max hadn't cared one bit that I was notorious for being fifteen minutes late my entire life. He wasn't trying to hear that excuse tonight, and I knew he was right.

As soon as I'd returned from my Hawaiian hiatus with Max, Coach pulled me aside after viewing the final edit of the Fox morning show segment. "Get ready. Things are about to change," she'd said, and boy was she right!

When the morning show segment finally did air, the producers had completely changed the spin to "The Rise of a Rookie." Everyone raved about the show, including the Diamonds franchise execs, who decided to go in a different direction and do some advertising spots with me and Rain and a few of the franchise favorites. In the end, they went with a national NBA "I Love This Game" promo that was shot using a green screen featuring me, Max, and Rain taking turns dunking during a Diamonds game. Kimber had phoned the commissioner and over drinks one eve had assisted him in discovering the potency of a cross-promotional alliance with such a dominating urban brand as Tru. The following week, Rain was in the studio dropping her vocals over a track that Tru's top producer crafted just in time for the league's playoffs campaign.

Things changed for Max, too. After our Hawaii trip, he'd been the team's highest scorer, amazingly averaging thirty-nine points a game.

If he was at the free throw line, it was guaranteed that his shots were golden, and after each one, he'd look directly at me and pull on his left ear and smile. During post-game interviews, he'd comment about his "inspiration," causing all the local papers to speculate about the exact nature of his relationship with "the adorable Doll." Max was packing the stadium to capacity and bringing out fans who hadn't been to a game since the Diamonds were in the playoffs six years earlier, which inspired local and even some national media to dub me the "Diamond Dolls Darling." It was this show of obsessive interest and support from the media and the general public that grossed the Chicago Diamonds more revenue than any other franchise in league history. Equity in the Diamonds brand soared, and between merchandising and ticket sales, the franchise machine seemed unstoppable. This same media hysteria and frenzied fan support had been the motivation behind the phone call both our coaches had immediately received instructing them to overlook the Golden Rule and additionally do everything in their personal power to see to it that "as long as Max and 'the Doll' are associated with the team brand, the engine must remain hot." Max and I were thrilled, though for very different reasons than the league execs; ultimately it meant we didn't have to sneak around or downplay the ridiculously obvious like so many other high-profile couples.

But not everyone was elated. Poor Kennedy was still struggling with anxiety over my leaving in three weeks. Once I'd accepted Kimber's offer, I put off telling her as long as I could. I knew Britt would be excited, but I'd been worried about Sweets from the very beginning. I'd even gotten Kimber to make several adjustments to the contract, one of which was my start date, which I was able to get pushed back to May just so I could have some additional time to spend with her.

Britt had been going back and forth to New York so much that she was now seriously considering getting a place there herself. On her most recent visits, she'd even traveled with her mystery companion, Poppie—and *Dallas* had thanked her privately for the first-class accommodations, mentioning that it wouldn't be so bad to live in the Big Apple and study at Columbia. But I still needed to see just how serious Britt was before I made any real decisions about which avenue I was going to call home. Tru had arranged to pay for me to reside in corporate housing at Trump Towers until I found exactly what I wanted after my attorney had gotten them to amend the maximum four-month housing accommodation with the coveted clause of perpetuity. But with each passing day, Kennedy's frustration grew into fearful angst.

Movado check: Shit! I needed to be in the lobby in exactly two minutes. I grabbed Kennedy by the arm and dragged her down the stairs with me. We had to step over the boxes that we'd all spent the last couple of weeks meticulously packing. None of us could believe that a whole year had gone by—just like that.

I dashed a sprinkle of food into Puma's tank before bending down to kiss it. "Mama'll be back as soon as the game is over."

Dr. Ivy had passed Puma's gills on to me at our last session. I'm still convinced that she'd gotten teary when she released me from her embrace. "You're gonna do just fine, Hannah. You've done all the tough work. Now it's time for you to have some happiness. You deserve it. Just remember: always stand up for yourself, and don't be afraid of confrontation, especially where it's warranted. And never let anyone take your power away from you." I'd gotten a little choked up when she walked me to her door. "Oh, and one more thing: take the damn fish. You're the only one around here I've ever seen him actually respond to." I was happy to get her sincere vote of confidence but even happier to get the *damn* fish!

Puma swam around the gold coral twice before surfacing to scarf down the fish food. I flicked his bowl and turned around to face my dearest friend.

"You know I'm not gonna leave you here, right, Sweets? Wherever I go, you go. No worries, remember?"

"Right, no worries. It's just that I really want this—really, really bad."

"And you'll have it. If it's meant to be, right? Now, who's the fresh face of Baby Phat? Come on now, who's my little Korean face of Baby Phat?"

"Me," Kennedy said, sheepishly.

"That doesn't sound like the voice of a budding supermodeling soap star," I said as I grabbed an apple from the island and headed toward the front door.

"Don't say that; you might jinx it."

"No such thing," I said, and opened the door to the ringing of the phone.

Kennedy darted for the cordless, and I could hear her screaming triumphantly into the receiver at Roxy.

"Bug! Bug—"

"Congrats, Sweets. See you in New York!" I yelled, smiling, as I waved my hand in the air and headed out the door.

SECOND OVERTIME

THE LOCKER ROOM WAS ON FIRE TONIGHT. ALL THE GIRLS WHO'D MANAGED TO make it through the tough season were proudly standing around in their signature two-piece whites like a rockin' cheerleading chick clique. We'd started out with twenty-five warrior goats and were now down to fourteen dazzling Dolls. We were the strong who had survived!

Most of the rookies had dropped off somewhere between the Thanksgiving/Christmas rush and the post–New Year's drag when the honeymoon came to a screeching halt. Around that time, Six caught the chickenpox and gave it to Elle before they both disappeared into the I-sort-of-used-to-be-a-professional-cheerleader-but-I-couldn't-quite-hack-it abyss. When many of the vets realized we didn't have a real shot at the playoffs, they officially resigned as well for one reason or another. Mona, on the other hand, who was still donning her nose splint, had tried to hang on as long as she could, but when her right cheek implant started to rotate under her skin, Coach politely nudged her out the Diamond Dolls door and respectfully asked her to never return—

but not before scribbling down the digits to a very reputable plastic surgeon in Beverly Hills.

I looked around the room and surprisingly teared up. Minnow was standing next to me, rifling through her locker for the Puffs, and Chloe was sitting on the bench on my other side adjusting Brooklyn's uniform. We all made jokes that it was cleaner and whiter than anyone else's on the squad. But they were just jokes, after all; it had already been decided that both she and Minnow were going to be squad captains next year. And Coach had been crystal clear from the very beginning that she didn't dish sympathy spots. Tonight was no different. Brooklyn was probably the most deserving and would've been on the court several weeks earlier if she hadn't asked for time off to shoot our sponsor's health club franchise fitness DVD. She'd trained hard and had even entered a few amateur fitness competitions. Her body was in amazing competitive condition, and as fate would have it, just around that same time, she'd boldly broken it off with Jack. "I know, Hannah, I know. But now, even more importantly, I finally know ME." And that was the last she ever spoke of him.

Katie, on the other hand, had been one of the vets who'd quit the team when she realized the playoffs wouldn't be in our immediate future. But she'd apparently not given up on dancing altogether and was recently rumored to be Mona's replacement as the other half of Sugar and Spice. Brooklyn had found that quite amusing and said it explained the receipts she'd found in Jack's wallet from "a place called VIPs."

"LET'S GO, DIAMONDS, LET'S GO!"

The first half of the game was nothing short of spectacular. The Knicks were in the lead, but it was tense. Max had been playing like a champion who was still fighting for a nonexistent playoff slot. When he neared triple double status, I figured he was playing with so much heart because he knew it would be his last game as a Chicago Diamond. Bittersweet!

As the final seconds of the second quarter ticked away, Max pulled up for a three-pointer that could have narrowed the lead and put the

Diamonds within two. The stadium went wild. True to form, he didn't
disappoint, and nailed the open hook. Screaming, I motioned to my
crew to head into the locker room so we could quickly change for our
final halftime routine. They didn't budge.

"C'mon, guys, we're running out of time."

No one moved an inch.

A hush swept through the stands, and I immediately felt twenty-
five thousand pairs of eyes staring directly at me, along with the cameras.

I turned around to look at Nana and Roman, who were sitting next
to Ali and the Brats in the courtside VIP seats Max had gotten them for
my final Dolls appearance. I quickly saw that in whichever direction I
turned, a camera lens was going to be there—waiting for me to move,
or not move, or halfway move.

Admittedly, over the past few months, I'd gotten used to the shutter-
bugs, but this was ridiculous, I thought. What was going on? I looked
back at Nana so she could share in my confusion. Roman patted her
hand while she dabbed at her puffy eyes.

I looked out onto the court past Shep, Styles, Mav, and Miles. I
couldn't find Max, even though I'd just watched him shake three
Knicks defenders five seconds ago.

The stadium went dark except for the bright white spotlight shining down on center court, directly on the center diamond.

"Darlin'—"

I heard Max's voice echo throughout the stadium and my heart
dropped into my bobby socks.

"I want to give you the world."

My eyes welled with tears, and I stood frozen in place with one
hand over my mouth and the other holding my stomach, trying desperately to keep from heaving all over my crisp freshly dry-cleaned two-
piece signature white. I looked around for him, but I couldn't see
anything except the bright blinding flashes from all the clusters of
cameras pointed at me.

"You are my perfection."

I tried to catch my breath between the falling drops of salty appre-
ciation.

"Definitely the perfect woman to handle all the idiosyncrasies that are my life. And I know for a fact that Noah, Cree, and little Zoey agree."

I didn't know where she was, but I could hear Zoey cooing in the background. My fingers were completely numb, and I didn't let the tears free-fall until I heard Nana snivel behind me.

"If you let me, I promise to love you and protect you, even after we grow old together and leave this earth. And even then my love will spill over, still needing to grow."

I could hear sniffles all around and could feel his presence even seconds before he appeared out of the darkness and was standing beside me.

"You are my light, and I need you to see, darlin'."

As he took my hand, a white light lit a path to the circular spotlight at center court. He squeezed my hand and led me to the middle of the stadium. And as we stood on the diamond he bent down to whisper into my ear. "Hope is a powerful, beautiful thing."

Hastily, one of the ballboys scampered onto the court and placed a stool behind me. Somehow I forgot that 24,983 people were watching the mucus bubble burst under my left nostril. Max wiped my nose with his thumb and picked me up to seat me on the stool. The spotlight disappeared, and the Jumbotron lowered. I looked up at him. He didn't take his eyes off me.

The four-sided oversized flat screen lit up with pictures and footage of me, dating back almost an entire year. Max had provided voice-over commentary for the professionally mastered video. The first segment was from my interviews at the cattle call auditions.

"I loved you from the first minute I saw you," his voice said, as the camera closed in on me standing frozen on the court that frenzied first day.

I grabbed his hand and squeezed it as hard as I could, trembling so much on the stool that I thought I'd tip it over. I looked at the screen and back at him.

"But when? But how? But—"

"Shh. Just watch."

He wiped away the tears, and I exhaled slowly, watching more footage of him studying me at that first game. As I cheered on the sidelines, he gazed at me and grinned at the frightful anxious look plastered across my face when my squad stood up to do the merciless mini-kick line.

"Even then, I couldn't imagine my life without you."

I locked eyes with Max and felt more connected to another person than I'd ever felt to myself. And for the first time, I truly understood what it meant to be part of a whole.

He moved behind the stool and wrapped both his arms around me as the video replayed that fateful halftime fall that exposed my notorious neon-orange doom. I tensed and wanted to look away, but he bent down and whispered again in my ear. "Watch."

One of the cameras had focused in on his reaction as he winced and bit down on his lip, watching intently before urging me under his breath to "get up, get up." And when I did, he smiled and applauded approvingly. There was no laughter at all, rather encouragement, support, and undeniable pride.

My mouth dropped, and I crossed both hands over my heart.

"And when she got up, I fell deeply in love with her."

He grabbed my hands from my chest and held them firmly in his.

He'd spliced in random footage from the security camera in my building of me coming and going, and once even hiding behind Dallas's desk, like an old-school *I Love Lucy* episode, watching as Max walked out the door with Cree on that misleading night, months ago.

"What's a real romance without a little confusion? She wanted me. Yeah, she wanted me bad. Look at that—she didn't even want me going out with my baby sister," the dubbed track boasted.

I pinched his arm and looked up at him, not quite believing that he'd gone to all of the trouble to do this for me.

"Watch."

I recognized the rest of the pictures from our amazing trip to Hawaii, until I saw footage of him in New York. I didn't remember any of this. Max was getting out of a limo. And Cree. I recognized her voice as she tried to balance the camera as he walked into Cartier.

Max breathed into my ear. "Stand up, darlin'."

Without taking my eyes from the screen, I scooted off the chair and watched as he looked at an enormous ring with Cree and a very appreciative saleswoman.

"No, I need something much bigger," he said to the out-of-focus redhead who was assisting him. "No, that's still not it. It has to really make a statement," he stressed to her again.

I could hear Cree agreeing in the background, and I watched as the woman walked back into the out-of-focus camera shot.

"No. Still bigger. And bolder—"

"—definitely with more caratage," Cree insisted.

"I think I've got the perfect ring for you, Mr. Knight," I heard her say as she disappeared again.

"Good, because my Love is perfect."

The screen faded to black, and our spotlight reappeared, but my stool was gone and Max was on one knee.

The crowd roared insanely, but I couldn't take my eyes off him.

Max patiently waited for them to settle down and stared helplessly at me. I watched a tiny tear fight desperately to hang onto his bottom lid between two ultrathick lashes.

"Hannah Marie Love, I think you are undeniably dynamic!"

I reached out to him and cupped his cheek in my moist, trembling hand.

"I have hoped that you would let me love you for a long time now."

My trembles quickly turned to shakes, and I was forced to keep one hand free to wipe my red swollen eyes and cover my gaping mouth as I stood on the diamond in the middle of the court in the Chicago Stadium in front of tens of thousands of fans.

"I'll follow you around the world. I just don't want to spend another day of my life without you by my side."

He reached for both my hands.

"Marry me, darlin'," he said, and slid a serious 9k platinum semi-pavéd ring with a single cushion-cut diamond onto my finger.

I watched him run his free hand through his curls and bite down on his bottom lip.

"OK, baby. OK," I agreed, through soft whimpers.

He stood up, lifted me into his arms, and slipped the ring from my finger to show me the engraving.

HOME IS WHEREVER YOU ARE. MAX

I was choking on my tears as Max secured the ring back onto my sticky finger. He nuzzled my wet nose and pressed his perfect pucker against my quivering lips. And as he flashed the world his infamously deep sweet dimples, the lights came up just enough for me to see that the crowd was on its feet. He spun me around in his arms, and I held on to his neck even tighter, wiping my snotty nose on his jersey. He continued to twirl me faster, and I threw my head back, watching the center diamond go round and round before one of my flying feet kicked an abnormally short cameraman smack-dab in the back of his balding head.

I looked high into the rafters and laughed at what Grandpa Red must have been thinking about all this. I could hear his approval through the electric noise that filled the dome. *"Somebody's gotta win, baby girl, somebody's gotta win."*

AND AS USUAL, GRANDPA RED WAS RIGHT. THE DIAMONDS DID WIN THAT night. And so did I.

About the Author

ERIKA J. KENDRICK is a Chicago native and graduated with a BA in psychology from Stanford University. After completing her MBA in marketing and international business, Kendrick moved to New York City to work for Island Def Jam. She has also interned for Clive Davis's J Records and worked at the legendary Apollo Theater. In addition to her familiarity with the music industry glitterati, Kendrick is no stranger to the glam world of professional cheerleading: She was once a Luvabull, a Chicago Bulls cheerleader.

The president of the New York chapter of the National Association of Black Female Executives in Music and Entertainment (NABFEME .org). Erika lives in New York City. Visit her website at www.erika kendrick.com.